THE WHISPERING NIGHT

TOR TEEN BOOKS BY SUSAN DENNARD

The Luminaries
The Hunting Moon
The Whispering Night

Truthwitch
Windwitch
Sightwitch
Bloodwitch
Witchshadow

THE WHISPERING NIGHT

SUSAN DENNARD

TOR TEEN

TOR PUBLISHING GROUP
NEW YORK

This is a work of fiction. All of the characters, organizations, and events portrayed in this novel are either products of the author's imagination or are used fictitiously.

THE WHISPERING NIGHT

Map art by Tim Paul, © Susan Dennard

A Tor Teen Book
Published by Tom Doherty Associates / Tor Publishing Group
120 Broadway
New York, NY 10271

www.torpublishinggroup.com

Tor® is a registered trademark of Macmillan Publishing Group, LLC.

The Library of Congress Cataloging-in-Publication Data is available upon request.

ISBN 978-1-250-33948-5 (hardcover)
ISBN 978-1-250-37240-6 (international, sold outside the U.S.,
subject to rights availability)
ISBN 978-1-250-33949-2 (ebook)

Our books may be purchased in bulk for promotional, educational, or business use. Please contact your local bookseller or the Macmillan Corporate and Premium Sales Department at 1-800-221-7945, extension 5442, or by email at MacmillanSpecialMarkets@macmillan.com.

First Edition: 2024

Printed in the United States of America

0 9 8 7 6 5 4 3 2 1

For Rachel,

my longtime friend and a loyal Wednesday bear

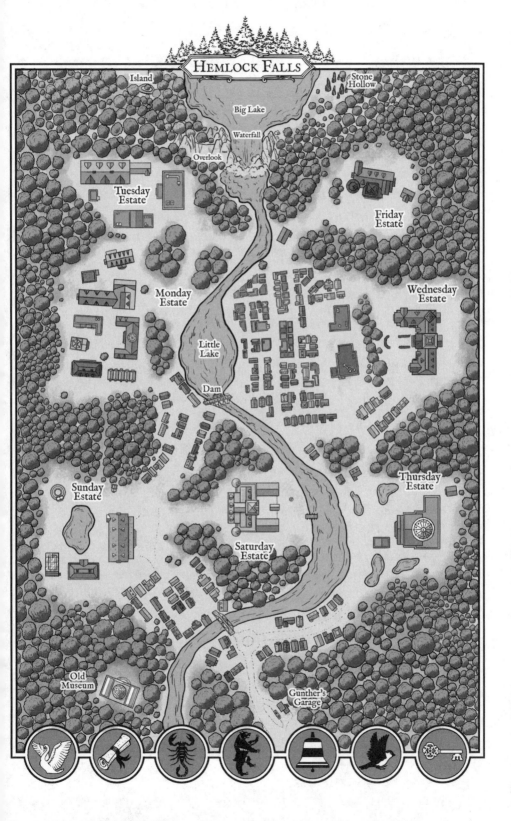

THE
WHISPERING
NIGHT

THE NIGHTMARE

The boy awakens beside a hemlock tree at sunrise. He has been here before, more times than he can count. More times than he can remember. The forest erases his human mind on the nights when it summons him. But this morning is different: a figure crouches over him. Trees drift and wave behind the man's head, releasing gray dawn light with each gust of forest breeze. A smell like bubble gum pierces the boy's nostrils.

"Hey," the man says. He has a low, growly voice, but kind. "I thought I might find you here."

The boy frowns, still groggy from the night he can't remember. He is in one of the three places he always ends up after the forest claims him, dressed in the same clothes he went to bed in: jeans and a thick flannel button-up. He has learned in the last two years that pajamas only lead to trouble. It's better to be fully dressed. This way, he will not freeze quite so quickly if he is unconscious for hours against a hemlock tree.

And this way, if anyone finds him, he looks less like a daywalker wandering from his bed and more like a kid who had too much to drink the night before. He has even started carrying a beat-up pack of cigarettes in his back pocket, just to complete the effect.

"How are you here?" the boy asks, his voice as rough as the broken soil digging beneath his boots.

"I've been watching you," the man replies, and he has the decency to look embarrassed as he says this. His teeth smack twice at bubble gum.

"I had a feeling something wasn't right, and . . . well . . ." He waves to the forest around them.

The boy nods. A strange feeling wefts through him that can't decide what it wants to be. Is it fear this man will turn him over to the Tuesdays? Or is it relief because now, finally, this misery will end?

He is so tired all the time.

He wonders if it will hurt when they kill him. It must have hurt that werewolf fifteen years ago. He thinks about that daywalker often, whoever they were.

The man blows a bubble, bright pink in a world of frosted gray. It pops. The boy flinches. Then the man offers him a hand. "Let's get you out of here before corpse duty finds us."

The boy stares at the man's hand, with its dried, seamed skin from constant sanitizer and latex gloves. Right now, the hand is simply pale, bare, and waiting for the boy to clasp it.

"Hurry." The man's fingers flex. He blows another bubble. It crackles with a triple *pop-pop-pop!* at the end.

"You . . . won't turn me in?"

The man shakes his head.

"But I'm a daywalker."

"No." The man glances to his left, into a stand of oak trees. "As far as I can tell, you're just a kid who got unlucky."

Oh. The boy doesn't know what to say to this. The relief his curse might finally end is replaced by relief that someone might be able to help him, to cure him, to give him back everything he had to give up two years ago. The bear and the bell he misses every single day. The aunt he can't confess to. The *life* he used to have.

He swallows, his throat dry from a night on the prowl that he will never remember. Then he nods and takes the man's hand. The grasp is strong, steady, true.

"Come, Jay Friday," the man says as he helps the boy rise. "Let's get you somewhere warm."

THE WITCH

The girl goes to the edge of the forest at twilight. She has avoided the call of the Dianas for three years, but she can avoid it no longer. She has failed, failed, *failed* to cast the spell from her sister. So if she wants to finish what her sister began—and finally learn why her sister died—she will need training.

Thus, when another summons comes, a small note that materializes inside her sister's old locket with coordinates in red ink, the girl decides to answer. The witches have been sending her these messages for the last three years, oddly unwilling to give up on her.

She is glad they've kept trying. After she failed for the thousandth time to do even the most basic of spells—a *mundanus* that creates a flickering flame—she has accepted she cannot do this on her own.

The inked coordinates lead her far from her clan's estate, and though the mist has not yet risen for the night, and she is outside the red-staked boundaries of nightmare danger, she still constantly checks her surroundings. She has crafted a plan, of course, in case a Luminary finds her here. A story about hunting mistcap mushrooms, and she has even brought a small sack with her for the filling.

But she encounters no one, and soon, she reaches the secret meeting place. Six minutes early because she is *always* six minutes early. She squints into the shadows. To her left, golden-leaf maples have turned to gray shadows in the darkness. To her right, underbrush and saplings are surrounded by fallen leaves.

Before her, the final grains of daylight vanish into gloaming. And behind her, a crow's face zooms in.

The girl jumps, a yelp escaping her as she lurches away from the head. It is not a true crow, but a person in a charcoal-colored mask marked with feathers and a metal beak, glittery and gold. The person wears black, almost scalelike armor. Then the person laughs, a wheezing sound that isn't quite human. And when she speaks, it is with an older woman's voice. "So you are ready to join us, are you? Why now?"

The girl swallows. Her heart is trapped somewhere beside her tonsils. She was expecting a question like this, of course—*why now?*—and she rehearsed several answers while wiping off eyeliner in her bathroom. But suddenly her various stories and excuses sound exactly like that: stories and excuses. And although she can see nothing beyond a glittering darkness where the Crow's eyes should be, she senses those eyes will see through any lies.

"Because," the girl finally replies, "I want to know what my sister was. What she did. What . . . what all of *this* meant to her."

"You mean you want to know why she turned on the Luminaries and chose their enemy?"

The girl nods. She does want to know why her sister would trade one controlling society for another—and what the Dianas have to offer that was worth giving up everything for, including her life.

The Crow laughs again, a round, hearty laugh that is fully human now. As if a switch has been flipped inside her throat. "I think there is more to your answer."

There is, but the girl will not say it out loud. *Cannot* say it. The spell her sister left behind—she doesn't know if it was a secret or if this witch before her was ever aware of its existence.

So instead, she says: "This is all I have. Please." Her voice is weaker than she wants it to be. "It's all I have, and so I have to try."

The Crow sighs, a sound that is neither amused nor mocking. It is simply the sound of someone who has heard what they needed to hear. "Yes," she agrees. Then she offers a black mask to the girl. It is wobbly without a human head inside and vaguely canid in shape. "This is yours now. Whenever you are summoned, you will wear it. Whenever you enter the forest, you will wear it. And whenever you work magic, you will wear it."

Work magic. The girl's heart finally releases from her throat. She reaches for the mask.

But the Crow skips it out of reach, wagging a finger. "This is for our protection as much as yours, child. Do you understand? Should the Lambda hunters ever find you, then you cannot betray us. You do not know who we are, you do not know our faces."

"You've seen *my* face, though. That means you can betray me."

"Yes, it does, Erica Thursday." The Crow bobs her head. "Now take the mask, child, and we will begin our first lesson."

To: *wednesdaywinonawednesday@internalsystem.luminaries.com*
From: *rachelgianawednesday@internalsystem.luminaries.com*
Subject: Home from the hospital

Winnie,

I've been home from the hospital for a week now, and I've been running training sessions every day since. You haven't been there though. Any particular reason why? Coach Rosa is great, but you've got to get in more movement than just Sunday estate training. At least if you ever plan to join the hunt.

I've said it before and I'll repeat it: you don't have to join the hunt. When, if—that's up to you. But I do think we need to catch up on some things. So I'll see you in the Armory tonight. I have gear for you, in case you do decide to train.

As for next week, we start at dawn every day to accommodate the Masquerade.

See you soon.

Rachel

C H A P T E R

1

The old cabin is neither old nor is it really a cabin.

Sure, it has four walls, a roof, and a general vibe that speaks of wolves eating little girls in red hoods, but if you step inside, you won't find grandmothers with big ears or big teeth. You'll find two lawnmowers, a compost bin that no one uses anymore, some canisters of gasoline, and an assortment of gardening tools that span the powering spectrum from completely handheld (a shovel) to fully battery powered (a leaf blower).

This is the landscaping shed for the Thursday clan, tucked against the northwestern edge of their estate, between the weeping willow on one side and the copse of dogwoods that will soon blossom on the other. The grounds appear deceptively untended here. As if the Thursdays don't want to be *too* conspicuously Thursday in a place where almost no one ever visits, but still they can't resist imposing order on nature's chaotic ways.

The grass is shorn. There are no weeds.

A large front door on the shed will release the lawnmowers from their pen like bulls at a rodeo, but it's to the smaller, human-sized door that Winnie Wednesday now tiptoes. The grounds are empty this early on a Friday, but she checks her surroundings anyway. And to be fair, with all that's happened to her in the last few weeks, she has good reason to never relax again.

Like ever.

Basically, if Winnie's life were a seesaw with "good stuff" on one side and "bad stuff" on the other, then it would definitely be tipped toward bad. In fact, the bad side would be so weighed down it would be underground.

For one, there are Dianas in Hemlock Falls. For two, those Dianas framed her dad four years ago, which in turn caused the ruin of Winnie's family. For three, those Dianas also have a self-feeding spell loose in the forest that's killing people, aka the Whisperer.

For four, her ex–best friends are determined to stay ex, and it's getting to be exhausting.

Yet despite the imbalance of Winnie's seesaw, she still feels happier than she has in weeks. Maybe part of that is because she can calculate pretty measurably just how far she has come since her first trial:

Number of friends a month ago? Zero. Number of friends now? At least six and counting.

Number of nightmare species fought a month ago? Zero. Number fought now? Eight, if you include werewolves as one of them—which Winnie does. Nine, if you include will-o'-wisps, which she doesn't.

Dianas faced a month ago? Zero. Dianas faced now? Three.

But perhaps more important than the empirical evidence that Winnie can track on a spreadsheet is the *emotional* evidence. Because for the first time in four years, she feels hopeful.

> *Hope is the thing with feathers*
> *That perches in the soul,*
> *And sings the tune without the words,*
> *And never stops at all.*

Winnie had to memorize that poem by Emily Dickinson for Ms. Morgan two years ago. Lately, the poem keeps surfacing like artifacts of data you can never quite scrub from a hard drive. And every time Winnie thinks of the poem, she imagines a will-o'-wisp in the forest.

And hope is why she has come here this morning, to the edge of the Thursday estate where a cluster of white flowers can watch her from beside the back door with judgment in their petals like pointing fingers. *Tsk, tsk, Winnie Wednesday. You really shouldn't be here.*

Trillium flexipes. The nodding wakerobin. They were Dad's favorite native flower in Hemlock Falls. No—they *are* his favorite flower because Winnie is going to find him. She is going to bring him home.

She shoulders into the shed. The smell of old grass wafts against her as she fumbles for a switch. Fluorescent lights wink on, revealing that nothing has changed since she last visited two days ago: an electric lamp still hangs on a hook in the corner with a folding chair and tiny bookshelf to stand solemnly beside it.

Winnie swipes the light back off again. It's too bright for what she needs to do. Then she hurries to the corner and drops into the folding chair. In seconds, she's yanking books off the shelf. Gone are the graphic novels and Percy Jacksons of four years ago. In their place are a varied assortment of bodice rippers with bent spines, historical Luminary textbooks with less-bent spines, and some philosophy and self-help books in Spanish that Erica's dad keeps giving her for her birthdays (these spines are not cracked at all; sorry, Antonio).

After she removes eight titles, a small line appears on the shelf's backing. It's where a false panel has been placed, shortening the depth by two inches. Since Erica did the same on all three shelves, it's not visible unless you know what to look for. Even now, knowing what to look for, Winnie has to squint behind her glasses and dig her fingers in. There should be a little divot. A little space to get leverage—

There.

She pulls. The false back peels away to reveal the latest findings from Erica Thursday—although, the two pages Winnie withdraws appear totally blank. And the honey smell that Winnie knows coats them is too weak to compete against the grass and gasoline.

From her back pocket, Winnie slides out a sheet of sketch paper—also deceptively blank—and presses it into the hidden compartment before returning the false panel along with each book in the exact order she removed it. And to make sure there's no difference in dust, she quickly tugs off, then replaces every other book on every other shelf as well.

Her top and bottom teeth click together, a physical manifestation of the nerves churning in her spine—until she shoves her tongue between. She has no reason to be nervous. She has done this three times now, her speed and finesse improving with each visit so that by now, she is basically a full-blown spy.

Agent Wednesday. Dad used to call her that sometimes when they played their secret code and cipher games. She had no idea then how much those games would save her. And maybe save him too.

On her way back out of the cabin, as Winnie folds the pages from Erica into her back pocket, her eyes catch on the old red vampira she and Jay painted five years ago. It has faded, so now only fangs and a single eye remain. Somehow the anatomical inaccuracy makes it more horrifying. Like a corpse left to rot until the forest has transformed it into a revenant.

Tsk, tsk, the trilliums scold as Winnie gently shuts the back door behind her and locks it with the key from Erica. *You really shouldn't be here.*

2

WTF Triangle: These three young adults belong to the Wednesday, Thursday, and Friday clans. Formerly best friends, two of them are now romantically involved while the third is a tentative ally. See also: Winnie Wednesday, witches, and werewolves.

When the WTF triangle met eight days ago, their first reunion in four years, it was awkward. And tense. And Winnie kept imagining spaghetti western music playing in the background, as if she were trapped in the graveyard climax scene of *The Good, the Bad, and the Ugly.* (She's pretty sure she was the Ugly in that scenario.)

But it was also undeniably productive.

If Winnie had brought a voice recorder to the cabin on that night, a transcript of the conversation would have read as follows:

[0:00]

Winnie: [standing below the window] Tell him, Erica. Tell Jay what you actually are.

Erica: [seated in the folding chair] No thanks. I'm good.

Winnie: Okay, then I'll tell him.

[Erica shrugs.]

Winnie: She's a Diana.

[Jay, leaning against a riding lawnmower, stiffens.]

Erica: I am. And Jay's a werewolf.

[Jay stiffens more.]

Winnie: This is a big deal, Erica. You do recall that you broke into my house to steal my dad's clues?

Erica: Because your dad took *my sister's* stuff. That dampener belonged to Jenna, thanks.

[Now Winnie is the one to stiffen. She pushes her glasses up her nose.]

[0:20]

Winnie: And you've known that for how long? Four years? You've *known* your sister was a Diana and my dad wasn't—

Erica: I don't know anything about what your dad was, okay? [lifts both hands] Maybe he was a Diana too. I have no clue. I just know that the dampener I found in your room belonged to Jenna, not him.

Winnie: But how did you even know the dampener was *in* my room?

[A pause while Erica crosses her legs at the ankles and smooths her jeans.]

[0:42]

Erica: I saw that map your dad left on the library shelf, and since I'm a Diana . . . I knew what I was looking at.

Jay: [snorts] So you aren't even gonna try to deny what you are?

Erica: Are you? It's not like you can call the Tuesdays on me, can you?

Winnie: Okay, but Jay didn't *ask* to be a nightmare, Erica—

Erica: [eyes narrowing at Jay] Yeah, how *does* that work?

Winnie: —while you voluntarily became a witch.

Erica: [shrugs] I only recently joined the Dianas, and only because I wanted to know why Jenna died. *How,* too. The official report from the Tuesdays says a vampira horde killed her on her second hunter trial, but I don't buy that. For one, Grayson said . . .

Jay: What? What did Grayson say?

Erica: He said he saw will-o'-wisps near her body when he found her. Not vampira. And for two, it just . . . it's never felt right. Her being on that trial, her dying in the forest. So once I learned she used to be a Diana, well . . . [Erica trails off.]

[1:34]

Winnie: So what—are you saying she was killed because of what she was?

Erica: I have no idea.

Jay: And how did you figure out she was a Diana in the first place?

Erica: How did *you* figure out you were a nightmare?

Winnie: [speaking at the same time as Jay] Stop deflecting questions, Erica!

Jay: [speaking at the same time as Winnie] Because I woke up one night in the forest with no clue how I got there. Is that specific enough for you?

Erica: [sniffs] I found a spell in Jenna's room. It was hidden in her diary.

Winnie: A spell for what?

Erica: I don't know.

Winnie: Do you still have it?

Erica: Of course not. With how nosy my mom is?

Jay: That still doesn't get us from point A to point B. So Jenna was a Diana—why did you become one?

Erica: [glares] They started contacting me. With Jenna's locket. I ignored it at first until . . . I didn't anymore.

Winnie: Wait, how does that work? [She fishes out her locket from her sweater.]

[2:24]

Winnie: This thing sends messages?

Erica: Yeah, the lockets send messages. A small piece of paper shows up in mine with words, sometimes in Latin. Sometimes not.

Jay: [under his breath] Pretentious.

Winnie: Does it ever heat up? And burn?

Erica: No. And that's a weirdly specific question. Does yours do that?

[Winnie doesn't answer. Just pushes the locket back into her sweater.]

[2:45]

Jay: Wait, I thought Grayson had your sister's locket. How did you get it back?

Erica: [bites lip] He gave it to me. After Jenna's funeral.

Jay: Does that mean he knew what Jenna was?

Erica: I have no idea. We didn't talk about it, and I didn't know what the locket meant when he gave it to me. [lifts hands in frustration] Jenna spent *all* her time with him the year before she died. When he showed up to give me the locket and invite me to a party at the old museum . . . Well, the only reason I wanted to go was so I could tell him off for stealing all my sister's time. But then my mom wouldn't let me leave the house, and that was that.

Winnie: But only a few weeks ago, you told me you'd lost the locket. Where was it?

Erica: [flushing] I just misplaced it. The latch is shoddy, and it fell off.

Winnie: Okay, so when did you get your first message from a Diana?

[Erica's lips compress.]

[3:28]

Jay: Come on, Erica. Answer the question.

Erica: Well, when did *you* become a werewolf?

Jay: [unfazed] When I was thirteen.

Erica: [Her eyes narrow again.] Okay, fine. I was twelve. And they sent a message every year after that, but I never answered until last year.

Winnie: Why last year but not before?

Erica: Because I wanted information. *As mentioned,* Winnie, I want to know why Jenna died. And how. [She flips up her hands.]

Jay: And do the Dianas have an answer?

Erica: I . . . don't know. Or at least, I haven't learned anything. Yet.

Jay: So why remain a Diana?

Erica: And why remain a werewolf?

Winnie: Because he can't just change what he is.

Erica: Precisely, Winnie.

[4:02]

Jay: [inhales audibly, then exhales] Give us one good reason we should believe anything you're saying right now, Erica.

Erica: [bounces one shoulder] I don't know. Maybe because I saved your life in the forest, Jay? I knew those witches were after you, but I led them away. Winnie can vouch for that. She was hiding *right* there.

Winnie: [winces, then nods] It's true. She did do that, Jay.

Erica: Look, the only reason I agreed to meet you here tonight is because I think we want the same thing. You want to know what happened to your dad; I want to know what happened to Jenna.

Winnie: And those are connected somehow?

Erica: Obviously. Your dad's map led to Jenna's dampener. *Without* the source inside. Do you know anything about that, by the way?

Winnie: You stole all my stuff. Did it look like I knew anything?

[Erica studies Winnie for several seconds.]

[4:37]

Erica: Okay, so this is why we need to work together. Pool our resources. I know about Dianas, you've got the clues from your dad. And you . . . [She looks at Jay.] I don't know what you contribute, honestly.

Jay: For starters, I'm someone Winnie can *actually* trust.

Erica: What are you trying to say?

Jay: I'm not *trying* to say anything, Erica. I am actively saying you're not trustworthy.

Erica: Oh, because trusting the Big Bad Wolf is a great idea—

Winnie: Enough. Both of you. [Winnie chops her hand at each of them.] Witch, werewolf, Wednesday.

Erica: Huh?

Winnie: Nothing. [She looks at Erica.] Jay is the F in our WTF triangle, okay? I'm not keeping secrets from him, and he *will* help us find what we need.

Erica: So does that mean we have a deal? I help you follow your dad's clues, and you help me find Jenna's source?

Jay: Hold up. I thought you wanted to know what happened to Jenna. You didn't say anything about finding her source.

Erica: [rolls her eyes] The two go hand in hand, Jay. Can't do one without the other. An empty dampener is useless.

Jay: And a full dampener is dangerous.

Erica: Jenna has been dead for four years. There's no magic left inside her source.

Winnie: Stop it, you two. Enough squabbling. And yes. [She extends a hand.] We have a deal, Erica.

[Erica shakes Winnie's hand, firm and businesslike. Jay simply digs his hands into his pockets and turns away.]

[End 6:16]

After that, the spy games began. Although admittedly it has mostly been only Winnie and Erica participating. Partly because there really isn't much that Jay can contribute. But mostly because he still doesn't trust Erica, even after eight days of proving herself useful to them.

And it's fine.

Yep, it's *fine* being caught in the middle.

Winnie didn't expect the WTF gang to become besties again overnight. Sure, she'd hoped for it. (*Hope is the thing with feathers!*) And yeah, she still daydreams of easy camaraderie, but even her loyal bear heart knows she has to approach this Erica alliance with wide eyes and hunter senses turned to max.

So for now, Winnie will be the W in a WT angle . . . and in a WF angle too. And maybe one day—hopefully sooner rather than later—those two corners will slot back into the three-sided shape they're meant to be.

CHAPTER

3

*Nightmare Masquerade: An annual tradition introduced in the 1970s
by Tessa Tuesday in which global Luminaries are invited to explore
Hemlock Falls. Over the course of a week, each clan hosts an elaborate event showcasing their clan's hard work and virtues.*

The high school rises before Winnie, with cars and jeeps and trucks
and bicycles pulling into the parking lot. Students converge, ejected
from parental vehicles or disgorged from their own. The morning is
cold, but the sun peeks up from the high school's south side. The days are
stretching longer now; a reminder that the forest can't steal everything;
that even summer comes to Hemlock Falls eventually.

Casey Tuesday drives past in his red Wrangler and howls at Winnie.

Because of course he does.

Four more howls reach Winnie as she coasts through the parking lot
and toward the bike rack at the front door. She doesn't acknowledge the
howlers, and they're almost static at this point. *Cosmic microwave background.* Now that the werewolf is presumed dead by the entire city—now
that Winnie knows the truth of that wolf and what really happened to her
under the crushing waterfall waves with the melusine and Jay . . .

Well, hope is the thing with feathers and she's feeling a lot of it these
days.

She doesn't even get annoyed by the giant Nightmare Masquerade
banner fluttering beside the school's front door. *Enjoy the celebrations*

and delight in the Floating Carnival! it declares in swirly golden script that Darian spent *hours* agonizing over. *Festivities begin Sunday April 21!*

That's only two days away now, and there's a dramatic illustration of a midnight-blue basilisk coiling around the Ferris wheel that floats on the Little Lake . . .

Okay, maybe Winnie does get a little bit annoyed. That basilisk has its poison glands in the wrong positions along its crown, and the tendrils coming off its cape are not accurate at all. Winnie would know, having seen one up close right before her glasses turned to stone.

Number of basilisks killed a month ago? Zero. Number of basilisks killed now? One.

She huffs a sigh and charges into the school. She is not going to let a poor anatomical representation of a nightmare ruin her day. She has new notes in her pocket from Erica to study later, and although her own just-delivered intel was nothing more than a rehash of things they already know, as far as secret alliances go, this one is working out quite well—and she really hopes Jay will recognize that soon.

When she passes Erica's locker on her way to homeroom and Erica happens to glance her way, Winnie offers only a nod. Which Erica returns in an identical interaction to what they would have shared a few weeks ago. Because they are not friends. They are barely acquaintances.

"*WINNIE!*"

The voice that screeches this is so loud and so close, Winnie is not prepared at all for the explosion in her eardrums. Or how very near Bretta Wednesday is when she flings her arms around Winnie and starts squeezing. Winnie is not a small person, and Bretta is not a large one, but Bretta easily lifts Winnie off her feet as she embraces her with all the ferocity of a Wednesday bear.

"WE DID IT!" This is a new voice and a second set of arms now squeezing.

"Did . . . what?" Winnie grunts out as Fatima's golden hijab presses against her left cheek.

"WE PASSED OUR THIRD TRIAL!" This comes from both Bretta and Fatima simultaneously, and it takes Winnie several seconds to take their jubilant screeching—which is *very loud*—translate it into words, and then process those words.

But eventually the neural pathways connect, and suddenly Winnie is screeching too. And jumping. They're all jumping. "OH MY GOD, YOU PASSED YOUR THIRD TRIAL! YOU PASSED YOUR THIRD TRIAL!"

"LAST NIGHT!" Bretta shouts.

"AND IT WAS AMAZING!" This is from Fatima, who is now pulling back. Bretta, however, still holds tight—and is still jumping. Her corkscrew curls spring while she chants: "We're hunters now, we're hunters now!"

Winnie pries herself loose, though it doesn't slow Bretta. Nor her sister Emma, who has joined their square and is managing a pretty decent jump despite her cast. "We're hunters now, we're hunters now!" She is singing along with her sister.

Actually, there are other people singing too—*You're hunters now, you're hunters now!*—because everyone in the hallway is feeling the ripple of exuberant Luminary joy. Becoming a hunter is a Very Big Deal; they all know that; and their smiles and fist bumps and applause parade by like the happiest of processions.

"We're celebrating after Sunday training today," Bretta says, finally pausing her jumps long enough to speak. Her cheeks are so bunched from smiling, the dimples within look fathomless. "You *have* to come with us! We're gonna go to Falls' Finest to *buy things*."

"Mom's out of town on networker stuff," Emma explains. Her own cheeks are just as round as her sister's—and her eyes may be a bit misty too. "She feels so guilty she missed Bretta's big moment that she's basically told us we can buy whatever we want."

"And," Fatima now inserts with a sly grin, her braces wrapped in bright orange rubber bands, "am I right in guessing you still don't know what you want to be for the Nightmare Ball?"

Winnie cringes—a melodramatic face she knows will make her friends laugh. And they comply, their voices lifting up to the paneled ceiling. "How about an anatomically correct basilisk?" Winnie suggests. "Complete with poison glands on its crown and tendrils that don't curl?"

Her friends are not impressed by this suggestion.

"Okay, you're definitely coming with us." Fatima hooks her arm in Winnie's and hauls her toward their shared homeroom. "Especially because I haven't even told you the most exciting news of all."

Something about the way she utters this makes Winnie's head cock.

Then makes her eyes narrow as Bretta laughs mischievously. "Oh, you're gonna love this part, Winnie!" she calls. "Just wait until you see."

"Um," Winnie asks as she follows Fatima into Ms. Morgan's room—and the bell starts its croaking. "Gonna love what part, Fatima?"

Fatima ignores her. Possibly because the bell is so loud.

"Gonna love *what* part?" Winnie presses once they're both seated in their desks. "Fatima, love *what* part?"

"That." Fatima points at the front of the room, where a grouchy-looking Ms. Morgan stands with a stack of papers in her left hand.

"Time to vote for your Nightmare Court," the teacher half moans, half snarls at the classroom. "These are the names that made it through to the final round of voting. Circle one person from each grade whom you think should . . . should . . . ugh, *represent* you on the Nightmare Court during the Masquerade next week. And please, for the love of god, my children, *do not* take it personally if your name isn't on this list. Winning one of these four crowns will have absolutely no bearing on your future in Hemlock Falls or beyond. It's an antiquated tradition that conflates popularity with success. Name a single Midnight Crown winner who has gone on to do great things?"

"Theresa Monday is a councilor."

"Patrice Thursday manages Falls' Finest."

"Hugo Sábado is the liaison with Mexico."

"Your own boyfriend, Mason, is the Lead Hunter—"

"Okay, okay." Ms. Morgan's head slumps. "I get it. Good lord."

The students don't stop, and more names ricochet around Winnie while Ms. Morgan plods like a pissed-off droll down each row and hands out papers.

Oh, Winnie thinks as one lands on her desk. *Now I see what's going on.* Forty names peer up at her, ten from each of the high school grades. Jay Friday is of course on the senior list, next to his fellow Forgotten band-mates: L.A. Saturday and Trevor Tuesday.

And right there, in the column next to Jay's, is Winnie's own name for year eleven. *Winnie Wednesday, junior,* it reads.

"I'm voting for you," Fatima whispers. "And then you're letting me do your hair when you win."

Winnie only glares at her friend. Then crumples up the paper and slouches back in her seat.

"Bravo, Winnie!" Ms. Morgan cries. "Let's all be like her, please, and refuse to engage! Who's with her?"

No one responds. Pencils and pens scratch furiously. Fatima snickers nearby.

As Winnie shambles out the homeroom door, Ms. Morgan pops up beside her. "Winnie, you dropped these."

A whiff of honey lilts up Winnie's nose—and her stomach slams so hard into the floor that she physically lurches forward two inches.

Because of course, Ms. Morgan is holding the two pages from the cabin. They might be blank, but all it takes is one person asking, *Hmmm, why does Winnie have paper that smells like honey?* and then conducting a Google search. They'll see real fast that honey is an easy way to write secret messages.

Winnie gulps. Then tries to *not* frantically yank the two pages from Ms. Morgan. *HOW DID THESE FALL OUT OF MY POCKET?!* she screams inwardly. Outwardly, she muscles a smile onto her lips. "Oh, ha! Thanks for finding those. Don't want to litter."

"Oh, are they trash?" Ms. Morgan's fingers tighten on the pages. "I can toss them for you."

The harpy laugh this pulls from Winnie's chest is so shrill, it actually hurts. Like, it *hurts* Winnie's lungs and it visibly hurts Ms. Morgan's ears. The teacher winces.

"Nope!" Winnie half shrieks. "I'll toss them myself. Thanks so much." *Tug.* Still no release.

"Actually, Winnie, now that I've got you here, there's something I've been meaning to say."

Oh god, there goes Winnie's stomach again. And her brain too, filling the milliseconds of silence with a thousand worst-case scenarios. *Why are you sending secret messages in honey, Winnie? Why are you sneaking around Hemlock Falls and the Thursday estate? Is Jay a werewolf? Is Erica a witch?*

"I . . . feel I need to apologize."

"Oh." This is so far removed from what Winnie was bracing for, she has to replay the words twice in her head. "For what?"

Ms. Morgan releases the pages. Winnie snatches them to her chest. *Play it cool, play it cool.*

Fortunately, Ms. Morgan isn't paying attention to the papers anymore. Her attention has slid sideways, following a pensive pucker on her lips. "Because I pushed you to apply to that art program at Heritage University a month ago. I had no idea you were going to attempt the hunter trials, and I thought . . . well, I'm sorry. I hope it didn't feel like I was saying you didn't belong in the Luminaries."

"Oh," Winnie says again, breathier this time. "I totally forgot all about that application. There's been a lot going on."

"Understatement of the year." Ms. Morgan sniffs. "It's not like Hemlock Falls is ever uneventful, but things have been especially bananas in recent weeks."

You have no idea. Winnie tries again to exit—she *does* have Algebra 2 to get to, after all. But Ms. Morgan lifts a hand.

"*But,*" she continues, dragging out that word, "I do have another application to give you before you go. This is one I think you're really going to like." She pauses to dig through a large pocket in her skirt. "Where are you, where are you . . . Lip balm, pharmacy receipt, aha! Here we go." She offers a wrinkled paper to Winnie.

Nightmare Compendium Illustrations Contest, it reads along the top, below which is a detailed drawing of a vampira heart (recognizable by the five chambers). *Submit your drawings to be included in the newest edition of the Nightmare Compendium.*

Winnie's heart skips a beat. Like, literally: it stops for the entire span of a usual heartbeat. "Holy crap," she breathes, and for a few seconds, she forgets about the honey-laced pages or that she's supposed to hate the Masquerade.

"Holy crap indeed," Ms. Morgan agrees. "This doesn't circulate until Monday at the Science Fair."

"Um, thank you?" Winnie ogles the flyer. Then flings her gaze up. "Wait—how did you even get this if it's not public yet?"

Ms. Morgan preens. "There are some perks to dating the Lead Tuesday

Hunter. One being that I get first dibs on dessert at clan dinner. Another being that I get sneak peeks and early access to competitions like this one."

"Wow." Winnie shakes her head. Then starts grinning . . . and grinning. "Thank you for showing it to me, Ms. Morgan. I'm really honored."

"Of course." Ms. Morgan grins right back. "All I ask is that you win, okay? So pick something *really* complicated to illustrate."

"I will." Winnie's mind is already leaping from one possibility to another. *Kelpie vascular systems are pretty incredible—oh, but spidrin spinnerets have microscopic spigots to create silk filaments.* Winnie slings her backpack around to stuff in the application. *And then there's the banshee claw, which I've studied firsthand!* But as she starts unzipping her bag, a thought erupts in her frontal lobe. If Ms. Morgan hears things before other people, then maybe . . .

"Hey, Ms. Morgan, um . . ." Winnie pauses, fighting the urge to click her teeth. This is a perfectly normal question; she has no reason to be nervous at all. "Has Mason ever seen anything weird in the forest?"

"I'm pretty sure *everything* in the forest is considered weird." Ms. Morgan snorts. "But you're talking about that thing that chased you, right? The Rustler?"

"The Whisperer," Winnie corrects, even though that isn't what she was talking about at all. What *she* was talking about were Dianas—including the two very dead corpses she left melted in the forest and whom absolutely no one has mentioned since.

It defies the third law of motion: for every action in nature, there is an equal and opposite reaction. In the Luminaries, that means when witches show up, Tuesdays assemble. Yet an entire week has passed since the forest burned and Jay nearly got taken by witches. Since Aunt Rachel *should* have died, but got saved by Jay while Winnie faced off to a powerful Diana leader. Yet there have been no broadcasts on the nightly news about witches, no warnings around town to be on the lookout for magical activity, and no sudden wails from the siren that stands next to city hall.

It defies basic physics.

Every day, Winnie has waited for an announcement to come. For the town to erupt with a droll-sized panic that would make their werewolf fears look unicellular in comparison. But every day, there's nothing.

And right now, Ms. Morgan doesn't seem to know about it either.

"Oh yeah. Whisperer, not Rustler." Ms. Morgan wags her head. "No, I'm afraid Mason's never mentioned anything about that. But hey, have you ever considered . . ."

That I'm crazy? Winnie thinks. *That it's all in my head? Because yeah, I worried about that for a while.*

". . . that maybe it isn't a nightmare?" Ms. Morgan shrugs. "I don't know. Just something to think about. You're the Luminary, not me!"

Winnie blinks at the petite, round-hipped lady who made her memorize poems two years ago. Ms. Morgan is shockingly close to the heart of the matter. *Pure Heart. Trust the Pure Heart.* Like, so close she has basically guessed what's really going on.

But maybe that's to be expected. Ms. Morgan is a non, after all. Her culture doesn't run thicker than blood, so maybe it's only natural she'd have an outsider's view on things.

"Thanks, Ms. Morgan." Winnie offers her a smile. It's tight, but real. Then she finishes shoving the application *and* her secret pages into her backpack (she digs those all the way down to the bottom; no falling out this time). "I really appreciate the application."

"Of course, Winnie." The teacher beams. "I'm always on your side."

4

The rest of Winnie's school day is blissfully uneventful. On the ride to Falls' Finest in the Wednesday family van after Sunday training, Winnie revels in the continued elation of Bretta and Fatima, who refer (in the cagiest of terms) to *our third trial that we have to keep totally secret.* Everyone laughs along willingly, Winnie loudest of all.

Although she can't help but notice Emma isn't *quite* as enthusiastic. So while they trace the brick sidewalks of downtown toward the glossy, glassy entrance of the main shopping hub in Hemlock Falls, Winnie hangs back. Emma might officially be off crutches, but she's still in a cast and always a few steps behind.

It doesn't help that the streets are extra crammed from an influx of foreign Luminaries here to enjoy the Nightmare Masquerade. The only two restaurants in town (the Très Jolie and the Revenant's Daughter) have lines stretched down the sidewalk. Plus, decorations cover everything: banners on the streetlamps, colored lanterns in the trees, garlands on benches and trash bins, and—annoyingly—that inaccurate basilisk poster everywhere.

Come on, Darian! Why wouldn't you consult your sister before printing that design in bulk?

"Hey," Winnie offers Emma quietly. "How are you feeling about . . . this?" She dips her head toward Bretta and Fatima, who bound forward, arms around each other like they're off to see the Wizard (the wonderful Wizard of Oz!).

Emma sighs. She doesn't need Winnie to elaborate on what *this* means.

"You know, I'm happy for Bretta. I really am. And I'm sure she'll leap right into training—"

Winnie's insides curdle at the word *training*. She definitely forgot about Aunt Rachel's email from that morning.

"—because that's how Bretta is. She sees what she wants and she just . . . Well, she goes and gets it. Even when we were babies, she walked a full month sooner than I did. Mom always says it was because Bretta was way too impatient and wanted to make sure she could get to our toys and have first pick. But . . ." Emma trails off.

Winnie lets a silence stretch between them, broken only by the ambient noise of other Luminaries milling about in the blustery downtown. Emma will say what she wants in her own time, and it's one of the things Winnie most appreciates about her. Emma is always intentional, in her words, in her movements, in her choices.

Sure enough, right when they reach the entrance to Falls' Finest, shoppers moving more speedily around them, Emma finally offers: "I think this might be another time where Bretta's ready to walk, but I'm still good with crawling. Does that make sense? I know I passed my third trial, and I know I felt ready before I went into it with you . . . But I didn't *like* being out there. And not because of the harpy or the werewolf or any of the other nightmares I saw. I didn't . . . well, I don't think I feel like Bretta does when she's in those trees."

Winnie nods. They have stopped walking. Fatima and Bretta are gone, swallowed up by the store along with all the other Luminaries who need last-minute outfits for the week of celebration.

"It definitely makes sense." Winnie reaches out to touch her friend's arm. Just a gentle brush above Emma's elbow. "And I'll support you whether you join the hunt or become a networker or give up entirely on the Luminaries." Her throat tightens on those last words. She *really* doesn't want Emma to give up entirely on the Luminaries.

Emma smiles. "Don't tell Bretta, okay? She still thinks I'm going to go full hunter mode as soon as I'm out of this cast. And hey—I might. I'll definitely attend some training sessions before I make any decisions. But . . ."

"But," Winnie agrees. "And don't worry: I won't say a word to anyone."

"I know." Emma briefly rests her head on Winnie's shoulder in a sideways half hug. Her braids smell like her favorite lilac perfume. "That's why I like you so much, Winnie. You're a great listener, and a steel vault for secrets. Sometimes, that's exactly what a gal needs."

While Winnie knows Emma's words were offered in kindness, they pummel and churn like stones in a harpy gizzard. *You're a great listener, and a steel vault for secrets.*

Yeah, Winnie is a steel vault all right. The kind that's really heavy and sinks down to the bottom of a lake. Probably the Big Lake while kelpies and sirens feast on her bones. First, Winnie has too many secrets of her own, ranging from dad-shaped to Diana-shaped to lying-about-a-banshee-shaped. Then she has all these other people's secrets too. Like Jay's bona fide status as a daywalking nightmare *werewolf.* Or Erica's unabashed, strutting-around status as a *freaking Diana.*

Fortunately, there's not enough space in Winnie's abdomen for guilt to wedge in. It's just *so stinking fun* to be with her new best friends. Plus, she hasn't been shopping in actual years, and on top of that, *she* isn't the one who has to pay for new clothes because according to Fatima, Winnie has access to the Wednesday clan's credit line.

"Mom told me I need to look good for all the foreign Luminaries coming to town." Fatima is studying the seam quality on a pair of cherry-red trousers as she says this. "Then she told me I should buy a few things for you too, Win. *Our local celebrity must look her best!*" Fatima shrugs, glancing at Winnie with clear apology in her blue eyes. "Not that you don't always look your best, I mean."

Winnie doesn't take it personally that Fatima's mom Leila *also* thinks her wardrobe sucks. Or at least, the truth stings a lot less once she has a pair of dark jeans, a fitted white T-shirt, and a wispy black dress with a pink flower pattern (that Bretta picked out for her) folded inside a paper bag. She even gets some black ankle boots she can wear with the dress *and* the jeans, and although Fatima insists Winnie should buy more stuff if she wants it . . .

Well, Winnie is pretty sure there's a point at which she's just being greedy. Besides, the one thing she really wants are new glasses, but that is beyond the purview of Falls' Finest.

Maybe it's time to try contacts again. Or not. (*Yuck*, touching your eyeball!)

Winnie spends so many hours with her square of friends that she barely has time to get home, change, and then pedal at maximum speed to the Wednesday estate for training, which is definitely *not* the thing she wants to do next. She hasn't gotten to read the latest messages from Erica; she hasn't eaten dinner; and she has a book report due tomorrow for a book she can't even remember the title of.

But for some reason, Winnie is pretty sure none of those reasons will seem valid to Aunt Rachel. Plus, Winnie can't deny she's ready to get this whole encounter over with. She has been avoiding her aunt for a week now, ever since their awkward debrief at the hospital, when Rachel basically said, *I will cover for you and Jay, and we'll all pretend that the werewolf is dead and you had nothing to do with those burned Dianas.*

So yeah. It's time to rip off this Band-Aid.

Tulips, newly erupted in vivid red, pink, and purple, flutter in neat rows beside the narrow green door into the Wednesday clan's Armory, i.e., the basement compound where hunters train. The evening sun shines, and rain clouds that had threatened to unload earlier have dispersed unemptied. The forest does that sometimes: breaks its weather promises right as you prepare for the winds to blow a certain way.

Although Winnie can't see it from this angle, she hears the beep and grind of power tools and construction gear. If she were to keep walking until she reached the gardens that sprawl behind the estate, she would see the assembly of pergolas and stages and tens of booths for the Hunters' Feast on Wednesday.

Each clan has their own celebration, and for the Wednesday bears, it's all about the food.

Winnie's breaths are shallow, her body warm from pedaling here on the family bike. She frowns at a flyer for the Nightmare Masquerade on the brick wall beside the Armory door. Then she considers if she should submit an anatomical cross section of a basilisk fang for the Compendium contest . . .

Then she accepts she is procrastinating and she charges through the un-locked door. Stairs descend before her. The spring sun winks away as she plummets down two steps at a time.

The first thing she notices is the smell—something floral, like a spa waits ahead and not an intense gym for the practice of killing monsters. Fluores-cent lights glimmer, gentle and unwavering and always at perfect brightness. Footsteps hammer, as does a sound like fists on foam targets. Then Winnie steps off the stairs into a wide space filled with hunters on the move. They leap, they roll, they swing at each other and block expertly.

Winnie stands on the second-to-last step while chills roll down her arms. This is what she wanted. *This* is what she dreamed of joining—more than the Masquerade, more than Sunday estate training, more than Wednesday clan dinners or even easy access to the Monday libraries . . .

Now here she is, and *wow*. She really has come so far in a month.

"Hey, kid!" Rachel's voice barks out over the din. It takes Winnie a few seconds to target-lock her aunt, who waves from behind a row of red punching bags. As Winnie jogs toward her, Wednesday hunters slow their workouts long enough to nod. A second cousin named Keifer throws out a hand for a fist bump, and it's such a casual gesture that Winnie's chest swells up like a puffer fish. Chad Wednesday, who made fun of Winnie on her first day of corpse duty—*Death is a part of life. Get used to it, Little Win-Win, or you won't last a week inside the forest*—hollers, "Nice to see ya, Winnie!"

He and Keifer aren't impressed by what Winnie did on her third trial. No one in this basement is, because they don't look at Winnie and see a celebrity. Instead, they see a new recruit joining the hunt.

For half a second, as Winnie nears Aunt Rachel—no sign that Rachel is the Lead Hunter beyond her general air of authority—a sadness grips Win-nie's organs. It wrings out her stomach, digs into her intestines. Because Mom didn't just lose her husband four years ago. Or her job or her friends. She lost her entire network, her entire identity.

Mom *used* to be a part of this, shouting orders and adjusting hunter form like Rachel does. She *used* to get fist bumps and welcome nods.

Then Winnie reaches Aunt Rachel, who, rather than acknowledge her niece, instead shoos Winnie over to the side so she can scope out two hunt-ers sprinting by on the indoor track. *Thump, thump, thump* go their boots.

In one hand, they swing their training bows. In the other, their training knives.

"First lesson," Rachel says flatly, watching them fly by. "If you're going to carry something in one hand, always have something else in the other. The human body evolved with bilateral symmetry." Her attention briefly flicks to Winnie's. "So if you only hold something on one side, your body is out of balance. And that, in turn, will slow you down."

"Oh." Winnie blinks, fastening her attention once more on the two hunters—who are somehow already halfway around the track. They've caught up to a slower mass of runners, and they dip and weave through the crowd before surging ahead again.

The taller of the two, Robin Wednesday (no relation to Winnie), is grinning as they gain ground on Jodi Wednesday (also no relation).

Rachel cups her hands to her mouth. "Tag her, Robin!"

Robin's grin widens. They double back and charge for Jodi, but Jodi is already diving into the mass of runners—who sway and scoot and duck to avoid Jodi. What ensues is one of the coolest things Winnie has ever seen. It's like watching bacteria crawl across a petri dish. The slower runners just keep jogging, veering as they must to avoid collision, while Robin and Jodi play an advanced game of tag.

All while holding their knives and bows too.

Then the bacterial mass has reached Winnie and Rachel. Boots and bodies thunder by. Jodi gets a punch at Robin's chest. Robin gets a kick into Jodi's low back. And Winnie has never wanted to play a game as much as she wants to play this one.

Perhaps because Winnie is grinning like an old family photo of Grandma Winona splattered with vampira viscera, Rachel says: "Don't worry, Win. You'll be part of that soon enough. You need better training clothes though. Here." She fishes a small key out of her hoodie pocket. "For your locker. Number eighteen."

Winnie swallows. Number eighteen. Mom's locker. For all of Winnie's childhood, that key hung on a hook beside her family's fridge.

Winnie accepts the key, slightly warm from Rachel's pocket, and finds a look in her aunt's eyes she has seen before: in the forest when Rachel really *wanted* to help Winnie and Jay, but her loyalty to the cause said she couldn't.

Winnie swallows a second time, but her throat isn't as willing to cooperate this time. Rachel looks away first, attention lasering onto her hunters. The brief glimpse of feelings is already gone, squashed beneath a Lead Hunter's frown and a hard, "Nicki and Tanaz, you're up! Jodi and Robin, to the bags!" She doesn't look at Winnie as she adds more quietly, "Get dressed, Win. We have work to do."

"Yeah," Winnie murmurs. She closes her hand around the key. One day—hopefully soon—Mom will be allowed to hunt again. Then Winnie will give her locker number eighteen, and the order of the world will be right again.

For now, though, this locker is hers. And for now, Winnie has work to do.

C H A P T E R

5

Winnie never joins the bacterial tag mass that thunders around the indoor track, but she still gets in plenty of movement for the next few hours. In fact, Rachel's regimen for her hunters makes Jay's tutoring sessions look like child's play. Like an *actual* child playing.

Winnie punches bags, she grapples other Wednesdays, she jumps hurdles and climbs ropes, and she repeatedly wonders, *Why did I want to do this?* She goes for at least two hours until her new black leggings and tank top are soaked through with sweat, and until eventually, Rachel slows the whole show down with a hollered, "Forest loop!"

Winnie doesn't know what that means, but she figures if she just follows everyone while they aim for the stairwell out of the Armory, she'll get her answer soon enough. She slots onto the end, jogging at an easy pace. Rachel falls into step behind her. They are the caboose to a long train of hunters doing everything Rachel commands.

Soon Winnie is up the stairs, out of the estate, and stamping steadily over gravel garden paths. The final rays of sunset laser over the Wednesday rooftop. Night will fall soon, and with it the mist will rise.

Flowers in full bloom melt past Winnie. A Monet painting daubed with blues and greens and purples—and fractured by a bright orange construction crane as well as a smattering of half-assembled food booths, each one proclaiming a different sort of delicious cuisine for free tasting.

Winnie is still the caboose on the Wednesday train, and she's okay with that. Her muscles are exhausted; her brain too; and not for the first time tonight, she dreams of her future dinner, which will probably be more PB&Js like her lunch.

Oh *boy*, peanut butter and jelly. It's basically dessert masquerading as a meal. In other words: delicious.

At the garden gate that feeds into old-growth forest and newer trees, the hunters narrow into a single-file line . . . then re-form into a more diffuse blob once they're on the path beyond. Winnie reaches the gate of wrought-iron bars attached to red brick. It wavers uncomfortably.

She shakes her head.

Soon, her boots stamp onto stepping stones. They're not yet illuminated by the trail's automatic lights. Twenty feet away, the stones fork into three paths. The right trail will circle Winnie to another trail. Left will loop back to the Wednesday estate. And straight will transport her to the forest.

Straight is where all the hunters go. So straight is where Winnie goes too.

Her breaths, which were labored before, now shift toward something pained. Something erratic. A cramp carves into her stomach, and for several moments, she thinks she hears music chasing behind her—a bass line trembling out into the night while magenta winks and glitters in the throng of hunters. Then suddenly it's masks she sees, charcoal-colored and canine . . .

You're fine, she tells herself. *You're just hungry. You just need food.*

But Winnie has never been good at lying, not even to herself. Her body knows the truth. *Number of people murdered one month ago? Zero. Number of people murdered now? Two.*

You're a murderer.

You killed them.

She makes herself keep going. The mist won't rise for another two hours; the forest is just a forest, no nightmares to escape. No hunters on the prowl.

Hunters like Jay because today is Friday, and soon he will be out there in the trees, putting his life at risk to protect not only Hemlock Falls, but an entire world who has no idea he exists.

No. Winnie can't think about this either. About Jay and how she almost lost him a week ago. *Just focus on the ground. On your stride. Bilateral symmetry, bilateral symmetry.*

Winnie doesn't notice her feet slowing. Stopping. She's just suddenly doubled over while the rest of the Wednesday hunters timpani-roll onward.

Red stakes wink like wicked candles nearby, marking the edge of the sleeping spirit's domain.

Rachel moves beside her, scooping a firm hand onto Winnie's shoulder and hauling her upright. "Keep going," she murmurs.

So Winnie keeps going. Although she doesn't make it far before she says: "You should be dead." She is panting. The words are strained.

"Yep," is all Rachel replies. Then she thrusts a water bottle into Winnie's grasp. She was clutching it in one hand while she jogged, and Winnie doesn't miss that in Rachel's other hand, she grips a small first aid kit—which she opens as soon as Winnie claims the bottle.

They are in the forest now. The nightmare forest, and although the last rays of pink try to knife their way in, here it is always shadow, always gray. Because this world belongs to the sleeping spirit. This world is infested with monsters.

Winnie sips from the bottle's squeeze top. It makes her footsteps lose their steady rhythm, but the cold feels good sliding down her throat. So she sucks in more, more, until she has drained most of the bottle and the sweat across her skin turns icy.

Her pace is so disrupted now, it's more walk than run. But since Rachel isn't stopping, Winnie isn't either. This is the way the mama bear goes, so the cub will follow.

"Eat this," Rachel commands, and Winnie finds herself blinking down at a gel pouch that proclaims it is *Hi EnerG!* In an *All-New Cherry Flavor!* It looks about as appetizing as *Chrysomya megacephala* maggots on a dead body.

"You need the calories," Rachel insists, and she rips off the top before Winnie can protest. The pouch presses against her lips and Rachel reclaims the water bottle. The gel turns out tasting as appetizing as the maggots probably would, but once Winnie gets it down, she *does* feel better.

The forest still looks like it wants to kill her, though.

Because it does.

"This . . . this shouldn't be so hard," Winnie pants out. "All the stuff in the forest—my trial, the Whisperer, the . . ." She can't make herself say *dead Dianas.* "It bothered me at first, but I thought I'd moved on." *I thought I'd learned to eat the pizza.*

Rachel snorts in a truly mama-bear fashion. "Yeah, that's not how trauma works, kid. Which is why we do this run." With no disruption to her stride, she straps the water bottle to a holster on her hip. Then the first aid kit too. "You're not the only one with bad memories of the forest. But the only way we can exorcise our ghosts is if we keep on facing 'em. Until you go out on the hunt again, this will be your exorcism."

"And if I can't exorcise? If I can't compartmentalize?"

"I never said compartmentalize." Rachel's arms settle into a steady, effortless swing. Like her hands are pendulums with no friction or gravity to act upon them. "That's a good skill to have, sure, but only while you're in the forest. Most of us—we can't compartmentalize forever. All the ghosts have to go somewhere. And if you can't find a way to exorcise them on your own, then we have trained professionals who can help you do so."

Winnie, her own arms most *definitely* affected by friction and gravity, lets her brain gnaw at Rachel's words. Nine nights ago, in the forest, Winnie decided the darkness that always drags at the light in Hemlock Falls must come from everyone eating their pizza, from everyone pretending pain, violence, and nightmares can never harm them. She decided, too, that Rachel must have a lockbox full of such ghosts.

And it's true. Rachel is saying as much right now. But she's also saying that she knows they're in there—and that she knows when to ask for help setting them free.

Winnie side-eyes her aunt. In this dim light, Rachel might as well be a younger version of Mom. And Mom, Winnie knows, has plenty of ghosts too. Except she never asks for help; she never even acknowledges their existence.

"You should be dead," Winnie repeats to Rachel.

And her aunt nods. "Many times over." A pause. A glance ahead to ensure they're still alone. Then, in a voice that is simultaneously harder and softer—like she's really straining to be gentle here, but the Lead Hunter part of her demands aggression: "Who else knows about Jay?"

"Just me and you." *Pant, pant.* "And Mario Monday."

"Mario knows?" A thoughtful frown folds Rachel's eyebrows. It's a look Winnie's mom makes with great regularity, particularly when watching reruns of *Murder She Wrote.* A look that says: *Well, that's a twist I didn't see coming.* "That explains why he was so ready to sign off on my Proof of Kill last week. I thought it was just because I was in the hospital and he didn't want to wear me out."

Winnie snorts. "Knowing Mario, that's probably what he wanted every-one else to think too."

"Have you talked to him about this?"

Winnie shakes her head. "Every time I try to find him, he's either out of his office with Science Fair stuff or Councilor Monday is right there."

Rachel winces at that because Theresa, as the councilor for the Mondays, is *definitely* not someone Winnie—or Rachel or Jay—wants noticing them.

"And what about . . ." Winnie hesitates. Wipes sticky hair off her sweat-ing brow. "What about the Tuesdays?"

"Yeah." This is all Rachel says at first, and it could mean a million dif-ferent things, ranging from *Yeah, they have come to talk to me* to *Yeah, I'm wondering why they haven't shown up yet* to *Yeah, they are indeed a clan in the Luminaries, Winnie.*

But then she finally elaborates: "Yeah, they talked to me, but it was weird."

"How so?"

"It was, ah, *spare,* I guess. Jeremiah came to my hospital room, asked a handful of vague questions, and that was it. No one has followed up with me since."

"Whoa." That could not have been more opposite from Winnie's experi-ence four years ago, when she thought the interrogations would never end. *Those* ghosts still haunt her today; she knows she will never exorcise them.

"My thoughts exactly." Rachel rubs her forehead with a sleeve. A lot *less* sweat drips off her than Winnie. "I don't like it, Winnie. And I wish I hadn't told Marcus that Dianas jumped me, because now he's terrified to sleep."

"Ah." Winnie wants to feel bad about that. She and her younger cousin shared a brief moment after Rachel nearly died . . . But it was short-lived. Marcus is back to pure, unadulterated goblin these days. "Has he told any-one about the Dianas?"

"No. I asked him not to, so we could keep from frightening the city. And the kid has kept his word."

"Well, maybe the Tuesdays are keeping it under wraps because of the Nightmare Masquerade? Like maybe, once the Masquerade passes, they'll investigate more publicly?"

"Maybe. But there was an awful lot of uproar over that werewolf."

Winnie almost trips at the word *werewolf.*

Rachel doesn't notice. "We had forums, we had testing sites and daily broadcasts. But Dianas are so much worse than a daywalker. They're *why* we have the siren downtown: to warn against our greatest enemy." She glances at Winnie, as if expecting Winnie to contradict this somehow. As if Winnie might have some insight that says, *Nah, Dianas aren't so bad.*

But Winnie's got nothing. She has been taught the exact same history as Rachel: back in the earliest days of Hemlock Falls, when the spirit had only *just* been born in the US, the Dianas fought to gain a foothold in the forest. It was ugly; people died; and the siren downtown—built to warn of Diana attacks—howled almost weekly.

In the end, the Luminaries of Hemlock Falls were stronger than the Dianas. The witches went back into hiding around the globe. The old siren fell into stale disuse, and later, it was repurposed to warn of nightmares escaping the forest.

But just because the siren hasn't howled doesn't mean the Dianas are gone—as Rachel and Winnie know all too well.

The Dianas still want to wake up each of the world's spirits.

They still want to overrun the world with nightmares and claim all the spirit magic for themselves.

So if *Danger to Luminaries* were plotted on a graph, with *Nightmares* on one side of the X axis and *Dianas* on the other, then all the data would *definitely* trend toward Dianas.

And this is why Jay doesn't trust Erica.

"All right," Rachel says with a heavy exhale. "I'm going to poke around a bit. Carefully, of course."

"And me?" Winnie asks. "What should I do?"

"Same as you have been for the last eight days: avoid attention, stay out of trouble, and keep training. Be the model Luminary you've always wanted to be."

Winnie has to fight to keep a grimace off her face. She's pretty sure leaving secret messages with her ex–best friend who is a Diana does not qualify as *staying out of trouble* or *being a model Luminary.* Nor does dating a werewolf.

Ahead, footsteps rumble. Rachel's lips pinch with part frustration, part disappointment. "We have to cut this short, Winnie. I see my hunters coming this way."

"Right," Winnie replies. She tries to swallow; her mouth tastes like cherry mixed with maggots.

"Don't forget dawn training this week," Rachel finishes. "And we'll chat more soon. Hey, Tanaz! Look at you, leading the pack. Not bad. But let's see if you can beat me."

"Mom! I'm home!" Winnie bangs at the kitchen back door. It is locked, which isn't a bad thing. Winnie was the one to lock it, after all. But this is a new behavior for her since discovering Erica stole all her stuff, so Winnie is now out here without a key.

Worse, the rain finally broke. No warning, of course, and with all the clouds seemingly gone until halfway on Winnie's bike ride home. *Kapow! Here you go,* the forest seemed to say, its thunder a maniacal laugh, and by the time Winnie reached the house, she was soaked through—as was the enormous bear flag still hanging off the front porch.

Winnie imagines she looks as limp and defeated as it does.

"Mom!" Winnie bangs harder. "Let me in! I locked the door and forgot a key!" Winnie knows Mom is home. The Volvo is parked on the front curb, and the light is on in her room.

A crow caws—loudly. Winnie jolts sideways, practically tripping over herself. But it's just the usual crow that lives on the roof, now perched on the recycling bin. Why it is out in this rain, Winnie can't say. But she shoos at it.

The crow caws again. Then nips at her, wings flapping.

"Eep!" Winnie shrieks at the same moment the back door finally swings wide. Winnie topples inside. "Did you see that?"

"I did." Mom slams the door shut before the crow can hop in—because it is *literally* trying to hop in. "It did that to me earlier! Do you think we should call Animal Control?"

Animal Control is really just Mom's second cousin Lauren and the five people Lauren gets to help her out with wildlife control. Vermin are vermin everywhere, even if sometimes the rats and raccoons become ghost-rats and ghost-raccoons in Hemlock Falls.

"No, leave Lauren alone." Winnie peels off her wet training gear. "The crow is probably just hungry."

"Oh." Mom blinks. "That's possible. Now that I'm working fewer hours at the Daughter, I'm not giving him as many hamburgers." She bites her lip and hurries to a notepad beside the swear jar (currently full after Mom got spectacularly angry over a pot pie that exploded last week). "Crow . . . food," she murmurs, pen scratching. "Hey, wait." Her head snaps up. Winnie is now down to her sports bra and underwear. There's a small puddle forming around her. "Why was the back door locked? I've noticed you've been doing that lately—and I've almost been locked out twice now too. You know we have a key hidden under the azalea, right?"

"I did *not* know." Winnie hastily grabs her wet garments—and then hastily stomps to the laundry room. She can't exactly say, *Well, Mom, I met Dianas in the forest a week ago, and they might try to break in and steal my stuff like Erica did—who, surprise! Is a Diana! As such, I feel that locking our doors would be a smart tactic moving forward.* On top of that, since Winnie is the worst liar in the history of bad liars, she is better off trying to deflect right now than respond.

"Did Jay call?"

"No." Mom appears at the laundry room door. She waggles her eyebrows. "But the night is young."

"Not for a Lead Hunter."

"Right." Mom's cheeks bunch up. "Tonight's Friday."

"Tonight's Friday." Winnie sighs, trying not to consider that these flies buzzing in her lungs must have flown in Dad's lungs too, every Wednesday night when Mom went out on the hunt. She slings open the washer door and dumps in her wet clothes. "Oh hey, how's the new job? Is being a Wednesday networker like you remember? Also did you get assigned an office? I would have come by to see, but I went to hunter training. And holy whoa, Rachel is *so* tough."

"She is," Mom concurs. Her eyebrows slope in unmasked longing. "How was it? What drills did she do? And did you get a locker?"

As relieved as Winnie is that Mom has completely and totally forgotten about the locked door, she also feels crappy over her choice of subject change. Because Mom's hunger for her old life isn't just evident in the acute angles of her brow; it's audible in her voice, slightly breathy. Falsely nonchalant.

Winnie dumps detergent into the washer. "Have you heard anything from the Council about when you can hunt again? Or is it still vague nothings?"

"Okay, that is way too much powder, my child." Mom scoots over and tugs the detergent from Winnie's grasp. "And this should be a delicate wash if you want those leggings to last." She hip-bumps Winnie aside. "As for the Council, it's still vague nothings. *Soon, Frannie. Don't get ahead of yourself! You're four years out of practice, after all.*"

Me too, Winnie thinks, recalling how winded she was at training while Rachel's sweat glands barely switched on.

"Oh, hey," Mom says, clanging shut the washer door. "Did you go shopping today? I saw a Falls' Finest bag on the couch."

"I did." Winnie grins slyly. "Apparently Leila wants me to look presentable for all these Luminaries coming to town, so I got to buy stuff on the Wednesday credit line."

"Dang, girl."

"I *know.* Want a fashion show?"

"Of course."

Winnie's smile stretches wider, and in under a minute, the living room has become a runway. And of course, Mom *oohs* and *ahs* at all the right moments. The rain might be falling, Winnie's muscles might be hurting, and she might have two pieces of paper covered in invisible ink that still need reading . . . but right now, Winnie is really, really *happy* to have this pocket of goodness.

All that's missing is Dad. He would perch on a couch arm, making his own fashion-related observations while wryly commenting that Mom and Winnie are kind of terrible at this. *In conclusion,* he would say, *take me and Darian with you next time you go shopping. I didn't win Best Dressed in high school for nothing.*

Then Winnie would laugh and say, *I do not want to shop with my dad and brother, thanks.*

Dad would shake his head in mock seriousness and say, *Your loss, Win-*

Ben. Your loss. And it *would* be her loss because it *has* been her loss for four endless years.

> *Hope is the thing with feathers*
> *That perches in the soul,*
> *And sings the tune without the words,*
> *And never stops at all,*
>
> *And sweetest in the gale is heard;*
> *And sore must be the storm*
> *That could abash the little bird*
> *That kept so many warm.*

It is almost midnight before Winnie can sneak downstairs and finally de-code Erica's message. She had to wait for Mom to go to bed, then wait an-other hour to ensure Mom was *fully* asleep. Winnie herself is half asleep and in her pj's (sweatpants and an ancient Charmander T-shirt) by the time she reaches the kitchen and lights the gas stove. Just one eye, one flame.

She pulls Erica's message from her pocket and waves it high, high over the fire. Not *too* high or there won't be enough heat. Not too low or the paper will burn . . .

There it is. The honey caramelizes. Words appear.

Still no news on who the Diana hounds were, and really no news anywhere. There was only that one message in the locket from Friday when I asked for help—and they said "no communication, stay hidden"—and nothing has come since. My guess is the Masquerade is forcing the Dianas to stay away. (Or forcing the Diana Crow if she's the only one remaining.) So many Luminaries visiting means more chances to get caught!

I do have other news, though. Katie Tuesday had too much hard cider last night, and she let it slip that her cousin Isaac saw Dianas in the forest. "Dead ones," she said. "And he claims he has pictures." Fortunately, she thinks he's just making it up. She also seemed to realize she should not have told me what she did. Isaac could get in huge trouble. Like outcast-level trouble for taking photos.

Katie made me swear I wouldn't tell anyone. Guess I'm already breaking that swear!

I'm going to try to find Isaac. Maybe those pictures will give us clues. Rumor is he eats lunch every day at the Daughter, so I'll try that tomorrow.

Thank you for going back over your dad's clues, but you're right that there doesn't seem to be anything missing. YARGH. I am getting so frustrated. I hope that book about secret messages arrives soon from Italy. Although at this rate, it'll just be another dead end. ~~Because of course that's my~~

I'll be busy with all the Luminaries visiting, so I'll have to write less, I suspect. But I'll keep checking to see if you've left any updates.

Winnie reads Erica's letter twice. Writing in honey water means the words are big and sloppy, with only a few paragraphs fitting to each page. But despite the mess of their "invisible ink," it's still Erica's handwriting. Familiar after four years.

It used to be that Erica would write Winnie notes all the time. They'd trade letters in class, finding fun ways to fold the pages and secret moments to slide them to each other. No one else could write in cursive, but Erica *always* used it—like she was some nineteenth-century heiress. She would even end every note with *Yours sincerely, Erica Antonia Thursday.*

She has not ended this particular letter that way.

Winnie homes in on the part that Erica scratched through. She can *just* make out the words *Because of course that's my.* And although that's all Winnie can decipher, she can fill in the blank: *Because of course that's my luck.*

Erica's old letters used to be part confessional, part diary. As if only by writing her feelings down could she extract their meaning. Her half sister Jenna wrote songs. Erica wrote letters. And Winnie . . . well, she drew. Her responses to Erica's letters would always be just a line or two of text, then she would draw. Cartoons of their teachers. A portrait of Erica's latest crush (which, *gross,* was briefly Peter Sunday). A crude diagram of a particularly juicy event in third period. All of it got sketched onto the page—and not only because Winnie enjoyed doing it but because her doodles *always* made her best friend laugh.

Winnie used to save all of Erica's notes. She had a giant, family-sized canister that smelled of its first life as an Earl Grey can (*Address me as "my lord."*). By the time Winnie was twelve, that thing was crammed completely with folded notes. Always, they were addressed to *Winona*, because Erica loved calling her that.

Dear Winona, guess what Peter said to me today in algebra!

But then Winnie's world collapsed, Erica walked away, and Winnie threw every single one of Erica's cursive confessionals into the trash.

Which is where she throws this latest one too. She is a human paper shredder, tearing the pages into smaller and smaller strips as she aims for the back door. Her mind whirls and spins. Isaac Tuesday took a picture, which is both super surprising and absolutely not surprising at all. It's human nature to want to cling to things—to stuff them into a canister for perusal at a later date. But Erica was also right: that sort of infraction could get him expelled from the Luminaries, a fate which Winnie would rate one out of five stars, thank you.

After a careful pause at the back door to ensure there are no stirrings from upstairs, Winnie eases up the lock. Then eases the doorknob sideways. The hinges creak, the wood resists, but she has done this enough times in the past week to recognize the door's rhythms. Here, if she lifts just a little on the knob, it'll squeal less. Here, if she goes a bit slower—

CAW.

Winnie jumps, flinging her shredded letter like confetti at the crow. It still waits atop the garbage, blinking as if to say, *Where the hell have you been?*

"Shoo," Winnie hisses at it. "Shoo, shoo. Dammit, *shoo!*" The crow does not shoo. It just watches Winnie gather up fallen pieces of paper and then toss them in the blue recycling bin. Then it continues its vigil as she returns to the back door.

"Do *not* caw at me again." Winnie waggles her fingers. "If you wake my mom, I will make sure she never gives you another hamburger, do you understand?"

Its eyes glitter—the only part of it that doesn't absorb light from the kitchen—and Winnie can't help but think of the *cornīx* in the forest, with her crow-shaped mask and anatomically incorrect golden beak. Winnie's fingers close around the doorknob. It's cold from the night and still wet from the earlier rain.

"I'm going to find him, you know." Winnie isn't sure why she feels the need to say this out loud. Only that speaking to this crow sort of feels like speaking to the witch from the forest. "If I have to go over every one of Dad's clues a hundred times or stalk Isaac Tuesday or . . . or track down every Diana who ever lived, I am *going* to find my dad. Just you wait. Soon enough, he'll be the one standing here giving you hamburgers."

The crow doesn't respond to this. It just continues to stare with such unblinking creepiness, it looks more nightmare than natural. Winnie's hand suddenly aches to draw it, from the gray feathers around its orbital sockets to the tip of its black beak.

Address me as "my lord."

Winnie pushes back into her house. The crow doesn't caw again.

7

Winnie learned her lesson after Erica broke into her house: never keep your musings in physical form. Handwritten thoughts can be stolen; sketched-out ideas can be used against you. So last week, after their meeting in the cabin, Winnie acquired a small marker board and as fine-tipped a dry-erase pen as she could find. Now, she sits at her desk in her bedroom, a lamp her only illumination against the night's shadows outside, and she draws out what she knows. Literally, she *draws* it as if she were writing back to Erica.

Her eyelids hang heavy. Her desk wobbles, a sign she needs to shove a new napkin under the left leg. And she desperately misses the feel of ink or graphite against paper; a marker is just too slippery against this laminate coating.

Still: safety first.

Winnie sketches out a scorpion. It might represent Isaac Tuesday or might represent Jeremiah. She hasn't decided yet.

Next, she draws nodding wakerobins, *Trillium flexipes*, fashioning each petal into the circle of a Venn diagram. Starting with the outer circles, she adds words: *Witches, Winnie, Spell.* Then she moves to the overlap sections: *Source, Sadhuzag, Dad.* Finally, she lands on the heart of it. The pistil.

WHISPERER.

This diagram, which she first made nine days ago, hasn't changed at all. But now, she knows who one of the witches is (Erica) and she knows there's at least one more witch in Hemlock Falls, hiding behind a crow mask. She also knows Dad was wrapped up with that Crow . . . but not guilty. He was simply in the Crow's way, so she took him out.

Winnie doesn't mean to fall asleep this way. She is just going to lay her head on her arms for a few minutes and rest her eyes. Then she'll get back to drawing. She *needs* to find more clues.

She startles when a knock sounds at the window. She has no idea what time it is or how long she has been draped here. Her muscles groan; her mouth tastes like dry-erase particles.

Another knock. Winnie snaps toward the curtain, but no shapes are visible. No hints of light to tell her the time outside. She flips off her desk lamp. Darkness falls—a pallid, blue darkness that sings of clouded dawn. One heartbeat passes. Two.

She knows who she *wants* to find at the window . . . and she knows who she fears might actually be there.

Another knock. Winnie's lens-less eyes are slowly adjusting to the shadows; a figure waits. And it's Jay—it *has* to be Jay. That athletic slant, that limber crouch.

Her breath whooshes out. She dives for the window, and in under a second, her curtain is drawn back . . .

And there he is, rain misting over him as he huddles beside the glass. Winnie hauls open the window and reels Jay inside. If he is surprised by the ferocity of her movements, he doesn't show it. He simply climbs in, as quietly and gracefully as a sparrow. He wears his usual buffalo flannel and jeans. Motorcycle boots too, with his hair wet from rain. And perhaps from a shower as well, since bergamot and lime radiate off him.

"The hunt," Winnie begins.

Jay shakes his head. "No." He doesn't want to talk about it.

So she replies: "Okay." Jay might keep all his secrets tucked away, he might live inside his head, quiet as the forest at midnight, but now she understands why. Now she sees the broken heart of him.

So Winnie slides her arms around Jay's waist instead of speaking. Here are the planes of his back, the muscled shape of his shoulder blades—his latissimus, his trapezius. Her fingers want to confirm he is intact. No injuries, no pain points, no scars. *He survived the hunt. He survived the hunt.*

As she touches him, his eyes rove over her face. His pupils swallow up the lambent gray. "Winnie," he murmurs. "May I—"

"Yes," she answers before he can finish.

His lips press to hers. Or maybe her lips press to his. Either way, all thoughts of the hunt fling out the window. Jay tastes like toothpaste and rain. Like spring and early mornings. His flannel is wet from the storm. His damp jeans rub against her sweatpants. His fingers twine in her hair.

He survived the hunt. He survived the hunt.

They kiss harder, an urgency taking hold. Jay's adrenaline from a night in the forest—it has to go somewhere, and Winnie is more than happy to receive it. She digs her fingers into his back and feels as he pushes, pushes until she has reached her desk. Until he has lifted her up so she can sit on the edge and wrap her legs around him.

Vaguely Winnie wonders if she's smearing all her marker sketches with her butt . . . Then she decides she doesn't really care. Venn diagrams are so deeply unimportant compared to this boy with his teeth and his lips and his need.

Until abruptly Jay pulls away. "Jesus, Winnie." His chest is heaving, as if he just emerged from a dive beneath the falls. "Jesus."

"Yeah," she agrees, also panting. Her heart hammers at double speed. Her vision spins, and dawn shadows swirl through her room like mist. Her legs release Jay, though not her fingers. She keeps her hands on his hips, her grip curled into his flannel.

He glances down and notices the marker board under her butt. "Oh crap. I messed up your drawings."

"It's fine." She lifts upward and slides out the marker board. "There's nothing new on here." She flips it forward so Jay can see, and he takes it in with eyes that now match the morning.

An uncanny stillness settles over him, murmuring of something not quite human. His lips are swollen. His face is flushed. Then he taps at the half-smeared word *Witches*. "Anything new from Erica?"

"Is that your casual way of asking if I still trust her?"

A faint wince. "Am I that obvious?"

"No, you're smart. One of us needs to not let Wednesday glasses turn their vision loyalty green."

Now Jay smiles, and he pulls Winnie to him so he can rest his chin on her head. "For the record, Winnie, I like your loyalty. And everything else about you too."

"But?" she asks.

"No buts." He laughs. "At least not with regards to you. But Erica . . . You're right I'm still worried about her."

"Still worried or *more* worried?"

He sighs. Then kisses the top of Winnie's head before pulling away. His fingers lace through hers. He draws her to the bed. The springs squeak. And here, with the pale light of a rising sun to creep through the curtains, Jay looks less nightmare and more boy.

"I've been digging through Grayson's stuff," he tells her. "Anything he left behind in his office . . . which is now *my* office." Jay shakes his head. "There's not much useful. I found all the clan banners he stole—three of which are Saturday banners because I guess he just thought it was hilarious to piss off Dryden."

"I mean, it *is* hilarious," Winnie says.

And Jay huffs one of his quiet laughs. "True. But I also found this." He shifts on the bed, creasing the blanket's sunflowers into yellow smears while he withdraws several folded papers from his back pocket. "These are just the first pages, but look. They're all from Monday research papers on werewolves."

"Oh." Winnie takes the pages and frowns at diagrams and tiny print, at theories and descriptions of werewolves from around the world. "You think . . . he knew what you are?"

Jay shrugs—but it's a falsely casual movement. "Maybe. Remember all that nightmare contraband you found in the office? The vampira blood and the mist we didn't understand? Well, I didn't collect most of that stuff. Grayson did."

"So maybe he was watching out for you? Protecting you, even?"

"Yeah. Maybe."

"He was a really good friend, Jay."

Jay wets his lips. He doesn't look at Winnie.

"It's all right to grieve him."

"It's not that. I mean, that's not the only thing bothering me. I just wish I could remember what happens in the forest when I turn, you know? Then I'd know if Grayson was helping me or not. I'd *know* what really happened that night when the Whisperer killed him."

Winnie sets the Xeroxed pages on her lap. Then she takes Jay's hands back into hers. They're cold. "When I jumped off the waterfall, I couldn't remember what happened for almost two weeks. And that hole—that *missing* time . . . It was awful." She shudders. "I can't imagine how hard it is to have hundreds of those holes you can't fill."

Jay doesn't answer.

"I'm here for you—"

"Yep." He pulls away. Springs squeak. Then his face pinches up and he shakes his head. "I'm sorry, Win. I know we said no more hiding things from each other. I'm just . . . I'm not ready to think about this stuff. Or Grayson."

"Okay."

"But I'll keep looking in the office. See if there's anything else . . ." A yawn takes over now. ". . . that might be useful." He yawns again, a full-bodied unfurling that sends his arms up and his back arching.

It's a pose that makes Winnie want to kiss his rib cage, his abdomen, his chest.

She very pointedly does not. And once Jay has folded back over, she says: "Thank you for looking, Jay."

"You don't need to thank me. It's not like I've found anything useful."

"But you're *helping* me. Even though you don't trust Erica—and that means a lot."

He shifts toward her, and Winnie thinks how very unsparing this light is. He's so clearly exhausted, so clearly hunted. She wishes she could make it better; she wishes she could cure the nightmare curse that suddenly struck him four years ago; and she wishes she could bring his friend back from the Whisperer who should never have claimed him.

Instead, Winnie kisses Jay. *You are safe here,* she wants her lips to say. Her hands too as they rise to cup his face. *I won't let the nightmares have you.*

Jay returns the kiss. Gentle, almost ghostly. Gone is the urgency from before. His touch is softer, matching the storm outside as it fades to spindrift. Until eventually they lie down. Until eventually, Winnie swivels so her back presses against Jay's chest. His arms wrap around her, and they fall asleep.

A lost nightmare from the forest.

And the hunter who found him.

CHAPTER

8

Jay leaves the same way he came in: via the window. Mostly because Mom wakes up—they hear her alarm—which makes Winnie *freak the eff out* and Jay alongside her. A night fighting against drolls, manticores, and vampira? Whatever. A morning against Mama Bear Francesca Wednesday? *Run for your life, Jay Friday.*

And he does. He was at least smart enough not to park his bike in front of the house, but still, when Winnie hears the engine rev a block away, she can't help but hide under her covers. Surely Mom will hear that. *Surely* she'll realize Jay snuck in and made out with her daughter.

It would seem Mom does *not* realize, and once Winnie's heart and breathing calm to healthy, sustainable rates, her eyes drift shut. She dozes off.

And finds herself in the forest.

It's a dream—she knows it's a dream, and she's glad for that. Because as real as it feels, she *knows* she will wake up, no matter what might come next.

What comes next is a white wolf. *Jay,* she thinks, except she can tell it isn't. This one has different eyes. He's smaller too. "Pure Heart," he tells her, although there is no movement on his canid mouth. Just a deep, rumbling voice worn ancient from grief and time. "Trust the Pure Heart."

"Yes," she answers. "I do." Even though this isn't true—the Pure Heart is the Whisperer, the center of her diagram, the pistil of her trillium, a *famēs* spell run wild in the forest. She doesn't trust it at all. Yet here she is, lying with frictionless ease: "I trust the Pure Heart completely."

She awakens to her locket scoring against her collarbone. She jolts up-right, grabs for it, fumbles it from her shirt . . .

But it's not actually hot. It's not actually burning, and whatever strange magic had claimed it in the forest when she faced those Dianas—it's not happening now. It's just a golden circle, with a moon and two stars, that once belonged to her grandmother.

A grandmother whom Winnie has thought of a lot lately. Because what does it mean if this really did come from Grandma Harriet, Dad's mom? And how can Winnie even confirm if such a thing is true when she has zero contact with the woman?

The house is silent now, meaning Mom has gone to her shift at the Rev-enant's Daughter. No rain pitter-patters against the roof. Instead there is only sunshine, aggressive in its brightness and revealing every scratch, fin-gerprint, and microscopic dent on the golden locket. Winnie doesn't open it because she knows it will just be a picture of her and Darian, and she has already withdrawn those photos to search for more clues behind them. There was nothing then; there is nothing now.

Erica might get messages in her locket, but Winnie never has. And on the flip side, Erica's has never gotten hot like Winnie's.

Winnie blinks. And suddenly an idea forms—one she can't believe she hasn't thought of before.

Part of her knows she should ask Erica first. Not for permission so much as guidance. But another part of her expects that if she does, Erica will instantly bark, *No*. And for once, Winnie would rather beg forgiveness in-stead of permission. (Oh, who's she kidding? When has she ever asked for permission?)

After snatching up a sketchbook, Winnie rips the top right corner off a blank page. It's a thumbnail scrap upon which she writes in silver pencil: *Is anyone there?* Then she snaps open the locket and places the message inside.

She feels silly as she squeezes the locket shut and says, "Let's see what you've got for me." But hey—she might as well give this a try. Her locket isn't like Erica's, but they've yet to test *how* differently the two golden necklaces might behave. And with all these dead ends and redundant Venn diagrams that grace Winnie's whiteboard each night, it's time for a little shakeup.

For several minutes, nothing happens. No warmth, no buzz, no sensation of magic to hermit-crab through the room. To say Winnie feels disappointed would be an understatement. She also feels even sillier, and heat creeps up her neck.

Until she finally just tears open the locket, and . . . nope. Her own handwriting stares up at her. She shuts the locket again. Then shoves away from her desk. The day beckons; she is going to be late if she doesn't pick up the pace.

Once downstairs, she finds a protein bar on the kitchen table with a note attached: *If you want real food, swing by the Daughter. LOVE YOU UNTIL THE END OF TIME—MOM*

Winnie would very much like real food. In fact, the thought of hash browns, eggs, and bacon sounds so delicious, she viscerally regrets sleeping an extra two hours when she could have vacuumed up diner food instead. Alas, she has not only missed a chance for a real meal, but the clock on the microwave indicates she is going to be super late to Luminary training if she doesn't get moving. And what was it Aunt Rachel said last night? *Be the model Luminary you've always wanted to be.*

Right. She can do that, even if it means she'll have to stay in her ratty sweatpants and rattier T-shirt proclaiming an undying love for Charmander. If this outfit was good enough for Jay Friday, then it's definitely good enough for the rest of Hemlock Falls. Although Winnie does tug on her leather jacket—which *still* smells new a full month after the twins gave it to her.

And she can't resist opening the locket one more time once she's out in the garden shed and retrieving the family bike. But the same message is right there. No magic, no reply.

Winnie sighs. Then she sets off for the Sunday estate, where culture can be mainlined into her blood. It might be the weekend, but if the forest never quits, than neither will Luminary training.

Winnie regrets her outfit as soon as she reaches her first class at the Sunday estate. She is three minutes late to Luminary history, which means the whole class stares at her as she scurries in. Her cousin Marcus loudly snorts, then mutters, "Charmander?" And for the ten thousandth time in her life, Winnie really wishes she could punch his teeth in.

Except then she feels guilty because the kid does have ghosts of his own right now. Diana-shaped ones he's diligently keeping secret.

At least it's not Professor Samuel standing at the whiteboard, since he went to visit a sick relative a week ago. Instead, the teacher eyeballing Winnie is a short, pale-faced woman who looks like she could bench-press Winnie with one arm while dominating an arm-wrestling competition with the other. She beams at Winnie, seemingly unconcerned by Winnie's tardiness, and after swatting a gray strand that has fallen from her mostly blond bun (pinned artfully atop her head in a way that Winnie wishes she could copy), she motions for Winnie to take a seat.

"As I was saying," Professor Alice declares with a barely there Norwegian accent, "I think you all will enjoy the lesson today." She points to the whiteboard, where words are written in thick, colorful markers that are easy for Winnie's bespectacled eyes to read: *The Importance of the Masquerade for Community Morale.* Below this are the seven clan symbols—each drawn in different colors. Not the best sketches, but clear enough to interpret. And a million billion times better than the listing of dates and names that Samuel always scribbles in tiny black ink.

"We will begin with the Floating Carnival. Does anyone know why it is beside the Little Lake?"

Marcus's hand shoots up. He doesn't wait to be noticed before half shouting: "To honor the aquatic nightmares of the Big Lake."

"Exactly." Professor Alice smiles. It is a very nice smile that fans lines around her dark eyes as she launches into a history of the Floating Carnival's most popular rides: the Ferris wheel, designed to look like a full moon. The Kelpie Carousel with assorted aquatic nightmares for riding. The Tilt-A-Whirl, which Winnie hates to ride because it makes her vomit.

Winnie is so lost in the lecture and taking notes—actual notes instead of just drawing in her notebook's margins—that she doesn't notice when the classroom door opens and a wheelchair wedges in. No one notices, actually, and Headmaster Gina has to cough twice to get everyone's attention.

And when Winnie meets Gina's eyes, the headmaster beckons a single finger.

A grenade goes off inside Winnie's stomach. *It's time,* she thinks. *The Tuesdays have finally come for me.* It had to happen eventually, after all. It's the third law of motion.

She thinks of melted hound masks. She thinks of ghosts and pizza. And her body goes numb as she rises and gathers her things. She distantly hears Headmaster Gina say, *I need Winnie Wednesday, please,* and Professor Alice reply, *Of course. She is all yours.* But the grenade is still echoing in Winnie's eardrums, so the words have a muddy, distant quality.

Winnie reaches the hall. "Ma'am?" She holds her books to her like a shield. They press against her locket, digging it into her sternum.

That's when Winnie realizes that it is not Jeremiah Tuesday striding down the hall, but Darian, her brother, followed by Councilor Leila Wednesday, followed lastly by Councilor Marcia Thursday—who is also Erica's mother.

Winnie feels all the blood return to her face . . . until she meets her brother's eyes and he mouths, *I'm so sorry.*

Sorry for what? she wants to ask. *And why is Marcia strutting toward me on patent leather kitten heels?* The woman is dressed in a black pantsuit, which makes her look like she's about to go to a funeral. Leila, meanwhile, wears a flowing almond-colored gown and a pistachio-colored hijab. Darian is the only one of them who isn't fancied up, but then, his default setting is "fancied up," since sweater vests and khakis are all he seems to own. (*That's not fancy, Winnie, that's business casual.*) He circles behind Leila and Marcia, letting them take the lead.

His face is as bloodless as Winnie imagines her own was a moment ago.

Marcia reaches Winnie first, and after a prim nod at Headmaster Gina, she places a firm hand on Winnie's shoulder and pushes her toward the school's front doors. Literally *pushes.* Which, okay, Marcia. Where the heck else is Winnie going to go right now? It's very clear this entourage is here for her.

Leila also mouths *I am so sorry* as Winnie is corralled past her.

Sorry for what? Sorry for what?!

"What is going on?" Winnie demands as Darian opens the school's double doors like he's a footman instead of a councilor's assistant. He even appears to be bowing. Spring wind batters over them. Ten steps away, shackled out of reach, is Winnie's bike.

Marcia points at a black Lexus SUV waiting at the curb. "Get in." This is all she says before releasing Winnie and strutting toward the driver's seat. Leila, meanwhile, gets in the passenger door.

"You're about to have to do some PR," Darian half whispers, half squeaks. He smells like spearmint toothpaste as he cattle-prods her onward. "And I am really sorry about it."

"P . . . R?" Winnie's first thought is pulmonic regurgitation—which is a frequent cause of death for a certain subspecies of velue—but her brain quickly points out that this makes no sense. *Public relations*, it provides. Then it adds, *Wait a minute, what?* Which Winnie blurts out loud: "Wait a minute, what?"

"I know, I know." Darian shakes his head. A smudge mars the left side of his glasses. It has been there for almost a week, which says a lot about Darian's current mental state. "I told them they should have warned you, Winnie. I told them this wasn't right, but I might as well be invisible for all anyone listens to me. I think she"—he jerks his thumb toward Leila, now firmly ensconced in the SUV—"is the only person who heard me say, *This is a bad plan.* And even she was like, *Sorry, Darian. We have to.*"

"Have to *what*?" Winnie practically screams. But Darian never gets to answer before Marcia barks: "Winnie, get in this vehicle right now."

Darian nudges at Winnie again, and this time, she lets herself be maneuvered onto the spotless, squeaking beige leather. A white suit hangs in a clear plastic bag on the opposite door. Winnie barely gives it a glance before shifting her attention to the rearview mirror—where Leila is again mouthing *I am so sorry.*

Then, as if afraid Marcia might catch her, Leila's mouth buttons up and she swivels around to meet Winnie's gaze head on. "We are on our way to the Luminary Welcome Breakfast at the Saturday estate. This suit is for you to wear—"

"Huh?"

"—because although I told Fatima to get you a suit yesterday, she obviously didn't listen. And in her defense," Leila quickly adds before Marcia can say something nasty, "I did not explain to her *why* Winnie needed new clothes. So she presumably thought the suit was just a suggestion and not a requirement."

"A requirement for what?" Winnie shoots a bewildered glance at Darian, then back to Leila. "Why am I putting on a suit, Leila?"

"Because," Marcia answers, icicles practically forming around her head, "congratulations, Winnie: you have won the Midnight Crown, earning more votes than anyone else in the entire school."

"I thought juniors wore a golden crown—"

"We've eliminated the rest of the Nightmare Court. There is only the Midnight Crown this year, and you've won it. As such, you are the new face of Hemlock Falls, which means you must impress forty-nine of the most important Luminaries in the world. And believe it or not, sweatpants and a leather jacket are not appropriate attire for such an event. So put on that suit hanging beside you. Then, put on some lipstick because, bless your heart, you look like a revenant."

No, Winnie thinks. *Do not "bless my heart." And no, I will not put on this suit or lipstick.* Except when she tries to say this, the only sound that comes out is the dying gasp of two lungs who've abandoned all hope.

She wishes she'd crumpled *every* ballot yesterday instead of just her own. Then she wishes she'd lit the entire ballot box on fire and flung it into the Little Lake.

Marcia stares at Winnie in the rearview. She has not bothered to turn around like Leila did, and it is honestly one of the most intense power moves Winnie has ever experienced in her life. *I don't need to face you to be in command. My reflection is enough to control you.*

Basilisks could learn a thing or two from that stare.

The next thing Winnie knows, she is tugging the suit off the ceiling handle while Darian shoves an assortment of unopened lipstick tubes at her. He looks as if he wants to crawl behind the seat and cower. Or else grovel at Winnie's feet and beg forgiveness. But since neither is currently an option, he simply claps his hand over his glasses and shifts his entire torso away.

"Wait, you expect me to get dressed now? Here?"

"Obviously." Marcia starts the engine.

Leila winces. "Yes, Winnie. I'm sorry no one warned you about this. We decided to tally votes earlier in the festival this year, and we only finished at midnight." It's very clear from her side-eye toward Marcia exactly *who* is to blame for Winnie's ignorance in the eleven hours *since* midnight.

Like, could no one bother with a phone call?

The SUV starts moving. The brick Sunday estate shrinks behind them. "Once we're at this breakfast? What's happening there?"

"You'll schmooze," Darian answers from behind his hands.

At the same moment, Marcia declares from the steering wheel: "You will engage with every Luminary who wishes to meet with you, and you will do so with a smile and a thank-you because it is an honor to serve your community and the greater Luminary cause.

"Now hurry up, Winnie. The Saturday estate isn't far."

CHAPTER

9

Some Luminaries like to call the Saturday estate the Versailles of Hemlock Falls. Typically, those people are Saturdays.

That said, if you shrank Versailles down to about a quarter of its size, took out all the mirrors, made it a little less classical and a little more Art Deco, then you would indeed end up with the Saturday estate.

As for the grounds, they really could give Louis XIV a run for his money. Even at this time of year, when spring hasn't quite clawed free from winter's shadow, the hedges and fountains and wooded trails sparkle. The sunshine, meanwhile, has strayed from aggressive toward downright bullying. It burns across the splendor of the grounds while the SUV crackles over the cobblestone driveway.

Because of *course* the Saturdays have cobblestones.

Winnie hasn't yet seen herself in the white suit, but she doesn't need a full-length view to know it will make a banshee weep. Someone like Fatima would have no problem pulling off the wide, billowy trousers and long blazer, but on Winnie, it looks dumpy. Worse, it sets off how much the sunshine has *not* bullied her since last summer. Frankly, her sweatpants and Pokémon shirt looked better.

It doesn't help that Winnie put on lipstick using only the rearview as a guide, and judging by Darian's wince, she didn't do a great job. Or maybe she just picked a bad color. How is *she* supposed to know if Flighty & Flirty is better than Sensual Seduction or Pouty Promises?

"I can't do this," Winnie hisses at Darian once Marcia has parked them before the enormous, awning-covered front door—where a valet awaits because of *course* they freaking do. Marcia and Leila have already exited, striding off to talk to Dryden, who now scuttles like a spidrin their way.

Spidrin: A catchall term for any nightmares resembling arachnids.

His approach gives Winnie a few moments alone in an empty SUV alongside her brother. "Darian, I can't do this."

"I know, Win, it's not fair." He spins a ring on his middle finger; Andrew has a match. *Spin, spin, spin.* "I know you hate the names everyone calls you. I know you hate all the attention, but the Italians are really obsessed with you. They want to meet you. And I'm pretty sure if you hadn't won the Midnight Crown, Marcia would have fixed it so you did."

Something about those words give Winnie pause. Then make her rear back. "Wait—she *did* fix it, Darian! Why else would Fatima have had orders to buy me clothes *before* the votes were counted? Oh my god, please, don't make me do this! It's a rigged vote, and people are going to *kill* me. Not only did I probably not actually win, but now the rest of the Nightmare Court has been eliminated."

Darian gulps so hard, his Adam's apple almost punches his chin. "I . . . hadn't put that math together, but you're right. And I really don't know what to say. Dryden and Marcia felt it would be easier without a full Court—"

"Easier for *whom*?"

"—and allow us to really show off your recent accomplishments."

"Since when is getting bitten by a werewolf an 'accomplishment'?"

"I think it's more the *surviving a werewolf bite* part." Darian scrubs at his hair.

"No." Winnie shakes her head. "No." She tries to remove the blazer. "I literally cannot do this because I literally did not win the Midnight Crown."

"Please, Winnie." Darian grabs her hands. He looks sick. Like, legit vomit-on-Winnie's-new-clothes sick. "I tried to tell them this was a bad plan. I really did. But they don't listen to me. I'm just that guy Marcia keeps calling David even though I *know* she remembers my real name."

Somehow, Darian looks even more sick. His skin is turning Wednesday green. "Please, *please* don't take off that blazer. They said you don't have to wear the crown if you don't want to."

"That doesn't make this better."

"Okay, then think of Mom."

Now Winnie pauses, her left arm halfway out of the blazer sleeve. "What does Mom have to do with anything?"

"They . . . *Marcia,* I mean, and Dryden too—they say they'll let Mom back onto the hunt ASAP if you do this. No more waiting, no more crappy office at the Wednesday estate—have you *seen* her office?"

"Not yet," Winnie mumbles.

"It's the smallest one on the networker floor. So small, I think it's probably an old supply closet. But Mom can be one hundred percent Luminary again. You—and me too . . . We just have to cooperate without complaint for the whole Masquerade."

"But we were made 'one hundred percent Luminary' over a week ago. Remember the big clan dinner? The one where Leila *literally* said the Council voted to let us back in?"

"I know, I know." Darian starts spinning the ring again. "They keep moving the goal posts. But if Mom can get back on the hunt, it's not like they can take her off it again."

Don't be so sure, Winnie thinks.

"This is only for one week," Darian says. "Well, technically eight days. But after the Nightmare Ball, you'll be done. And Mom will be back on the hunt as if the last four years never happened."

Winnie lets her arm slump back into the sleeve—because let's be real: she already knows how this scene will end. It doesn't matter that she has done so much for her family over the past month. It doesn't *matter* that adding in a Midnight Crown just feels like an unnecessarily cruel cherry to plop on top of everything. In the end, Winnie is a Wednesday bear. She is loyalty through and through.

So she swallows. Clears her throat. Then tugs her blazer fully back into place. "This isn't fair, Darian, and I'm not happy about it."

The relief on her brother's face is startling. His skin blends from green back toward olive. "Thank you, Winnie. Oh my god, thank you. And trust me: I'll do everything I can to make this painless for you."

10

E ither Darian's definition of *painless* is not like Winnie's, or else he was lying. Winnie chooses to believe the former, although she can't help but suspect the latter as she's hauled into the Saturday estate.

It has been well over four years since Winnie last stepped inside, so her memories of the grand foyer have been rubbed down to vague splashes of gold and purple—just streaks of color on the page. Reality is so much sharper. Lush tapestries on the walls give way to gilded woodwork. Keys glitter across a black-and-white marble floor, stamped in gold upon each tile, and the towering foyer that holds it all is framed by a gilded staircase that circles up one side. A chandelier winks coyly overhead, each crystal carved into a key.

Leadership in deed and word, reads one large floor tile at the center of the room. *Persuasion is power.*

"We're going to the ballroom," Dryden barks from the front of their marching line. "Winnie, you will enter with me."

"And me," Marcia purrs, her manicured nail poking into Winnie's spine at the perfect angle to make Winnie feel like a wind-up doll. *Crank, crank.* Now dance, Winnie! Dance!

She doesn't dance, but she does go as directed into a hall lined with windows. Leila offers more apologetic glances, but she never actually steps in to help. Meanwhile, Darian is furiously texting someone about, Winnie suspects, an order of beef tartare he keeps muttering about.

As Winnie soldiers down the long hallway, floor-to-ceiling windows reveal a terrace outside covered in potted flowers—as well as an enormous fountain with river sylphids shooting water. Beyond that, on a lawn that rolls down to the river, the Nightmare Stage is currently under construction on the grass. When finished, it will be an ornate assemblage of gold, silver, and Saturday purple.

Winnie's Converse are silent next to the clattering heels of her drill sergeants. Leila, knowing that Winnie bought new boots the day before, had wrongly assumed Winnie would wear those boots today. Now Winnie's white pants, which are way too pinchy in the waistband, drag over the tiles. Mirrors offer her glimpses of herself as she is prodded past closed doors that might lead to Rumpelstiltskin or maybe just to a bathroom.

She does not *look* in the mirrors, since she knows with absolute certainty she won't like what she sees.

When they at last leave the hall for the ballroom, it feels as if Winnie really is stepping into a fairy tale—except the macabre kind where everyone dies at the end. For one, the room is classically designed and peak Versailles. But now draped over it are dark silks and laces, feathers and crystals, fairy lights and paper lanterns. If Winnie tried to bedazzle a room like this, it would look tacky, but the Saturdays have managed to keep it classy.

And holy hellions and banshees, are there a ton of people in the room. Clearly *forty-nine of the most important Luminaries* does not include all the aides, family members, and general hangers-on who have accompanied them. They all stand about, mingling in a way that is more mixer and less breakfast—although people do hold plates of food.

Different languages bounce and ping around the room, but where Winnie expects all eyes to turn to her as she is thrust inside like livestock, no one seems to notice her. And now that Winnie is looking behind, she realizes only Marcia and Dryden are actually still with her.

Good job, Darian. You're running great interference here.

Winnie scours the room for anyone else who can come to her rescue. All she finds are seven tall tables draped beneath velvet tablecloths. Upon each is an ice sculpture in the shape of a clan sigil. A green tablecloth with an ice bear for the Wednesdays. A purple cloth with an ice key for the Saturdays. All the colors, all the animals, all the symbols.

And at the scarlet table with the ice scorpion stands Jeremiah Tuesday.

He hasn't noticed Winnie yet because his back is to her, revealing the same red buzz cut she remembers from four years ago. His shoulders are broad, his limbs thick, long, and he wears what he always wears: black fatigues, as if he is never off duty. As if he takes his motto of *Strength, we hold the line* so seriously, he must always be ready for an attack.

It has been four years since the last time Winnie saw this man, deep in the labyrinthine underbelly of the Tuesday estate. He rarely leaves his own grounds; he rarely emerges from the scorpion hole.

Please don't notice me, Winnie thinks. Her bodily functions have halted. No heartbeat, no breath, no digestive gurglings in her abdomen. For eight days, she has been bracing for him to show up before her; now she is walking right up to him instead.

Without a word, Marcia hooks her nail into Winnie's blazer collar and directs Winnie to the right. Which is fine by Winnie. Anything *away* from the Tuesday councilor is good. She glances over her shoulder twice; Jeremiah never notices her; and soon all the other people filling the ballroom block him from view.

What she needs is an escape. A distraction. A hotspot of nightmares that will form *right here* and start spewing out monsters . . . in the middle of the day.

Winnie is so deep in her fantasies—she can totally imagine a hidebehind in that shadowy corner—that she doesn't realize she has reached a podium until suddenly she is being strong-armed up to it. In her defense, it doesn't actually look like a podium but rather a slightly elevated table with a key motif carved into the dark wood. It's also not on a stage, but rather a rug so plush it lifts Winnie up a full four inches.

"Here are some words for you to read," Marcia says, and she shoves an index card onto the podium.

"Wait, *what*? I have to speak?"

Darian's head pops up and Winnie realizes her brother was ducked on the other side of the podium, hooking in sound equipment.

"Mic," he whispers. "Pretty easy to use. Just, you know, talk into it."

"Thank you, David." Marcia doesn't sound grateful. "The speech is short, and when you're done, Winnie, you'll welcome Councilor Saturday to the podium. Then you may exit stage left."

"I don't know what that means, and since when do I have to give a speech?"

"Go that way, Winnie," Dryden inserts, and he points to the open glass doors leading onto a separate terrace—where sure enough, a long buffet awaits with servers in tuxes behind it. The poor people look cold, despite the sun's glare.

"Now, let's get started," Marcia says, and once more, her fingernail is screwing into Winnie's back. *Crank, crank.* Speech, Winnie, speech!

Darian turns on the mic. Instead of feedback to squeal across the room, there are only three harp-like notes to rise from speakers Winnie can't see. The room quiets. Tens of faces turn her way, and she's almost sad there's no technical issue to buy her a few more seconds.

Someone coughs. Winnie's eyes snap that way. The morning sun spears across her glasses. It backlights everyone watching her, so she can't tell who's who.

She feels the weight of Luminary curiosity, though, like a thousand tons pressing down. Like the waterfall pushing her, fighting her, keeping her from rising—

"Read," Marcia snarls.

Winnie gulps. Her teeth have been clicking this whole time behind lips that are supposedly flighty and flirty. She's grateful the words on the index card are typed in BIG ALL CAPS LETTERS because her glasses are starting to slide, and everything is getting a little woozy. "Welcome," she begins.

And there goes the feedback. Nails on a chalkboard. A kelpie shrieking on land. But the feedback is gone as fast as it begins.

"Welcome," Winnie tries again, "to Hemlock Falls. I am Winnie Wednesday, the . . . Girl Who Jumped. The Girl Who Got Bitten. The Girl in Green. Or some of you may even know me as . . ." *Oh god, please don't make me say this.*

She glances at Marcia, at Dryden. They definitely will make her say this.

Winnie chokes out: "Wolf . . . Girl." And okay, it actually doesn't taste that bad. At least people aren't howling. And there are even two different people translating her words into sign language, as well as gentle whispers suggesting others might be verbally translating her words too.

"As this year's winner of the Midnight Crown"—*barf*—"I'm here to welcome you on behalf of the Council and the entirety of Hemlock Falls. We hope you enjoy the Nightmare Masquerade. We have many special treats in store for you—including beignets outside?" She doesn't mean to lilt this like a question, but also . . . *really?* She's advertising for beignets? "Now, may I introduce you all to our host for the day's breakfast: Councilor Dryden Saturday."

Polite applause follows. Then Dryden pops up beside Winnie, practically shoving her from the podium—not that she needs shoving. She topples away from the thing as fast as she can, feeling all the eyes follow her even though Dryden is now speaking. Marcia, meanwhile, is pointing toward the open doors—*stage left!*—and yes, Winnie thinks stage left looks amazing.

She wants a tea. She wants a beignet. She wants for this circus to be over. *Do it for Mom. Do it for Mom.*

Morning air sweeps over her. Winnie sucks it in as she stumbles to the buffet, except buffet is *way* too plebeian a word for what awaits on the long, wrought-iron table placed beneath baskets of hanging begonia, verbena, and fuchsia.

Dad would have loved those flowers.

"Tea," she tells the nearest server, whom she's pretty sure is a Wednesday. "Earl Grey, please. And a napkin to wipe off this lipstick."

CHAPTER

11

If Winnie thought the speech was bad, what follows Dryden's long-winded introduction is actually so much worse. She should not have gotten tea. She should not have eaten two beignets. She should not have passed Go and collected two hundred dollars. Instead, she should have fled while she had the chance, even if it meant stealing a canoe from the Saturday boathouse and paddling upriver to the Little Lake.

Painless, Darian? You call this *painless*?

When she was at the podium, there were a hundred and fifty Luminaries slightly hazed by morning sunlight. Faceless, nameless—just eyes bearing down on her like all those will-o'-wisps in the forest. Now, however, she is having to *meet* all of them, and they are no longer faceless. No longer nameless.

It feels like hours of being carted around by Dryden and Marcia to different Luminaries. Because of *course* the groups aren't separated by their clans or nations—that would be too easy! Instead, they are dispersed and mingling like multicolored gumballs dumped on the floor. So at the Sunday table, Winnie meets a Norwegian Søndag, then an Italian Giovedì, then a Mexican Miércoles . . . Then it's over to the Monday table, followed by the Tuesday table.

The Tuesday table.

Winnie is almost glad she is so overwhelmed, because she doesn't have time to freak out about Jeremiah Tuesday. Instead, she is an asteroid caught in his planetary orbit, and while she definitely senses her slow approach toward him, she's still in outer space. There are too many faces, too many names, too many hands, so she can't fully focus on the knots in her intestines.

At least not until the gravitational pull of Jeremiah Tuesday is too strong and she has burned into his atmosphere.

"Ms. Wednesday," he says in a deceptively soft voice that always makes him sound like a radio host introducing jazz fusion to the night's listeners. "It has been a long time."

Winnie's teeth start clicking. *One, two, three.* She stops them. "Yes." She refuses to drop his blue gaze. Refuses to do anything other than look at him like an unabashed bear while he shakes her hand.

He has a firm handshake.

She makes hers firmer.

"Councilor Tuesday." She pulls her hand back. *Do not wipe it on your pants, do not wipe it on your pants.* "May I meet your guests?" She veers her attention to the stunning woman at Jeremiah's left, who has silvery hair in loose curls. It is artfully messy, and her fitted black dress makes her look like she stepped out of a black-and-white film from the '50s. "I'm Winnie Wednesday, ma'am."

"Caterina Martedì," the woman answers, and a slow smile spreads over her Sensual-Seduction-red lips. Her fingers clasp Winnie's. "Lead Liaison for the Martedì clan."

They are warm and strong. And they are familiar.

Then there it is: a faint burn from Winnie's locket. A heat to sparkle against her collarbone and transport her back in time to that night inside the forest, when fires burned and witches died. When Jay had to drag away Aunt Rachel to save her, and when Winnie—whether she will admit it or not—became a murderer. Because she *had* to. Because it was the only way to fight against the Diana Crow trying to destroy her.

The same Diana who now stands before Winnie and holds her hand.

Cornīcēs: These elected witches maintain roles of leadership within Diana society. To be eligible, one must have both skill and experience.

"It is so wonderful to finally meet you, Winnie. I have been waiting such a very long time." The signora speaks with an accent—which she did *not* have in the forest—and for a split second Winnie wonders if maybe she's got it wrong. If this signora is only smiling so widely because she's happy to be here . . .

But then Winnie's locket heats a second time, and Winnie *knows* she is facing the crow from the forest. The *cornīx*. All that's missing is the mask.

Signora Martedì smiles, like she can hear what's happening in Winnie's brain. "It is so very commendable, all you have done for this town—and for the global *Luminari*, too."

Winnie's mouth opens. Then closes. She wants to say something like, *I guess you would know*, but all her words are splitting apart at the seams. They are nuclei bombarded into fission. If Winnie tries to speak, only gamma photons and radiation will come out.

For ten days, Winnie has been braced for fallout over what happened in the forest. Tuesdays coming for her or for Rachel or Jay or Erica . . . But on none of Winnie's bingo cards was there *ever* a square that read: *Diana leadership shows up in a room full of Luminaries.*

And there absolutely, 100 percent, most *definitely* was never a square that read: *Diana is also a powerful Martedì who can openly walk in front of Jeremiah Tuesday.*

A Lead Liaison. Someone who can travel all over the world, to any Luminary outpost they want to visit, without anyone batting an eye.

Winnie knows she needs to say something. She knows she needs to emit coherent words with her tongue, lips, jaw, and pharynx. But instead, she just keeps glancing around her like, *Oh my god, is anyone else seeing this?* Which of course they aren't seeing this because they don't know that there are Dianas in Hemlock Falls and that this elegant woman in her tailored dress and perfect lipstick tried to kill Winnie ten nights ago.

Except . . . Jeremiah Tuesday.

He knows.

Not about Winnie, maybe, but he knows about the Dianas in the forest. He *knows* there were dead hounds, murdered by flame. He *knows* that Aunt Rachel fought against them. And he knows he has swept it all under the rug for over a week now.

And oh crap, there go the nuclei in Winnie's brain again, except this time they're undergoing fusion, forming helium from hydrogen and powering an entire solar system of ideas. *This explains why Jeremiah barely interrogated Rachel. This is why there has been no uproar over the Dianas, no ringing of the alarm. Jeremiah Tuesday is keeping it all hush-hush for this powerful Luminary beside him.*

The question is, though, does Jeremiah know what Signora Martedì really is? Is he, in fact, working with her? Or is he just a pawn, pushed around the board by her witchy whim?

A sharp poke screws into Winnie's spinal cord. Marcia has her claws out again. *Crank, crank.* Answer, Winnie, answer! Dryden, meanwhile, is sucking his teeth impatiently, and Jeremiah is looking at Winnie with a thoughtful, borderline worried gaze that transports Winnie back in time to a cold, concrete interrogation room underground.

Only the signora seems unsurprised by Winnie's stunned silence. There's even a flicker in her dark eyes that says, *Oh, I know exactly what you're thinking right now, little bear, and it's delicious.* She is still holding Winnie's hand, too, and seems to be in no rush to release it.

Winnie forces her brain to find words. Then she forces her tongue, lips, jaw, and pharynx to formulate those words loud enough for others to hear. They aren't the best words. They aren't even *smart* words. But they're kind of all she has right now: "Oh, wow," she says, her grip tightening on the signora. "You look really different in this light, ma'am. I almost didn't recognize you."

A collective lifting of eyebrows. A small grunt of confusion from Dryden.

The signora smiles. Her pressure on Winnie's hand increases. Her pointer finger curls inward in a move that would be sensual if this were a romantic situation; instead, it's unambiguously threatening. "Ah, but I do not believe we've met before, Winnie. You must be mistaking me for someone else. I do have one of those faces."

"Right." Winnie slides her hand free. It's shaking a little, so she pushes it into her blazer pocket. "Sorry, ma'am. I guess you look like someone I've met before." Since these words aren't a lie, they come out strong and clear—and Winnie feels strong and clear saying them. The nucleic reactions in her brain's language centers have settled; she is finally regaining control.

Which is why she twists away from Caterina Martedì like the woman is just *any* old Luminary who showed up from out of town. "Where to next?" she asks Dryden. "I haven't met the Wednesday visitors yet."

It's clear that Dryden and Marcia can sense something Very Strange and Possibly Worrisome has just unfolded before them. Yet it's also clear their minds can't evaluate what. Winnie and this powerful Luminary knowing each other? That would be as plausible as eyeballs inverting or nose hairs combusting.

A small frown puckers on Marcia's mouth. Dryden's nostrils flare repeatedly.

Marcia pulls herself together first, flashing her most beneficent smile at the Crow. "Enjoy the breakfast, Signora Martedì. We are so glad you're back in Hemlock Falls for pleasure this time, instead of business."

"Yes," Dryden agrees, hastily cramming himself into the conversation. "And do try the espresso. We imported it all the way from Italy *just* for you, so it should taste better than last year's." He gives her an obsequious smile, then his hand comes to Winnie's shoulder, Marcia's claw digs into Winnie's back, and Winnie is carted away from the Tuesday table and a scorpion made of ice.

12

Both carnivores and herbivores are essential for a healthy ecosystem, and this author posits that so too are our disparate societies of Dianas and Luminaries. The question however is: Which society is the predator? And which society is the prey?

—*Understanding Sources: A Brief History and Guide*
by Theodosia Monday

When Winnie was a toddler, her dad taught her a very important lesson: if there was ever something she couldn't do, then she should simply turn to the nearest grown-up and say: *I need an adult!* Apparently Winnie took this lesson so deeply to heart that she went on the warpath. She demanded adult intervention for literally everything, ranging from picking up a stuffed octopus that *she* had thrown across the room to insisting Grandpa Frank put spoonfuls of strawberry ice cream into her mouth so she wouldn't have to lift a finger. *I NEED AN ADULT!!!*

Dad thought it was hilarious; Mom did not; and Darian can't remember these alleged misconducts.

Right now, as Winnie is herded toward the Wednesday table, that old lesson is all she can think about. *I need an adult! I need an adult!*

Distantly, Winnie knows this is a panic response. That her brain is actually trying to protect her from mental overwhelm. Because of course she is *with* adults. Tens upon tens of them, none of whom she can actually speak to about what just happened at the Tuesday table.

It doesn't help that Winnie can feel Signora Martedì's eyes, boring into her with the strength of two high-powered drills. It takes all of Winnie's self-control *not* to look in the woman's direction. *Not* to see if Jeremiah Tuesday is watching her too. *Not* to simply crawl under the nearest table and wait for this whole breakfast to end.

On and on Winnie moves, drifting like a dinghy at sea. At the Wednesday table, with its ferocious ice bear, Leila tries too hard to be smiley! and bright!, as if she's overcompensating for Winnie—who is emoting about as much as an actual dinghy at sea. Next is the Friday clan with its sparrow sculpture. Jay's aunt Lizzy looks pained as she introduces Winnie to nearby visitors, and she gives Winnie a squeeze on the shoulder that is probably meant to be supportive . . . except Winnie has dissociated so far from her body, she hardly feels it.

She continues onward. Drift, tip, float. She shakes more hands and forces more smiles and blesses more (figurative) babies with the Saturday clan, where Dryden handles the whole situation as if *he* were the winner of the Midnight Crown who survived a werewolf attack and jumped off the waterfall. Then Winnie is led to the Thursday table, its ice bell melting so artfully, it somehow looks *more* like a bell now than it probably did four hours ago. *Don't piss off Marcia*, it seems to warn. *Do what she commands, little bear.*

Yeah, except Marcia is the least of Winnie's concerns right now, thanks. And if Winnie had any doubts remaining that she was incapable of compartmentalizing—or of exorcising her ghosts—then this breakfast has shattered that illusion. She's terrible at it. Time compresses and expands, feeling interminable and also too fast.

Until there are suddenly no more hands left to shake or names to forget. Winnie is *finally* finished with this breakfast, and she is left with only Darian at her side.

Yet if she expected safe quarter from her brother, she instead finds only a frazzled young man with powdered sugar smudged on his lip. "I'm sorry, Win. I did try to call this morning to warn you, but no one answered the house phone."

"And you couldn't call a second time?" Winnie's voice sounds like it's coming through two tin cans and a string. "I was home all morning, Darian. So was Mom."

"Well, it's not *my* fault if you . . ." His lips purse. He shakes his head. "No, you're right. I should have called more than once. But I was busy and distracted, so I didn't."

Bingo, Winnie thinks, but she doesn't have the energy to say it out loud. Her mind is still shouting for an adult, and in the end, Darian was just looking out for Mom. Which is exactly what she's doing too.

Darian withdraws a stack of blue papers from his pocket. They are folded vertically but otherwise smooth—as if he only just printed them off to deliver to her. "This is your schedule for the week. I've divided everything by day. So here's where we start. Today is Saturday the twentieth." He taps at the words on the first page: *Welcome Breakfast at Saturday Estate—Winnie does speech. Dress is elevated business.*

Elevated business? Is *that* what this suit is?

"After this, you've got the day free. Tomorrow, though, you'll need to attend training at the Sunday estate. The Sundays are moving the hours around to accommodate Masquerade events, so only a few days this week will conflict with your schedule. If I may make a suggestion about your wardrobe—"

No, you cannot.

"—you'll want to wear something jewel-toned for the parade. There will probably be a lot of cameras, and jewel tones show up best on film. If you need to do more shopping, Dryden actually put in a line of credit for you at Falls' Finest, in addition to Leila's. Since I guess Fatima didn't do a good job—"

"Do *not* bring her into this."

"Right. Forget I mentioned her." Darian shakes the papers. "I tried to be as clear as I could in my event descriptions, about what you'll be doing and how long you have to do them. But, of course, feel free to reach out if you have any questions."

"'Feel free to reach out'?" Winnie's voice sounds less echo-y now. "Are you my brother or my publicist?"

Darian blanches. Then bristles. "Honestly, Winnie, I'm both. And I don't know how many times I can tell you 'I'm sorry.'"

It's rare to behold Darian lose his temper. He and Dad are two calm peas in the same calm pod. Snaps of temper and flares of annoyance—those are more Winnie's and Mom's speed. And sure, Winnie has some sympathy for Darian's predicament right now. She just got walked around by Marcia and Dryden like a marionette with wood for brains.

And *sure,* Winnie can also acknowledge she is using this moment to express her frustration from a different situation—one regarding a certain Martedì fifty feet to her left. But hey, this is why she needs an adult: because right now, she's flailing and lost and really, *really* alone.

"I see there's no Saturday Spaghetti Night on the schedule," she says as she takes the blue schedule from Darian's grasp and shoves it in her blazer pocket. Shove, shove, *shove.* The papers crunch and the pocket bulges. "I guess our usual dinner is canceled? *Again?*"

Darian looks like she just kicked his puppy. And honestly, it *was* kind of low for her to bring up their usual Saturday-night dinners—the ones he has repeatedly canceled as of late. His rib cage deflates. His shoulders sag. Winnie would almost pity him if she weren't so startlingly mad. "I'm leaving, Darian. Don't try to stop me."

His mouth works like a fish's. The publicist side of him visibly wants to keep arguing—to retrieve the schedule from Winnie's pocket and smooth each page. But the brother part of him . . .

"Fine, Winnie. Fine. I'll cover for you if Dryden or Marcia notice you're gone."

"Thanks," Winnie grudges out before spinning on her sneaker heel and aiming for the garden exit. She barely makes it ten steps before she feels a buzz at her collarbone.

Her locket is warming in a familiar way she desperately wishes *weren't* familiar. Then there's Signora Martedì, coalescing like a nightmare from the mist. The woman's eyes are hooded, but in a smug way. In a way that says, *You can't hide from me, so be a good girl and follow.*

Nearby, Dryden and Marcia wear smiles so forced, Winnie thinks their eyeballs might pop out from the pressure.

"I wish to try this famed espresso, Signorina Wednesday. Escort me?"

The Crow's right hand comes to Winnie's back. Her left hand sweeps toward the doors leading onto the patio. And Winnie's blood curdles, her skin crawls. She feels like she's being attacked by a changeling all over again, except now there are all these witnesses . . . yet no one able to help her.

A scent like lavender tickles her nose. Pleasant and sickening at the same time. The signora is a small woman, and morning light reveals the faint glitter in makeup that has settled into the lines around her eyes. Her arms are bare, save for a golden shawl she has elegantly draped across her shoulders.

Dryden all but thrusts Winnie toward the doors. "Enjoy!" he half shouts, half snarls, and his eyes bore into Winnie's face as if to *demand* she go get that espresso and enjoy it right away.

Winnie does move her bear feet, although not for Dryden's sake. Not for Mom's either. And certainly not for this repulsive woman's, whose pumps click on ballroom tiles. No, Winnie shuffles along like a dog to heel, because while her body is rebelling and her brain is telling her *YOU NEED AN ADULT!*, the Agent Wednesday part of her senses she's faced with an opportunity.

The heat in Winnie's locket recedes as she nears the patio doors. Spring wind purrs against her. She smells beignets and coffee and wet grass.

"*Due espressi,*" the signora declares once they are beside the food tables. The tuxedoed barista nervously leaps to work. Winnie pities her. If these *espressi* aren't the best things ever tasted, she is going to hear about it.

The signora inhales with audible self-congratulation, opening her arms to the view of the Saturday gardens. "What a beautiful estate, Winnie. Almost as lovely as the Martedì estate in Torrente di Cipresso. That is where *our* branch of the Luminaries is located."

"I know." Winnie is amazed words can exit her mouth.

"Signora," the barista says, and Martedì swirls around gracefully to accept the espresso cup upon its little saucer. She then nods for Winnie to take the second drink—and Winnie wants to. She really does. It's right there, promising a jolt of caffeine to her veins that she desperately needs.

But she doesn't take it because listen: even Team Petty needs a win sometimes.

Winnie does feel bad for the barista though as she pointedly turns away, her chin held high. *I reject your espresso, witch.*

The signora laughs. A sound that is almost impressed, but mostly just amused. "Follow me," she declares, and she doesn't wait to see if Winnie does.

Within seconds, it's clear where the signora is aiming: the famed Saturday maze. It's a place Winnie hasn't visited in years, but that she likely knows better than most Saturdays.

Because Dad designed it.

For months, Winnie would see the sketches of it on his desk by the family computer. A hundred different shapes and layouts he crafted for Dryden, none of which were up to muster. In fact, it was working with Dryden that pushed Dad into abandoning his passion for landscape architecture and shifting to just . . . well, landscaping. Gardening. Tending the plants someone else designed. Because although people might be the worst, plants never let him down.

Besides, he would say whenever Winnie would ask him about why he gave it all up, *I didn't move to Hemlock Falls for my degrees, Win-Ben.* She always thought that was the most romantic thing she'd ever heard.

Now here Winnie is, walking into that maze with the woman who ruined Dad *and* ruined the wife he came to Hemlock Falls for.

The yew hedges swallow them. The sun's rays, vicious acute angles on the horizon, vanish. Shadows and cold lay claim. Brick pavers give way to tumbled gravel. The Saturdays have added purple streamers with heavy golden keys for the Masquerade. It gives the maze an almost circus-like feel, as if Winnie isn't merely stepping into a hedge labyrinth, but a magician's secret tent. *Or a witch's.*

Winnie wishes she'd grabbed the espresso. Her mouth is dry. Her brain is scrambled. *Team Petty has now become Team Thirst.* She keeps sizing up the woman beside her. She's so tiny without a crow mask. She's so fragile. Winnie could take her, if it came down to it . . . right?

"You can't," the signora says, and suddenly her accent is gone. No more Italian flair, no more gracious smiles of a Luminary in power. She is a Diana again. *The* Diana *cornīx* from the forest. "You're wondering if you can beat me, aren't you?" She glances at Winnie, her earlier smirk now spreading into a Cheshire cat smile. "It's what I would be thinking, and the answer is no. You can't."

Winnie swallows. Her heart hurts because it skipped at least two beats while she frantically worried the woman had read her mind. But no. Of course not. There are limits even to what Diana magic can do. Or at least Winnie sure hopes there are.

They have taken four turns into the towering hedges. Noises from the breakfast have faded. There is only Winnie and the Diana and the design

Dad conjured almost a decade ago. He would be delighted to see how well it has grown, how dense the yew branches have become.

It is quiet as the forest when the mist rises.

A bench waits here for weary Luminaries, and beside it is a rolling ball water fountain that should be soothing, but is instead *really* ugly because Dryden insisted it be made from purple granite. Winnie keenly remembers Dad's disgust. *Purple granite? Is he serious?*

"Where's my dad?" These are the only words Winnie wants to make sure she gets out, and she's pleased by how level her voice is. How calm her gaze.

Annoyingly, the Crow is just as calm and level back. "I don't know, Winnie. If I knew that, then I wouldn't be here right now trying to conduct a private conversation where no one will walk in." She gives a flick of her wrist, and though Winnie doesn't see it, she hears the word *obvolvō* coast against her eardrums.

Somehow, the space around them becomes even quieter.

"You told me you 'dealt with him.'" Winnie sets her jaw. "In the forest, you said those exact words to me. Now you're telling me you don't know where he is?"

"I don't." The signora shrugs, boredom hanging off her like her shawl. "He was clever four years ago. He got away before I could subdue him. And now, believe it or not, Winnie Wednesday, we want the same thing. You wish to stop the spell in the forest, right? Jeremiah told me you call it the Whisperer?"

"You don't want to stop it."

"Oh, but I *do*. It's only a matter of time before people realize what it is, and I can't have that happening. It's a nuisance, and I need it eliminated."

Winnie's head pitches back. "You *made* it."

"No, Jenna Thursday made it."

Somehow Winnie pitches back even more. "You're lying."

"Unfortunately, I am not. And it gets more complicated, for you see, Jenna bound the spell to her source, so until I find *that,* I can't stop the . . . the Whisperer, was it?" She opens her hands in a ballet-smooth shrug. "And thus, Winnie, we are not enemies at all."

Winnie forces herself to exhale through her nose. That was a lot of bombshells in the span of twenty seconds. "You . . . tried to kill me."

"After you killed two of my witches, so I think we're even." The Crow smiles, but it doesn't reach her eyes.

And Winnie *really* wishes she'd taken that espresso. "It was self-defense." Her words sound weak. Like a lie, even though she knows they're true. For some reason, a taste like *Hi EnerG!* cherry fills her mouth.

The Crow splays a hand to her chest. "And I was simply defending myself against *you*."

Winnie's first instinct is to snap, *No, you were hunting Jay!* But her jaw is smarter than her throat; her teeth grind together so no mention of Jay can break free. She doesn't want to draw attention to him. She doesn't want to remind this Diana of what her target was.

The woman remembers anyway. "I don't care about your boyfriend—he *is* your boyfriend, right?" She draws her shawl more tightly to her shoulders. "I can find other daywalkers to absorb magic from, Winnie."

Surely it's not that simple, Winnie thinks. *Surely you didn't go to all that trouble just to get Jay's daywalking magic.* But she has no time to call the Crow's bluff—not before Martedì says: "What I want is the same thing Erica Thursday wants."

"Erica?" Winnie forces out instead. "What does Erica have to do with anything?"

"You really are bad at lying." The Crow slopes away, sliding farther into the maze. Her heels somehow do not get eaten by gravel. "I want what Erica wants and what *you* want, Winnie: to find out where your father's clues lead."

The witch's voice cuts off here—and the muted quality that had ensnared Winnie vanishes. Whatever spell the Crow is using, Winnie is no longer inside it. And though Winnie *hates* herself for it, she stomps after the woman and her magical dome of silence.

Static brushes over Winnie. Words resume: "He was clever. He got away from us that night four years ago, before we could get answers. And he took Jenna's source with him."

More bombshells. More white noise in Winnie's brain. "I . . . don't believe you."

"Smart. Because, unlike you, I'm an excellent liar." The signora claps her hands to her cheeks. Her face visibly blanches. "*Winnie Wednesday is a*

Diana like her father! Lock her away. And her brother and mother too. Such disloyal bears!"

This is the largest bombshell of them all. A flash grenade going off in the forest, so that Winnie suddenly understands how nightmares feel. She suddenly understands how you can be abruptly blinded and deafened, scrambling to regain the sensory control you had only moments before.

She feels like she's twelve years old again, watching as Tuesday scorpions overrun her home. Watching Erica and Jay walk away from her. She'd felt so helpless then—and she feels just as helpless now.

Winnie wets her lips. Then shakes her numb, senseless head.

"Here is what will happen, Winnie: you and Erica and—what is his name? The Friday boy? You will continue exactly as you have been, trying to track your father's clues. Except now, when you find Jenna's source, you will bring it to me."

"No." It is incredible that any word ejects from Winnie's lips.

"Then I'll simply take it from you."

"And we'll . . . simply . . . turn the Whisperer onto you."

The Crow laughs, startled. "You do have gumption. I'll give you that. But this is a fight you can't win. We are *allies* here, Winnie. And we want the same thing—I promise."

Never.

"So be a good Wednesday and figure out where your father hid that source. Then my witches and I can get the *famēs* under control and leave this wretched place." Her nose curls up. If Winnie didn't already hate her, she'd *definitely* hate her for glaring at Dad's maze like that.

"How many of you are there? How many witches are in Hemlock Falls?"

"*So* many, my dear. And we'll be watching you and your friends and your family." She reaches out a single arm, almost as if she wants Winnie to kiss her hand. But then she pats Winnie on the head instead. "Now I really must get back." Her Italian accent has suddenly returned. "Jeremiah will be wondering where I have gone. Oh, and in case you're wondering: no one can know about our little bargain here." She makes a gesture that is almost like a parting wave. Words Winnie can't hear skate from her lips.

There is the static again.

And there is the locket, heating up—cranking so hot, so fast that Winnie gasps and doubles over.

"Ciao ciao!" the Crow calls, and for a full two seconds, a maniacal cackle bounces around Winnie like she's trapped on cartoon railroad tracks while the villain twirls his mustache. Until at last the Crow departs, her laughter chasing away as she vanishes into the yew hedges.

13

Anyone could be a Diana.

A Diana could be anyone.

This is what Winnie considers as she slowly straightens. Her locket's burn has cooled. It's just a glowing ember now, a faint reminder of what happened, like a puddle after a storm.

She is cold. She is thirsty. The waist on her pantsuit is starting to cut off circulation to her vital organs, but she finds she can't leave the maze yet. She needs to think without eyes upon her or Luminaries begging to shake her hand.

After all, anyone could be a Diana.

A Diana could be anyone.

This isn't Winnie's first time facing such a truth. Four years ago, her dad was caught as a Diana—and she truly believed, for four agonizing years, that he was one. Then ten nights ago, Winnie discovered Erica was also a witch. Then right after that, she fought three Dianas in the forest, leaving two of them burned to crispy pulp.

Winnie pushes out a hand. She wants to feel the wall the signora backed her against. It is both solid and . . . not. This is no sturdy hemlock, no majestic oak. Nor is it a wild bush, with space for wind and creatures to weft through. The leaves and branches absorb Winnie's palm's pressure—but they don't let her in.

She wishes Dad could see how much his maze has grown. The hedges consume all sight, all sound. His sketches across the family desk are a full-grown, proper maze. And honestly, the purple granite fountain doesn't look *that* bad.

This is a place to get lost in.

And it is also a place to get found again.

At that thought, the last of Winnie's demands for an adult slide away. Sand in an hourglass. Because one thing most people don't realize about her is that she doesn't like to be cornered. Tell her she is an outcast from the Luminaries and she must serve a punishment for ten years? Okay, fine. She'll train on her own, enter the hunter trials, and get it done in four.

Oh, you want to hunt her ex–best friend and try to kill her aunt? That's right: Winnie will *literally* burn you alive.

Big or small, high stakes or low, Winnie doesn't like to have her back pressed against a wall. But it's in those moments, when everyone looks at her and sees only weakness, that Winnie always, *always* finds her strength.

Or maybe it's just spite. Never underestimate the power of Team Petty, after all.

Either way, the Crow made one hell of a mistake confronting Winnie here—right in the maze that Dad built. She'd have been better off leaving Winnie hanging after that breakfast introduction. She should have simply walked away and never initiated further conversation. Then the whole *not knowing what the Diana wants* would have sent Winnie into a stressed-out tailspin.

Instead, Signora Martedì cornered Winnie in a maze and literally pushed Winnie's vertebrae, sacrum, and skull against a hedge wall. So now like oxygen and hydrogen leading to H2O, total clarity washes through Winnie's brain. She has developed harpy-keen vision; she has grown banshee-fast muscles; she has earned vampira-sharp fangs; and most important of all, she has the loyalty of a bear that she isn't afraid to use.

No one threatens Winnie Wednesday's friends and gets away with it.

And *no one* threatens her family.

Winnie pushes away from the hedge. Its leaves rattle goodbye. The fountain burbles *ciao ciao*. She won't leave this maze the way she came in—Dad made three secret exits, and if she simply pushes a bit deeper, she will find one of those hidden portals out of here.

The sun rises behind her, bellicose and unyielding. Except now Winnie appreciates it. *Warm me,* she thinks as she digs her hands into her pockets. *I've got a long walk ahead.*

C H A P T E R

14

The smell of heaven washes over Winnie as she steps into the Revenant's Daughter. She is ravenous as an actual revenant—which, for the record, cannot have daughters.

"Winnie!" Mom pops up at the restaurant's front. She looks as frazzled as Darian, and comparably worn down too. As if, after four years of putting up with whatever crap the Luminaries threw at her, her skeleton and organs have finally surrendered. It doesn't help that the Daughter is *packed*, mostly with foreigners who want to enjoy greasily authentic American cuisine.

"What are you wearing?" Mom asks, taking in Winnie's suit with visible horror.

Winnie swats the question aside. She neither wants to explain the Midnight Crown, nor does she have the time. "Is Isaac Tuesday here?"

"Isaac Tuesday?" Mom's eyes thin. "Yes. I just served him a Swiss melt. But Winnie, he's, like, twenty-five. Way too old for you."

Winnie does not respond to this because frankly it does not deserve a response. Mom knows she and Jay are together. Also, *gross.* Isaac Tuesday. She instead provides Mom with her flattest-eyed stare and asks: "Where is he?"

"Last booth, by the kitchen."

"Thanks." Winnie launches off, ignoring the vocalized outrage that chases after her because she has one thousand percent just cut in line. *That'll keep Mom busy,* she thinks. Then she feels bad because she is only adding to Mom's overwhelm—and isn't she supposed to be helping Mom by playing a nice Midnight Crown?

As promised, Isaac sits in the booth by the door. Winnie spots his red hair first, which is so much like Katie's, they could be brother and sister instead of simply cousins. He is chomping into his Swiss melt when Winnie pops into the seat across from him.

He stares at her, the sandwich paused halfway into his mouth.

"Hello, Isaac. I'm not sure we've met before. I'm Winnie Wednesday."

He resumes chewing, an air of befuddlement settling over him like a cloud. From what little Winnie knows of him, this might also be his default expression. Katie has described him as *the definition of a himbo*.

Isaac swallows. Then grabs for a napkin from the dispenser on the table. "I know who you are. And I have a girlfriend already."

"Yuck." It's bad enough for Mom to misconstrue the situation; it is less fine for Isaac to think Winnie is into him. She taps the side of her chin. "You missed a spot."

He scrubs. His fair cheeks redden, almost matching his hair.

"I'm here because I know what you saw in the forest, Isaac, and I know you took pictures of it too."

Now all the blood drains away. So fast, it's like watching a time-lapse of a vampira sucking its target dry. "I . . . don't know what you're talking about." He has about as much charismatic skill as Winnie does when *she* lies.

"I don't have time for the denials, Isaac. I need what's in those photos, and I need them now. So hand me your phone."

His eyes dart sideways, as if searching for an escape route. When he sees there is none, he withdraws the phone from his pocket. "There's nothing on here."

"Of course there is." Winnie yanks it from his grasp, and he doesn't try very hard to stop her. "What's your passcode?"

"There's nothing on there."

She sighs. Then plugs in *1–2–3–4–5–6*. It unlocks immediately. *Himbo indeed*. While she moves to his photos (it takes her a minute; she's not used to smartphones . . . or any other variety, really), Isaac picks up his ham-and-Swiss melt. Then puts it back down again. Then starts tapping the table with a knuckle.

"See?" he says after a while, when all Winnie can find are photos of his dog and his girlfriend. (Shelly Thursday? *Really?* Girl, you can do so much better.) But Winnie isn't fooled. She finds his albums, scrolls down, down . . .

She taps "Hidden" then pops his password in again.

Isaac gasps audibly. "No." Now he looks worried. He grabs for the phone.

"It's okay, Isaac," Winnie murmurs, "I don't care about your gym selfies." She doesn't. And to be fair, there aren't that many on his phone. Just a few photos of him flexing in front of a bathroom mirror, and then . . .

Ah, there they are: the dead hounds.

Winnie feels her own blood drain at the sight of them. A feeling she should have anticipated, except her spite has been focused so sharply . . . Well, she forgot about her ghosts.

Winnie's fingers tremble; she hides it by quickly sending the photos to Erica's phone. Then immediately deleting the messages.

Isaac, meanwhile, is hyperventilating on the other side of the table. "I could lose my job," he rasps. "I could get thrown out of the scorpions—"

"You could get thrown out of the Luminaries," Winnie corrects as she next deletes each photo one by one . . . then navigates to his trash folder and empties it. "And ten out of ten do *not* recommend. But here. I've saved your butt, and now there will be no record of your lapse in judgment."

She offers him the phone. Her hand still shakes—although not nearly so much as Isaac's. "What are you going to do with those?" he asks. "What do you want from me?"

"I want access to everything the Lambdas are doing right now in the forest."

Isaac looks at Winnie with a combination of horror, incredulity, and his default himbo confusion. "I'm an Alpha scorpion, though. We fight escaped nightmares and clean up kill sites. Lambda scorpions are the—"

"Witch hunters. Yes. I'm intimately familiar. But you all work in the same underground bunker of offices. So you're going to get me those records from the forest." Winnie points at Isaac's phone. "And then I won't share these photos you should never have taken."

"But I can't get you that!"

"Ah, but you don't really have a choice, do you? I can assure you from personal experience"—Winnie snags one of his potato chips; *crunch, crunch*—"that being an outcast sucks."

"I repeat," Isaac says, leaning onto the table. His left elbow lands in pooled condensation. "I can't just *access* Lambda records, much less give *you* access."

"Find a way." Winnie shrugs.

It is at this moment that Erica appears next to the table. She is dressed in a sleek gray dress, her hair in a tight ballerina bun. She wears her school backpack, as if Sunday training only just ended. "Ah, so this is why I got some fascinating text messages." She flashes her phone at Isaac.

And the poor guy gags. Like, full-on *gags* and has to shove a napkin against his mouth to keep the vomit in.

"Awesome," Winnie says, scootching out of the booth. "I think that means we're done here. You've got Erica's phone number and you've got your orders. Text her when you're done, Isaac." Winnie hooks her arm in Erica's and drags her toward the kitchen.

And to Erica's credit, she acts as if this is a perfectly normal interaction for them. Meanwhile, in a whisper snarl only Winnie can hear, she demands: "What are you doing here?"

"The same thing as you, I assume: tracking down our only lead."

"Which I said I would handle. What if someone sees us together?"

"Don't worry." Winnie shoves them through swinging doors. A steel counter laden with plates of greasy joy winks up at her. "We have a lot of catching up to do." She reaches for a plate of fries.

"Winnie!" Mom leaps up behind them like a Whack-A-Mole. "*No stealing food!* I still need this job, you remember."

Yes, Mother. It's why I'm wearing this pantsuit. "Fine, then. Can we get an order of fries to go?" Winnie spins and claps a hand on Erica's shoulder. "Also, I need more clothes, so we're going shopping. And yes, Mom, Erica and I are friends again so you can stop staring."

"It's not *Erica* that's making me stare," Mom mutters. "It's that godawful blazer—and by the way, Winnie, you sat in mustard."

15

W hat the hell is going on?" Erica asks this while power-walking next to Winnie on the downtown sidewalk. Fries rattle in a takeout box, a perfect soundtrack to Winnie's *glorious* spite that has now fractured into all-out panic.

"The siren is thought to be an evolutionary ancestor of the melusine," Winnie answers as they weave around visitors and locals alike. Dogwoods and redbuds are just unfurling their spring attire. The Masquerade lights twinkle in assorted clan colors, even in the afternoon. "Since DNA tests show phylogenetic matching." She shakes her head. *This is not what I want to say! Why can't I talk about the Crow?!* "Much like apes eventually evolved into humans, sirens were likely a precursor to the melusine."

"Winnie, stop." Erica grabs Winnie's shoulder, reining her to a halt. They are just outside Joe Squared. The scent of coffee drapes across them with no-good, lying promises of comfort. "I know you don't want to talk to me about melusine. I mean . . . you don't, do you?"

Winnie shakes her head. Or rather, she *wants* to shake her head, but she can't seem to move it at all. She also wants to pull out her locket, since she and Erica have previously discussed the lockets and their differences. Surely Erica could look at the locket and do the math. *2 + 2 = Winnie is bewitched.*

Because that's what is happening now, right? That final wave and whisper from the Crow—it must have caused this. A spell to keep Winnie from talking about what happened in the maze. But of course, Winnie can't withdraw the locket any more than she can move her head. She is completely

cemented in place while Erica stares at her, first in bewilderment. Then in
curiosity.

But bless Erica with her brilliant Thursday mind because it only takes
her the distance of one block before she cracks the puzzle. "You're under a
spell, aren't you? Is that what you're trying to say?"

Winnie can't nod, of course, and the harder she tries, the louder a buzzing grows in her ears, like a wasps' nest loosed into her skull. "Contrary
to popular belief," she squeezes out, "in the non world, vampira do not
require an invitation to enter a home."

"Right." Erica gnaws her lip. Then she grabs the takeout box, tears it
open, and gnaws a fry instead. All while staring at Winnie as they stride
ever closer toward Falls' Finest. *Chew, chew, chew.* "Definitely a spell. Obviously cast by a Diana who is somewhere in the city. Seeing as you were just
at that Saturday Welcome Breakfast, then it's got to be someone who was
there. Unless . . . it happened before? In the night maybe?"

"I didn't see anyone last night." Winnie's breath hitches. Those words
came out no problem—and now that she considers it, everything she said
to Isaac was easy too.

Another fry vanishes in Erica's mouth. "Okay. You were able to speak
just now. But what happens if you try to talk about what's happening? *Is* it
a spell, Winnie?"

"The origin of this myth," Winnie answers, "is attributed to the bellwether, since a vampira horde will not enter any space until the bellwether
does."

"Got it." Erica stuffs in three more fries. "Definitely a spell, then." She
glances around to make sure no one is listening. They are now outside the
glass doors into Falls' Finest, where the fancy lettering on the windows has
a sign boasting: *20% off all Evening Wear, This Week Only!* The few people
trickling in and out are too wrapped up in being tourists to spare them a
glance.

"I'll be honest," Erica continues through a mouthful of starch, "that I
have no idea what kind of spell this is, and I *definitely* don't know how to
neutralize it."

"And I'll be honest." Winnie scowls. "I'd really rather you weren't so
calm about this because I am freaking out." *Okay, I could also say that.*

Erica sniffs. "I'm a Thursday. We're always prepared."

"Does that mean you have a plan for how to never run from a banshee—grrrr."

More fries get vacuumed into Erica's mouth. *Chew, chew, thoughtful chew.* "I mean, it seems to me we still need to find Jenna's source. Yes?"

Winnie nods. Then is *way* too relieved she can make that movement. "And we also need to find any clues my dad left behind." Success! "That way, hellions often hunt in packs—*YARGH.*" She snags a handful of fries and starts chomping too.

"It theems," Erica mumbles through a fry that isn't fully chewed, "that you can talk about anything"—swallow—"related to Jenna or your dad. So . . . let's stick to those topics for now."

"If that's the extent of your plan—"

"Give me a second." Erica glares. Then grimaces. "Okay, give me a few hours. I need to think."

"Fine. And *I* need to go shopping. So can you help me?"

Erica's eyes narrow. "I guess this means that whoever did this to you already knows we're in cahoots. Am I right?"

Winnie wants to nod, but yet again, she cannot—and yet again, the wasps screech louder in her ears. "Cahoots is a funny word," she offers instead. Then, "Can we go inside? It's cold out here."

She aims for the doors, feeling weird—uncomfortable even—that she was just here yesterday with her square of friends. They laughed, they shopped, and the seesaw of Winnie's world seemed so bright. Now here she is, verbally hogtied by a Diana *cornīx.*

At the store's entrance, Erica stops long enough to toss the now-empty takeout box into a trash bin. "Are we being watched?"

Probably, Winnie wishes she could say. Instead, she spits out: "Though seemingly small, no wider than a cobra, the basilisk can in fact stretch up to forty feet long."

"Right." Erica dusts salt and grease off her hands. She has more animation than Winnie has seen in . . . *years,* actually. And Winnie doesn't think it's because of all those fries. "We'll figure this out, Win. Every spell has limitations—even the ones I've never heard of."

Winnie tries to smile, and is delighted when her lips can actually obey. But before she can offer a sentimental reply, Erica grabs the door and shoves it wide. Perfume scents and pop tunes river over them.

"Come on. Let's get you some more clothes because while I look great in a pantsuit, you do not. Also, the mustard, Winnie. The mustard."

Once upon a time, when Winnie was nine years old, she and her best friend Erica Thursday pretended to be Dianas.

They wore navy bedsheets draped over their bodies in imitation of the navy cloaks Dianas had supposedly worn in their secret meetings centuries ago, and they each picked out what their source would be. Winnie's was a simple rock she found in the garden that looked vaguely like a human metacarpal bone. Erica, meanwhile, went *all in*. She stole a spherical piece of obsidian that sat in her family's cold, modern living room on a side table beside the grand piano—and that her mom really loved and was super pissed to later discover had been removed.

That was part of the fun, though. Pissing off Marcia, waiting for her to notice when her younger daughter misbehaved. Erica had an incredible ability to weasel out of punishments. It was 25 percent manipulation mixed with 75 percent airtight logic.

You can't just take things, Erica! That crystal costs hundreds of dollars. You get no allowance for a month.

Ah, but Mother, if I don't have an allowance, my friends will notice—and what if they tell their parents?

Winnie, who was even worse at verbal manipulation than she was at lying, would always observe her friend with wide-eyed awe and high-grade envy. Because *wow*, Erica would articulate an argument so impenetrable, even a jury would stand up to applaud—and Erica did so without ever breaking a sweat. Winnie, meanwhile, fumbled over her words and usually abandoned all hope at first sign of resistance from whomever had scolded her.

Not that Winnie got scolded often in those days. She liked rules and she liked following them—and any activities to the contrary happened pretty much *exclusively* on Thursday grounds where no Wednesday bears dared to tread.

On this particular night seven years ago, there were no Fridays treading either since it was actually a Friday and Jay was at clan dinner. Looking back, those Friday nights were often Winnie's favorite of the week. Not that she didn't love Jay—she did, and in quite a different way than she loved Erica—but having it be just *her* and her best *girl* friend . . .

Those really were the best times.

And there they were, wrapped in bedsheets in the old cabin on a hot midsummer night holding their sources and pretending to cast spells.

Eye of newt and blood of stone, Winnie improvised.

Tongue of harpy whispering home, came Erica.

Then together, they sang the one line they *did* know went in a Diana's spell—or at least, that was what Katie Tuesday had told them the week before (and she would know because her cousin was in Lambda training). *Sumus ūnus in somnō et somniīs.*

We are one in sleep and dreams.

When they uttered those words, they felt a charge brush over them, like static cling after going down a plastic slide. It prickled and crawled and made their hairs rise until they both reached out to touch each other . . .

And *spark!* A little burst discharged between them.

At the time, they decided it had to be magic. *Real* magic, and they would swear to Jay the very next morning that they had cast an actual spell. Later though, as the years would pass, Winnie would decide it was nothing more than the sudden flow of a current between two charged objects brought in contact. In other words, electrostatic buildup.

But there would still be a little part of her that wondered . . .

Until the day when Winnie learned Erica really *is* a Diana who can cast magic. That Erica really *does* have a source, and it is hidden where no one will ever find it. Or at least where Winnie hopes no one will ever find it, since the Tuesdays are a constant threat—and that threat is only growing after what happened a week ago in the forest.

Two witches burned alive.

A third witch who got away.

It sounds like the beginning of a nursery rhyme: *This little witchy went to market. This little witchy stayed to play. These little witchies got burned alive, while this little witchy got away. And this little Luminary screamed "wee, wee, wee" while the forest chased her as prey.*

Sumus ūnus in somnō et somniīs.

We are one in sleep and dreams.

16

While Winnie and Erica buy an entire wardrobe of clothes, actual progress regarding what happened at the breakfast or getting this spell off of Winnie's words—that goes absolutely nowhere. Winnie tries writing words on paper, spelling them out in sign language with her limited knowledge of the ASL alphabet, and even singing them.

Nothing works. Nightmare Compendium factoids reign supreme.

At least, though, throughout each experiment, Winnie's furious spite cranks back into place. Then cranks *even higher* because dammit, she will not let the Crow win. She will *not* be a weak target for the Crow to crap on. And it is that spite that delivers Winnie and Erica to the cabin after sunset.

Together. At the *same time*. No hiding. No sneaking. No secret spy messages to trade off.

And over the course of an hour, they form a plan. One that Winnie actually feels good about, because Erica is not only a Thursday, but also one of the smartest people Winnie knows. Plus, they now have the photos from Isaac's phone—which is the first real clue they've acquired in over a week.

Mostly, Winnie feels good because this plan is a real middle finger aimed at that Diana. *You want to threaten me in the maze my dad built? You want to keep me from talking about you and turn me into an audiobook narrator for the Nightmare Compendium? Well, then I'm going to find every Diana in this town and reveal them. Every single one.*

"Okay," Erica murmurs. "So it's hard to see on my laptop screen, but . . ." They are in the dark with a sheet draped over their heads like they used to do as kids. If anyone walks in, hopefully they just assume Winnie and Erica are making out or something. Not studying images of witches.

The scent of cut grass is especially sharp thanks to a mowed lawn that afternoon. It feels like childhood. It feels like safety.

"Still, it's better than the phone." Winnie crooks her neck toward the screen. Her heart is lodged somewhere in her throat. Her glasses creep down her nose. For the last hour, she has mostly been able to talk unimpeded by the spell. No wasps in her ears. As long as they stick to Jenna or Dad topics, she is a fully functioning Winnie Winona Wednesday.

The first of Isaac's photos loads. There are seven in total, and this one shows a blurred and blackened streak of earth. Probably an accident as he tried to surreptitiously get the phone high enough for a secret shot.

The next photo is a foot. The rubber on the shoe melted, and Winnie hears Erica swallow at the sight. She swallows too. Her throat hurts with her heart stuck there. Her stomach is wound up tight. Her teeth start clicking.

The third photo is the whole corpse, and Winnie can't help but gasp. A wheezing sound because she killed this person, and it's impossible to pretend otherwise when faced with the vivid, full-color evidence. When she left the burned scene, the mist had not yet risen—which meant the sun hadn't either. There wasn't much to see, and her body was pumped so full of adrenaline . . . Well, she hardly stuck around to explore the scene.

Only now is she realizing how much of a blessing that really was.

"It was self-defense," Erica murmurs, her eyes fixing on Winnie for several seconds. Then she clicks her trackpad, and the next photo pops up.

It's both bodies at once, charred and smoking. The masks that were once shaped like hounds are melted into near nothing. Only plastic ears remain on the left body, only part of a snout on the right.

"You did what you had to do." Erica rests a hand on Winnie's shoulder. Then a second hand on Winnie's arm. It is meant to be comforting. Winnie wants to flinch it away.

She closes her eyes instead.

"Do you see anything recognizable?"

"No." Erica withdraws. Her voice softens as she angles back to the screen. "But that's not surprising. We're taught to never give anything away. Our faces, our voices, and even our bodies—they're all hidden or modulated. And like I told you, this was one of the only nights where I actually met anyone. Usually everything I learned came in messages from the . . ."

"The locket." Winnie forces her eyes open. In all the chaos of the last twelve hours, she has forgotten until *right now* that she put a message inside her own.

Not that it did anything. When she quickly pops it open, the words *Is anyone there?* stare up at her. She snaps it shut again and returns her attention to the screen. The bodies look the same as they did before; they're just bodies. Inanimate as the nightmares she collects on corpse duty. As the nons she has seen mutilated and ruined countless times.

Death is a part of life. Death is a part of life.

"Can you zoom in?"

"Yeah." Erica clicks a few times and the details expand, expand. It's not a high-quality photo—there wasn't enough light—but at least zoomed in, it's easier to emotionally detach. Winnie is a scientist seeking answers. She is a detective looking for clues.

For several minutes, Erica scrolls over the photo, moving side by side in organized rows. She begins at the melted shoes. Up, up they go. There is nothing specific. Nothing to stand out. So much is burned and shapeless. Whoever these Dianas were, they are nothing more than overcooked meat in this photograph.

Death is a part of life. Death is a part of life.

The air under the sheet feels heavy. The grass smell is sickening.

"Wait." Winnie lays a hand on Erica's, pausing Erica's methodical side-to-side tracking. "Go back."

Erica obeys, and the slight variation that had caught Winnie's eyes reappears. "That." She points at a line of silver. The first light of dawn glints on it, and there's the unmistakable glare of glass.

It's a pair of glasses, tucked into what was a pocket before most of the shirt burned.

"I . . . know those glasses," Winnie says, although it's becoming increasingly difficult to actually get those words out. And not because of the spell, but because of building nausea. Because of thickening horror. "I know who they belong to."

Erica gapes at Winnie. In the blueish light off the screen, the russet tone of her irises is almost purple. "Well? *Who is it?* And how can you possibly recognize them?"

"Because I hated them and wished I could break those glasses every time I saw them." Winnie leans forward to rest her head on her hands. Her eyes close again. "That bigger corpse right there is Professor Samuel from Luminary history. I killed Professor Samuel."

Winnie doesn't get home until midnight, and because she is the actual worst, she doesn't even realize she has missed Jay's regular Saturday-night show until she finds a note from Mom on the kitchen table.

Tried to stay up to see you, but guess Forgotten show running late. Love you, Winnebago!

Winnie immediately grabs the family phone. Jay doesn't answer. She tries again three more times, determined *not* to freak out. Because after all, his silence could mean all sorts of things that are not death-by-Crow or death-by-Tuesday or death-by-fellow-nightmare. Heck, maybe he's simply mad at her. (Although admittedly, she hopes that's not the case either.)

On the fourth try, she lets the phone click over to voicemail. Then she listens, teeth grinding, to Jay's recorded voice: "Leave a message."

"Hey, Jay, it's me. Can you call me back, please? I'm so sorry I missed your show tonight. Like, I'm so, *so* sorry. Okay, yeah. Call me back. Oh, and this is Winnie." She hangs up.

Then forces herself *not* to call a fifth time and instead carry herself upstairs. Once in her room, she sits at her desk, grabs paper and her favorite 0.5 pen, and with nothing but her lamp for illumination, she starts sketching. Not trilliums tonight; they will lead her nowhere. *Tsk, tsk, we can't help you.*

No nightmare anatomy for the Compendium competition either. Instead, Winnie lets her right hand and the two hemispheres of her brain connect without any intermediary of consciousness. She lets the stress and intensity of all that happened today—the Midnight Crown, the Crow, the photographs of dead hounds, and the glasses tucked into a charred pocket . . .

It comes pouring down her arm, like she's a little teapot shrieking to be tipped out.

Yet it's not the images of her day that form on the page in sharp lines. It is Jay as a boy, all feet and gawky limbs draped across his living room couch after a night with just the two of them playing Mario Kart.

"Winnie?" he asked.

"Yes, Jay?"

"Do you think, when we're grown up, we'll still be friends? Me and you and E?"

"Why wouldn't we be?"

"I dunno. Just seems to me lots of people don't stay friends once they're old."

"My mom and Rachel are still best friends."

"Yeah, but they're related. They have to stay friends. But Aunt Lizzy and Erica's mom—they used to be tight, remember? And now they don't talk at all."

"Right. I always forget about that. But . . . they're not us, Jay. We won't be like them."

"Promise?"

"Promise."

Winnie stares at the boy before her. This was before he was summoned by the forest—by a wolf's jawbone mysteriously tucked beneath his pillow. Which is a method of mutation Winnie *never* heard of before Jay's description of it, and neither had Mario. Nightmare mutations are spread by bite; not because the forest simply *decides* one day you'll be a nightmare.

Except that's exactly what seems to have happened to Jay.

Her right hand starts moving again. The pen scratches and scrapes across the paper.

"Winnie?" Jay asked her four days ago, as they sat together on his bed at the Friday estate.

"Yes, Jay?"

"I want to kiss you."

"Now?"

"No, in three years and sixty-seven days. Preferably in the afternoon, if you can make it work—ouch. Punching someone on the arm isn't nice, Win."

"If you qualify that as a punch, then you aren't worthy of your Lead Hunter title."

"I mean . . . I'm not worthy of it."

"I'm sorry. I shouldn't have said that."

"I'll forgive you if we can go back to the subject of kissing. I do want to kiss you three years from now. But also right now too. Basically, I want to kiss you always. It's like . . . it's like homeostasis, and it's just this constant, steady state inside my system. 'Kiss Winnie,' it says. 'Kiss Winnie.' Wait— why are you looking at me like that?"

"Because I'd like for you to say 'homeostasis' again, please."

"Homeostasis."

"Ah, Jay."

"Wow, that's so much nicer to hear than 'Ugh, Jay.' I guess this means I should talk nerdy to you more often. Homeostasis."

"Ah, Jay. Do it again. Say something else."

"No, no. This time you have to pay the toll—ouch! Okay, okay. You've really got to stop hitting me. You're stronger than you look."

"Or maybe you're weaker, Jay Friday."

"I am when you kiss me."

"Like this?"

"Just like that. Can I have another?"

"No, now you have to pay the toll."

"Wait, so you won't pay it but I have to?"

"I paid, Jay! Here, I'll kiss you again. And again. And here, on your neck. Your jaw. Your ear . . ."

"Ah, Winnie."

"Now it's your turn. I expect payment."

"Homeostasis. Biome. Mitochondria. Uh . . . binary fission? Okay, if you keep doing that, Win, I'm not going to be able to think of any more science words."

"Don't worry. I have more than enough for the two of us."

A black-and-white wolf lies upon the page. It is Jay in the forest ten nights ago, when Dianas and Luminaries hunted him. His eyes are closed; he is curled into himself and dying. Blood smears his fur.

Winnie abruptly shuts the sketchbook. She doesn't want to relive that night. She doesn't know why her teapot mind wanted to draw it. *That is the night you became a murderer. That is the night you killed.*

Winnie kicks away from her desk. Her swivel chair squeaks and spins as she shoots to her feet. As she drags her skeleton to bed and hides beneath her blanket. The sunflowers on it are so much brighter than any that will ever grow in Hemlock Falls.

The last thing Winnie does before she closes her eyes is check her locket. Still no message inside, so she rips out the paper she wrote on. She crumples it. Drops it to her floor. Then Winnie falls asleep—and far more easily than she expects to. Her mind drifts; her teapot is drained; and there is just enough space now for Jay's song "Backlit" to creep in. To tickle at her amygdala like a prophecy.

With heat on your skin I spin until I can't see us
I find no relief, inside I'm still a hopeless curse
I miss you more now
Now that it's been so long

WINNIE'S SCHEDULE FOR
THE NIGHTMARE MASQUERADE

SUNDAY

10:30 A.M.: *Floating Swan Parade*
- *Winnie is expected at the dam, where she will ride in the lead boat for the Sunday parade*

11 A.M.: *Floating Carnival*
- *Opening of Floating Carnival—Dress is casual, but Darian recommends jewel tones.*
- *Winnie will open the gates to the Carnival along with the Luminaries.*
- *Expect photographs.*

12 P.M.–5 P.M.: *Sunday estate training*

5 P.M.–7 P.M.: *Sunday Dinner*
- *Enjoy dinner at the estate with the Sunday clan and visiting dignitaries—Dress is still casual, but Darian recommends polishing up*
- *Be prepared for interviews and photo requests at any moment!*

9 P.M.: *Floating Carnival*
- *Sunday firework display on the Little Lake*
- *Winnie expected for photograph with Gina Sunday and visiting Sundays beside the Ferris wheel*

C H A P T E R

17

They say the best party in the world is the Nightmare Masquerade in Hemlock Falls. Perhaps it's because spring has finally sprung, elbowing in with green that's lain dormant too long. Or perhaps it's because here, April showers don't bring May flowers so much as a softening inside the forest.

Oh, the monsters will still kill you, but they'll do so with a gentler touch.

Of course this particular spring is already proving more deadly than any spring before, going all the way back to Hemlock Falls' first founding a century ago. Funny how everyone seems to be sweeping that under the rug in favor of their beloved Masquerade . . .

It won't stay funny for long—at least not for anyone but a certain *cornīx*.

The sun is halfway up the eastern horizon, just lifting over the enormous carnival that throbs and glitters along the Little Lake's pier. The Ferris wheel—crown jewel of the Carnival—shines brightest of all, spinning on its floating platform. From where Winnie is, folded into the shadow of an oak tree on the edge of the Sunday estate, she can *just* see the wheel if she squints hard enough. It's meant to look like a full moon; they even pump out dry ice to add to the grandeur.

Crowds seethe even though the Sunday Parade won't start for another hour. The best places to watch—and catch tossed candy—are on the dam, where the boat parade begins, or along the western shoreline of the Little Lake, because all the boats and floats will loop there before ending their journey at the Floating Carnival.

When Winnie was ten, she created a petition to stop the littering that ensued from all the poorly flung candy. Either by bad aim or bad catching on the shoreline, it was certainly *thousands* of little sugary tidbits and their wrappers that sank underwater never to be seen again.

SAVE THE FISHES, her petition read, and the logo she drew looked a lot like the "Save the Whales" one on her hoodie—which yes, she already owned when she was ten. (It fit very differently back then.)

No one signed Winnie's petition except Jay and Dad. Erica thought it was "embarrassing." Darian said her fish looked like a whale (fair). And Mom . . . well, she simply said, "Later, hon," and never got around to it.

Right now, as Winnie eyes the dam—where she must be in forty-five minutes so she can clamber onboard a swan-shaped pontoon boat next to Headmaster-and-Councilor Gina Sunday—she wonders if maybe she should start a second petition. After all, now that she's "famous," people would probably want to sign it just so they can breathe the same oxygen as Wolf Girl for fourteen seconds.

Hello, Signora Martedì. How do you feel about carp and sunfish? Would you be willing to sign this? And maybe remove this spell on me, while you're at it?

"Good morning."

Winnie whirls about to find Erica gliding toward her, dressed in all black. With her signature steel-toed boots, she channels Sophisticated Catwoman—and she cringes at Winnie's own outfit of emerald-green sweater and black jeans. "You're very bright."

Before Winnie can snarl, *You helped me pick this out yesterday, remember?*, Erica squares toward the Sunday estate and sets off.

Right. So they're back to this version of Erica. Marcia 2.0: all business, all ice, and glares for miles. Winnie wanted to open the morning with some good-natured ribbing on the fact that Erica wasn't her standard six minutes early. Instead, she scampers to catch up—and waits until they're almost behind the estate to ask: "Hey, have you talked to Jay today?"

Erica gives her a look that says, *Why the heck would I?*

"It's just I forgot about his show at Joe Squared last night. You and I were at the cabin, and it slipped my mind. Then he never called me afterwards. So now I'm worried—"

"Whatever." Erica rolls her eyes and slides out her phone. "Text him."

"Thanks." Winnie tries for a grateful grin, but Erica isn't looking at her anymore. Although she does say, in a deceptively flat way: "Jay doesn't like me, does he?"

Winnie swallows. "Um . . ." She reaches for the phone.

Erica doesn't release it. "That's what I thought."

"He doesn't *trust* you. There's a difference."

"Is there?"

"Sure. I mean, you and those witches went into the forest to kill him eleven nights ago."

"Except I tried to help him," Erica points out. "I led the Dianas the wrong way."

"And he knows that. I've told him lots of times."

Erica doesn't respond to this. Instead, she fastens her dark eyes onto Winnie's and asks, point-blank: "Do *you* trust me?" They are both still holding the phone.

"Yes," Winnie answers, and to her surprise, this assertion doesn't sound like a lie. It *should* be a lie because she told Jay yesterday morning that she, Winnie, was too loyal. But then . . . well, yesterday afternoon sort of changed things, didn't it? The Crow showed up; she bewitched Winnie and set her an impossible task; and then Erica and Winnie spent the whole day following clues, buying clothes, hiding in the cabin under a bedsheet, and finally, making a plan that has led them here.

Now Erica is the one to visibly swallow. She finally releases the phone to Winnie's custody. "Thanks," she murmurs, and although she offers nothing else before resuming her stride toward the school, it's enough. Because, just like Winnie's *yes* a moment before, it felt real. It felt true.

Thanks.

With awkward thumbs, Winnie quickly types out a message to Jay. *This is Winnie on Erica's phone. I am sorry I wasn't there lass tnight. We have al ot to catch up on. Meet me at thefloating carnival?* She hits send and then almost trips on a step because she's staring so hard at the screen, telepathically begging Jay to respond. She missed that they were to the stairs leading up to the locker rooms.

"You coming?" Erica calls. Her voice drifts down the stairs before getting sucked into the nearby stretch of muddy track that leads to a maze of high walls where Luminaries train.

"Yep." Winnie scurries after, and once Erica has pocketed her phone, they finish the climb to the locker rooms. From this height, on the hill where the Sunday estate resides, she can see the entire obstacle course and training lake beyond. The indoor pool with its glass roof—and the edge of the soccer field too.

Erica pushes open the door. "Anyone in here?" she calls.

Only echoes respond. So she thrusts all the way in, Winnie right behind, and warmth sleeks over them from a vent. "How did you know the door would be unlocked?" Winnie whispers.

"Lucky guess," Erica replies, her voice its usual volume, and Winnie can't tell if Erica is being serious or sarcastic. Either way, she clearly isn't frightened about getting caught, and she moves with the practiced ease of someone who has done this before.

Winnie can practically hear Jay saying, *Maybe you should be worried about why she's so good at this.* But Winnie shoves that caution aside.

In seconds, she and Erica reach the locker room exit. This time, Erica doesn't call anything, but before she can slip through the swinging door, Winnie stays her with a hand. "Wait," she whispers. Then she grabs her locket, tucked beneath her green sweater and white under-tee.

The gold is warm from natural body heat and nothing more. If the Crow is here, Winnie's locket isn't giving its usual warning. "No Crow," she wants to say, but instead declares, "Also called the praying mantis of the forest, vampira move on stilt-like feet that rest atop the soil."

"Yes. Yes, they do." Erica frowns. "About your condition, I had an idea last night."

Winnie waits for Erica to elaborate, to regale, to spin a tale worth listening to, except nothing more comes. "Um," Winnie nudges. "And?"

"And nothing." Erica's lips cinch sideways. "I'll tell you more if I can figure out how to break the spell. Can we *go* now?"

Marcia 2.0 indeed. Winnie waves her on.

The estate is eerily quiet. It's not a place Winnie has ever entered while empty—because it is rarely ever empty. The only reason there's no teacher or student or colorful librarian here now is because all Sundays are expected in the same parade as Winnie. But once that's done? They'll head back here. Luminaries training happens every day. *If the forest never sleeps, then we can't either.* And as Darian's schedule revealed, the Luminaries will move around training hours to ensure their youths miss nothing.

Clan banners hang in shadow. The Wednesday bear looks particularly grumpy—as per usual—because he is perpetually displeased by Winnie's choices. *Bold of you to come here, girl. You did kill the man.*

"Because he was going to kill *me.*"

"Huh?" Erica asks.

"Nothing." Winnie aims pointedly for the stairwell at the hall's end. She already has too many feelings to get to the bottom of—dead Dianas in the forest, the Crow at the breakfast, the spell currently choking her throat. Throw in a professor whom Winnie hated, and nope. Her brain really can't grapple with that right now.

"Come on," she commands when Erica lags. She clutches once more at her locket—still cool. "Let's see what Professor Samuel was hiding."

18

What Professor Samuel was hiding is not obvious when Winnie and Erica reach his office on the third floor. Like all the other Sunday offices, there is no door—and therefore no lock. It's as if the Sundays wanted to make an open floor plan inside a building that was not designed for it.

Or maybe their swan hearts just don't like privacy.

Samuel has . . . no, *had* a corner space, giving him two windows: one which overlooks the parking lot and another which stares off toward the Monday estate. The brick campus is just visible over a stretch of trees. And somehow, despite the morning sun muscling in, his office is colorless and cold. There are no decorations on the wall, no photographs of family, and when Winnie opens Samuel's filing cabinet, she finds nothing except tests, papers, and grade sheets.

Obviously Winnie knew they weren't going to find blatant Diana paraphernalia, like rowan-wood medallions or a hound-shaped mask . . . And no, she wasn't expecting a directory labeled *Who's Who: Dianas of Hemlock Falls*. But still, this whole space is more barren than a desert in a drought. The only thing of interest in the entire wooden, un-carpeted space is a small telescope facing the northern window—and even that looks lonely and sad.

A worn book called *Shooting Stars: Identifying Asteroids, Comets, and Meteors* sits on the windowsill, but a quick flip through reveals no dog-eared pages or highlighted passages. As far as she can tell, Samuel just liked shooting stars. *And now he'll never see one again. Because of me.*

"Find anything?" Winnie makes herself ask, shoving the book back onto the sill.

"Nope." Erica offers this in a way that also declares, *Just like I told you we wouldn't last night.* Which is true: she had said, *Only a fool would keep their Diana stuff in their office.*

"Think outside the box," Winnie says. "What's some inconspicuous stuff a Diana might have? What are some things *you* have?"

Erica's mouth seams shut. Her arms fold over her in a physical manifestation of a castle portcullis lowering.

"A box of Band-Aids?" Winnie means this as a joke.

Erica doesn't laugh.

"Look." Winnie yanks off her glasses. Erica blurs away, her castle eroding to wind and weather. "I don't really care what you *can* do or *did* do, E. What I want is to find your sister's source before were-creatures, when in their animal form, are almost unkillable. *Oh my god.*" Winnie clenches her teeth so hard, her eardrums hurt. Then, with the same care she would apply to crossing a rope bridge over a ravine, she adds: "I . . . want to find Jenna's source. But more than that, I want to know who in Hemlock Falls is a Diana." *Anyone could be a Diana. A Diana could be anyone.* "So help me out here. Does anything look weird in this room?"

"I don't *know.*" Erica says this with siege engine force. "I was taught early on to keep my stuff in separate, unexpected places. Spots with no obvious connection to me in case—" She breaks off as a rumble vibrates into the room.

Winnie and Erica spring toward the eastern window. "Shit," Winnie says at the same time Erica murmurs, "Well, this is bad."

The *this* to which Erica refers are the five Tuesday Hummers now parking outside. Uniformed scorpions scuttle from each vehicle, carrying flattened cardboard boxes—although only three scorpions per vehicle because apparently Tuesdays can't carpool.

Exiting the nearest Hummer—and the only scorpion without a box—is Jeremiah Tuesday. He glances up to Samuel's office. His eyes meet Winnie's.

"Shit," she repeats, dropping to the ground beside Erica, whose reflexes were a split second faster.

"Did he see you?"

"I don't know. Maybe."

"It's darker in here than out there." Erica's tone is more hopeful than convinced. "Let's go."

"Wait." Winnie's eyes leap around the office while her mind leaps through every drawer she just opened. Erica doesn't know the Tuesdays are in cahoots (still a funny word) with Dianas. She doesn't *know* that the Lead Liaison to Italy is a Diana *cornīx* with Jeremiah Tuesday in her pocket.

That means Erica can't solve for the same *y* that Winnie can. Erica likely thinks Jeremiah is here to find evidence, while Winnie is 99 percent sure he's here to destroy it.

"Keep looking," she commands.

Erica coughs. "Are you off your rocker? There's nothing here, Winnie, except Tuesdays who would love to lock us up for a very long time."

Except there is something here. There has to be. Winnie crawls on her hands toward the desk. They have only minutes before the Lambda scorpions get up here, but she *refuses* to leave. She's like a horse who's just had blinders slotted on: there's nowhere she can look but ahead, and ahead is Samuel's desk with three drawers.

Stapler. Scotch tape. Another stapler (unnecessary). Package of black dry erase markers (opened). Package of colored markers (untouched). Post-its. While Winnie digs through, cataloguing everything mentally, Erica launches toward the cabinets. The metal drawers clang open. Clang shut.

"Nothing," Winnie says, shooting to her feet. "There's *nothing* in his desk."

"And there's nothing in his files. I mean, there might be." Erica's voice is rising—not in volume, but in pitch. As if she's sucking back helium from a balloon. "But I can't go through every single paper or grade sheet in the *one minute* we have left before Tuesdays show up. We're stuck here now, Winnie!"

"Not yet, we aren't." Winnie zips toward Erica, barely avoiding a collision with the telescope. "Maybe if we camp out in another office we can see what they grab."

Erica pales. "Uh, they're going to grab everything because they must have finally figured out Samuel was the dead guy in the forest. All of this is evidence."

At those words, they simultaneously realize the office is in disarray around them—and they simultaneously burst into action to clean up. By the time the last drawer is closed, there's a vibration quavering into Winnie's feet, so she hooks Erica by the arm and propels them both into the hall. They cut diagonally into a different office. Curtains blanket a window that would otherwise stare at the obstacle course and training lake. Without discussion, both girls hurtle behind the desk and crouch there.

It smells like chai latte, which Winnie recognizes as *L'eau de Professor Il-Hwa*. And unlike Professor Samuel's room, there are plenty of portraits of family. *People would mourn her if she died, while Professor Samuel has no one.*

Winnie shakes off that thought. She likes her spite blinders; she wants to hang on to those as long as she can.

"Last office on the right." Jeremiah speaks with the same voice he always uses, and somehow, the fact that he sounds so appealing, so smooth, only makes him that much more terrifying. Like this is just one more task on his to-do list: *Get milk; drop off mail; destroy Diana evidence.*

Boots tramp faster. Louder. Then stop at Samuel's office, which audibly fills up like a can of sardines. Grunts take over the soundtrack. Fabric rustles. Cardboard scrapes as boxes are assembled.

None of the scorpions speak. And Winnie and Erica definitely don't either.

Entire galaxies are birthed and collapsed during the time they huddle there behind Il-Hwa's desk. Winnie's brain, of course, wants to latch on to its usual refrain of Nightmare Compendium factoids. *Changeling: These daywalkers can perfectly mimic any human they see, though claws give them away.*

Except now she hates the Compendium. She *hates* that it's always going inside her brain and that a spell has hijacked it. Worse, Diana trivia sneaks in there too. *Sagitta aurea: These spells are used to kill or maim a target. Famēs: These spells are self-feeding and sustain themselves in the forest.*

On and on it goes, until at last, the sound of scraping cardboard ceases. Drawers stop slamming. And one by one, people stamp past Il-Hwa's office, their steps more labored now, as if they carry heavy loads.

After a full minute of quiet, Erica shifts to rise. But Winnie grips her sleeve, head shaking. She can't say why she's certain they'll be seen . . . but she is. There's a coil of cool air in the office when there should only be heat. Like a scorpion waits at the door.

More nebulae form into stars. Then become red giants. Then supernova. Then lastly, black holes.

A creak. A squeak. Another coil of air that doesn't mingle with the rest.

Erica's eyes are enormous and white. Winnie's lungs, meanwhile, have become two balloons she can't deflate.

The footsteps patter away. Only after a full three minutes of *real* silence—counted in one hundred and eighty Mississippis—does Winnie finally nod. Finally breathe normally again. "Come on," she whispers.

"Where?"

Winnie doesn't answer. Instead, she runs tippy-toed to the door, pokes her head out, finds the hall beautifully, *deliciously* empty, and darts right back into Samuel's office. Everything looks as it did before, since Samuel had nothing on display to be confiscated. Nothing but the telescope and the shooting-stars book, both now gone.

And why take them, unless . . .

Winnie slithers to the parking lot window, slotting herself just out of sight so she can peer through the glass. Sure enough, there's Jeremiah Tuesday with the telescope stretched over his shoulder. "Gotcha." Winnie grins and finds Erica's eyes across the tiny room. "Did you happen to see where the telescope was aimed?"

"The . . . sky?"

"That's helpful."

"Well, did *you* see where it was aimed?"

"Fair point." Winnie sidles to the northern window, but there's nothing to observe beyond trees and, as Erica said, blue sky. "Could he have hidden something inside the telescope?"

Erica is biting furiously at her lip, a frown pinched on her brow. "I guess he could have. Anything's possible."

This time, Winnie doesn't reply with a sarcastic *That's helpful.* Instead she asks, "I don't suppose Isaac has texted you? Maybe he can find out why they took the telescope."

"If he had texted, I would have said something."

"Fine. And . . . Jay?"

Erica snaps her head. *"Nada."*

Winnie frowns. She doesn't like that—not merely because of her guilt over missing Jay's show. But because it really isn't like him to go this long without contact. "Well, can you tell him to meet me at Sunday training? If he can't make it to the Floating Carnival before noon, I mean?"

"You should really just get your own phone." Erica glares. But she also obediently types out a message while Winnie's thoughts vortex inward. Trillium flowers form across her brain. *Whisperer. Sources. Dianas. Dad. Jenna. Lockets. Silencing spells.* It's all feeling disconnected and meaningless. Like there's no longer a Pure Heart at the center she can rely on. All the connective tissue has been frayed by a crow-shaped razor.

Neither girl speaks again while they navigate through the Sunday estate. A cold morning greets them outside the locker room. Wind rattles down from the forest.

19

Winnie outright refuses to throw candy from the pontoon-boat-turned-swan.

Dryden tells her she must. She tells Dryden *CANDY KILLS*, and to her surprise he drops the subject. Possibly because she literally bares her teeth at him like a nightmare. He also—wisely—does not make Winnie wear the Midnight Crown. It's exquisitely detailed—made from painted metal to look like woven pine branches with an ouroboros sliding through—and way too freaking heavy.

Headmaster Gina—who is also on the boat with Winnie since it's *her* clan parade—doesn't seem to notice any of this exchange since she is too busy arguing with their boat's driver over his poor navigation skills. Twice, they almost crash into one of the other swan-shaped boats. And the docking at the Floating Carnival is a real testament to Gina's Sunday patience because they not only *do* crash into another boat (Hey, Professor Funday! You look really, *really* bright today in that magenta sweater!), but they also hit the pier hard enough to knock an entire plastic bag of individually sized chocolate bars into the Little Lake.

RIP, Winnie thinks as she, Gina, and Dryden are finally helped off the swan by the driver, who now decides to reveal his second profession as a blogger. "I interview famous Luminaries! Will you answer some questions for me?"

"No."

"Did you wish you had a parachute when you jumped off the waterfall?"

"Not sure it would have helped me."

"Does hypothermia hurt?"

"I don't know. I was unconscious."

"Did the werewolf have teeth bigger than a great white shark?"

"Depends. Is the shark a juvenile?"

Winnie is saved by (of all people) Marcia Thursday. Erica is, as expected, already at her mother's side, and she gives Winnie a look so cool, Winnie actually needs a double take. They *were* just together, right? Winnie didn't just imagine that whole encounter at the Sunday estate with Jeremiah Tuesday and the telescope?

As Dryden and Marcia discuss the next events on the agenda—*Winnie, are you listening?*—Winnie takes in the Floating Carnival around her. Water laps gently against steel pilings. Streamers in clan colors twinkle over clapboard stands and stalls. Voices churn, hailing from volunteers and workers. There are games and competitions, treats and crafts, and everywhere Winnie looks, she spies happy Luminaries with no idea that Dianas have taken over Hemlock Falls.

Banners flutter. Music plays from a calliope. And to the north, the Ferris wheel spins, spraying out reflected light each time a car hits its zenith.

"Come," Dryden commands. "The world is waiting for you."

Winnie looks again at Erica.

This time, Erica blinks in solidarity.

Marcia's hand lands on Winnie's right arm. Dryden's lands on her left. And once more, Winnie is nothing more than a marionette being lolloped around on wooden legs.

"Smile, Winnie," Marcia declares once they reach the striped tent that marks the carnival entrance, where a large silver ribbon awaits. Winnie obeys, not because she wants to smile, but because it's the closest thing she has to a suit of armor. A sea of bobbing heads and gawping faces await her beyond the silver ribbon, so smiling at them feels safer than recoiling.

When people lined up to be tested for werewolf mutation, they'd formed helpful, single-file queues outside the striped tent. Now they are a mass. A swarm. A nest of manticores ready to attack. And somewhere in there, the signora must be waiting, scheming, laughing like the cartoon villain she is.

Anyone can be a Diana. A Diana can be anyone.

Morning sun glints on Winnie's glasses, garbling all the faces into splotches on the page. "You'll cut the ribbon," Dryden tells her, "once I declare, *Enjoy the Carnival*. Do you understand?" He doesn't wait for a reply before pushing enormous scissors into Winnie's hands. Like, hilariously *enormous*. To the point that she feels even more like a puppet now, holding these human-sized scissors.

"Welcome!" Dryden calls, a megaphone abruptly appearing at his mouth. With the pince-nez on his nose, there is something almost ringleader about him. "Welcome to the fifty-fourth annual Floating Carnival!" Cheers erupt outside the tent, and as Darian's schedule promised, cameras flash.

Winnie smiles wider. She is a bear. She is untouchable.

"We hope you enjoy the festivities this year," Dryden continues, "and remember! Although death may be a part of life in Hemlock Falls, *life* is a part of it too! Life and pleasure and defiance against the night!"

Now the crowds really cheer, and Winnie has to admit, what Dryden said wasn't half bad. The energy, the noise, the animation of it all—it reverberates inside her with a truth she has felt before. *That is why we're called the Luminaries, Winnie. We are lanterns the forest can never snuff out.*

"Cut it," Dryden growls. *"Winnie, cut it!"* Judging by the circumference of his eyes, he might have been snarling this for several seconds. But—did he say *Enjoy the Carnival*? Doesn't matter now. He wants her to cut, so cut she will.

Winnie hefts open the scissors and arranges them around the ribbon. *Crank!* The ribbon doesn't cut.

"Uh . . ."

"Again," Dryden snarls. *"Again."*

Winnie cranks the scissors again. Nope. Again. Still nope, and oh god, this is turning into a bad dream. *Please, please, please, forest spirit, let them work this time—*

The ribbon splits. Cameras flash. Luminaries cheer.

And the Nightmare Masquerade finally begins.

Augustus Saturday's Ferris Wheel: Often called the "jewel" of the
Floating Carnival, the central spoke of the wheel is made to look

like a golden full moon. The carts circling are black with silver stars, so when the wheel spins, it looks like a galaxy hovering above the Little Lake.

To Winnie's vast surprise, she ends up wearing a *real* smile shortly after the ribbon cutting. Dryden sets her loose to "mingle" and she almost immediately runs into Bretta and Emma at the goldfish toss. As always, they look amazing. Bretta has on a pistachio maxi dress under a black moto jacket. She munches from a bag of her favorite salt-and-vinegar chips. Emma, meanwhile, wears a jean skirt, thick tights, and a T-shirt with the Goblin King from *Labyrinth* on it—no chips.

"Winnie!" Bretta waves her over while beside her Emma unsuccessfully tosses Ping-Pong balls at fish bowls. Emma laughs when one of the balls bounces off the attendant's head.

"Please stop doing that," Arthur Sunday (senior class) says.

"It's not on *purpose*." Emma rolls her eyes in Winnie's direction. "Obviously it's not on purpose. I just really want a goldfish." She tries again; the ball hits Arthur again.

He scowls.

"Maybe just give her a goldfish?" Bretta suggests with a flirty smile. "Then at least she'll stop bonking you."

"Or," Emma counters, leaning onto her casted leg, "I'll try a different angle—"

"*No you don't.*" Bretta shoves the chip bag onto Winnie, then swoops in before Emma can put all her weight on the leg. "Dr. Dara literally said yesterday that you're doing that too much." She tucks an arm under Emma's shoulder, shares her biggest smile for Arthur (who is too busy picking up Emma's wayward Ping-Pong balls to notice the vibes Bretta is sending his way), and then hauls a complaining Emma onward. "Come on, Win!" she calls without waiting to see if Winnie actually follows.

But of course Winnie follows. For one, she is now Carrier of the Chips. For two, she is grateful for the distraction. Her eyes can't stop searching for Jay, while her brain keeps catapulting back into Samuel's office. It was *so* empty. And now it will always be empty.

Because of what Winnie did.

And where is Jay? Why isn't he here?

As if reading her mind, Emma asks, "Hey, where did Jay go last night?"

Winnie's feet slug to a halt. "Huh?"

"Last night. Jay didn't come to the show at Joe Squared."

"L.A. was so *pissed,*" Bretta adds. Then she grabs the chips back to her and resumes munching.

Winnie's whole body freezes over. They are beside the Nightmare Puppet Stage, where a sign declares the show will start at one o'clock. People stream around Winnie and the sisters. One guy glares.

"What do you mean *Jay didn't come to the show*?" Winnie doesn't mean to shout this, but she definitely shouts this.

"Exactly what I said." Emma's face pinches up with apology. Bretta's face, meanwhile, is a mishmash of indecision while she chews: Does she think Jay is an asshole for skipping his own show? Or is she worried like Emma clearly is?

"He *was* there," Emma explains, "but then he left. Like, right before the show. With Councilor Tuesday and an Italian lady. He said he'd be back, but he never showed up. Normally he's such a reliable Friday—"

Bretta snorts her doubt.

"—and we tried to find you last night to tell you he was gone, but . . . Well, you weren't home."

No, because Winnie was with Erica staring at dead bodies and spewing useless Compendium facts.

"You need a phone," Bretta says. "Because we were actually pretty worried, Win."

"Was Jay with you?" Hope lifts Emma's eyebrows.

"No." Winnie's voice is back to being stuck in a tin-can phone. She is a chocolate bar sinking to the bottom of the Little Lake. "Jay wasn't with me." *And I wasn't with him because I am a terrible person.* "Did you," she begins, "ask his aunt Lizzy if she's seen him?"

"Councilor Friday?" Emma shakes her head. "No, but Trevor did call her last night during the show. She didn't know where he was either."

Winnie's head detaches from her spinal column. Her gaze fixes somewhere on the quantum space between Emma and Bretta. *I should have been there. If I had been there, this wouldn't have happened.* "You said he left with Jeremiah?"

"Yeah, Councilor Tuesday and an Italian lady. Hey, Winnie, is he okay?"

"Probably." This is a lie, and the twins can hear that. "Thanks for letting me know," Winnie adds. "I'm going to go find him right now." She walks away, despite her friends shouting after her. Despite them calling, "Should we do something?"

Maybe he just got pulled onto an extra hunt, Winnie's brain suggests. *Or maybe he turned into a werewolf and is still sleeping it off.* It's the same list of possibilities Winnie conjured last night, except now she has actual evidence to push against her. The Crow promised to harm Winnie's friends and family; now the woman has probably followed through.

People try to stop Winnie as she roves the Floating Carnival. *Can I get a selfie? Hey, will you sign this?* She ignores every request. Every face. Brilliant streamers and glittering lights smear around her. She passes the carousel with kelpies instead of horses. The funnel cake stand. The Tilt-A-Whirl. She hears Andrew call out from a Ring-the-Bell stand, where his mallet swing has only gotten him up to the third level. *Sylphid.* He groans. Then waves.

Winnie doesn't wave back.

Anyone could be a Diana. A Diana could be anyone.

Calliope music follows her like a horror movie gone wrong. Her fingers straighten at her sides. Her stride lengthens. Her harpy-sharp vision scans and searches for the one face she needs.

She thinks of her sketches of Jay. She thinks of the boy, an orphan and so alone. She thinks of the wolf, cursed and terrified.

Winnie is almost to the Ferris wheel, where dry ice tentacles over the dock, caressing the full moon of the wheel like forest mist. A line is cordoned off—and there, *right there,* is the target of her hunt: Signora Caterina Martedì stands beside Marcia at the front of the Ferris wheel line.

"Signora," Winnie declares, "allow me to join you on the jewel of our Floating Carnival." Shouts of protest erupt from the people waiting in line. Until someone points out: "It's Wolf Girl! The Midnight Crown!" That shuts everyone up.

"No, no, Winnie," Marcia says through a pained smile. "*I am* riding with the signora."

The Crow smiles serenely. She was clearly expecting Winnie to confront her. "Of course, Signorina Wednesday. What an honor to ride the Ferris wheel with you. You do not mind, do you, Councilor?"

Marcia's mouth bobs open. She can't exactly say no, and Winnie can't pretend she doesn't feel a lemon twist of triumph over dominating Marcia so easily.

"Thank you, Councilor Thursday. *Ciao ciao.*" The signora offers an arm to Winnie, as if they are longtime friends. As if *touching* each other is a totally normal thing to do.

Winnie takes the Crow's arm. *I'm not afraid of you.* Then she smiles—a fake, cold smile. Her locket, she notes, isn't warming at all.

Strangely, this close, the Crow reminds Winnie of Grandma Harriet— a woman Winnie barely knows and hasn't seen since Dad disappeared. Harriet and the Crow have similar coloring, similar bearing. They have similar style, too: a scarlet, ankle-length gown undulates dramatically in the breeze. Martedì's loafers click next to Winnie's sneakers. A black shawl drips over her shoulder. Her gray hair is loose and wavy.

An attendant whom Winnie vaguely recognizes from Wednesday dinners hurries over to help them strap into a cart. Lights gleam on the Little Lake's water, pulled like strands of caramel by the current. A chemical, musty smell from the dry ice fills Winnie's nose. Then she is seated in the cart and the Diana is seated too, straight-backed and elegant, beside her.

"*Grazie,*" Martedì says as the attendant lowers a bar across them.

The Ferris wheel engine kicks on. The wood and metal groan. Winnie and her enemy begin to rise up from the fog. *Pick your nightmare, spin the wheel! Or you'll end up a Diana meal!*

"Where is he?" These are the first words out of Winnie's mouth. "What have you done with him?"

"You will have to tell me who you mean, Winnie." The witch has lost her accent again. She stares with calm curiosity over the lake and Hemlock Falls expanding before them. Two weeks ago, Winnie thought all the lights of downtown were liars. Swamp fires pretending to be fairies. Now she *knows* it's true.

There is no safety in Hemlock Falls. There is only death and Dianas and monsters.

"Cut the act." Winnie leans toward the Crow. A scent like lavender cuts into her nose. "I know that Jay was with you last night, and that he never showed up for his band's show. So where did you take him?"

"My, my." The Crow clucks her tongue. "You are making a lot of assumptions here. Yes, I spoke to Jay Friday last night—just as I spoke to *all* the Lead Hunters." She motions to the crowds. They are high enough now that everyone has become miniature. "But Jay left along with the rest of them—including your aunt—the moment we were finished. If he disappeared after that, well . . ." A shrug of her shawled shoulder. "That had nothing to do with me."

"I don't believe you."

"I don't really care if you do. Have you found Jenna's source yet?"

Winnie recoils. Wind sweeps against her face. It smells like funnel cake and a lingering tendril of dry ice. "Of course I haven't."

"And why not, Winnie?"

"Because you only gave me the task yesterday."

"But you were searching long before that. And as you know, every minute you waste is one more minute that the Whisperer can use to kill people."

"Is that a threat?"

"Of course it is." The signora grins. "Do not mistake me for a patient Sunday swan, willing to wait until *you* decide you're frightened enough to make a move." She motions to the swan pontoon, regal and bright next to an array of colorful floats from the parade. "I am a Tuesday scorpion, and there's venom in my sting."

"You're a cartoon villain, is what you are."

The signora chuckles. Wind flings her hair across her face, but she lets it flutter there, unbothered. "I'm giving you until Wednesday morning. If I don't have Jenna's source by eight A.M., then your boyfriend really *will* disappear—along with everyone else you care about."

Wednesday morning. Winnie feels sick. The Ferris wheel moves too fast. The lying lights of Hemlock Falls melt together. *Like hound masks.*

"That's not enough time," Winnie croaks.

"For someone as industrious and *illustrious* as you? Surely it is."

"I . . . need help, then." Winnie can't believe she's squeezing this out. She can't *believe* she's sitting here giving this woman what she wanted all along: Leverage. Power. Control.

"You want *my* help?" The signora's thick eyebrows rise in mock surprise. "Well, you certainly aren't very polite about it."

"Get rid of this spell on me. Let me tell Erica about you. And Jay—let me tell him too." For the first time since leaving the maze, Winnie can say all of those things freely. No trivia replaces her words.

"You're cute, but no."

"Why not? Clearly you can turn the spell off at will, right? You're letting me talk freely right now."

"I can, Winnie, because it's helpful to me. It is *not* helpful to me if you talk to your friends. Or anyone else, for that matter."

"Okay *fine*," Winnie powers on. "You're a Tuesday, so can you get me records of the night my dad vanished? That would help."

"That I certainly *cannot* do."

"Cannot or will not?" Winnie stares down at the carnival, oblivious and gorgeous. *And a bunch of sitting ducks.* "Then . . . then tell me what happened. You were there that night, clearly."

"And I wasn't the only one."

"You mean other Dianas?"

"I mean your mother." The smile returns, predatory now. A scorpion about to attack. "Maybe you should start with her, Winnie. Little Franny has even more secrets than you do—ones Jeremiah could never pry loose. But you . . . well, *you're* her daughter. Maybe she'll share them with you. And if not?" The signora shrugs. "Wednesday morning will be here soon enough."

20

As far as Winnie knows, on the night her dad disappeared, events unfolded as follows:

It was a Monday, and Mom was supposed to be gone until 8 P.M. with hunter training. She sprained her ankle, though, so she left Aunt Rachel in command and came home early. Winnie was at Erica's house doing homework. Darian was on his second date with Andrew (they went for coffee at Joe Squared).

When Mom reached the house, she found Dad in the middle of the living room with a glowing light in one hand and a piece of paper in the other. The paper vanished the instant she stepped into the living room; the light did not.

"What are you doing?" she demanded, total shock mixing with rigid horror. "Is that a source?"

"You shouldn't be here," Dad replied. His hair was apparently a mess. "Fran, you can't be here."

In the time it took him to say those words, Mom realized there was magic all around. She smelled it, she felt it. Dad tried to run. She tried to give chase, but her ankle was busted. She barely made it five steps before he was through the kitchen and opening the door.

He looked back once. The light around his hand spread. An explosion, Mom thought, before it hit her. She blacked out.

When she came to, she dragged herself to the Tuesday estate. Not that Darian or Winnie knew this. They came home; they went to bed; then they were both awakened by Tuesday scorpions hours later and locked into handcuffs.

The rest . . . ah, well, the rest is shitty history. Winnie and Darian were hauled underground at the Tuesday estate and blasted with Jeremiah's probing questions—in separate rooms, of course. *Were there burn marks on your dad's fingers? Did you ever smell strange things in the house? Did he have small wooden coins in his possession?*

No, no, the answer to everything was no—including the biggest question of all: Can your family still be in the Luminaries?

Four years later, after months in denial, then years in rage . . . then the sudden flip of the script in which Winnie learned Dad *was* actually framed . . . Now here Winnie is, and everything has been flipped all over again.

Dad *was* framed, and maybe Mom has always known about it.

It makes a frowning, chewed-up sort of sense. After all, Mom never really fought the punishment passed down from the Council, even though it ruined her life and her children's. She just kept her gaze forward, never complained, and trudged on.

And then there was always that nagging question of why Mom kept the birthday cards that mysteriously appeared in the mailbox each year. *What if,* Winnie now wonders, *there were more than just birthday cards? What if Mom found other things too?*

Winnie's mind is alight as she walks through the Carnival and the calliope music nips after. One turn on the Ferris wheel was all she endured before she got right back off again. The Crow trilled, *"Ciao ciao!"* while Marcia leaped into Winnie's place. Winnie ignored the Crow—and ignored Marcia and everyone else too. She simply set off, walking south. Then once she reached the carnival's exit, she strode through and didn't look back.

She wants to go to the Friday estate and search for Jay.

She wants to track down Mom and confront her.

And she *wants* to pound that Diana's face in, then pound in Jeremiah Tuesday's too.

But it's time for Sunday training, and so back to the Sunday estate Winnie will go. By foot. She will walk and walk and walk because there's something about the steady pounding of her feet that seems to fire up her brain. Like one of those bicycle-powered engines: as long as her wheels are spinning, her brain has computational function.

People slow down to offer her rides. Casey Tuesday in his Wrangler. Fatima in her Mom's Taurus. But Winnie waves them on. It's not that she doesn't want company right now (although she doesn't) so much as her brain can't spare the processing power. She needs to think through what it might mean if Mom has always known. She needs to *feel* what it might mean if Mom has always known.

Could that mean Mom also knows where Dad is right now?

Winnie pushes into a jog, savoring how her Converse slap on pavement. How her breaths get shallow and fast. Heat saturates her muscle fibers. She has to stop at one point to pull off her green sweater, revealing her white tee now speckled with green fuzz. She holds the sweater in one fist, losing her bilateral symmetry, but the challenge feels good. Like it used to feel when she would run and run and *run*, thinking only of the hunter trials ahead. Knowing only *she* could save her family by passing them.

What if Mom could have saved them all along? What does that *mean* for Winnie and for Darian?

It's too much for Winnie to reckon with, so she just keeps slamming one foot in front of the other until she reaches the middle of the dam. No floats or boats are here now. Just water and cold.

At this point, her emotions are running along familiar fault lines. And frankly, if she could have her way, she'd just skip the whole *feeling things* quake and jump straight into the aftermath of dusty stillness.

Winnie cranks out her arm, sweater still clutched there, and imagines dropping it into the Little Lake, where it can sink down and join all the plastic candy wrappers. And also the Tuesday Hummer Grayson Friday drove in there four years ago.

Four years ago. Why did so many things happen four years ago?

At that question, a memory surfaces in a way the candy bars and Hummer never will. A conversation on the roof of the old museum, where Jay lay draped on shingles while grief and vape smoke enclosed him.

"Grayson was on his second trial," Winnie says to the water, where wind sketches a chevron pattern. White chop on dark waves. "When he stole a Tuesday Hummer and drove it off the dam."

The second trial was the same trial Jenna was on when she died. Jenna, who was Grayson's girlfriend. Jenna, who created the Whisperer. Jenna, who gave Grayson her locket for reasons no one understands.

And Grayson, who tried to reach out to Erica four years ago, only for her to essentially throat-punch him away. He told her that he'd found Jenna on her trial and tried to revive her. Assuming that's true, what happened next? Why did he steal a Hummer and drive it off this bridge right there?

Winnie is still gripping the green sweater, holding it over the water as if she really does plan to drop it. In her brain, her three-petaled trilliums are morphing into four-petaled poppies.

Dad, Mom, Jenna, Grayson. On the surface, they should have nothing in common. And yet, four years ago something happened that connects them all.

Mom and Dad. What does Mom know? This is a conversation Winnie will have tonight, when she can gather the needed supplies and corner Francesca Wednesday alone.

Jenna and Grayson. What did Grayson know? Winnie thinks of the photograph she found in Jay's office—of Grayson wearing Jenna's locket. Then she thinks of Jay, still missing—or at least not answering her messages.

Winnie reels in her arm. The sleeve of the green sweater flutters like a fishing line that's lost its catch. After tying the sweater around her waist, she resumes her run. Symmetrical now. Faster thinking, better processing. Until eventually the Sunday estate appears before her. Until she is once more at the oak tree where she met Erica only a few hours before.

Luminaries percolate from vehicles toward the front doors, pulled by the gravity of their culture. There might be a carnival with cotton candy and goldfish, but there is also a forest that wants to kill them. Winnie lets her footsteps slow so she can search for a Wagoneer. For Jay's pale head and signature flannel.

He isn't here, though, so she looks instead for Erica and the Porsche. Winnie will call Jay directly. She will hear his voice, and maybe then she will feel less worried about him.

Because of course, there are other things than the Crow that might have harmed him.

Winnie shoves inside the Sunday estate—so full, so alive now—and continues her wild search for Jay's face, for Erica's. Her feet lead her without conscious control to Luminary history, where Professor Alice is waiting at the door.

Because of course, Professor Samuel is dead.

Because of course, Winnie killed him.

"Ah, there you are," Alice says with a smile that reveals lipstick on her teeth. "I have been told to escort you out of class."

Winnie blinks at Alice. She is panting and sweating, and her neural pathways are primed for instant panic—*What is it this time? Did they learn Erica and I broke in earlier? Oh god, what if they have security cameras!*

Except now Alice chimes: "You're being moved to new classes, Winnie!" She grips Winnie's biceps with the strength of a droll and whirls her around. "I'll be seeing you at the end of the day moving forward, instead of the beginning."

"Ma'am?" Winnie is surprised this comes out without cracking.

"You're being bumped *up*, Winnie. Don't you want to be around students closer to your own age?" Alice's smile falters. "Wait—why are you so sweaty? Did you run here?"

Winnie nods.

"Well, all the more reason to advance you. Come on."

"So . . . I'll be with my grade now?"

"Oh, no, I didn't say *grade*." An apologetic smile. "The headmaster felt you were too behind in Luminary history for that, but she did move you to the tenth-year class during third period. And for first period, you'll be moving into twelfth-year physical training."

"Oh." Winnie doesn't really know what else to say to this.

"You passed all of your trials," Alice explains. "Which means you're more than ready to train with the seniors. But if you don't feel comfortable, I'm sure Headmaster Gina can rearrange things—once our day of Sunday festivities is over, of course. I hear you will be at our Sunday dinner tonight?"

"Uh, yeah." Winnie finds herself swallowing and shoving at her glasses. Alice has led her to the locker rooms, and the door looks very different with body heat and voices to press against it.

"In you go." Alice grins. "And I'll see you in third period!"

Winnie feels detached from her body as she moves to her usual locker. She just jogged from the Floating Carnival while her brain attempted to run complex computational formulas. Now here she is, back in the Sunday estate locker room where the lights are too bright and a handful of seniors are staring at her with expressions she can't sort through. Are those fangirl smiles or mocking ones? Or are these girls all just changelings who want to eat Winnie and wear her skin?

She has just wriggled into her black training T-shirt, when *bam*. Someone is standing beside her.

L.A. Saturday snorts at Winnie's flinch. She wears the same training gear as everyone else, but she has made it wholly her own by cutting her T-shirt into a crop top and adding a small tutu over her track pants. She looks ready for the roller derby. "Care to explain why your boyfriend didn't show up to our show last night?"

No, Winnie thinks. *I really don't.* She retrieves her glasses from a nearby bench and shoves them on. She doesn't think L.A. has ever directly addressed her in her life.

And she certainly has never directly scrutinized Winnie like she's a *Chrysomya megacephala* larvae under a microscope.

"Well?" L.A. prompts.

"I have no idea why he didn't show." This is true. Completely true, but either Winnie's tone isn't very convincing or else her own panic over Jay is coming through, because L.A.'s posture softens.

Though only momentarily.

"Well then, what's this about you winning the Midnight Crown, even though you're not a senior? Some of us have worked really hard to get a crown, you know. Then you just show up and win *all* of them."

"I had nothing to do with that. The Council were the ones who shrank the Court to one."

L.A. cocks a single eyebrow. "The *Council* did it, huh? And you had *nothing* to do with it? It wasn't *your* idea to just skip the Golden Crown meant for juniors and go straight for Midnight?" The sarcasm dripping off her voice is practically forming a puddle around her boots.

Frankly, Winnie doesn't care. L.A. has confronted her, clearly hoping for a fight—and you know what? Winnie would *love* to go toe-to-toe right now. Which is why she says: "I guess if you wanted the Midnight Crown, L.A., you should have gotten more votes."

The entire locker room audibly sucks in at those words. As if no one has ever talked back to L.A. Saturday before. The only person who doesn't gasp is L.A. herself. Instead, her other eyebrow leaps up to join the first.

"I have no doubt I actually did win. I won the Bronze Crown, the Silver Crown, and the Golden Crown. There's no way in hell I didn't also win Midnight."

"So what are you saying? You want me to just give it to you?"

L.A. shrugs as if to say, *That works for me.*

And Winnie shrugs right back. "Welp, can't say I have it on me, Louisa Anne. But hey, check back at I-give-zero-fucks o'clock, okay? Maybe I'll have it by then."

Another gasp through the locker room.

L.A. opens her arms, smiling a feral smile. "Cute."

To which Winnie responds by tugging back her right sleeve to reveal pale scars for all the senior class to see. "If a werewolf couldn't take me down, then I can promise you can't either."

L.A. doesn't look at the scars. She just holds Winnie's gaze, her blue eyeliner thick and vibrant.

The entire locker room is holding its breath.

Then L.A. relaxes. A laugh barks from her throat. She starts nodding as if Jay has started a bass line. "Okay, okay. I hear you. Don't fuck with the Wolf Girl." She laughs again, a brighter sound this time, filled with real amusement, and the entire space deflates like a balloon.

L.A. flips up both hands. "I'm excited to see your moves in the hot room." She pivots away. The final bursts of trapped air escape, and the unexpected shakedown ends.

But rather than feel relief at L.A.'s departing back, Winnie feels only fury gathering. Spinning like a hurricane. This is one more person trying to back her into a corner—and one more person who has *severely* underestimated what Winnie Wednesday can do.

L.A. picked the wrong target. She picked the wrong day. Winnie just faced down a full-blown Diana *cornīx,* and L.A. is such small fry in comparison, she's basically microscopic.

"*Meu Deus,* that was rough," Coach Rosa says when Winnie finally storms onto the grounds behind the Sunday estate. The midday sun asserts its dominance across the obstacle course. The small lake ripples with spring-cold waves.

"You just watched everything that happened and didn't interfere?" Winnie glares at the coach's signature yellow scrunchie around her ponytail. Then at Rosa directly.

Rosa grins. "L.A. needed to be taken down a notch—like most Saturdays—and you managed it without even breaking a sweat. Well . . . without getting any sweatier." She studies Winnie's face. "Why *are* you so sweaty?"

Winnie wants to scream, *BECAUSE EVERYONE IS OUT TO GET ME TODAY.* But she chomps on her tongue instead and focuses on where Coach Rosa is now pointing. Tens of twelfth-grade bodies sprint and leap and swing.

"We're racing to the hot room," Rosa says. "You're blue"—she shoves a velcro strap and flag into Winnie's hand—"and the later you get in there, the harder it is to survive. Especially since I'm guessing you'll be everyone's target right now."

21

The hot room sounds so much nicer than it actually is. You might imagine a sauna or steam room—and that's a start. But now ratchet up the heat and steam to Level Relentless, and instead of a spa with cucumbers for your eyes, imagine an underground maze where everyone wants to destroy you.

Filled with columns, walls, ditches, mounds, and a long pool of varying depths, the hot room is meant to mimic the forest when the nightly mist rises. It is, in other words, meant to mimic hell.

Winnie hasn't entered the maze in over four years, and back then, she and her fellow sixth graders only ever did the most basic of maneuvers to acclimate themselves to the steam.

There's almost no light beyond five white bulbs spaced throughout, and the obstacles are changed weekly so no one can memorize the layout. Sometimes the classes split into teams, sometimes it's every hunter for themself. *Last Hunter Standing,* it's called, and the goal is to eliminate all other students by ripping off their flags.

That's the game today, and Winnie is going to win. She couldn't pound in the signora's teeth, but she can probably get in a few swings at L.A. *Come at me,* she thinks as she navigates the outdoor obstacle course into the woods behind the Sunday estate. *Back me into a corner, L.A. I dare you.* The same goes for the rest of the class too. They don't get to watch Winnie get bullied like it's Shakespeare in the Locker Room.

Steam drifts out of the mausoleum-like entrance to the hot room. Trees cast shadows. Winnie forces herself to drop low and take each step into the darkness slowly. Because she's last to arrive, there will inevitably be an ambush at the bottom of these stairs—and those seniors will inevitably be expecting Winnie's head high. So if she's *really* quiet and *really* low, she should be able to slip right under.

If she's unlucky . . . well, some grappling might be in her near future. But that still won't compare to getting stuck in the middle of a vampira horde during the *real* forest mist, and Winnie doesn't care how many Saturdays go full alpha-hole on her. Divas are easier to take down than a sadhuzag.

The intensity of the steam rolls over Winnie, thick and hot. It steals her sight and forces her to rely on senses she didn't know she had until that night on her first trial a month ago. She *does* have those senses, though, and if the run from the carnival was a cardiac warm-up, then the obstacle course toggled all her reflexes to On.

A kiss of cold hits her skin. She hears a scrape like shifting fabric. The steam thickens against her lips.

Winnie scoots off the final step and drops to the concrete floor—right as two arms sling out where her torso was. A red flag is hanging at eye level; Winnie rips off the flag and sidles left, searching for a wall she can use both as cover and guidance. She never even sees a face.

The sounds of remaining ambushers pinball from behind. Grunts. A *Hey, no fingernails!* And a *What the hell, bro?* It's distracting—both for Winnie and the girl she almost runs into: Clarissa Thursday, a second cousin to Erica, who is now materializing in the steam.

"Sorry," Clarissa says, and she charges Winnie with the grace of a ballerina and speed of a banshee.

But Winnie really, *really* has something to prove, and for all Clarissa's undeniable skills, she's not an *actual* banshee. Winnie's muscles move without command. She punches upward with both hands, knocking Clarissa's outstretched arms. Then she whirls in close, snatches off Clarissa's orange flag, and keeps on moving.

Clarissa squeals, a sound both frustrated and delighted. It makes Winnie smile. *Number of flags grabbed a month ago? Zero. Number of flags grabbed now? Two and counting.*

Winnie passes three more Luminaries, but they never realize she's there before she has their flags. And with each new ribbon to shove into her pocket, the more Winnie is convinced she's going to win this. She's going to be the last hunter standing, and L.A. Saturday can savor the taste of defeat.

Boohoo, I got your Midnight Crown and your flag, Louisa Anne.

Winnie moves around a column, under a low archway, and over two "streams" made of rustling plastic—the second of which Winnie doesn't quite avoid. Two Luminaries leap at her. One wears a yellow flag, the other a green, and Winnie ducks behind the yellow right as the green lunges.

They take each other down, which Winnie derives great pleasure from, even if it isn't sportsmanlike. And she especially enjoys plucking off both their flags while they're tussling. She slinks back into the steam before they can stop her. Obscenities chase behind.

Winnie's grin expands, steam pushing into her mouth and between her teeth. Eventually she'll have to meet L.A., and she can't wait for that moment to come. Don't fuck with Wolf Girl, indeed.

Winnie reaches the central pool. It is the one element of the hot room that never changes, its waters supposedly kept the same temperature as the shallows of the Big Lake. The air breathes differently here, slightly cooler, slightly thinner, and she senses no movement in the steam that beads on her skin. She circles the pool, moving cautiously. No one is here, leaving her to wonder if maybe she's already the last hunter standing—if maybe she got L.A.'s flag without realizing it.

She hopes not. She really wants to see L.A.'s face when she clobbers her.

At the pool's end, a column blocks Winnie's way. She can continue left, skirting dangerously close to the pool's edge, or she can go right—the safer option, so long as no one else is around.

She decides to risk left. Cold air tickles her scarred arm. She forgot to roll down the sleeve. Her toes inch along a narrow lip beside the water. Scoot. Slide. Scoot. Slide.

She realizes half a second too late that someone else has had the same idea. Their feet touch. Then their hands. Then they're both grappling for each other's flags. Winnie can't even see what color it is; she doesn't care. She's not going down.

Except that right as she does manage to find the flag—gray, it's gray— her feet slip. She loses her balance. She falls backward into the pool. Her body crashes under the cold, lungs expelling every drop of air.

And Winnie knows right away that she's in trouble.

It's an atavistic terror that electrifies her muscles, her brain. *Not again,* it seems to say. *Not these ghosts again.* She is back beneath the falls, sinking and numb. She trusted the forest, and it only froze her in return. Her life is plucking away from her.

She thrashes, trying to swim, but the green dress is tangled around her like kelp that will never release.

No. Not the green dress. You're in the hot room.

Her body doesn't care. It's trapped under the falls, while water roars. She is so cold. She is so numb. *Why* did she trust the forest? The Whisperer is coming. The Pure Heart can't save her. She didn't find the source, and now everyone in Hemlock Falls will die like Grayson did—

"Winnie," someone shouts at her. "Winnie, you're okay. Winnie, Winnie." They are shaking her, and she is no longer submerged. She's not even in the water, but draped on the inclined exit at the pool's other side. Someone has hauled her all the way here. They drip water onto her, their face backlit by a foggy light bulb. "Winnie, you're okay. You're okay. Hey, it's me, Win. It's just me."

Bergamot and lime. It's Jay. *Always* Jay.

"You're here," she chokes out, trying to sit up. But Jay is tugging her too tightly against him.

"I'm sorry I pushed you in," he says into her wet hair. "I didn't know it was you."

"You're here," she repeats. And this time, she digs her forehead into his shoulder. He is so warm. "Is there . . . anyone else left?"

"I doubt it. You're the first person I've run into in a while. And again," he insists, "I didn't know it was you."

"I believe you." She is shivering. "D-do you know what time it is?"

He shifts, as if to study his dad's watch in the darkness. At this angle, he is a black-and-white sketch with shadow eyes and wet-dark hair. "It's half past."

Winnie groans. That means there's still thirty minutes left in class. "I can't do it, Jay. I can't go back out there and deal with everyone."

A zipper hisses. Then Jay's hoodie—wet, but warm—drapes over her, followed by his arms again. Safe, certain. One part of the forest she can always trust.

"And you don't have to go back out there. We can leave, Winnie. Just walk out of here. There's a door nearby. It leads to a pump room we can use to sneak out."

"Spoken like someone who has used this tactic before."

He doesn't deny it. Just explains: "Grayson showed it to me a while ago. Probably because he . . . knew what I was. What I am."

Winnie sighs. A sharp, cold thing. Grayson Friday continues to prove a mystery. *He was a hard person to describe,* Darian once said about him. *And at the end of the day, I don't think anyone really knew him.*

As much as Winnie would like to use Grayson's private escape right now, she knows she can't abandon the blue schedule; she *knows* she can't skip all the tasks she has been set as the Midnight Crown. For all the secrets Mom might be hiding, she is still the most important person in Winnie's life.

"I'll just run out the clock in here," she murmurs. "And you can explain to me why you missed your own show last night. You were at the Tuesday estate? Is that right?"

"Ah." Jay hugs her more tightly against him—like he's the one who's afraid the forest will claim him. His nose presses into her wet hair. "It was a long night, Win. And as usual, I can't remember a thing."

Another cold, sharp sigh levers up from Winnie's abdomen. "It's happening more often, isn't it, Jay?"

"Yeah." A nod. Another squeeze. "Yeah, it is. And for longer times too. I barely made it out of the Tuesday estate before the mutation took hold. What happens if I change while other people are around me, Win? Then what? What do I *do?*"

You die, she thinks. But she doesn't say this out loud because Jay already knows this is the answer. *Witches, werewolves, Wednesdays.* Three petals, four petals, messages in honey ink, and nothing that Winnie can find to connect them all.

She shivers again. Then kisses Jay's neck. Just a gentle pressure below his ear to remind herself that he is real, he is here, and that the shadows of the forest haven't claimed either of them quite yet.

C H A P T E R

22

After a day of confrontations, Winnie does not expect that the hardest one will be her mom. After all, it's *Mom*. Literally her favorite person in the whole world. Literally her *hero*. Not a Diana pretending to be a Tuesday, not a Saturday wanting to bully her in the locker room, and not ghosts from the forest wanting to drown her.

Yet here Winnie sits, at the kitchen table, her heart all stutter and no flow. She's dressed in the green sweater and jeans from the morning, because after counting down the clock with Jay, she took a blessedly hot shower in the locker room and once more became the Face of Hemlock Falls.

Jay, who was still recovering from his lost night in the forest, left at Winnie's insistence to visit Mario. Because if his transformation is happening more often, maybe the Monday scientist can help.

Please let Mario help.

Classes blurred by, and Winnie felt like a child being carted along at the zoo, forced to eyeball exhibits she didn't care about while all the critters she *did* want to see were behind crowds of people taller than her. By the time she reached Sunday dinner, she had vowed seventy-three times she would insist that L.A. should have the Midnight Crown instead. But every time her chance came with Dryden or Marcia, Winnie wussed out.

Now here she is, on her only free two hours, between dinner and the fireworks. She wasted thirty minutes of that time navigating from the Sunday estate to her house—which would have taken even longer if Headmaster Gina hadn't offered her a ride. Now she has wasted another fifteen minutes waiting on Mom, who had no shift today at the Daughter and so should be home by now.

Winnie debates cracking open a can of ginger ale. Then decides, no. Those are for special occasions only. Then she decides actually, never mind, she does want one because her pesto pasta dinner is threatening to reroute via her esophagus . . .

And that's when the engine of the Volvo gurgles outside. A wyrm with indigestion to match Winnie's. Seconds later, Mom is shoving in through the front door.

Winnie lurches to her feet. Her mouth is dry. Her teeth are like clattering typewriter keys. She kind of wants to run away. But instead, she makes herself sweep up the eight red envelopes on the kitchen table and hold them out like a fortune-teller with tarot cards.

Mom doesn't notice when she first strides in. She still wears her driving glasses. "Hey, kiddo. How was the dinner at the Sunday . . . oh."

Now she's noticing.

Her face goes pale. Revenant pale. She drops the Volvo keys, and they thwack on the ground by her feet.

"Mom," Winnie says, enunciating carefully, "what are these?"

"Oh dear." Mom lets her purse slide off her shoulder to join the keys. "You've opened them."

For half a heartbeat, Winnie feels bad about that. Then she shakes the guilt free. It's not justified; Mom hid these for four years. "They have my name on them."

"And . . . Darian's cards? He knows too?"

Okay, now Winnie does feel crappy—but again, the emotion grips her for a mere split second before logic barrels in. "Darian doesn't know these exist, Mom. And I had to open the envelopes because . . ." Here Winnie wavers. Not because she's worried about the silencing spell or the factoids that will projectile out, but because in the four years since Dad vanished, Mom and Winnie have never talked about what happened.

Literally, *never.*

Mom and Darian have talked about it. Darian and Winnie have talked about it. But Mom and Winnie? No way, no how. They haven't merely snuck around the subject, so much as hammered in stakes, draped tarps, and then unspooled some barbed wire.

Winnie's teeth click twice. She watches as Mom rubs at her thigh—where an old banshee scar still gleams. She used to scratch at that thing all the time.

"Was Dad framed?" The question is a catapult, taking down barbed wire and a stretch of tarp in one blow.

Some stakes must still be standing, though, because Mom doesn't answer. Instead, she asks: "What do the cards say?"

This is not what Winnie is expecting. She frowns. "Uh . . . they wish us happy birthday. Me and Darian."

"Right." A nod. Then, with visible yearning widening her pupils, Mom adds: "And nothing else? No other messages?" Unspoken: *No messages for me?*

Lots of other messages, Winnie thinks. *The secret kind, and not for you.*

"He drew pictures for Darian. Of the family."

"Ah." A protracted sigh slides out. Mom plods to the kitchen table, finally towing off her driving glasses. She sits. Winnie sits. And when Mom holds out a hand, Winnie slides one of Darian's cards into it.

Paper crinkles as Mom tugs the card from its envelope. It is the most recent of Darian's birthday cards, so the hand-drawn Winnie is all grown up in it.

"Oh," Mom says, and her eyes redden as she takes in the sketch of the family. "It's like the old photo that used to hang in our living room. Except . . . Bryant aged us up, didn't he?" The question is rhetorical; Mom's voice is distant, her gaze lost in an alternate timeline where Dad never disappeared.

Winnie answers anyway: "He talks about that photo in the cards to me." She taps an envelope, but doesn't withdraw the card. "But you took the picture down years ago."

"I did." Mom's lips compress. She sets the card onto the table. "It's in my office now. At the Wednesday estate. Because . . ." A pause here. A careful chewing that carves crow's-feet into the skin around her eyes. "Because it's not . . . I mean, there isn't . . ." Another pause while Mom's mouth bobs open. Bobs shut.

Winnie can *see* words want to come, but it's as if Mom's lungs are black holes and no air can get past the event horizon.

Except that's when it happens: enough speed for Mom's words to break free from gravity. And so many, that once they start coming, they absolutely cannot stop. "Many aquatic nightmares will drag prey to depths where little light penetrates."

"Huh?"

"When hunters get dragged into the Big Lake by such nightmares, they are often disoriented and lose track of where the surface is."

"Huh?" Winnie says again—because these words are *almost* like the entry in the Nightmare Compendium on aquatic nightmares. But not quite. They're changed enough to scrape at her brain. To push and rub like a jigsaw piece being shoved into the wrong slot.

Winnie's face scrunches up. For the first time since leaving the Sunday estate, her heart finds a rhythm—and it matches the theme music to *Jeopardy!*. Doo-doo-doo-doo, doo-doo-doo!

"To determine which way to swim," Mom continues, her face cinching up just like Winnie's—"exhale into your hand and feel which way the bubbles move. Air will always rise. Follow the bubbles, and you can find the surface again."

Mom leans back. She is finished. She has reached the end of what she wanted to say, and she sets the card on the table like it's the ace in a winning hand. Except she stares at Winnie with an apologetic smile that says, *Don't worry: I know you won't understand what I'm saying.*

Winnie does understand, though. Sure, it takes her a moment of gawping blankly. Of running Mom's words through her brain like some internal search engine. *Not the Compendium, so what else is there?* Then a result appears. Match = 100 percent.

Mom isn't quoting the Nightmare Compendium. She's quoting the abridged version that all hunters carry into the forest. Because if there is any tome crammed into Mom's brain the way the Compendium is crammed into Winnie's . . .

Well, the Abridged Hunters' Compendium would be it.

Little Franny has even more secrets than you do, the Crow said at the carnival, *ones Jeremiah could never pry loose.*

Yeah, Winnie can see why. Mom is clearly stuck under the same spell Winnie is. It's incomprehensible. Unexpected. A plot twist even Jessica Fletcher on *Murder, She Wrote* could never have seen coming. But what other explanation is there?

However, there's one problem: the Crow didn't seem to know about this.

Sure, the Crow could have lied. Pretended she didn't know Mom was bewitched. But Martedì wants what Winnie wants, and it doesn't help her to block Winnie from getting there.

Yet if the Crow didn't put this spell on Mom, then who did? And how the *heck* is Winnie going to discover anything if she and Mom can't have a real conversation?

"I understand," Winnie says. "You . . . can't talk about this with me."

Mom blinks. And Winnie can practically see fresh words trying to escape the event horizon. "How?" Mom manages to croak out. Then: "How do you know?"

Winnie sucks in a shallow breath. She can't shake her head—although she definitely tries. But it just makes her ears buzz, buzz, hum.

"Who . . . did this to you?" Winnie grinds out instead.

Now Mom is as stiff and silent as Winnie was, implying she also wants to speak, but the rules of the spell won't let her.

Until suddenly Mom *is* moving. Until suddenly she is outright laughing, a high-pitched, almost painful cackle while she waves the card before her. "Four years," she says between strained giggles. "Four *years*." She pushes off her seat and yanks Winnie close for a hug. A weird, uncharacteristic, slightly suffocating bear hug.

"Winnebago," she says into Winnie's hair, still laughing—though more quietly now. "I don't know what to do. I have *no* idea what to do. It's been four years, and I am just as lost now as I was then. But hunters injured in the forest must first be checked for signs of blood." She withdraws, gripping Winnie hard by the biceps. Boring into her with a stare. "And if blood is found, then it must be stanched. Immediately. Otherwise, nightmares will scent it and hunt you down.

"And that's why we have to be careful, Winnebago: hunters are never, ever safe in Hemlock Falls."

That night, as Winnie watches fireworks sparkle above the Little Lake, as she smiles and pretends she just *loves* wearing the heavy Midnight Crown, a crow watches the same fireworks from atop a black-shingled roof. He is cold. He is hungry. He isn't sure why he has made his home here when there are plenty more comfortable places around town.

But then the woman with sad eyes comes outside and offers him a grilled cheese, and he feels briefly happy. Briefly warm. He really likes melted cheddar on toasted bread.

Meanwhile, miles north in the forest that never sleeps, a spell stirs. It is hungry too, and this is not the sort of hunger that cheddar will ever satisfy. *Pure Heart. Trust the Pure Heart.*

The Whisperer goes hunting.

WINNIE'S SCHEDULE FOR
THE NIGHTMARE MASQUERADE

MONDAY

8 A.M.: Monday Science Fair Kickoff
- *Winnie is expected outside the Monday Science Library— dress is casual, but Darian recommends jewel tones.*
- *Winnie will open the gates to the Science Fair along with Theresa Monday.*

8:30 A.M.–11:30 P.M.: Science Fair Judging
- *Winnie will be guided along with six other judges to compare the greatest feats of the Monday clan from this year.*
- *Again, expect photographs.*

12 P.M.–1 P.M.: Monday Lunch
- *This is a buffet-style meal held in the primary Monday banquet hall for presenters.*
- *Expect photo requests and possible interviews.*

1:30 P.M.–3:30 P.M.: Science Fair Judging

4 P.M.–5 P.M.: Science Fair Awards Ceremony
- *This too will be held in the banquet hall.*
- *Winnie will be expected to stand on stage with other judges.*

6 P.M.–9 P.M.: Monday Awards Dinner & After-party OR Nightmare Forest "Safari"
- *Winnie will meet at the Monday estate, and you can decide if you'd rather attend the dinner/after-party or attend a "safari" through the forest.*

- *FOR PARTY: Dress is cocktail/fancy.*
- *FOR SAFARI: Dress warm and wear shoes for hiking.*

9 P.M.: *Floating Carnival*
  - *Monday firework display on the Little Lake.*

23

Under normal circumstances, Winnie would be thrilled by an entire day at the Science Fair. In fact, this is so on-brand for her, she is legitimately angry she can't spend the hours enjoying behind-the-scenes access to all the new Monday inventions. Like, this is the only perk of winning the Midnight Crown, but rather than gush over technology, she spends every minute with a countdown timer in her head.

T minus forty-eight hours until the Crow makes good on her threats.

Sure, it sounds like a lot of hours . . . until you start carving out chunks for awards ceremonies and races (see the Tuesday schedule for details). Which is why Winnie has strapped on an old Timex dug out from the bottom of her closet: so she can keep track of exactly how much time she has before eight A.M. on Wednesday morning arrives.

As she tromps around from booth to booth, stage to stage, green room to green room, Winnie scowls when spoken to by any councilor (yes, even Leila Wednesday), smiles only for photos, and spends every tick-tocking moment pretending she doesn't hear Dryden when he snarls at her, "Hurry *up,* Ms. Wednesday! There are more exhibits to see and judge."

Marcia is, of course, less gentle, screwing a Philips-head fingernail into Winnie's spine whenever Winnie dares question a Monday about their invention. *Wow, so you're modeling this suit after kelpie anatomy? How do you make the circulatory system preserve warmth without a pumping mechanism?*

Screw, screw, screw.

Tens of booths, tens of inventions, and Winnie can't enjoy a single one.

Her only "relief" comes in the thirty-minute bathroom break she gets before lunch. She's at least got access to a VIP toilet, and it's right as she's about to stride in that Darian springs.

"There you are," he pants, his cheeks red as if he already got started on the Tuesday Olympics. "I've got something for you." He reaches into a leather messenger bag at his hip—one Winnie recognizes, but has never seen so sloppily stuffed before. But then he pauses. "Oh . . . you bought more clothes."

For the first time since the Big Bang created the universe, Winnie is actually better dressed than her brother, and she can see he is having trouble processing this. He smooths at his rumpled pale pink sweater—which actually looks a lot like her sapphire-blue sweater (jewel tones!) that is brand new, and therefore doesn't need smoothing. She has paired it with the same jeans as yesterday, and though she knows she'd look better in literally *any* other shoes in her closet, she opted for combat boots this morning. Because come on: Nightmare Safari? She ain't hiking in the forest without proper footwear.

"Erica helped me," Winnie says, the implication being *You didn't.*

It flies over Darian's head. He blinks behind his glasses (no longer smudged). "You're friends again?"

"Why? Want access to Marcia?"

Now he grimaces. "You're still mad at me, huh?" Genuine shame collapses his skeleton like a folding chair. For a brief moment, he is not only worse dressed, but also the shorter sibling too.

And now Winnie feels bad. Because it's not really him she's mad at. That's the Crow, whom Winnie has seen neither feather nor talon of today. Still, she lacks the energy to apologize, so she simply says, "Did you need something? Because I've really got to pee."

"Oh, right." Still frowning, Darian digs into his bag and withdraws a scuffed-up flip phone of the not-smart variety. "This is for you. I guess Fatima raised it with Leila that you should have a phone, and so Leila said I could pull one from the city hall supply closet." Darian smiles tentatively. "So . . . yay? It's ready to go, with my number in it, and Dryden's too. Just in case."

Just in case what? Winnie thinks. Even if the sleeping spirit were to wake up and all of Hemlock Falls were to disintegrate beneath a mass of seething nightmares, Dryden Saturday would still not be a person Winnie would call. Nonetheless, she makes herself match Darian's smile—though hers is more *pained* than *tentative*—and accept the phone from his grip.

"You push that button there, with the face-looking icon, to access contacts."

Winnie pushes said face-looking icon. Sure enough, numbers pop up. Except there are more than two. "You put Andrew's number in here."

"Yeah." Darian's smile spreads into something more natural. "And the house number's in there. And Mom's new office line. Oh, and Leila suggested I include hers and Fatima's numbers, so then while I was at it, I tossed in Jay's. And, ah . . . how's it going with you two?"

Winnie snorts. Since there is literally no way for her to explain that her relationship *would* be great if Jay's life weren't under constant threat by a nightmare mutation and a Diana *cornīx,* she instead opts for: "I think you should be more worried about your own relationship, Darian. I saw Andrew at the Carnival yesterday, and he was so very aggressively alone. Like, the poor guy was banging the hammer at the Ring-the-Bell by himself. No one to cheer him on." Winnie doesn't add that she didn't cheer Andrew on either. "So . . . you know. Maybe you should take him out for a nice time at the Carnival? Or I don't know, take off Wednesday and do the Hunters' Feast together."

"Right." Darian looks faintly ill, which Winnie is starting to recognize as the look he gets whenever he peers into the crystal ball of his future and sees only Dryden Saturday staring back.

Exchange *Dryden* with *Witch,* and Winnie can relate.

"Fraternal failures," he mutters to himself as he shuffles away, "and ruined relationships. Great job, Darian the Destroyer."

Okay, now Winnie *does* feel bad. Darian only alliterates when he's at the farthest end of his stress spectrum.

Once she has relieved her bladder, washed her hands, then snuck back into an empty stall so no one can talk to her, Winnie pulls out her "new" phone. Texting is even more awkward without a proper keyboard, but she's able to fire off a message to Jay.

This is Winnie. Got a phone. How was last nite?

She sits and waits for a reply, but none ever comes. Which she tries not to freak out over. She also tries not to imagine him once more transformed in the forest, where either hunters or nightmares might kill him. Or once more sucked into the Crow's and Jeremiah's clutches over pretenses Winnie can't protect him from.

She sends Fatima a message too while she waits.

This is Winnie. Thanx 4 asking ur mom 4 phone 4 me

People come and go in the bathroom. Minutes ooze past, too slow and yet too fast since Jay isn't responding. *Werewolf. Witches. Wednesday. Whisperer.* Flowers germinate, bloom, wither across Winnie's brain. Her fingers itch to draw.

Until at last, the phone makes a ding.

It isn't Jay—much to Winnie's disappointment. It's Fatima. *Yay! A phone! Where are you? I'll be at the Monday lunch with my mom. Sit with me?*

Winnie sighs. Her heart is booming, and she hates herself for wishing this were Jay. She hates herself even more when she realizes, as she pushes off the unused toilet, that she's no better than Darian. That her own friends have been just as abandoned as Andrew.

Winnie saw Emma, Bretta, and Fatima in Nightmare Anatomy yesterday at the Sunday estate, but she barely spoke to them. She didn't update them on Jay, and she *definitely* didn't apologize for suddenly striding off in the middle of the Carnival. Yet not once did they push or pester her. They gave her space to be silent and sulky. And they also gave her a goodbye hug before she had to break off into her new Luminary history class during third period.

Here she is, telling Darian to be more attentive to his boyfriend, when she herself has been a Grade A Crappy Friend.

True, Winnie can't talk about what's going on because all these secrets in her life aren't hers to share—and then there's a freaking silencing spell on her to boot. But there are also plenty of innocent topics she could chat about, like Fatima's costume for the Masquerade and all the epic stuff Winnie saw during the first half of the Science Fair.

Oh, and there's the Compendium Art Competition, which did get officially announced today, exactly as Ms. Morgan promised.

With more pep in her step than she's had all day, Winnie abandons the bathroom. As she walks, she considers how kelpie circulation could be applied to one of Fatima's costume designs—how she might draw such a system, each artery and vein a gentle stroke across the page.

But her pep is short-lived. She's like one of those cartoons that comes to such an abrupt halt, they leave smoking skid marks behind. Because in the long hall where lunch is being served, buffet style, Winnie finds Signora Martedì. A cartoon all her own, but of the evil, mustache-twirling variety.

And right now Martedì is twirling her mustache directly over Fatima.

Winnie spots them from three tables away. The hall, which is normally used for Monday dinners, has high rafters and skylights to glare down a garish light. Where the Wednesdays have a massive, elegant fireplace in their dining room, the Mondays have a podium and blackboard meant for guest lecturers.

Right now, the blackboard reads *WELCOME TO THE NIGHTMARE MASQUERADE!* Then below that is the same message in all the other languages of the Luminaries. *Bienvenidos al Festival de Máscaras de las Pesadillas,* 악몽의 가면무도회에 오신 것을 환영합니다, *Добро пожаловать на Маскарад Кошмаров,* خوش آمدید به تقریب یک خواب نورارڈ , and on and on.

And ten steps away from the podium, at a round table with diners and food, sits Fatima . . . with Signora Martedì parked right beside her, laughing and clapping and patting Fatima's shoulder as if they are the *bestest* of friends.

Winnie stares for several seconds, her teeth rolling out a rhythm behind her lips that would make a snare drum proud. Her first instinct is to stomp over to Martedì and scream at her to *back the hell off!* But she knows this would make A Scene, and A Scene isn't something Winnie wants—at least not for Mom's sake. She also wouldn't be able to explain herself to anyone.

Why did you just scream at one of the most important members of the Martedì clan?

Because will-o'-wisps lure their prey with lights! That's why!

Winnie's toes inch forward. Her second instinct is to turn tail and run. Just text Fatima an apology and seek refuge once more in the bathroom. Not because Winnie is scared of Caterina Martedì (although, let's be real: she is), but because the woman loses all her manipulative sway if Winnie never *sees* her asserting dominance over Winnie's friends.

And that's clearly what's happening here: the Crow wants Winnie to know she can and *will* get to every one of Winnie's closest friends. *Wednesday morning will be here soon enough.*

That's when Winnie feels it: a heat against her sternum. Her locket is warning of magic, warning of the Crow. Martedì knows Winnie is here, even if Fatima hasn't noticed yet.

The Crow looks up. Her eyes meet Winnie's, and she smiles. Then her hand, currently placed on Fatima's shoulder, tightens. It's a movement that could be interpreted kindly, supportive, endearing by anyone on the receiving end. But Winnie knows it for what it really is.

She knows because she feels a whisper of power scrub down the back of her neck. Feels her locket blare all the hotter. And *sees* Signora Martedì's smile turn threatening.

Then Martedì straightens. Withdraws her hand from Fatima. And in a swirl of black shawl and silver hair, she pivots away.

Which is when Fatima finally spots Winnie too. She waves, eyes brightening. "Winnie! I got a sandwich for you. Hope you like veggie medley because that's all that was left."

Winnie shambles forward, her eyes locked on the Crow's retreating back. Her shawl gives her the look of wings, and Winnie would bet big money that's intentional. Slowly, Winnie's locket cools.

She drops down next to Fatima. Her heart is giving her snare-drum teeth a run for their money. "Hey, who . . . was . . . that talking to you?"

"Oh? Signora Martedì? She's the Tuesday liaison, and wow! She's *so* nice, Winnie. She told me she studied fashion for a few years in Milan, when she wasn't sure if she wanted to stay in the Luminaries or not. And *then* she said she'd come look at my Masquerade Ball designs this afternoon. How cool is that?" The gleam in Fatima's eyes is decidedly heart-shaped as she continues gushing.

And Winnie finds herself caught once more in the Crow's feathery clutches. She can't warn Fatima; she can't scream, *STAY AWAY!* But there's also no way in hell she's going to gush alongside her friend and say, *Oh yeah, Martedì is the absolute best. I just love her!*

So Winnie sits there instead, mouth bobbing and heart drumming, and tries to find a way to veer Fatima away from praising a villainous Diana who wants to ruin Winnie's life. *Tick tock, tick tock. Wednesday morning will be here soon enough.*

T minus forty-four hours.

As Fatima continues to recap every *awesome word* that Caterina Martedì uttered (which included so many compliments on Fatima's own style), Winnie shoves a veggie sandwich down her gullet. It's *way* too much mayo. Her tongue sticks to the roof of her mouth. But when Fatima pauses to bite into her own sandwich, Winnie leaps at the chance for a subject change.

"I thaw"—*gulp, swallow*—"some really cool inventions today. Maybe you can incorporate them into one of your designs. Like, there's this one armor that covers only the chest—but it can be extended downward over the thighs with the simple push of a button."

Now Fatima is the one to gulp and swallow. "Whoa. How does that work?"

Excellent. "The layers of the armor are modeled after the keratinous shell on turtle-wyrms, but specifically the head flap. Here, I'll show you." Winnie grabs a napkin, Fatima hands her a pen, and in seconds, Signora Martedì is forgotten.

Or at least, she's forgotten for Fatima. Winnie hasn't forgotten the Crow at all, and it's probably not a coincidence that she and Fatima end up designing a costume they name *The Hunter* . . .

Which is a gown stylized after the ancient Roman goddess Diana. Yes, *that* Diana whom the witches are named for—but who was actually a symbol for the Luminaries on the hunt before that.

Winnie isn't backing down from the Crow. She isn't going to let Martedì scare her. And with a real hunting bow in one hand and a real knife sheathed on a jeweled belt at the waist, Winnie's sketched figure with Fatima's design overtop is pure, unadulterated *badassery.*

Winnie is just finishing the sketch (okay, the model's hands kind of look like popcorn) when Fatima's phone dings. Winnie's too. When they look, they find messages from Bretta. Except on Fatima's phone, it's a group chat that also includes Emma. On Winnie's . . . Well, it's just a message from a number she hasn't saved yet.

Party tonight at the old museum. We going?

"Hmmm." Fatima glances Winnie's way, frowning. "Do you want to go? Because honestly, I'd rather stay home and work on my designs."

Winnie hesitates. She wants to respond: *If we go, would that keep you from meeting with Martedì this afternoon?* But this is silly, so Winnie instead shakes her head. "Naw, I'm tired. I'll just turn in early."

"Really?" Fatima's eyes narrow. "Is that really your reason?"

"Um, yes?" *Oh crap, that sounds like a lie.* "Why wouldn't it be?" *God, that sounds even worse.*

"It's just . . ." Fatima runs her tongue over her braces. "You've felt kind of distant lately. And you've been hanging out with Erica Thursday a lot. Which is fine, you know, but we can *all* be friends. You don't have to choose her over us."

Winnie stares at Fatima. She feels sick. She feels guilty. Worse, there's so *very little* she can actually say to explain what's going on. "It's not like that," she insists—and because this is true, it comes out with the necessary amount of emphasis. Of friend-shaped panic. "I promise it's not like that, Fatima. Erica and I—it's just . . . there's some stuff I have to do with her, okay? But you and Emma and Bretta are still my best friends. I promise."

"Okay." Fatima huffs a tense laugh. "I'm glad to hear it." Now she smiles and lifts up her phone. "I'll answer for the both of us, shall I? No . . . party . . . for me . . . or Winnie. Maybe . . . next . . . time. Oh, but hey—are you going to hunter training tomorrow at dawn?"

Winnie groans. *Right.* Hunter training. She one thousand percent forgot about it this morning. "Are you?"

"Not tomorrow, but Bretta wants to start on Wednesday. So I think I'll go then. How was it for you last Friday?"

"Intense," Winnie admits, although she doesn't elaborate. She's still wriggling with shame. "Hey, um, I haven't thanked you yet for the phone. I really appreciate you telling your mom I needed one."

"Aw, you got it, Win. Anything for our besties, right?" Fatima smiles once before her thumbs start flying again across her phone. And Winnie, feeling *even worse,* twists away so she can scan the crowded room filled with the brightest lights of the Luminaries.

The Crow is nowhere to be seen. She and her wings have retreated to the shadows, and when Winnie touches her locket, she finds it cold as a candle blown out. Cold as a lantern forgotten on the Big Lake's spring shore.

Jay Friday, 1:35 P.M.
How do I know this is really Winnie?

Winnie, 1:37 P.M.
Ugh Jay

Jay Friday, 1:37 P.M.
Okay, verified. That was easy

Winnie, 1:38 P.M.
When can I c u?

Jay Friday, 1:39 P.M.
Why are you texting like a grandma?

Winnie, 1:39 P.M.
Old phone

Jay Friday, 1:39 P.M.
So your new phone is an old phone. For some reason, this feels very appropriate for you

Winnie, 1:40 P.M.
I am insulte
d

Winnie, 1:44 P.M.
Did u talk 2 Mario?

Jay Friday, 1:44 P.M.
Yes, but he's busy with the fair today. He said to come back tomorrow

Winnie, 1:44 P.M.
Can u wait that long?

Jay Friday, 1:45 P.M.
One more night won't do anything

Winnie, 1:47 P.M.
I hope ur right

Jay Friday, 1:47 P.M.
Don't worry, Win. Everything will be fine

Winnie, 3:31 P.M.
Any progress on my condition? This is Winnii

Erica Thursday, 3:37 P.M.
So you finally got a phone. Thank god. And no. No progress yet.

Winnie, 3:37 P.M.
2 bad bc my mom has same condition

Erica Thursday, 3:39 P.M.
WHAT
I'm sorry, what?

Winnie, 3:40 P.M.
Can I call? Have ceremony soon

Erica Thursday, 3:40 P.M.
No. I'm with my parents right now. ☐

Winnie, 3:40 P.M.
Did u use emoji? I see only empty box. Phone is 2 old
4 emojis

Erica Thursday, 3:41 P.M.
Of course it is. Jesus, Winona. You are the opposite of a
Thursday

Winnie, 3:42 P.M.
Is that a compliment?

Erica Thursday, 3:42 P.M.
No.
And yes, I included a skull emoji with my text because I am
slowly dying as I endure nightmare anatomy

Winnie, 3:43 P.M.
U r wrong. That's best class of day

Erica Thursday, 3:44 P.M.
☐☐☐☐☐☐
That was 6 more skulls, for the record. And here are 6 more.
☐☐☐☐☐☐

Winnie, 3:44 P.M.
Got 2 go 2 ceremony. Talk more l8r

Erica Thursday, 3:45 P.M.
Jesus, reading your texts causes me actual pain
Chat more later, xo ☐

Winnie, 4:15 P.M.
Mom, I got a phone

Francesca Wednesday, 4:17 P.M.
Who is this?

Winnie, 4:17 P.M.
Your dauter

Francesca Wednesday, 4:18 P.M.
I don't have a dauter

Winnie, 4:20 P.M.
DAUGHTER WITH A G AND AN (a?) H

Francesca Wednesday, 4:20 P.M.
Ah, yep. That's Winnie alright
How is the science fair?

Winnie, 4:21 P.M.
Would b better w out crown
Phone is old
Slow 4 text

Francesca Wednesday, 4:22 P.M.
Ah, okay. That explains the robot voice
Boop-beep-boop. I. Am. Winnie. Dauter Model 1.6.

Winnie, 4:22 P.M.
Buy me new phone?

Francesca Wednesday, 4:23 P.M.
Cute. But money doesn't grow on trees, kid

Winnie, 4:24 P.M.
It does n Brazil forest
Predatory tree w bark made of pure gold

Francesca Wednesday, 4:24 P.M.
Welp, you've proven your identity
When will you be home tonight, Winnebago?
I have an early shift at the Daughter tomorrow
Daughter with a g and an (a?) h

Winnie, 4:25 P.M.
B home after safari

Francesca Wednesday, 4:25 P.M.
Okay, sounds good. Have fun.

I LOVE YOU FOREVER AND THEN SOME
But really, I do.
And thanks for sharing what you shared last night. We'll figure it
all out, okay?

Winnie, 4:26 P.M.
Ok, Mom
Love u 2 4ever

C H A P T E R

24

Obviously given the choice between an after-party or a nightmare "safari," Winnie will always choose the safari. Not merely because it allows her to wear her combat boots while the other requires "cocktail/fancy attire," but also because this will give her a chance to talk to Mario Monday.

Alone.

Or so Winnie thinks until she steps onto the bus that will carry her and twenty-three other nightmare wonks into the forest. As soon as she climbs aboard, she is pounced upon.

"Oh, Winnie!" Professor Funday declares, leaping up from her seat in the back row. "Oh, sit with me, sit with me!"

Seeing little alternative, Winnie obeys. Which is fine; she genuinely likes the woman. And for the first time probably *ever*, the librarian is not dressed like a coral reef vomited onto her, but rather like a forest did. Not *the* forest of Hemlock Falls, of course. This is more Disney forest with bright, rapturous shades of green ranging from summer pine to bursting meadow. Even her boots have been painted (yes, painted) the shade of a fir tree in winter. Her silver hair is tucked beneath a beanie that skews neon, and her eyeliner sweeps out from her eyes in sharp branches.

It's a lot.

"Winnie," Funday says, almost breathlessly, "I've been trying to find you since last week, but with visitors arriving and the Sunday floats to prepare—I do most of the decorating you know—"

Winnie did not know, but that tracks.

"—I've just not had a moment to reach out. But that book I ordered from Italy finally came in. The one on moon and stars symbology. You remember it?"

Winnie's lungs wheeze. Then wheeze again for good measure because oh boy, does she remember it. She has been anxiously awaiting that book's arrival for over two weeks now and has been calling the Monday library every morning since day three. *No, no books here for a Winnie Wednesday.*

"The Mondays delivered the book to *me,* even though I very clearly told them it was to be delivered to *you.* Winnie Winona Wednesday, I said, our very own Midnight Crown. Although, of course, you hadn't won yet. Wait, where is your crown?" Funday blinks expectantly.

And Winnie blinks back. Because she gives approximately zero craps about the Midnight Crown and approximately *all* craps for more information on this book. "The book. Where is it now, Professor?"

"It's at my house."

"Can I get it from you? Like, tonight? After this? Or we could even skip this and just go grab it now."

"Oh, well, about that." A slight chuckle. The fuzzy green squirrels dangling from Funday's earlobes bounce and sway. "I didn't realize the book would be in *Italian,* so I'll have to translate it for you. Unless you know Italian?"

Right. Italian. Because of course the freaking book would be in Italian. *I could ask the Crow for help reading it,* Winnie thinks as a hysterical laugh squeaks from her mouth. "Nope, can't say I know Italian."

"Alas. I've been attempting to translate each night, but honestly, my Italian is so rusty. If you could tell me something specific you would like to focus on, then that might move things along more quickly. It's a *big* book and there are so many chapters. Chapter one is on the initial need for the symbols. Chapter two is about actual constellations that inspired—"

Pop, pop, pop. Mario boards the bus. Everyone falls silent.

Like Funday, Mario has traded his signature look (in which a laboratory vomited upon him) for more practical gear like khakis, hiking boots, and a brown fleece. He has not, however, abandoned the signature bubble gum.

He spots Winnie at the back; gives a tiny wave; then launches into: "Welcome, locals and visitors alike. I'm Mario, lead nightmare researcher for the Mondays and foremost ecology expert in Hemlock Falls. Although." He throws a mischievous smile Winnie's way. "The winner of our Midnight Crown back there—"

Every head whips toward Winnie.

"—has quite the advanced knowledge herself. So if I'm ever too busy to answer a question about our local fauna, then feel free to ask Winnie Wednesday instead."

No, thinks Winnie, dread shoveling through her. *Do not feel free at all!*

But it's too late. The damage is done. What should have been a mindless meander through the forest before dusk—in which she tries *not* to repeat her panicked meltdown from Wednesday training or the hot room pool—is now going to be filled with foreigners wanting selfies and asking questions.

She is going to murder Mario. Or at the very least, shove him off the overlook into the falls.

Mario continues with a description of where they'll be walking (western shore, departing from the hunters' parking lot) and what they can expect to see (prime manticore nesting habitats, kelpie formation spots, the kill site for a recent droll). "And if we're lucky, we'll finish in time to enjoy that open bar at the after-party! All right." He claps his hands, gnawing at the gum he cannot subsist without.

Then one huge bubble precedes a final grin for Winnie. "Let's get going, friends! Into the woods to Grandmother's house!"

Wow, Winnie thinks. *That sounds ominous.*

She feels lingering stares upon her. She fidgets with her glasses and focuses *very* hard on Professor Funday's face. "The chapters," she squeezes out. "Can you tell me more about them? Because yes, there are some specific things I'm interested in from the book."

Funday nods. Her eyelids batten shut. Then she ticks off her fingers one by one in a way that suggests she's reciting something memorized. "Why Luminary Symbology Evolved, The Original Constellations, The Evolution of Symbols, The Appropriation of Symbology by Dianas—"

"That," Winnie blurts at the same instant the bus engine revs. Funday doesn't hear her.

"—A Dictionary of Common Symbols, Putting the Secret in Secret

Society, and . . . oh, what was that last chapter called?" Funday's eyes crack open. The bus is now puttering across the parking lot. "Think, Teddy, think."

"No, it's fine, Professor." Winnie shakes her head. "I'm mostly interested in the appropriation by . . ." Oh gosh, should she finish this sentence? Should she say the word *Dianas*? Her family is still so closely associated with witches. What if Funday thinks, *Why, this is odd,* and alerts Jeremiah Tuesday to Winnie's probing?

Although, would it matter if Jeremiah did find out at this point? He knows Winnie is just following wherever Signora Martedì wants her to follow—which is therefore where Jeremiah must want her to follow too, right?

T minus thirty-eight hours until the Crow makes good on her threats.

Winnie doesn't have to finish her sentence because Funday fills in the blank for her: "Dianas." She smiles a crinkly smile. "You want to know how the witches appropriated the symbols?"

Winnie thrusts again at her glasses. "Yep, and, uh, I guess . . . the dictionary would be useful too."

"Ah, that's right. Your locket!" Funday smacks her forehead—which ends up being a full-on karate chop because at that moment, the bus yaws hard to the left.

Bonk!

The librarian grimaces. Then shakes her head as if there are tiny canaries flying around it. "Ouch. Where was I? The locket. Um, can you show it to me again, Winnie? I don't remember what it looks like."

Winnie obeys, digging the locket from her Save the Whales hoodie, which she traded her sweater for. (She also added her leather jacket to the ensemble because the schedule *did* say to dress warm.) The locket glints in the evening light.

"Ah yes." Funday adjusts her glasses so the bifocal parts of her lenses rest higher on her nose. "A pretty straightforward design," she murmurs to herself. "A waning crescent with three stars. Typically three stars would stand for *nuntius,* which means *message.*"

"So . . . that's all this means? *Message*?"

"Well, it was usually the beginning of a message, and then more moons and stars would be added after that. So for example, after the first moon and three stars, a moon and four stars might follow. Which would literally mean *yew tree,* or more symbolically *danger*—because hunter bows were made from yew. Five stars, meanwhile, referred to rowan trees for protection . . ." Funday trails off here as she flips around the locket. "Nothing on the back of the locket . . . and . . ." She snaps it open.

A scrap of paper flutters out.

Winnie's heart, again, skips several beats. Especially because, with Funday in the way, she can't reach the paper to retrieve it. And *especially* because the way it falls is apparently the perfect angle for Funday to snatch it up and read. "My apologies, Winnie," she says. "I didn't mean to knock out a lover's note. *How romantic,* though."

For several more missed heartbeats, these words are meaningless to Winnie. Then two thoughts collide at once: *She must think Darian is my boyfriend, not my brother, since his photo is inside.* And: *But wait, I thought I pulled the message out on Saturday night?*

Winnie grabs the paper, pasting a very fake, laughably huge grin across her face. "So romantic," she agrees. Then she flips the paper to read it on its way toward her pocket.

And oh, now Winnie understands. *Now* she sees why Funday might consider this romantic. Evening sunlight, filtered by a dirty bus window, reveals a message that isn't at all what Winnie snapped in there two days ago. Because she really *did* pull that out on Saturday and toss it on the floor.

Museum, it reads. *11 P.M. tonight.*

"Nightmare Safari" is a deeply misleading label for what happens over the next three hours. For one, there are no nightmares to see because the mist hasn't yet risen. Therefore, the forest is nothing more than . . . well, a bunch of trees. Yes, there's a definite creep factor that regular trees don't possess—and there *is* that sense of Something Watching that everyone knows is caused by the sleeping spirit at the bottom of the Big Lake. But with no actual creatures to behold or photograph, the "safari" is more like a late-evening hike while the sun sets.

Not that Winnie minds. She's such a bundle of panicked energy, she is frankly glad she can expel that energy here instead of wasting hours at the after-party—or worse, all by herself in her bedroom.

Museum. 11 P.M. tonight.

Before Mario can drive the transport bus fully out of civilization and into the forest's clutches, Winnie blasts off a text message to both Jay and Erica: *Meet at old museum at 10:30.*

She doesn't know if they get the message, since neither respond before the magic of the spirit eliminates all signal. That doesn't stop her from checking the device every twenty seconds to see if *maybe* a little blip of city service can sneak through.

It can't, and for the next three hours, Winnie finds herself forced into the role of unofficial assistant tour guide. And despite her early reservations, it actually ends up being a solid distraction. Because these visitors really *are* nightmare wonks with the ecological, evolutionary, and biological questions to prove it.

So if she's freaked out by the fact that they are slowly heading toward the northernmost shore of the Big Lake, which is *slowly* getting them closer to an area where two Dianas were burned to death . . .

Well, those ghosts are quieter than Professor Funday, who fires out enough questions to keep both Winnie *and* Mario busy.

And if Winnie's entire circuit board is lit up by a single question—*WHO SENT THE MESSAGE IN MY LOCKET?*—then too bad. Winnie is here, in the forest, and the nightmare factoids bursting from her mouth aren't forced there by a spell.

When they reach a stretch of shore shaped like a half-moon, Winnie can't help but think of Grayson Friday. Of the funeral that happened for him right here, a little over two weeks ago. It was the same day Jay became Lead Hunter. It was the same day Winnie first realized maybe she wasn't so great at exorcising her ghosts.

A stream burbles far too cheerfully at the farthest edge of this secluded beach. Next to it grows a silvery rowan tree, its branches flaunting new purple buds. *Some Dianas,* Winnie thinks, remembering words from Theodosia Monday's book, *will craft small coins from rowan wood that has been harvested in a spirit forest, believing such amulets can protect against nightmares.*

Such a tree certainly helped her escape a sadhuzag two weeks ago.

"Manticores frequently rise here after the mist," Mario explains as he guides them onto the silty beach. "Because the females are attracted to this softer soil for their nests."

"And what about the males?" a visiting Tuesday asks. "Also, how does mating work for local manticores?"

"A great question, Señora Martes. Winnie, do you want to take it?"

"Sure," Winnie says because what the heck else is she going to do right now? "Mating for manticores in this forest is a lot like scorpions in a non-magical ecosystem. The males begin the courtship with a behavior called 'juddering,' which creates vibrations in the ground. The females follow that."

On and on, question after question—like a pop quiz to end all pop quizzes—twenty-four pairs of eyes watch Winnie with rapt attention. Mario too, because these people don't actually care about Winnie's Midnight Crown. They just want to know about the local nightmares in as much detail as two human encyclopedias can offer. And much like the Science Fair earlier, this whole thing *should* be fun. Winnie *should* be reveling in this chance to show off her knowledge and chat with fellow nerds.

Instead, she has never hated Signora Martedì more. And she can't help but wonder if the signora is the one who sent the message in her locket. Except why? Martedì can just talk to Winnie directly. No need for subterfuge or lockets.

T minus thirty-six hours until the Crow makes good on her threats.

Or, another thought prods. A feathery, hopeful voice. *What if the messenger is Dad?* If three stars mean *message,* maybe he wanted Winnie to contact him with the locket all along.

Winnie is so distracted by her inner spiral and outward quiz bowl, she almost forgets the main draw for coming out here tonight: talking to Mario. And it's only once they're wrapping up the safari on the overlook beside the waterfall that she finally gets her chance.

Pop, pop, pop!

Far below the wooden decking, in a river churning with untamed waves and white chop, is where the melusine healed Winnie. *Beside* the river is where Jay dragged her out after she should have died.

To the west, a thoughtful violet sky is shifting toward hungry gray. Forest branches fracture it, like a frightened kid peeking through their fingers. The mist will rise soon. The forest and its monsters will awaken, and maybe the Whisperer too.

Winnie pivots away from the overlook. The ghosts are too loud; Jenna's old song won't stop playing in the back of her brain. She wishes she could seal up that song in bubble wrap. And the ghosts too. And all the endless, *relentless* feelings that go along with them. Then she could shove it in a box in the attic, right next to that box of photographs from when her family used to be whole.

Hope is the thing with feathers.

T minus thirty-five hours.

"Hey," Mario says. He has followed Winnie away from the overlook, and now he offers her a stick of gum. She takes it, and for several seconds the sugar overwhelms her salivary glands. She chews. The intensity recedes, and the scent of forest detritus creeps back into her nasal cavity.

"Why is Jay getting worse?" Winnie's voice floats out like a will-o'-wisp.

Mario glances behind them, but they're alone here, twenty steps from the overlook.

"He told me he didn't used to change this often," she continues. "Maybe once a week. But lately, it's almost every day."

Mario shoves a fresh stick of gum into his own mouth. It mixes with old gum, and when he speaks, it's around a mouthful of rubber. "No inspired theories of your own, Win? No wagers you want to make?" He tries for a grin.

But Winnie can't grin back. The Winnie of a month ago, who just *desperately* wanted to feel relevant—to know someone was listening to her, no matter how unlikely her theories got . . .

That Winnie is gone, replaced by one who is *too* relevant. Who is trapped in the center of a Venn diagram, with every circle dependent on her, whether or not they know she exists.

"I have a hypothesis," Mario continues when Winnie doesn't answer. He slides his hands into fleece pockets. "It's possible the severity of Jay's mutation is responding to increased inflammation."

"But . . . why would there be increased inflammation?"

"Same reason there would be in a human." Mario blows a bubble. *Pop!* "Stress, Winnie."

"Stress?"

"Jay just became Lead Hunter, right? Plus, he, ah . . ." Another glance to verify they're alone. "He almost died in his wolf form a week and a half ago, so it's possible the mutation is responding to heightened cortisol."

"But why does he even *have* the mutation?" Winnie thinks back to all those Monday papers Grayson had gathered. Each one referenced were-wolf mutation as only spreading through bite. Yet Jay was never bitten. On top of that, when he bit Winnie—only a hundred feet from this spot right here—the mutation didn't spread to her.

The question hangs in the air while Mario's jaw works. While a bubble inflates . . . then pops, and he slides his hands into his fleece pockets.

"Well?" she presses. "I can tell you have an answer, Mario. Want to share it with the rest of the class?"

Now Mario winces, and to her shock, rather than blow more bubbles or shove in more gum, he withdraws a shiny wrapper . . . then spits the pink wad from his mouth into it. "There have been records," he answers as he wraps up the gum and returns it to his pocket, "of nightmare mutations that can spread genetically. It's rare, since so few daywalkers have a human form—and even fewer live long enough to produce offspring. But . . . it has happened before. And you may recall that seventeen years ago there was a—"

"No." Winnie doesn't mean to say this. She doesn't mean to say anything, but she also can't let Mario finish his sentence. She can't let him draw the line he's about to draw.

"It's just a theory," he insists, but now Winnie lifts her hands. "No," she repeats. The more she learns, the harder this will be to compartmentalize.

But it's already too late, isn't it? Her brain has drawn the line without Mario's input, connecting the werewolf who was killed seventeen years ago to the boy Winnie loves today. *Jay doesn't know who his father was. His mother never shared the name before she died.*

Winnie sways.

"It's just a theory," Mario repeats, more emphatically this time. "I have no actual evidence, Winnie. Not to mention, my theory doesn't explain the jawbone Jay says he found under his pillow four years ago. So there's a good chance the genetic connection *isn't* the root cause of his mutation, but rather something we've never heard of—"

"*Signore! Signore Mario, mi scusi!*"

Mario pales. It's clear he doesn't want to end this conversation with Winnie, but he also has no choice. "Yes, Signora Lunedì?" he calls over his shoulder. "Do you have a question?"

"*Sì, sì.* I want to know about Diana sources and their, uh . . . oh—how do you say? *Impact* on forest ecology. Does the source location impact the local ecosystem?"

"That's a great question, Signora. I'll be right there." Mario grits out an apologetic smile. "Sorry, Winnie. We'll have to finish this later."

No, Winnie thinks, *I'd rather not.* "I'm going back to the bus," she tells him quietly. But Mario doesn't hear. He has already left her. He has already abandoned her to the forest and any new ghosts who might want to claim her.

C H A P T E R

25

Winnie, 9:25 P.M.
Will be late 2nite
Visiting twins

Francesca Wednesday, 9:25 P.M.
Okay, Winnebago. Thanks for letting me know.

When the safari group returns to the Monday estate, fireworks are about to begin over the Little Lake. Everyone exits the bus, except Winnie, who holds her seat and pretends to focus *really hard* on her phone.

Dusk has blossomed into night, as have lanterns strung across the parking lot. They emit a brown-tinted glow, each one marked by the outline of a scroll for the Monday clan, and beneath which are names too small to read from here. Too small, even, to read from the pavement beneath each lantern.

But everyone knows what names are on there: Monday hunters lost to the forest.

Winnie digs her locket from her hoodie. The message within hasn't changed; it still reads *Museum, 11 P.M. tonight*. So she slides her Monday schedule, folded into quarters, from her back pocket. Next, Winnie retrieves a pencil. It's just a short yellow one from a supply Mario had for the tourists who wanted to keep notes during the safari. The tip is too soft against her leg; the marks left behind on the page are clumsy. But that's fine. She isn't going to draw tonight. She is simply going to think. Then she'll shred up this paper and toss it into the nearest bin.

What I know:

1. Four years ago:
- *Dad went missing and was framed as a Diana*
- *Grayson drove a hummer off the bridge during his second trial*
- *Jenna died on her second trial after ~~vampira typically consume the top halves of bodies~~ NO*

2. Dad's map led me to:
- *Jenna's empty dampener in the stream where Grayson died*
- *A granite hole in the forest stained with blood*

3. Mom knows more than she can say about Dad, but she is under a spell

4. I am also ~~in the forests surrounding the Earth's oldest spirits~~ NO NO NO

5. Erica can maybe help with #3 and #4

6. Tuesdays are in cahoots with ~~from afar, they appear as gnarled, elderly women~~

7. Jay is a werewolf, and it's getting worse
- *His father might have been*

Winnie stops writing here. Her lungs swelling with an inhale. *It's not relevant,* she tells herself. *Jay's father isn't relevant to your list, and Mario's theory probably isn't right anyway. So you can stop writing now. You don't have to finish the sentence.*

She doesn't finish the sentence. Instead—and with a firm leash on any wayward ghosts—Winnie starts a second list.

What I don't know:

1. *What my locket does*
   - *If three stars means MESSAGE, was I supposed to use it for contacting Dad all along?*
   - *Why did Grandma Harriet have the locket—or did she really?*

2. *What S. hid in his office*
   - *Is the telescope important or not?*

3. *Why Jenna created the ~~in Norway, revenants are called draugr~~*
   - *Why Jenna went on her second trial*

4. *What Mom knows and what happened four years ago*

5. *If any of Mario's theories about Jay are true*
   - *How Jay got a wolf's jawbone under his pillow*

6. *WHO AM I MEETING AT THE OLD MUSEUM????*

Technically this second list is shorter than the first, but that fact coaxes no triumph from Winnie's chest. Instead, her eyes dart from *wolf's jawbone* to *MEETING AT THE OLD MUSEUM* to *What Mom knows.* Back, forth. Up, down. A quick glance at *telescope important or not?* Then it's back to *wolf's jawbone.* Back to *MEETING AT THE OLD MUSEUM.*

Winnie hears her breathing pick up speed. She *sees* her pencil start shaking against her thigh. And she knows what's coming next—except this time, it's not only ghosts unleashing. It's also the *overwhelming sense* that she is up against more than she can handle. That her Don't Know list is *too long* and there is *too much* for her to reckon with inside of Hemlock Falls.

Because the Crow isn't the only bad guy out there, is she? There are other Dianas too, and there's the Whisperer, churning through trees and nightmares and people as easily as Winnie will soon tear through this paper . . .

And oh god, now that Winnie considers it, if Jenna created the Whisperer and the Whisperer killed Grayson, does that mean Jenna killed Grayson? The boy she loved? Somehow, that is almost as awful as learning there's a chance Jay's father was the werewolf who slaughtered people seventeen years ago. There's no escaping tragedy in Hemlock Falls. Death really is a part of life, and the forest really does break everything.

Wolf's jawbone.

MEETING AT THE OLD MUSEUM.

What Mom knows.

Telescope important or not?

Winnie drops the pencil. She doesn't hear it clatter to the bus floor. Doesn't hear it roll, or feel when it bumps against her boot. She leans forward until her forehead hits the back of the seat in front of her. Her glasses press into her brow. Her eyelids close, pinch, squeeze until she sees shooting stars. *Shooting stars like the ones Samuel used to observe through his telescope.*

No, Winnie can't think of Samuel either. She can't think of the other dead Diana, totally unknown, left smoking on the forest floor. She can't think of the lanterns bobbing outside, with the hundreds of Monday names lost over the century. And above all, Winnie can't think about Dad.

Because what if it's *not* him at the old museum tonight? What if he's also dead and gone forever just like everyone else on her list? Like Grayson, like Jenna, like both Jay's father *and* mother? And what will Winnie do if all her sleuthing and searching leads her to absolutely nothing but a *famēs* spell with no end?

Winnie tastes cherries in her mouth. She feels like the bus is moving, though it's not. She wishes Jay were here to wrap her in his hoodie. She wishes Aunt Rachel were here to give her water. Hell, Winnie would even take Ms. Morgan right now, just to hear the lady say, *I'm always on your side.*

A whistle sounds outside. Then a crackle like bubble wrap. Then a thunderous boom that means the fireworks have begun.

For several seconds, Winnie lets the noise hammer into her. It's a battlefield. A thunderstorm. She feels the light off the fireworks, even though she knows her eyes are shut too tightly to see them.

The human eye can detect a single photon of light.

She can't remember where she learned that fact, but she does remember being flabbergasted. A photon of light is the smallest packet of electromagnetic energy in existence. It's not a particle, it's not a wave. It has no mass, no diameter. It is one dimension of energy, momentum, and angle.

Yet the human eye can detect it. A *single* photon traveling along a line at the speed of 299,792,458 meters per second—the human eye can sense when it's there.

Winnie wets her lips and pushes backward until her vertebrae, sacrum, and skull can rest against the bus seat. The fireworks blast and zoom outside in a boisterous display of defiance. *You cannot snuff us out tonight.*

She wonders if the nightmares see the lights and hear the noise. If they gaze in awe or cower in fear. She wonders too what the hunters must think; is it a distraction? Or is it a reinforcement of the mission that propels them each night?

Above all, Winnie wonders what all this noise must do to the sleeping spirit at the bottom of the Big Lake. If such a noise cannot awaken it, then what in all the universe can?

The cherry taste recedes from Winnie's mouth. She rises, her blue paper clutched in one hand, the pencil forgotten on the floor. Then with careful, contemplative steps, she exits the bus. The night outside is warmer than she expects. The fireworks are louder, their colors brighter. Luminaries trickle into the parking lot, exiting the after-party to watch the glittering show.

Winnie spots Dryden, fireworks reflecting colors on his pince-nez. And oh, there's Darian snuggled close with Andrew. *Good.* Everyone smiles— even Marcia, whose face wears an unfamiliar serenity as she leans against Antonio. She looks less like his *Antonio-nym* (as Winnie and Erica used to joke) and more like a partner very much in love. A wife, a mother, a councilor just doing what she can for Hemlock Falls.

For several seconds, Winnie feels wholly suspended in time, in place. Her teeth feel no urge to click. Her breaths come steady and full. There's no panic, nor onslaught of ghosts.

Instead, she thinks of the oceanic bathypelagic zone, where the water is so deep, not even a single photon can penetrate. Where the pressure is so intense, few creatures can survive. And yet, life still goes on there at the pure heart of the ocean. The fish and squid and microbes manage to see and find each other.

Because they create their own light.

"Ah," Winnie sighs, and her skeleton softens within its fascial suspension. All this time, when she thought the lights of Hemlock Falls were lying to her—they weren't, were they? They were *never* swamp fires pretending to be fairies, but instead bioluminescence inside the ocean.

Winnie twists again toward the Little Lake and the fireworks. A breeze coils against her, coming not from the forest, but from the east with smells like funnel cake and gasoline. Like gunpowder and cotton candy. Beyond the boats wobbling as they launch fireworks, the full moon of the Ferris wheel spins. *Aspire to become me,* it says to the waning gibbous in the sky.

The last time a waning gibbous hung, Winnie was beginning her first trial. She was an outcast. She was alone. Now here she is, one month later, literally surrounded by other people.

In a finale of color and chaos and joy, the last fireworks launch into the night. The cheers from nearby Luminaries build, competing in Winnie's brain for acknowledgment, and she finds she's holding her locket in a fist she doesn't recall making.

Number of people depending on Winnie a month ago? Two.

Number of people depending on Winnie now? Thousands.

Her phone vibrates in her pocket. She doesn't check it. Instead, she turns away from the Little Lake and sets off toward the family Volvo. She feels taller; she feels fuller; and she realizes this must be what Aunt Rachel meant when she talked about exorcising versus compartmentalizing. It's what Ms. Morgan meant too, when she talked about eating the pizza.

Winnie might have ghosts to haunt her—some of which aren't even her own—hovering like all these stamped lanterns bobbing on the breeze. But right now, at this particular moment, Winnie can't look at the lanterns. She can't listen to the ghosts.

Because the human eye can detect a single photon of light.

And that light is what she needs to be following.

As Winnie walks, as she methodically shreds her blue paper—*rip, rip, rip*—a feathery hope fills her ribcage. And far to the north, a will-o'-wisp watches the same fireworks, its own pure light shining into the trees.

CHAPTER

26

As far as venues go for rowdy meetups away from snooping adult eyes, you can't really beat the old museum. Art deco and white stone, it's got four long galleries, seven side chambers, a glass conservatory, and—the most popular spot of all—a domed rotunda perfect for booming bass lines.

Winnie of course knew from Bretta's text that there would be a party here tonight. What she wasn't expecting was for it to be a masquerade.

This isn't like the grand ball coming on Saturday, where a string quartet will play and all will marvel at the elegant, elaborate nightmare costumes that people like Fatima have designed. This is a party for teenagers, where booze flows in abundance (along with nightmare contraband), and the costumes are comparable in quality to what you'd find at a Halloween party for nons.

And although some of the costumes tonight are indeed mimicking nightmares, most are just . . . well, there are a lot of sexy nurses, sexy pirates, and sexy superheroes in attendance.

Winnie is, at the moment, the only *not*-costumed partygoer—which doesn't seem to bother anyone, since they haven't actually noticed her lurking against a column near the entrance with her hood pulled over her face and her hands stuffed into her pockets.

Except Casey Tuesday, who *has* managed to spot her and now stands uncomfortably close. He's dressed like Dracula (which has no connection to actual Luminary lore, for the record, although some historians do speculate the Count might have been a Diana tapping into vampira magic).

"Punch?" he asks. His breath plumes; the warm breeze from before has fled. Forest cold dominates again. "It has vodka in it."

"No punch." Winnie tugs her hood lower and wonders how the heck Casey noticed her. She's far enough from the main entrance that none of the disco or strobe lights can reach her. Only music does, blasting from speakers she knows hang inside the main rotunda.

Casey tips back his cup. A scent like nail polish remover and strawberry sears up Winnie's nose. Casey chokes. Then coughs. Then rubs at his now-tearing eyes. "So, I, uh . . ." *Cough, rub.* "I hear you and Jay Friday are dating. Is that true?"

Winnie grunts. If only she had some garlic with her. Or some holy water. Or hell, a wooden stake. Maybe if she waved it at Casey, *that* would get him to leave in a way that social cues never do.

He wipes his mouth and conspicuously does not sip more punch. "So if you're dating, does that mean Jay's taking you to the Masquerade Ball? Because I still don't have a date."

"I wonder why," Winnie murmurs.

Casey nods enthusiastically. "I know, right? I've asked like sixteen people. But hey—you know what they say about lucky number seven . . . teen. So what do you say? Want to go with me to the ball?"

"No," cuts in a new voice. "She will not go with you to the ball."

As one, Winnie and Casey whirl toward a nearby shadow, from which Jay manifests. Maybe he was standing there all along; maybe he only just arrived on silent boots. Either way, his skeleton is at its tallest and there's a cant to his jaw that would send most nightmares running.

Not Dracula, though. "Oh, hey, Jay. Want some punch?"

Jay ignores the question. "Winnie is my date for the ball, Casey. Are we clear?"

Winnie blinks. She's been standing here for half an hour, fretting and freaking that Mario's theory might make her view Jay differently—or worse, that it might make her blurt out something backed by *zero evidence* that he absolutely doesn't need to know. But she shouldn't have worried. Seeing Jay makes her feel as it always does: three parts extreme attraction + two parts deep respect for his air of competence + one part intense frustration.

"Ugh Jay!" She shoves off the column. "You haven't actually invited me to the ball. So no, I'm *not* going with you."

Jay rounds toward her, eyebrows shooting high. "I didn't . . . know I had to invite you?"

"Of course you have to invite me." Winnie glares behind her glasses. "For all you know I have plans on Saturday night."

"Do you?"

Winnie shrugs. "I might. Casey here has invited me to the ball twice now, so maybe I *will* go with him."

"Really?" Casey is so excited, he sloshes out punch. Alcohol whiffs through the night. "I have a mask that looks like a velue, so I'll need *you* to get a dress in teal to match it. Also, I spent all my allowance on the new *Call of Duty,* so I won't be getting you a corsage."

"She's not going with you, Casey. She's told you that twice now." Jay offers this without breaking eye contact with Winnie. His pupils have swallowed up most of the irises, making him look more animal than human. A puzzled animal with its head cocked to one side. "I'm confused, Winnie. If you're my girlfriend, aren't we supposed to do things together—"

"*Girlfriend?*" Winnie yanks off her hood. "You *also* haven't asked me to be your girlfriend, Jay! These sorts of developments require conversation. You don't get to . . . to just *claim ownership.*"

"I'm single," Casey inserts. "So if Jay's bothering you, Winnie, I will gladly step in."

Now Winnie is the one to snap: "Oh my god, Casey. No." Then, because she feels he deserves an explanation, she adds, "I'm not going to the ball with you because you spent four years being a total dick to me while I was an outcast."

"No, I didn't!"

"You toilet-papered my house."

"Not by myself! I was with Peter, Dante, and Astrid!"

"Point proven. Now, if I may offer a suggestion: return *Call of Duty* so that you can get your future date a corsage. Oh, and go away."

"But that game has *hours* of content, Winnie. A flower will wilt before the night is even over—"

"*Casey,*" Jay says. His pupils briefly shrink; the silver irises almost glow. "You need to go now, and give me and Winnie some space."

Casey finally listens—because of *course* he'll listen to a fellow male. Though he doesn't stomp away without an assortment of swear words and a glare so petulant, it would give Marcus a run for his money. And if not for Jay stepping closer, Winnie would probably chase after Casey and dump fruit punch all over his costume. But as it stands, Jay *is* in fact stepping closer.

Way closer.

"Please, go with me to the Masquerade Ball, Winnie."

"No." She pushes her glasses up her nose. "You don't get to *command* me to do things."

"That wasn't a command. It was a question."

"Except that questions begin with a predicate, not a subject. Such as, '*Will you* go with me to the ball?'"

"Okay, *will you* go with me to the ball? Say yes, and then be my girlfriend too."

"Oh my god, Jay, what don't you understand about *questions*? *Will* you be my girlfriend?"

"Okay, Winnie. I'm sorry." Jay moves even closer. So close now, Winnie has to tip her head all the way back. "Let me try this one more time. I have liked you since we were kids. You were the first person I kissed, and for four years, that kiss haunted me."

"Oh."

"And if I'm being honest, Winnie, it still haunts me. Because *you* haunt me. Waking up next to you Saturday morning, after a night on the hunt, was probably the best feeling I've ever had in my whole life, and I want to do it again. And again. And again. For as long as you want to do it with me too."

"Oh," she repeats.

"You've asked me a million times about where I take girls to make out, and the truth is I don't have anywhere. Because no one has ever been you, Winnie. So *please*, will you be my girlfriend? And then will you go with me to the Masquerade Ball on Saturday? Oh, and . . ." He reaches up to remove her glasses. "Will you let me kiss you?"

"Yes," she tries to say. Except all she can manage is a shaping of her mouth. A curt, almost desperate nod.

But Jay doesn't kiss her. Not right away. Instead, he lifts a single finger and taps her nose. "Boop."

Then he kisses her.

So hard it pushes Winnie's back against the column. Or maybe she's the one pulling Jay. It's impossible to tell, and she definitely doesn't care. All that matters is how her shoulder blades rub against cold stone. How the boom of the music vibrates into her ribs. How Jay's hip bones feel so pronounced as they press against her.

Here is his waist, defined and firm. Here are his lips, kissing not just Winnie's mouth, but her jaw, her neck, her collarbone.

She feels like she did when she drank melusine blood. Her whole body sparkles. Her neurons light up with the need for more Jay, more nightmare, more forest. She can't think, she can't breathe, she can't do anything but pull Jay harder, harder against her.

His teeth tug at her earlobe. "Homeostasis," he murmurs, and a laugh bubbles up from her lungs.

"Ah Jay," she murmurs on cue. Then he is kissing her again, his tongue meeting hers while her fingers explore his back.

The night's cold is gone now. Winnie is hot enough to scald. She is a phoenix burning into something new. A lantern shining against the night.

Until a voice charges over her: "Oh my *god,* you guys. No one wants to watch that. *Please* just get a room."

27

I'm sorry, Winnie," Erica says in a tone that is decidedly *not* sorry. "But when were you going to tell me you put a message in your locket?" She stands with her hands on hips, several paces from Winnie. A strobe light from one of the few windows not boarded up flashes over her like a thunderstorm. "We've been together *how many hours* in the last few days? And still you couldn't bother to mention this?"

"I didn't keep it from you on purpose." Winnie lifts her hands. Now that the whole WTF gang is here—and actually standing in an approximation of a right triangle—Winnie has explained why she summoned Erica and Jay to meet her. "I assumed it didn't work. Because it didn't until tonight. And well . . . there's been a lot going on."

"But it *did* work." While Jay sounds less pissed about this development than Erica, it's clear he too feels Winnie should have kept them updated.

Although, that rasping strain on his voice might also be from what he and Winnie were just doing two minutes ago. Like, Winnie still has her back against the column (which shall henceforth be known as Location #1 on the list of Great Make-Out Spots in Hemlock Falls), and Jay's lips are visibly swollen.

"So who answered the message?" Erica demands. "Show it to me." Unlike Jay, who is dressed as always in jeans and flannel, or Winnie in her ancient hoodie, Erica has actually put on a costume: cat ears. This in combination with the same all-black ensemble she wore yesterday, and she really has transformed into Catwoman. Which adds one more Sexy Superhero to the party.

Winnie pulls the message from her hoodie. "I have no idea who sent this, E. Only that it says 'museum, eleven P.M.' . . . Wait, now it doesn't say anything at all." She pushes out of the column's shadow to hold the paper into the blinking light, but no. There's nothing written there.

Erica doesn't seem surprised. In fact, she rolls her eyes so aggressively, her head swings. "You have to put the paper back in the locket, Winona. It's like an auto-deleting text message—"

"Those exist?" Winnie asks.

"—and if you keep it out of the locket, the message vanishes. Here." Without asking permission, Erica scoots in and snaps the paper back into the locket. "Now we wait a few seconds."

Erica's hands remain clasped around the locket. Her eyes go hazy, as if she's staring into the future. Or maybe just counting to ten.

Jay clears his throat.

"Shut up," Erica replies, accurately anticipating what Jay is about to say. (So maybe she *was* staring into the future.)

"I don't like this." Jay fastens a stare onto Winnie. "I don't feel good about it, and I think it's a trap. Secret notes in lockets and magic spells that auto-delete—this all feels like a really bad combination."

Now Erica is the one to stare at Winnie. "Please remind Jay that he's the one who's a werewolf."

Winnie swallows. She has successfully kept Mario's baseless theory about *why* Jay is a werewolf tamped down inside her brain. Now is not a good time to start chewing on it again.

Erica flips open the locket. "Awesome. There you are, Mr. Message. Except . . ." She angles the paper into the light. "It says *second floor*. That's not what it said before, is it?"

All thoughts of werewolf mutations scatter. Winnie snatches the paper from Erica, and sure enough, it now reads: *Second floor, 11:05.* "Whoa. This is new since I left the Monday estate."

"And it's eleven oh five now." Erica's eyes bug. "Put the note back in the locket, and let's *go*." She spins on a boot heel, ready to march away.

Until Jay sidles a long leg into her path. "Nope. We're not going up there, Erica. Following messages from an unknown *witch* seems like a guaranteed way for all of us to end up dead."

"Don't make assumptions." Erica pins him with an Ice Queen stare.

"Winnie asked the locket for help, and that's clearly what we're getting. For all you know, it's her dad sending the messages, and we're about to *finally* get what we've been looking for."

Winnie's mouth dries at those words. Her tongue thickens.

"Or maybe," Jay counters, "it's that witch who tried to kill me and Winnie in the forest. Remember her?"

"You don't know the *cornīx* wrote this. There are probably more Dianas in Hemlock Falls than just her, and someone bewitched Winnie with a circling-words spell—"

"Wait, what? What spell?" Jay stares again at Winnie, but it's not like she can explain to him what's happening, so she simply shrugs helplessly back.

"She can't talk about it," Erica fills in, and there's a smugness to the up-tilt of her jaw. She knows more than Jay, and she's savoring it. "Any time Winnie tries to tell me about it, random nonsense spews out."

Now Jay's expression is one of betrayal. *Erica knows this but not me?* But again, it's not like Winnie can say or do anything to explain herself. All she can manage is a tight-knuckled fist around the message and a furious exhale entombed by spring-cold fog.

Overhead, the strobe light keeps bouncing.

"Are we all good now?" Erica asks with pretend sweetness. "Because if so, it's now eleven oh six, and we're late." She sets off again toward the museum's entrance, and oh, Winnie is now noticing a tail attached to her jeans.

"I'm sorry," Winnie tries, but Jay isn't paying attention. His phone is lighting up in his flannel pocket, a secondary strobe to clash against the party. When he tugs it out, he groans. First at the phone. Than at Erica's disappearing figure.

Given that the time is now 11:07 according to Winnie's own phone, and that Erica has fully vanished from sight, Winnie mutters a rough "I'm sorry" for Jay. Then she scampers after the T in their WTF triangle.

Jay, half shouting into his phone so he can be heard, prowls after. "Can you—no. Please, L.A. Just wait, okay? It shouldn't take long. Yeah, fine. Fine. I can meet you in the rotunda."

That's the last Winnie hears before the party subsumes her.

She has been to the old museum before, of course. On the night of Grayson's funeral for a party so massive, there were at least double the people here celebrating his life. But whatever this party lacks in scale, it makes up for in enthusiasm. Music careens over Winnie like a wrecking ball. Or like the disco balls that dangle in the main rotunda where once upon a time, a life-size droll skeleton hung. Black lights turn graffiti into glowing art displays across the marble floors and transform a wide, winding staircase into river rapids of dancing Luminaries. So many masks, so many painted faces, Winnie recognizes no one—and she herself remains unseen, pulled so far inside her hoodie, she has basically morphed into a turtle-wyrm.

Turtle-wyrm: Like the name would suggest, this subset of wyrm is able to retract its head into its body during times of danger or distress. (See also Cueille-Aigue, where one such wyrm managed to escape and survive for three years before Martedì Alphas tracked it down and killed it.)

For a chaotic, thudding moment, as Winnie tries to shove up the stairs toward the second floor, she loses Erica. She loses Jay. And she loses herself too, to the darkness, darkness, light of the Luminaries.

Then Winnie is at the top of the stairs and shoving into more crowds. More bodies. The heat mauls. Smells overwhelm, alcohol emulsifying with perfumes and deodorants and sweat. Winnie can't see Erica, she can't see Jay, and now that she's on the second floor, where is she supposed to go?

With elbows and a cast-down head, she bludgeons her way into a familiar anteroom, where Grayson's memorial was set up scarcely two weeks ago. The easel still remains, but there's no crappy printout of Grayson's face, no *We will miss you!* written in permanent marker.

It's just a room where more people dance, a few make out, and most hunch together shouting over the music or sharing drinks. No one looks at Winnie, and soon she finds herself before the window that will lead onto the roof. It's open, though only enough to suck in a purl of air.

Winnie pulls her phone from her pocket. Her fingers shake as she fumbles out a message to Erica and Jay. *By roof window.* Then she waits.

And waits.

And waits some more while nothing happens.

Nothing except her locket vibrating against her chest. She jolts against the window. Then hastily checks the locket, where a new message reads: *Closet by bathroom. Now.*

Winnie doesn't move. Her body hums with music and movement, but it's not the work of her muscles. Not fibers contracting and stretching at the command of her brain. *Closet by bathroom. Now.* She's pretty sure she knows where that is. There are bathrooms on this floor, and between the men's and women's is a door. The sort of door you expect to hold mops and toilet cleaner and extra paper towels. She can reach that door in mere moments if she aims east and into a darker, emptier gallery of the museum.

Winnie isn't stupid though. Yes, she tromped into the forest on her first trial completely unprepared and nearly got killed by a banshee. And yes, she followed Emma into the forest when she had literally no weapons or proper footwear. And oh yeah, she did go after Jay after he was shot by Wednesdays and all she had for protection was nightmare contraband.

Still, she isn't stupid. Each of those instances had high risk, but much higher reward. She got her family back into the Luminaries; she saved Emma's life; she saved Jay's life; and now, *right now* inside the shadowy, forgotten part of the museum . . .

Winnie thinks of Dad's face, so much like Darian's. Of his auburn hair that she inherited from him. She thinks of the sketches he drew in the birthday cards. She thinks of Mom, sitting at the kitchen table, trapped by the same spell that controls Winnie. She thinks of fireworks and Ferris wheels and the honest lights of downtown. Then she thinks of blue paper and stiff pencils and a don't-know list that isn't shrinking.

All she has to do is walk a hundred feet and see what's there. She doesn't have to *approach,* she doesn't have to *talk* to anyone, and she certainly doesn't have to remain if the whole thing feels wrong.

Winnie pulls out her phone. *And sweetest in the gale is heard; And sore must be the storm; That could abash the little bird; That kept so many warm.* She texts Jay, then Erica: *2 floor bathroom now.* And finally, Winnie rocks away from the window. Her decision is made; the photons are guiding her this way.

Unfortunately, she doesn't sense the night air trying to hold her back. Because it has no substance. It has no voice. It has only a whisper scratching to life nearby.

The party rumbles on.

C H A P T E R

28

There's no one there.

That's what Winnie sees when she reaches the long gallery that once held Luminary historical portraits. There are dark spots on the gray wall that mark where frames used to hang. There are couples in discreet shadows. And there's a small group at the farthest end of the room sitting round robin and playing cards.

As for the bathrooms—both of which Winnie can see from here, along with the closet between them . . . Well, there's no one there. Absolutely *no one.*

She hovers at the edge of the wide archway into the room. The party pulsates behind her; lights flash stochastically against music she can't quite hear. It's just bass and boom and bodies.

She checks her phone again. Nothing.

She checks the locket again. It's unchanged. *Closet by the bathroom. Now.* Winnie's face screws up. Is there another bathroom on the second floor? Or could this message mean the *first*-floor bathrooms? Do *they* have a closet nearby too?

She propels herself onward. *Step, step, step.* A rhythm that doesn't match the party. She adjusts her glasses three times. *Step, step, step.*

Nothing happens.

There's still no one there.

Winnie gets all the way to the ladies' restroom with its doorless entry into darkness and a stick figure in a dress (that someone has modified to be gender neutral by removing half the dress). And there, right next to it, is the closet door.

It's about as innocuous as a door can get. Rectangular. Wooden. A brass knob on the right. It's the sort of door you're not supposed to notice, and there's not even a sign on it to indicate what, once upon a time, it might have been for. Storage? Cleaning supplies? Secret portal to Narnia?

Winnie stops walking now. By her estimation, she is ten steps from the closet—and there is still no one. She doesn't hear water running or toilets flushing. (Although, to be fair, she's not sure the pumps are operational.)

Her phone quakes.

Her heart blasts into the stratosphere.

And with clownish fingers that have forgotten how to mobilize, she bumbles her phone from her pocket. It's Erica. *Where are you? Did you leave the roof window?*

Crap. Winnie's previous text to her didn't go through.

She looks again at the closet. Again at each bathroom door. Then again at the round-robin crew twenty yards away. Someone just got a full house; they're howling their joy into the gallery.

No, she types out. *2 floor bathr*—

She doesn't get a chance to finish. Not before a figure oozes from the bathroom like an oil spill. They are small, yet shapeless in a gray robe.

On their head is a hound mask.

Winnie drops her phone.

She doesn't mean to, but seeing that mask transports her straight into the forest. She is once more watching as golden arrows fly and phoenix fire ignites to roast two witches alive.

Canēs: These are the lowest level in the Diana hierarchy, specialized in hunting nightmares for spells and spreading the Diana cause.

"Winnie," the voice says. "Winnie, these are for you." The hound offers something that smears the shadows with red.

Winnie's eyes track down. And although her glasses slide, she manages to find what the witch is holding.

Red envelopes. One, two, three, four, fanned out just like Winnie fanned them out when she confronted Mom. Two have Winnie's name. Two have Darian's.

This person is not Dad, though. Whoever stands before Winnie is half a head shorter and with robes that billow like a Sith Lord's. They are *not* Winnie's dad.

"Who," she begins, without taking the cards, "are—"

No.

Heat erupts from Winnie's locket like a gunshot. A cry cuts loose from her lungs. Her knees wobble beneath her.

No, the voice that isn't a voice repeats in Winnie's brain. It has no gender, no shape, no weight. It's just a word slicing through her mind like a guillotine. It's just fire blazing on her chest like a poker.

Yet Winnie knows that voice belongs to the Crow. Her locket never responds to anyone else this way.

The hound stares down the gallery, their snout aimed at a distant window Winnie would have sworn was closed only a few moments ago. Then light spears through that open window, and the hound tackles Winnie.

Sagitta aurea: These spells are used to kill or maim a target. Just as the Dianas are named for the Roman goddess of the hunt, these spells are modeled after Diana's preferred weapon of golden arrows.

Winnie and the hound crash against the closet door. Screams erupt across the room. Light flares, golden as a summer sun and overwhelming Winnie's vision. Then smoke scores into her nose.

Because the golden arrow has hit a nearby wall, and now that wall is burning.

The hound grabs Winnie's arms, frantically tugging her to her feet. "Run," they say, shoving the red envelopes into Winnie's hands. "Winnie, you have to run!"

Hotspot: These extensions of the sleeping spirit's domain can appear anywhere within several miles outside the spirits' typical boundaries. Like mushrooms that have fungal connections extending and branching below the earth's surface, the spirits also grow and reach and spread.

Mist rolls toward Winnie like the ash from a volcanic eruption. It comes from the gallery's end—from the window where the golden arrow appeared. Hot and magicked and unstoppable. It engulfs the room so fast, she can do nothing but let it come for her.

The heat shears her skin. Her eyesight vanishes. And deep, deep inside her, a hysterical version of Winnie laughs like a hidebehind. Because the Sundays think their hot room is like *this*? How adorable, how precious. They clearly know nothing about what the forest can really do.

Hidebehind, Winnie's inner Compendium spurts. *These thin daywalkers are native only to the northernmost spirit forest of the Americas. They stalk prey by hiding behind trees, and the only warning of an attack is the high-pitched laughter emitted when they pounce.*

"Winnie!" she hears Jay roar from behind. *"I'm coming!"*

Then there he is, an inhuman blur morphing into a hunter beside her. His hand claps onto Winnie's arm. "Move," he commands. "We have to keep moving."

Yes. This is the one lesson Winnie really should know by now after how many times in the mist? After how many nightmares have formed around her?

Later, she will marvel that she had the physical capacity to not only hold on to the red envelopes when the mist thundered across her, but to shove them into her hoodie pocket. Her phone might be long gone, but these cards are prizes she refuses to give up.

With fingers latched like pliers, Jay hauls Winnie back toward the antechamber—or at least, she thinks that's where they're going. She can't see; she no longer smells smoke from a burning wall; and she can hardly hear. Yet of course Jay makes it all seem so easy. This might not be the forest, but nightmares and mist are his natural habitat. And Winnie, Winnie, Winnie—oh, what do you *think* you're doing here? What do any of these silly little Luminaries in their silly little costumes think they're doing here in this domain that the forest has suddenly claimed?

Those same silly little Luminaries scream. Winnie sees shadows forming in the mist. And uselessly, her brain emits: *The only warning sign of a hotspot's formation is the flight of local fauna.*

Someone grunts and rolls. A nightmare snarls. "Winnie!" Jay's voice twists around her in horrifying ways. "Hellion on your left!"

Yes. There it is, lunging at her with fangs bared. She has seen hellions so many times, but always dead, always damaged by hunter bolts or shrapnel grenades. She has just enough time to think, *My what big teeth you have!* before its front paws land against her.

She falls to the wooden floor, her chin barely tucking inward to avoid concussive contact. Heat sears against her, mist and snarling saliva and a breath that reeks of carrion.

Fangs lurch close, along with eyes as fiery as the pits of hell the beast is named for. *This is what killed Grandma Winona. This is how she died.*

Jay slams into the hellion's side, and it flings off Winnie—although not without claws shredding over her leather jacket.

A gust of wind punches in from the nearby roof-access window, clearing mist and revealing Jay and the hellion locked in a match of strength that Jay is not going to win. Winnie scrabbles to her feet, half crawling across the room to the easel. "Sorry," she says to the future dead, yanking the wood to her. One kick at the right leg, then another for the left.

"Jay," she barks. "Catch!" She flings one of her two newly made stakes his way.

And for a fraction of a second, she remembers doing this before: throwing a stake at Jay. Except he was a wolf then, and she was trying to kill him instead of save.

The memory is gone before it can fully form. Jay catches the stake as the hellion's teeth lock onto his forearm. *Punch.* The stake stabs into the hellion's neck. *Punch.* He stabs this one into the skull.

The hellion releases, and Jay shoves the nightmare off him. He's bleeding, but when Winnie crouches to help him, he waves her off. "More nightmares." He points with his bloodied arm toward the rotunda—where yes, the screams and shouting and a building roar are impossible to miss.

As are the people sprinting into this antechamber, one of whom is L.A., dressed as a zombified nurse. She catches sight of Winnie and Jay aiming her way and shouts, "Droll! There's a fucking *droll!*"

Droll: A humanoid nightmare that can range in size from four hundred pounds to almost four thousand. They are best avoided or, if conflict is necessary, then dealt with by many hunters at once. Firearms recommended.

Winnie and Jay do not have firearms. *No one* in this museum has firearms.

When Winnie and Jay—and now L.A. with them—push through the crowds into the rotunda, the mist has fully cleared, and the droll stands exactly where the old skeleton used to hang.

It's a big one. Definitely in the thousands of pounds range.

Jay sprints ahead of Winnie, taking stock of the situation faster than Winnie can possibly absorb it. Her brain is still trapped in the gallery where a Diana *canis* gave her birthday cards and saved her from a golden arrow. *Except, why was a golden arrow coming for me? Why would the Crow want to hurt me?*

"L.A.! Trevor!" Jay shouts, flying for the stairs. "Aim for the knees!"

Jay jumps. Right off the staircase and leaping the balustrade like it's nothing. He lands on the droll's shoulder, and the nightmare twists its ugly head toward this obnoxious human—who is somehow *still* shouting orders.

It's incredible. If there weren't actual lives on the line and actual nightmares in the middle of the old museum, Winnie would just stand here at the top of the stairs and marvel at her boyfriend. *Youngest Lead Hunter in Hemlock Falls.*

No wonder he is though.

Jay drops off the droll's shoulder, landing behind the monster in time for his bandmates to charge in with makeshift weapons. L.A. has a chair leg and Trevor just has the whole chair.

They slam against the droll's knees. Its bellows writhe all the way into Winnie's bone marrow, propelling her into action while Jay's voice somehow pierces the chaos. "Imran, the ribs! Marisol, the face—get it in the fucking eyes!"

Winnie bolts for the stairs; they're shallow, and she flies down two at a time. Meanwhile, Jay dives and rolls around the droll. His arm sprays blood.

Winnie is halfway down the stairs when the droll turns toward her. Its eyes, huge ogling things, lock onto her and she would swear it laughs. That its grotesque mouth stretches wide, and chuckles bounce out.

It reaches for her on the stairs, hands as large as her torso and arms longer than she is tall. It's just like the arm she retrieved on corpse duty weeks ago. And its wrist is *just* like the wrist she always draws during class. (So soothing, all those carpal bones.)

A meaty hand grabs her, and Winnie doesn't have to think. *Lunate bone, capitate bone, hamate bone.* The spike goes in. The droll screams, high-pitched and pained. Then Winnie reclaims the stake, satisfaction surging through her like a champagne bottle uncorked. Her hunter senses are toggled to max. She wants *more.*

She gets her wish a heartbeat later when Jay appears. He snags the stake from her as he passes, then, just as he'd done before, he clears the balustrade to land on the droll's shoulder.

This time, though, it's not a distraction. One stab—that's all it takes. Right into the ear.

And Winnie finds she is grinning. Jay may never go to school, but hell if he doesn't know his nightmares. *Droll ears are particularly sensitive, their cochlear and vestibular nerves sitting closer to the surface than humans'.*

The droll's ogling eyes start rolling. It's really screaming now, yet Jay is still barking orders. "Winnie!" he shouts from the ground floor, pointing with his bloodied arm toward a nearby room called the nightmare gallery. *In there,* he's saying. *Help in there.*

Like every other hunter here, Winnie obeys without question. She clears the rest of the steps in four leaps. She no longer has a weapon, but she'll figure that out once she sees what she's up against.

Which happens moments later: the nightmare gallery is almost completely cleared of people, save for three bodies wrapped in sticky white web . . .

While *six* spidrin scuttle and spin across the room.

"*Spidrin!*" Winnie shouts to anyone who might hear in the rotunda: "*SPIDRIN WITH PREY!*" That's all she has time for before the nearest spidrin darts her way and launches a web.

Winnie drops sideways, barely getting low enough before sticky silk flies where her body just was.

Spidrin: A catchall term for any nightmares resembling spiders. They will always possess eight legs and produce webs; some feature human body parts as well.

These ones definitely have the human body parts. Their thoraxes are shaped like a human's—some female, some male, one that is even a child's. Then they all have eight hairy brown legs, and heads with eight eyes and mandibles clacking.

These truly are the stuff of nightmares, and Winnie can't help but think, *This should be my entry for the Compendium contest.* Then her thoughts are silenced by more web pitching her way.

Winnie levers herself at the nearest spidrin, one with a well-muscled thorax and chest hair. *Actual* chest hair. She sees each curl as she dives closer. *In close quarters, the spidrin will resort to physical combat instead of web deployment. Beware of possible venom.*

Mandibles zoom in, but Winnie bypasses the creature and aims for a table filled with booze. Up she springs. Smash goes the nearest bottle. Then she rounds and stabs the bottle into the spidrin's back.

It is entirely too human.

And Winnie *hates* herself for thinking of Professor Samuel in that moment. This is not a place for ghosts to rise.

"Duck!" a voice calls, and Winnie obeys, rolling under the booze table.

Then she watches as a flaming bottle arcs through the air, lighting up the dark gallery that used to display illustrated nightmares instead of real ones.

The bottle smashes onto a spidrin. The monster hisses and writhes and burns alive, while legs spasm inward, just like a real spider.

Winnie thinks again of Samuel.

Until Trevor gallops by and barks, "Help the victims, Winnie! Get them free!"

Right. Priorities. Winnie grabs for another bottle. *Smash.* This time, she turns her blade onto the web-bound prey. Just like a real spider, these nightmares save their food for later. She stabs the broken glass into thick silk.

But at that moment, a charged, feral sensation swipes over her spine. It's like a live wire dragging down a chalkboard. *No,* she thinks. *It can't be. Not here, not now.*

She finishes carving the web; Casey stares up at her with vacant eyes. He's alive, he's breathing . . . but he's definitely not moving.

Winnie wracks her internal Compendium for an antidote. Isn't there something in the addendum about dissolving the web in water that—

"I've got this!" a new voice shouts. Winnie glances up, startled.

"Bretta?"

"I got this," she repeats, pushing Winnie aside and grabbing at the webbing around Casey.

"Is Emma here too? Is she okay?"

"She's fine." Bretta spares Winnie a brief glance. Her eyes are huge in the dark room; her skin shines with sweat. "She's outside and calling the Tuesdays for help right now."

"Why are you here?"

"Why are *you*? And with Erica, I saw." There's a harshness to Bretta's voice that Winnie has never heard before—at least not directed at herself. And she can't help but acknowledge, *This is fair.* After all, she said she wasn't coming tonight. She said she and Erica weren't friends. Now here she is, unable to explain anything.

Wind sucks against Winnie like a miniature wormhole; like a nuclear warhead detonating. She knows exactly what it is. She just prays it isn't inside the museum.

"I'm sorry," Winnie tells Bretta. That's all she can offer, all she has time for. The Whisperer is coming, the Whisperer is *here,* and only Winnie knows about it. No, she can't stop it, but maybe if she can find it, she can distract it. Keep it away from the rest of the museum.

Away from Bretta, Emma, and everyone else she cares about.

Winnie lobs to her feet and aims for the exit. The live wire on the chalkboard writhes hotter with each step. She reaches the gallery's end and veers into a room filled with couches ripped to shreds like they were nothing more than teddy bears caught in a lawnmower.

Winnie crosses the room in seconds, knowing on a visceral level where the Whisperer will be. She can't say *why,* but it just makes sense. Everything keeps going back to her dad, doesn't it? So now, where the Whisperer must await will be in Dad's favorite room.

Winnie reaches the conservatory and steps inside.

30

When Winnie steps into the conservatory, she can't see anything. Not because the room is too dark—if anything, it's brighter here, with the moon to shine through a glass ceiling and reflect on white tiles. Rather, Winnie sees nothing because there is nothing to see.

There is nothing to hear, either. No blenders eating xylophones, no engines dropped down a mineshaft. It's as if a winter coat has been draped across the conservatory, and it reminds Winnie of the muffling spell the Crow cast in the maze.

The Whisperer *is* here, though. The static of its magic scours like a backward comet against Winnie. Her teeth feel as if they're detaching from her gums, and the urge to retreat fires through her muscles in short bursts of *SOS* and *Get the hell out of here.*

Winnie holds her ground, fingers tightening on the broken bottle.

She winds her arm back. Then flings. If the Whisperer really is here, it will shatter into a glass hurricane. Instead, the bottle whistles in a perfect arch like a rainbow after a storm. It clatters to the ground and slides over three tiles.

But that is when the sound finally does arrive: the whispering Winnie knows so well. That she thought for days was from a nightmare, before she finally figured out it was from a spell.

Famēs: These spells are self-feeding and sustain themselves in the forest.

The sound—so quiet next to the battles from the rest of the museum—rustles louder, and Winnie finds she's squinting. Staring hard at where the Whisperer *should* be, but where empty air still remains.

The whisper boils louder until she can no longer hear the rest of the museum. A cheese grater starts flaying across her skin. Vertigo takes root inside her cranium. But she doesn't run, and she doesn't look away. Because why, why, *why* is the *famēs* so still—so concentrated in this place, like a flower folded inward?

Winnie can't pinpoint when the singing begins. Only that somewhere, in all that radioactive chaos, a melody assembles. It's like one of those psychedelic pictures that look totally meaningless until you stare at it long enough for a 3D shape to emerge.

What emerges here is Jenna's song. Still wordless, still only melody, but it's *the* song that Winnie hears when she dreams. That she still thinks saved her while she was beneath the waterfall's waves. She once thought Jenna wrote songs that could break you—but that always put you back together again.

This one, though, isn't going to fix Winnie. This one seeks only to destroy.

"Jenna?" The name drips off Winnie's tongue, wholly silent because the Whisperer can't help but consume it. "Jenna, is that you?"

A hand claps onto Winnie's shoulder. She heard no footsteps, felt no shifting in the air to herald a person's approach, but now there is a *hand on her* and it is gripping so hard she can do nothing but be towed away on a riptide of unseen muscles.

PURE HEART, the Whisperer says in a voice that is not a voice at all, but a melody shattered by space-time and regret. *THERE YOU ARE.*

The Whisperer launches into full power. No music. Only hunger and violence and death.

And finally, Winnie listens to the hands—finally she twists into them and lets herself fall into a frantic run beside Jay. Just in time too, because behind them, the conservatory shatters. It is an explosion of glass and iron and lawnmower-flavored bloodlust. The stink of burning plastic keens so hard into Winnie's nose, her eyes water. She almost trips over the remains of a couch cushion.

She can see, through tears and filthy glasses, that Jay is shouting something. But she can't hear him. All that fills her ears are the whispers. Haunting, relentless whispers.

They reach the nightmare gallery, where only two spidrin remain, fighting against costumed Luminaries. Now though, the spidrin are fleeing too, scurrying on their knobbed legs at a speed no hunter can match.

"*RUN!*" Jay roars, and Winnie realizes she can hear him once more. They must have gained enough ground, so the *famēs* can no longer eat their words. But it's not *enough* ground, and worse, Jay is stumbling. Stopping. Bending over.

Oh god, no.

He is changing. Before Winnie's eyes and with mist to pour off him, his nightmare mutation is taking hold. His clothes absorb into his body as if they never existed. His muscles ripple and shift.

Jay has just enough time to lift his face. To find Winnie with eyes that glow like the moon. There is so much pain there, so much fear. "I love you," he tells her. "I'm sorry."

Then the mist spews wide. Jay vanishes entirely within its grasp. And worse—somehow worse—a chemical smell is acidifying Winnie's nose hairs again. Sound is once more vacuuming away. And there, *there* are the helicopter blades of fury to thunder against her skin.

The Whisperer has caught up to them.

Mist retreats from Jay as fast as it erupted, sucking inward until only a massive white wolf remains. He looks at Winnie with silver eyes. "*Run,*" she screams at him. "*Run!*" But the Whisperer eats everything, even her voice.

So Winnie shoves at Jay, her skin so electrified she can't feel his shining fur or canine muscles. She *shoves,* and then she uses that momentum to carry herself forward too. They will follow the spidrin. She and Jay will get out of this gallery before the Whisperer can destroy them.

Jay isn't following, though. He has turned away from Winnie to face the smeared distortion of the *famēs* spell. His hackles are raised as if he's growling, as if he plans to fight this thing that cannot be defeated.

Winnie skitters to a halt, ready to surge back after him, except now L.A. Saturday has arrived. Her zombie nurse costume is torn and tangled, while her face is reddened with exertion and her eyes are hollowed out by fear. Winnie sees her mouth move, shaping words that might be *Come on, Midnight Crown!*

Now here is Bretta too, lurching in. Each girl grabs one of Winnie's arms, and Winnie has no choice but to be towed along, just as Jay towed her earlier. Except she *let* Jay pull her, and she does *not* let Bretta or L.A. They don't understand what is happening; Winnie can't let the Whisperer have Jay.

She screams and fights, but now there are more Luminaries grabbing her. Trevor. Emma. Katie with a gash across her brow. And there's Erica too. *Erica will understand, Erica will listen.*

"Jay!" Winnie screams, still fighting. *"Jay is back there!"*

They are halfway through the rotunda when she feels it.

The quiet sating of the Whisperer.

And the silencing of the wolf that filled its belly.

WINNIE'S SCHEDULE FOR
THE NIGHTMARE MASQUERADE

TUESDAY

8 A.M.: *Tuesday Olympics All-Terrain 10K*
- *Winnie is expected at the Tuesday estate—participation optional. Dress is sportswear, if you decide to join.*
- *Winnie will fire the starter gun along with Jeremiah Tuesday.*

9 A.M.: *Full Olympics Begin*
- *Winnie will watch the different sports events of the day—choices range from footraces to wrestling matches to archery. You can decide!*
- *Again, expect photographs.*
- *When not watching, please mingle in the VIP area.*

12 P.M.–4 P.M.: *Sunday Estate Training*

4 P.M.–7 P.M.: *Olympics Continue*
- *Again, your choice on what to watch.*
- *When not watching, please mingle in the VIP area.*

6 P.M.–7 P.M.: *Olympics Awards Ceremony & After-party*
- *Ceremony will be held on the main sports field.*
- *Winnie will be expected to stand on stage with the Council.*
- *After-party will follow in Hangar A.*

ALL DAY: *Public viewing of Tuesday gear*
- *If you need a break from the sports, you can explore the Tuesday weapons, armor, and assorted vehicles in Hangars A–F.*
- *Expect photo requests and possible interviews.*

9 P.M.: *Floating Carnival*
- *Tuesday firework display on the Little Lake*

31

Interview with Wednesday (Winnie) Winona Wednesday

[0:00]

Jeremiah: [seated at interrogation table with open manila folder before him] Interview begins now at 6:45 A.M. on Tuesday, April twenty-third. Ms. Wednesday, eyewitness accounts place you in the second-floor east gallery when the hotspot formed at [glances at notes] 11:16 P.M. on Monday, April twenty-second. Is that correct?

Winnie: [stares at hands folded on table; expression is vacant] I don't know. Probably.

Jeremiah: We also have three reports of . . . Open quote. A golden arrow flying across the room. Close quote. And one person said, open quote. It looked like magic. Close quote. All four reports mark you as the source of the magic.

Winnie: Okay. I wasn't, but okay.

Jeremiah: Care to elaborate?

Winnie: Not really.

[Jeremiah takes a sip from a nearby coffee mug. Then leans back in his chair.]

[1:03]

Jeremiah: Ms. Wednesday, you're in a lot of trouble. As I'm sure you know because we've done this before. [waves hand at interrogation room] Except last time, it wasn't *you* standing accused of magic and witchcraft. It was your father—

Winnie: And you know damned well my dad was framed. That it was really the banshees who have vertical pupils, greenish skin, and claws with needle-like points.

[Jeremiah frowns. Then taps at the folder on the table.]

[1:25]

Jeremiah: I'm not sure I follow.

Winnie: [tilts forward now, visibly angry] Bull *shit,* Jeremiah. I know what you are and what you know. The basilisks possess hollow fangs that inject venom much like natural snakes. *FUCK.*

Jeremiah: Calm down, Ms. Wednesday—

Winnie: *You* calm down! I didn't ask to be here. I, like everyone else, was trapped inside a fucking hotspot while nightmares tried to kill me. But now, somehow, it's all *my* fault.

Jeremiah: It's not?

Winnie: You *know* it's not, just like you *know* I'm not a Diana. And you *know* my dad was never a Diana either. We're all innocent and the examination reveals algal hair and a bulbous body—*no.* [She breaks off with a sob. Then crumples forward to land on her hands on the table.]

[2:06]

Jeremiah: Here's what I know, Ms. Wednesday—

Winnie: [muffled] Call me Winnie. My name is Winnie.

Jeremiah: We found this phone in the gallery. It appears to be yours, and you have a message to Jay Friday telling him to meet you there, as well as an unsent message to Erica Thursday.

Winnie: [lifts head and audibly swallows] Have you . . . seen Jay?

Jeremiah: No, Ms. Wednesday. But if you're worried about his secret, well . . . cat's out of the bag. Or should I say wolf?

[Winnie sways.]

Jeremiah: And as for Ms. Thursday, she was questioned at the museum—and she was a great deal more forthcoming about last night.

[Winnie doesn't answer. Just crumples over again.]

Jeremiah: Ms. Wednesday—

Winnie: *Winnie.*

Jeremiah: —I need you to sit up. You're going to want to see these.

[He pulls four red envelopes from the manila folder. Then opens the envelopes and withdraws white cards.]

[2:50]

Jeremiah: These are birthday cards, aren't they? Signed as if from your father. *Are* they from your father?

[Winnie snaps upright. Then catches self on table. Jeremiah, meanwhile, lays out four cards side by side.]

[3:08]

Jeremiah: Let the record show I have placed four cards for Ms. Wednesday to view, and the cards all contain birthday messages. Two are for Darian Wednesday, two are for Winnie Wednesday.

Winnie: [voice shaking] My dad is gone. How could he send me birthday cards?

Jeremiah: I'm wondering the same, Ms. Wednesday. I'm also wondering what these mean. To what framed photo is your dad referring in this card? And why write the birthday year so strangely? Happy one dash three dash T H birthday?

Winnie: You'll have to ask my dad what it means because . . . well, it's all one big cipher to me. [She slouches back in her chair and gazes left.]

[3:47]

Jeremiah: Come now, Ms. Wednesday. These were in your pocket at the museum. Why have birthday cards that are meaningless?

Winnie: Because . . . [She swallows.] The . . . well, a
person gave them to me.

Jeremiah: And you took them from this [makes air
quotes] person? Willingly?

Winnie: I mean, they offered the cards to me, and
yeah. I . . . didn't know what was going on, okay? I
went to that gallery because I was . . . I was following some messages. [sighs, possibly with relief] And
the messages led me to the gallery, where a person met
me who had these cards.

Jeremiah: And *that* person cast the *sagitte aurea*
spell?

Winnie: No. They protected me from it. They wore a
hound mask. [Her eyebrows lift, as if surprised.]

Jeremiah: A hound mask? Because it was a costume
party?

Winnie: Don't pretend you don't know what a hound mask
means.

Jeremiah: In other words, *you* know what a hound mask
means.

[He smiles and withdraws a photograph from the folder.]

[4:32]

Just like these hound masks from two bodies in the
forest.

[Winnie coughs. Then pulls off her glasses and sets
them on the table.]

[4:47]

Jeremiah: Let the record show the photograph is of
two corpses in the forest, their bodies burned beyond
recognition. They each wear a mostly melted hound mask
like Diana *canés* wear. Now, Ms. Wednesday, I am going
to guess by your reaction that you know who these Dianas are. That, in fact, you were with them when they
died.

[Winnie shakes her head.]

Jeremiah: You can protest all you want, but I know you
were there [taps photograph] because of . . . oh, where
is it. [He searches the folder while still speaking.]

You see, we found signs of a changeling on the morning
we found the dead bodies. But the changeling itself
was missing. Until the *following* night, when the Thursday hunters found it and killed it. [He slides a second
photograph onto the table.]

[Winnie gags. Then turns away.]

[5:25]

Jeremiah: Let the record show this is a photograph
of a dead young woman who looks exactly like Winnie
Wednesday, except for the telltale claws that indicate
it's actually a changeling. So what happened that
night, Ms. Wednesday? Did you kill your fellow Dianas,
and then decide to attack the old museum too?

Winnie: [voice weak] I didn't attack the old museum.
You know I didn't.

Jeremiah: I don't know anything, actually, because
whenever I press you for answers, you fill the air
with trivia. Which is—I can only assume—a tactic your
mother taught you. But you know what, Ms. Wednesday? I
have time. I have lots and lots of time.

[Jeremiah picks up his coffee mug and sits back in his
chair. He takes several sips, watching Winnie. She sits
slumped in her own chair.]

[7:20]

Jeremiah: I have witnesses too, Ms. Wednesday, of you
and your friend Jay Friday. So if I want, I can lock you
up forever—and have him killed as soon as we find him.

[Winnie sighs. Then rests her forehead on the table.]

Jeremiah: I won't do that yet though. Instead, I'll
wait. Because there's obviously a network of Dianas
here in Hemlock Falls, and I intend to find out who
they are. Each and every one of them. Let the record
show I am now withdrawing a book from the folder. Do
you know what this is, Ms. Wednesday?

[Winnie looks up as Jeremiah places a paperback book
on the table.]

[7:56]

Jeremiah: This is called *Shooting Stars: Identifying
Asteroids, Comets, and Meteors*. Do you recognize it?

Winnie: [sighs again] Yeah. It was in Professor Samuel's office.

Jeremiah: So you know what he was.

Winnie: I do, although not for the reason you're implying. And *you* know this already. Just as *I* know you went to Samuel's office to destroy evidence.

Jeremiah: I'm sorry, to do what now?

Winnie: Why else would you go there?

Jeremiah: Because it took us almost a full week to ID his body, and we were hoping to find evidence of other Dianas. This is all we found though. Now tell me: What's important about this page? For the recording, I am opening to page 273, where the spine is split and worn. It's a page dedicated to the Lyrids, a meteor shower that happens each April.

[Winnie swallows and stares at the book.]

[8:33]

Jeremiah: Well, Ms. Wednesday?

Winnie: I don't know. It's April now, *Jeremiah*, so I guess the professor was enjoying the meteors.

[Jeremiah frowns.]

Jeremiah: So these constellations, Lyra and Hercules, mean nothing to you?

Winnie: Obviously not. I didn't even know they were constellations until right now.

Jeremiah: Sure you didn't.

[He glances at his watch. Then closes the book and returns it to the folder.]

[9:18]

Jeremiah: If you want to play coy, Ms. Wednesday, then that's fine. I'm not going to torture you for answers. I'll give you time to think over everything we've covered, and when I come back tonight, I expect you'll have more to say. Now, if you'll excuse me, I have an All-Terrain 10K to win. In the name of scorpion pride, "we hold the line."

[Jeremiah returns the photographs and birthday cards to the folder before him. He stacks it all neatly, then pushes to his feet.]

[9:49]

Jeremiah: Interview concluded at 6:55—

Winnie: [voice muffled by table] I'm the Midnight Crown. [She lifts her head.] People will wonder where I am.

Jeremiah: No, Ms. Wednesday. I really don't think they will.

[End 10:00]

32

I f Jeremiah Tuesday thinks he is torturing Winnie, then he has no idea how good she is at torturing herself. He leaves her alone in the interrogation room with nothing but water and silence to keep her company, and she gets a *great* head start on self-inflicted wounds. For hours, she has nothing else to do but go over what happened at the old museum.

A thousand times. A thousand thousand. *What happened at the old museum? Where did it all go wrong?*

There was Jay, as a human. *I love you. I'm sorry.*

Then there was Jay as a wolf while the Whisperer frothed with hunger.

Then there were her friends, who, logically, Winnie knows were only trying to protect her. Were only trying to get her away from a monstrous, unstoppable whirlwind that they finally understood was very real.

But Winnie hates them. All of them. L.A., Trevor, Katie, and yes, even Bretta. Even Emma. Even Erica. They took her away from Jay, and now Jay is gone because of it.

Maybe he isn't gone, her brain spurts every five seconds, a caricature of the first stage of grief: denial. *Maybe he isn't gone, and the Whisperer didn't destroy him.*

"Except I felt it," she tells the interrogation table. "I *felt* it."

You don't know what you felt. It might have been adrenaline.

Winnie wants it to have been adrenaline. She *wants* it to have been an awful dream she will wake up from, with the words *Trust the Pure Heart* echoing across her brain. But this isn't a dream. The *Pure Heart* echoes are real because the Whisperer briefly had a voice that spoke to Winnie.

It made music too. Somehow, impossibly, it made music. And now the song that once belonged to Jenna is the soundtrack to a scene Winnie can't stop playing in her head. Every time she finishes imagining each moment, each beat at the old museum, from Casey Tuesday in his Dracula costume to the kiss against the column with Jay, to the Diana hound in the bathroom with cards from Winnie's dad . . .

To the voice at the gallery's end that must have been the Crow . . . Then all the way through to that moment when Winnie felt Jay's life vanish.

Every time Winnie reaches The End, her brain circles back to start the track anew while Jenna's haunting song plays on.

Eventually, Winnie is escorted several hallways over to a cell with cinderblocks for walls, a squeaky cot with no blanket, and a toilet with a bare-minimum privacy screen. It's so *prison cliché,* Winnie would find it funny.

Except nothing is funny right now. She simply drops to the cot, rests her head on her knees, and drapes her hands over her neck like she's in a tornado drill. And that's definitely what this feels like: a tornado. All that's missing are the sirens.

It's like these nightmares only show up when you're around, Winnie. Mario said that to Winnie half a month ago at the dockside werewolf testing site. *Or like you've got some special power that only lets you see them.*

Well, this power sucks then, she answered. And it does. Even now when other people have seen the werewolf and the Whisperer . . .

This power sucks. Winnie wants it gone from her body, from her brain.

She has no idea how long she is in the cell like this. Only that it is enough time for her to start rubbing at another stage of grief like the scratch-off strip on a lottery ticket. *Bargaining,* the ticket reads.

What if I hadn't followed the messages? What if I hadn't asked Jay to meet me? What if I hadn't lost him in the crowd? Would he still be here?

But denial is the coin that's doing the scratching, so that still fills her skull too. *Maybe he's not gone. Maybe you didn't feel the Whisperer consuming him. Maybe he's just fine and on the run from the Tuesday scorpions.*

Clearly Jeremiah knows that Jay is a werewolf. Presumably because someone at the old museum saw Jay change and told the Tuesdays.

Repeat track. Start the scene over again.

Winnie can't hear anything in her cell. It's so well insulated, she might as well be at the earth's core. Or in outer space. Or locked inside the Whisperer.

She stands. She paces. Three times, they bring her water and crackers. Once, she pees in the ridiculous toilet.

Repeat track. Start the scene over again.

After at least three hours—maybe a hundred—she forces her brain to stop. To *STOP*. Unfortunately, the shield she flings up is more like a ramp. It doesn't block so much as deflect. Her thoughts leave the old museum, sure, but then they slide right over to her family.

Because what does it mean for Mom and Darian if Winnie is here inside a cell? If she's accused of the witchcraft her dad was framed for four years ago? Obviously Mom's chance at rejoining the hunt must now be burned to cinders. And Darian—he'll have no shot of ever becoming a councilor if he is believed, yet again, to be related to a witch.

Winnie can still remember how it felt when she was released from the interrogation room four years ago. Mom was being drilled in a room nearby; twelve-year-old Winnie was totally, *terrifyingly* alone while a scorpion in full armor marched her up, up into the dawn.

The dregs of night still clung to the sky, and it was always at those twilight moments when Winnie's eyesight was—and still is—at its worst. When the cones and rods in her eyeballs play tug-of-war and neither side can seem to win. She had also been crying that night, which meant her skull hurt. Her tear ducts ached.

And then there was Darian before her. He'd just finished with his interrogation too, and now he stood in the gravel parking lot of the Tuesday estate, cast in matutine grayscale. He held the Volvo keys in one hand. An opened bottle of water in the other.

He looked more shocked and lost than Winnie felt, dressed in his flannel pajamas. His eyes were latched onto a space ten feet in front of him—but his actual focus was galaxies away. Until he looked up. Until he saw his sister, and he changed. The same folding-chair-of-a-skeleton pulled itself into shape before Winnie, joint by joint.

He opened his arms.

Winnie ran into them.

And that hug—that ferocious, almost brutal compression that his muscles branded onto her bones . . . It was *the thing* Winnie needed in that moment. It was *the reminder* that they were a family, that they were bears, and that whatever came next, they were doing it together.

"Mom can't leave yet," he told her, still hugging. The water bottle's cheap plastic crackled against Winnie's back. "So I'll take us home."

"How long will she be here?" Winnie asked.

"I don't know." Darian pulled away, and god, he looked so much like Dad. Especially when he forced a smile and asked, "Was it just me, or did Jeremiah's breath smell like pickles?"

Winnie laughed. A broken, freeing sound. "It smelled *so* much like pickles!"

"Right? I mean, like, I enjoy a dill for snacking, but it's the middle of the night, my dude. Brush your teeth!"

Winnie doesn't mean to start crying here, four years later in this cell. But it's the only logical conclusion. Scratch too long at the lottery strip, and eventually you'll hit paper. Then flesh. Then blood vessels and muscle and bone.

She drops back onto the cot. Her head falls again between her knees.

People always act as if the stages of grief happen in clear, orderly steps. Like you really do just scratch off until you get to the next layer. But instead, it kind of happens all at once. A jumbled mass of feelings to get dumped on you. This one over here is shaped like denial. This one over here looks like rage. This one over here is bargaining and depression mashed into a single lottery ticket. And over here, we're back to rage.

For ten hot, vicious seconds, Winnie lets her tears fall. Unfettered. She will cry—for herself, for her family, for Jay—and then she will pull it together, just like Darian did four years ago.

Darian, you should have seen Jeremiah's mustache. He totally had creamer stuck on one side. I spent the whole interrogation wanting to wipe it off.

Winnie's tears stop. She lifts her head. Her glasses are on the cot beside her, dropped there as soon as she came into the room. She grabs them now. The cinderblocks sharpen. Jenna's song is elbowing back in, carrying the old museum and its ghosts along with it. *I love you. I'm sorry.* Except now, Winnie's brain is snagging on one moment: when the Whisperer seemed to say, *Pure Heart. There you are.*

Her teeth start clicking a methodical beat. A replacement for the pacing to power up her brain. *Pure Heart. There you are.* She hadn't really considered what those words might mean in each of her replays, but now she processes them like they're holes on a punch card being fed into an old computer.

Who was the Whisperer referring to? *Who* was the Pure Heart? There were only two people in that conservatory: her and Jay. And the Whisperer didn't wake up until Jay arrived.

Winnie's neurons start firing in all new directions now, a conspiracy wall forming inside her mind, complete with red circles and lines made of yarn. *The night the Whisperer chased you off the waterfall, Jay was there too. And the night Grayson died because of the Whisperer, Jay was there.*

And when Winnie and Jay went in the forest and found that granite hole, Winnie *felt* the Whisperer wake up nearby . . . And oh no, if she goes back—way, way back—to the first time she sensed the Whisperer, it was that night on her first trial. *And Jay was there.*

The only night she can't line up is the night the Whisperer killed all those vampira in the forest. But what if Jay was there then too? What would it mean if he was always nearby when the Whisperer was hunting?

Winnie's teeth stop clicking. For the first time since she got locked in here, since L.A. and Trevor, Bretta and Erica, and everyone else dragged her from the museum, she has hope. It makes no sense because nothing on her conspiracy wall would suggest Jay is still alive. Or that her family will come out of this mess unscarred. Or that Winnie has any future filled with photons ahead of her.

But for some reason, she feels a feathery spark brightening in her chest because maybe, just maybe . . .

"Okay," she murmurs to the door, a cold, metal thing across the room. In four strides, she reaches it. "I'll talk now!" she shouts, her voice rebounding off the metal into her face. Her breath ain't great, but at least it ain't pickles. "I'll talk now, but only to Isaac Tuesday!"

It is very clear that Isaac was expecting Winnie to summon him. Or if not *expecting* it, he certainly imagined this scenario, and so now he is taking steps to mitigate harm to himself. His steps look like:

- *Shutting himself alone in the interrogation room with Winnie.*
- *Leaning so far over the table that when she leans as well, they are basically touching heads.*
- *Whispering so no one outside can hear them.*
- *Turning off the usual recording device so truly,* no one *can hear them.*

"What do you want from me?" he asks. His eyes skate frantically around, and Winnie's face is so close to his she can see where he missed a spot shaving.

"You know what I want, Isaac. I need to get out of here."

He gulps. "I can't do that. As bad as those photos I took might be for my future, if I *help* you out of here . . ." He gulps again, and this time his eyes close as if he might pass out.

Winnie places a hand on his. "Hey now, Isaac. Let's stay in the present moment. Here's what's going to happen. You're going to describe the layout of this underground nest to me. Then you'll escort me back to my cell"—she waves to the door, metal and cold just like her own—"and tell whoever is in charge right now that we're finished."

"The Lead Hunter. Mason Tuesday. He's the one in charge."

"Great," Winnie says. "Tell him, then." Part of her wants to add, *And please tell his partner Ms. Morgan that I'm here because she said she's always on my side.* Except Winnie is 99 percent sure Ms. Morgan didn't have *Prison Bust* on her list of *Ways to Help Winnie.*

"Once you reach the cell, Isaac, you'll push me in, but then you won't lock the door behind you."

His eyes are still closed. He swallows loudly once more, and Winnie takes pity on him. "Hey," she murmurs. "Look at me, Isaac."

He opens his eyes.

"Am I correct in thinking most Tuesdays are up at the Olympics right now? That there's a skeleton crew down here because Jeremiah probably doesn't want anyone to notice the drama happening underground?"

Isaac nods. He's sweating now.

"So just tell me how to get out of here, what spots to avoid, and I'll do the rest. All *you* need to do is escort me, tell Mason I had nothing to say, and forget to lock the door. Super easy."

"Then . . . then we're even?"

Winnie lifts one hand. "I swear. On my mom, on my dad, on my brother: I swear, we'll be even then."

"And your friend, the one with the photos—she'll delete them?"

"Absolutely. Although . . . speaking of Erica, do you know what she told Jeremiah? Or what anyone else from the party said to him about what they saw?"

"No—I don't have access to that kind of information. Like I've said before: I'm at the bottom of the food chain in here."

"So you're a cockroach."

"Huh?"

"That's what scorpions eat."

Isaac looks sick all over again, and Winnie quickly adds: "But no one will eat you, okay?"

"Are you sure? Because right now, they're all wondering why you asked to see *me*."

"Tell them I'm friends with Katie, so I trust you."

"No one's gonna believe that."

"I promise they will, Isaac." Winnie lays her hand on his again. "Katie was at the party last night, so it'll make enough sense at casual glance. Plus, you're going to act totally clueless if anyone asks for more details. You'll shrug and say, *She just said Katie told her about me.* And they're going to believe it."

"But when they realize you've escaped—"

"I'll wait, okay? I'll wait until you've been gone a while, and then I'll make my move. Then it won't look like we coordinated anything. Now hurry, Isaac: we're losing time. Tell me how to get out of here."

I t's not that Winnie intends to lie to Isaac. As she was telling him her plan, she really did *believe* she would give him time to exit before she snuck out. Unfortunately, logistics and sheer terror make a liar out of her.

Because while Isaac walks Winnie down "prison cliché" hallways to her cell, she glimpses nary a single guard. On top of that, the one guard who first answered the door at Winnie's pounding is busy brewing herself a pot of coffee in the lounge area when Isaac marches Winnie by.

It's mind-boggling. All these terrifying Tuesdays, and yet most of them are upstairs duking it out inside the boxing rings or sprinting across a soccer field. So for a single day, their security is *so* deeply lax, a sixteen-year-old can evade it. Or, at least, Winnie sure hopes she can.

And to be fair, if she didn't have a newly assembled map imprinted on her brain of this subterranean lair, the odds of escape would be stacked against her. Plus, there's the undeniable fact that once out of the Tuesday underground, any escaping prisoner would have an entire town of nightmare hunters to contend with. So really: only a fool would try to break out of this place.

Or a Wednesday bear with literally *nothing left to lose* and absolutely *everything to gain*. If L.A. was small fry to the Crow, well, the Crow has now become small fry to the great whites circling Winnie's raft.

With a silent apology to Isaac, Winnie cracks open her door a mere minute after his departure. He's gone. Which means it's time for Winnie to get gone too, before her single guard finishes brewing coffee.

Here's what Winnie knows about the layout: all halls are arranged like a grid. No space is wasted. Which, if she were going to be nitpicky, that makes it more like a *beehive* than a scorpion's nest. But whatever. It makes busting out of here a whole *helluva* lot easier.

One left. Two straights. One right. One left. Three straights. And then on the right there will be a stairwell. Two flights up, and Winnie will reach Hangar D, where Isaac has told her assorted Tuesday vehicles are stored. Since the hangar is laid out like a mechanic's shop, she will be ejected into the grease pit used to access car underbellies—which should be empty right now, since the hangar is currently open to the public. On the opposite side of where Winnie will enter, there will be one more staircase, which she can use to join the throngs of excited Luminaries.

From there, Winnie just needs to blend in long enough to get the hell off the Tuesday estate.

The first stretch of hall goes without hiccup. Although Winnie's heart is pounding so hard, she's shocked she doesn't develop real hiccups. But by the time she reaches the end of the hall and makes her first left, her heart has settled into a more reliable rhythm. Her muscles have warmed up too. And while her full hunter senses haven't switched on, she does at least feel competent.

She's also desperate, and damned if Shakespeare wasn't right about diseases desperate being relieved by desperate appliance. (*Aren't you proud, Ms. Morgan? I remember my Dickinson and my Shakespeare! Now please don't be mad if your boyfriend gets in trouble because I'm escaping on his watch.*)

It's during the long stretch of three straights that Winnie is finally forced into evasive action. The sound of voices sends her twirling down an unplanned intersection. Then into a darkened bathroom, where she mistakes her reflection for a person and almost faints.

But it's just herself, and after puffing out a breathy, pained laugh, she forcefully looks away from the mirror. That shadowy reflection looks too much like the dead changeling from the forest.

And that dead changeling looked very, *very* much like peering ahead into a horrible future she can't avoid.

With a little shake to rattle such visions loose, Winnie makes herself use the moment wisely. First, she zips off her leather jacket. It's got a gnarly gash across the front pocket from the hellion. Then she wiggles out of her Save the Whales hoodie. That thing is familiar enough to be iconic at this point.

She turns the hoodie inside out, changing the faded green exterior into a dark, fleecy shade that melts into the bathroom's shadows. Then she slides back into her leather jacket.

Next, Winnie braids her hair, tucks it inside her collar, and finally she tows up the hood. Since she is still dressed in her Nightmare Safari gear of dark jeans and boots, she actually looks like any old hunter or Luminary about to head out for a snack.

Lastly, Winnie removes her glasses. It's not ideal, but she's also not *so* vision-impaired that she can't see where she's going. No, she won't recognize faces on the street, but given that *she* doesn't want to be recognized either . . .

This is safest.

Plus, if she could go almost her whole third trial without glasses in the *nightmare* forest. At *night.* Then navigating the scorpions' hive and the Tuesday Olympics will be easy-peasy.

Winnie gives herself a quick, blurred once-over in the dark mirror. She doesn't look like the changeling; she doesn't look like herself.

She resumes her march through the halls, getting back on track in mere seconds. At one point, a person requires her to stop and "tie" her shoe while they stride past. "Morning," they say.

Winnie only grunts in return. A second person sends her retreating deep, deep into her hoodie. But they're so focused on their phone, they don't look up. And a third person almost does corner Winnie when she hurries into the stairwell to Hangar D. They're coming downstairs dressed in full scorpion gear with their helmet hiding all features. "Hey, Asteria. Aren't you supposed to be suited up?"

Winnie coughs. Then, still coughing as if she choked on her own spit, ekes out: "Yep"—*cough, cough*—"I'm about to." She explodes up the stairs, passing the suited scorpion before they can wonder, *Wait a second, was that really Asteria?*

The two flights blur past, and then there it is: a long stretch of room that sings of *Almost Freedom.* Light cuts down at strange angles, carried in from the hangar above and shaped by vehicles parked over inspection pits. Noise simmers in, following the same odd lines. Everything smells like grease and oil, but actual grease or oil—or gasoline or tools or even a single forgotten screw—are nowhere to be seen. The Tuesdays would never allow *mess* inside one of their facilities.

Stairs lead out of each inspection pit, and shelves line the walls with tool boxes, tires, and countless bottles of various liquids.

A voice shouts behind Winnie. It is not a *nice* voice, and if she had to guess, it's the scorpion now realizing it wasn't Asteria they met and that a prisoner has gone missing from her cell.

Winnie pitches herself into a sprint. Zero to sixty miles per hour in less than 0.4 seconds. Her combat boots squeak on the spotless floor. Her weak eyes scour for the quickest path to an exit. She just needs to get out of here. She just needs to lose herself in the crowds above.

Except when she is halfway across the space, rounding a shelf of barrels, she hears another shout—this one from ahead. And there's a staticky, clicking sound too, as if radios are turning on. Turning off. As if scorpions are being sent after an escaping Wednesday in a grease pit.

Winnie is not going to make it to the exit.

But that's not the only way out of here.

She changes course, leaping onto the nearest set of stairs out of an inspection pit. There is a vehicle in the way. A Hummer, by the looks of it, but Winnie puts her odds of freedom at 50 percent going this way . . . and 0 percent if she keeps running down below.

She slithers her body sideways, spins twice like a crocodile on a riverbank, and then she's out. She's no longer *under* the vehicle (yes, a Hummer) but instead beside it and scrabbling to her feet. Two middle-aged Luminaries and a child ogle her, clearly wondering if Winnie is part of the exhibit or a visitor who ignored the *No Touching* signs slammed everywhere.

"All good here," Winnie declares as she slings herself over an exhibit guardrail. "I got the check engine light turned off, and you won't need another oil change till next year. If you feel so inclined there's a tip jar on the other side."

She smiles at the kid, who wears her hair in what are honestly the *cutest* pigtails. Then Winnie pulls her hood low, *low,* hunches her shoulders, and grapevines into the crowd.

The Tuesday estate is more army base than fancy mansion. As a clan who prioritizes strength above all else, they have approximately zero interest in flowery grounds or elegant miniature palaces. In fact, there's not much aboveground worth seeing. Just the big hangars, and a long brick building that looks like it could be a high school, a prison, or a warehouse.

This means that converting the estate into a huge sporting event, complete with fields and tracks and bleachers, is easily done every year. And always, always, on the south side of the field, a long, brightly lit, lushly appointed VIP section stands—which is where Winnie now aims.

Because the great thing about Marcia Thursday is that she is predictable. It's why Erica always had such an easy time playing games and manipulating her mom. The Marcian theorem, Winnie liked to call it, because if you input *x,* then you will always get *y.*

Which means that—despite the fact Erica was nearly killed at a party last night—Marcia will still expect her daughter to attend the Tuesday Olympics. And *that* means, if Winnie wants to find Erica, she just has to go where her own blue-papered schedule had directed her: the VIP section.

Somehow, it is early evening when Winnie exits Hangar D. The sun didn't rise today, so much as carve the sky in half like a magician with a new trick blade.

T minus fourteen hours until the Crow makes good on her threats.

The light burns low enough on the horizon to confuse Winnie's cones and rods. Every face she passes is an unrecognizable, backlit smear.

And there are *so many* unrecognizable, backlit smears. She can't believe it. Surely, *surely* the news must be out about what happened the night before. There were so many people at that party; many weren't locals.

Of course, the longer Winnie dives and weaves through the crowds, the more she realizes the wolf *is* truly out of the bag—although perhaps not the actual wolf part. Everywhere she sidles, she hears the excited tales from someone who knew someone who knew someone who had a cousin at the party. Or someone simply discussing the hotspot they heard about from Johnny Saturday on the news.

Darkness, darkness, light, Winnie thinks as she tries to row her dinghy ever closer to the VIP area of the sports field. There is no greater display of that Luminaries juxtaposition than right now: many of the society's youths almost died, so let's savor the fact that they didn't by sprinting for trophies.

And now that Winnie is really honed in, there's no missing the *over* brightness of it all that isn't simply caused by a brutal sunset. People are dressed in their clan colors, laughing and clapping and cheering and shoveling in hot dogs or funnel cakes like they might never eat again. Because . . . well, here in the Luminaries' world, they might not.

Winnie thinks of photons.

She thinks of the bathypelagic zone.

She also thinks of scorpions, since there are several, fully armored, floating through the crowds in search of Winnie. Given that she stands out almost as much as they do, she makes it her first order of business to sneak into the 10K All-Terrain Race registration tent—now closed, of course, since the run finished hours ago—and steal a new shirt. She then uses a rubber band holding bibs together to pull her hair into a tight, borderline painful bun over which she places a stolen All-Terrain Race baseball cap. Lastly, she finds a tub of red body paint (*scorpion pride!*) and slathers it all over her face and hands.

For almost thirty seconds, once her new disguise is in place, she stands there pinned down by indecision. *Keep the hoodie and jacket? Or leave them? Keep or leave? Keep or leave?*

She decides to leave—although it causes her actual pain to do so. She has had that hoodie for six years, and the leather jacket is one of the most special birthday gifts she has ever received. But Winnie can't be stupid. She can't let sentimentality get in her way. So she shoves the clothes under a table, sets her jaw, and once more braves the Olympics.

Cheers from the current event (soccer, she thinks) are loud enough to smash out all others. The people are so tightly packed too, that Winnie eventually *does* have to put on her glasses just to locate gaps for wriggling through.

At last, though, she reaches the edge of the cordoned-off VIP seating area.

The first thing Winnie notices is that Darian isn't here. This startles her. Then terrifies her. It makes the four-year-old hug branded on her bones physically sear. As if her skeleton wants to crawl out of her body and search for the brother that *should* be at Dryden's side.

She will never forgive herself if Darian is underground right now. If Mom is too, and Winnie just escaped without finding them. Without even *searching*.

The next thing Winnie notices is that Jeremiah Tuesday *is* here, clean and dressed in his usual fatigues. No sign of the morning All-Terrain Race on his body—or of the interrogation in his nest from before that. He smiles and laughs, chatting with a Vtornik Winnie vaguely recognizes from the Nightmare Safari.

The Crow, however, is as absent as Darian. Which doesn't make any sense. That woman is pulling Jeremiah's strings, right? So she should be here, twirling her mustache and laughing evilly. Or maybe even actively searching for Winnie with her magic . . .

Except now that Winnie considers it, now that she gnaws at her lip and gazes at Jeremiah's oblivious, chuckling face, what was it Signora Martedì said on the Ferris wheel? When Winnie asked for records of when her dad disappeared?

Cannot or will not? Winnie replied.

The Crow never answered, but what if . . . what if the answer was *cannot* because Jeremiah doesn't know what Martedì is? He said in the interrogation, *There's obviously a network of Dianas here in Hemlock Falls, and I intend to find out who they are. Each and every one of them.*

If Jeremiah really doesn't know, if the scorpions really *aren't* the tools of Signora Martedì . . . then that changes things, doesn't it? Winnie isn't sure *what* it changes, but something.

As Winnie scans more faces, searching for Erica, her gaze finds L.A. Saturday instead, dressed in a gorgeous purple gown. On her head is the Midnight Crown, but rather than look happy that she finally has what she wants, she looks trapped in that nightmare gallery of the old museum.

She looks, in fact, like Winnie must have in the Tuesday cell, when last night's events looped and re-looped across her brain.

L.A. saw what Jay turned into.

She saw, yet all she could say to Winnie before the Tuesdays took Winnie away was: "How did I never realize what he was going through?"

Yeah, Louisa Anne. Winnie can totally relate; she too wonders how for four years, she never saw what Jay was going through.

Right now, though, Winnie's focus is on Erica, whom she finally finds slumped in a chair beside her mom. Marcia, hilariously, looks less like a sports fan and more like a person cosplaying one, complete with a foam finger on one hand, a foam bell on the other, and so much maroon-and-silver gear, her skin looks that color. Actually no, her skin *is* maroon because she has put on body paint too.

Wow, Marcia. Way to take it to eleven.

Erica, meanwhile, is dressed in a black outfit not so different from yesterday's. Minus the cat ears and tail. Actually, maybe it *is* the same outfit—and maybe Erica hasn't slept any more than Winnie has.

Yet *x* always leads to *y,* and here Erica is anyway. Her dad too, mingling with less blatant Thursday spirit in a group of Jueves visitors from Mexico—or at least, Winnie thinks that's who they are because she's pretty sure she recognizes Erica's uncle in the group.

With very little finesse, Winnie scoots right up to her friend—opposite side of Marcia, of course—and says, "Hey."

Erica glares at her, clearly planning to laser-beam whomever would dare disturb her. But when she takes in Winnie's getup, then fastens on Winnie's face, her eyebrows rocket skyward.

"We can't talk here," Winnie adds before Erica can say something loud or dangerous or conspicuous.

But of course, she's not giving her friend enough credit. "Duh," Erica replies. "Meet me at the bathrooms." A dip of her head toward an array of fancy portable toilets nearby. Then she swivels away as if Winnie really is beneath her notice.

Winnie follows the command, and in seconds, she and Erica are ensconced behind a toilet. The crowds, meanwhile, are absolutely losing their minds because—based on the *especially* loud cheers for Friday—the Friday clan must be dominating the Tuesdays on the pitch.

"They let you out?" Erica has to yell to be heard.

And Winnie's snort definitely isn't audible. She points at her face paint. "Does this look like someone who got let out?"

Now Erica's jaw sags. "You're on the *lam*? Holy crap, Winnie. How did you break free?"

"Long story." Winnie shakes her head. "And you're the only person I know who can help me."

Erica rears back—and Winnie cringes. Not because of Erica but because her whole body is vibrating with a growing roar of *Friday, Friday, Friday!*

It makes her think of Jay.

It makes her think of the Whisperer.

"I'm sorry, E," she continues. "Things are bad—"

"No shit."

"And I need a ride out of here. Is your car here and can I have the keys? If anyone asks, just say I stole it."

"My car isn't here—" Erica breaks off as a cheer erupts that could literally puncture eardrums. The toilets sway, and Erica leans close enough to shout right into Winnie's ear: "My car isn't here. But meet me at my mom's car. It's in the VIP lot, black Lexus with the bell on the windshield. I'll get us out of here."

"Us?" Winnie shouts back.

And Erica smiles.

C H A P T E R

34

The official story is that you got hurt last night at the hotspot and you're a hero who has graciously handed your crown to L.A." This is the first thing Erica says once she hits the unlock button on the Lexus—which Winnie now recognizes as her ride to the Saturday breakfast a few days ago.

"Uh, trunk for you!" Erica snaps, when Winnie aims for the passenger seat. "You're covered in paint. Also, what if people see me driving you out of here?"

Both points are good ones, so Winnie crawls into the trunk space as soon as the door is wide enough to fit through. Then she lies on her back and folds up her legs.

God, she's tired.

In seconds, Erica is backing them out and resuming her story—though louder now, to be heard over the crunching gravel and car engine. "Only me, L.A., Trevor, and Bretta really saw that Tuesdays took you, not Monday ambulances. And . . . well, we've all been threatened with cell time if we say a word during the Masquerade."

What about after the Masquerade? Can you blab then? Winnie doesn't ask this. "What about my mom? Or Darian? Do you know where they are?"

"No." Winnie can hear the pity in Erica's voice. "I haven't seen either of them all day—oh *shit!* They've got a blockade at the exit, Winnie. There are scorpions raising their hands for me to stop."

Winnie screws her eyes shut. "Stop then, E. When they find me, act like you didn't know I was in here." *Maybe this time I can look for Mom and Darian before I escape.*

Erica does not stop. Instead, the SUV lurches. So hard, inertia yanks Winnie back against the door. She hears gravel spray like firecrackers. Then she hears furious shouts and yelps rebound off the SUV.

Erica whoops: *"HELL YEAH."*

And Winnie shoots up to a seated position, jaw to her sternum as she gapes out the tinted window at four scorpions chasing them down the road. One is also bellowing into a radio.

"They're going to come after us!"

"Yep!" Erica grins into the rearview mirror. Her eyes look slightly unhinged; her energy leans toward *chaotic neutral.* "But you know what they say about Thursdays!"

"Your clan is too uptight?"

"Never without a plan!" Erica bangs both hands against the steering wheel. "And believe it or not, Winona, I actually have a plan for a day like today!"

"When Tuesdays would chase you through Hemlock Falls?" Winnie doesn't mean to sound screechy, but she definitely sounds screechy. "Because there is a Hummer pulling out of the estate now!"

Erica laughs, also a screechy sound, except it's less *panicked bear* and more *overzealous bell.* "Not quite that, but trust me: I got this."

Winnie wants to trust Erica. She *really* wants to trust Erica—especially because she has no seat belt on and they are currently accelerating to warp speed on a residential road. Which is basically what *all* roads in Hemlock Falls are. The roads are also all peppered with approximately three billion stop signs.

One of which Erica blows right through. *Hi, Monday estate! Bye, Monday estate!*

Well, at this point, Winnie supposes she has no reason to remain in the trunk. They are both fugitives now. *Agents Wednesday and Thursday on the run.* She clambers over the seat into the back seat. "They're still behind us."

"I can see that. But it's just one Hummer."

"For now." Winnie feels the lock on her seat belt engage. Oh, and there goes another stop sign—with a car in the intersection too.

Who is, understandably, laying on the horn.

"Where exactly are you taking us?" Winnie demands, grabbing the oh-shit bar. She's seated diagonally behind Erica, and if she weren't already *totally alarmed* by everything going on, the excited flush currently rising up Erica's cheeks would definitely worry her.

Erica is having fun right now.

Like a lot of fun.

Winnie adjusts *chaotic neutral* to *chaotic evil*.

"We're going here," Erica replies right as she slams on the brakes and executes the kind of turn Winnie thought was only possible in a Fast & Furious film. The tires scream. The SUV drifts, drifts, drifts. *Vrrrooom.* And now they're revving into the Sunday estate. Erica hurtles them right up to the front of the school. "We're going inside. Follow me!"

Given that the Tuesday Hummer is also rushing into the parking lot, Winnie sees literally no alternative. Aside from arrest, of course. So she chases Erica out of the Lexus, and into the school—which appears to be open for Sunday hunter training.

As the double doors swing shut behind them, she spares a glance backward.

Okay, three more Tuesday Hummers are zooming into the parking lot. Awesome.

Fortunately, the main hall is fully lit and fully empty. Erica's boots squeak; Winnie's too. And if Winnie thought the stares on the clan banners were disapproving on Sunday morning . . . well, ha. *Ha.* She's pretty sure the Wednesday bear would climb down and tackle Winnie right now if it could. And that Tuesday scorpion definitely wants to eat her.

At the locker room, Erica slings inside. "Grab your training gear," she orders. "You look like you were in the prom scene from *Carrie.*"

This reference flies past Winnie, but she obeys all the same, and in seconds, she and Erica are sprinting onward again. Erica has a black duffel; she crams Winnie's clean clothes inside. Except now, rather than lead Winnie toward the back door and the shadowy freedom of encroaching night, Erica pulls Winnie toward Coach Rosa's office. It's just past the showers, right before the door to the obstacle course.

The window beside the door is dark; Rosa is at hunter training, of course.

Erica tries the knob. It resists, but that doesn't slow her. She digs out a single key from the duffel she had in her locker, and with practiced ease, she slides the key in. This time, the knob turns. This time, she shoulders in easily before tugging Winnie along.

Once they're both in the dark, Erica locks the door. And in case this wasn't already too much for Winnie's brain to keep up with—although yes . . . she's starting to remember how *comfortable* Erica was sneaking into the school on Sunday—Erica is now hissing, "Come on, Winnie. Come *on*."

"Where?" Winnie asks. It's a room with only one door! No. Wait. She spies a second, much tinier door in the room's corner, tucked next to a filing cabinet. It's the kind of door that would block a crawl space, and honestly, Winnie would never have noticed it if not for Erica. It's the same boring beige as the wall.

But now Erica is opening the hatch with the key she used to access the office, and . . . now she's crawling into total darkness. "Come *on*," she snarls again, and though Winnie would really like to ask, *WHERE DOES THAT GO, THANK YOU?!* she also understands the stakes of her situation. Right now, she is wanted by the Tuesdays for witchcraft *and* breaking out of their bunker.

It's safe to assume that Tuesdays are pouring into the school. They will search everywhere, including this office. And if they are actually good at their jobs (unlike poor Isaac), they will also circle behind the school to close off locker room exits.

In other words, Winnie is trapped and the only way out is through that hatch.

So Winnie gets on her hands and knees and starts crawling. She shuts the hatch behind her with an awkward hook of her heel on the knob. All light falls away. And Winnie's rods freak out. If there are any photons here, her eyes sure aren't finding them.

Until a light flips on—small. Targeted. Winnie recoils. Her cones go haywire.

"Sorry," Erica whispers. "There's a ladder straight ahead. We've got to go down."

"To where?"

"Pump room," she replies before chomping onto her phone with her teeth and continuing to crawl. Her light, now aimed straight down, doesn't offer much guidance to Winnie's eyes. Still, it's so much better than the darkness, she could cry from relief. Or maybe that's stress that makes her eyes prickle. Or exhaustion. Or the adrenaline that has been pumping in her veins since she fled her Tuesday cell.

The light ricochets. Erica whispers, "Here's the ladder." Then Winnie hears a metallic clanging replace the previous rustle of clothing.

Moments later, Winnie reaches the ladder too. *Pump room,* she thinks, remembering what Jay said when he found her in the steam two days ago. He offered to sneak her out of class this way.

"What if scorpions check where we're going?" They must know the pump room exists.

"They won't." Erica's voice is breathy from exertion. Or perhaps elation.

"How do you know?"

"*Because,* Winona. Remember what I said about having a plan?"

"Hard to forget, given that I'm currently being dragged through it like tin cans on a *just-married* car. But you know what would help, E? If you *told* me the plan. And then explained why you have one in the first place."

"Patience, please." Erica's voice sounds different now. More solid, like the walls have changed shape around her.

Which they have, because now Winnie has also reached the ladder's end and the pump room spans before her, lit only by Erica's swinging flashlight. Pipes stretch and loop, connecting vats and heaters in a complex embroidery of copper and steel.

"This way," Erica murmurs, hefting the duffel onto her shoulder. "And *yes,* Winona. Before you nag me again: once upon a time, I became a Diana, and the first thing they taught me was to make sure I hid my stuff in weird places."

Once upon a time, I became a Diana, and the first thing they taught me was to make sure I hid my stuff in weird places. Places that have absolutely nothing to do with me, so if anyone ever finds my mask or—god forbid—my source, they won't have any way of tracking it back to me.

My mask was easy to hide because it's flimsy and foldable. I put it in a Ziploc, put that Ziploc in another, and finally hid it inside a toilet tank on the second floor of the history library.

No, Winnie, that isn't gross. The water in a toilet tank is clean, okay?

As for my source, that was riskier to hide. Because unfortunately, when hiding a source, you need it to be contained by running water—yes, I know. I thought of the toilet tank trick again, but when you put a source in its dampener, it's too big for a tank.

And the source has to be in the dampener if you're going to do magic with it. It not only prevents Luminaries from finding the source, but it also preserves the magic within. Which, I mean . . . I was definitely trying to do magic, even if I wasn't really succeeding.

Yeah, that means I was burying my source in the forest regularly to absorb spirit magic.

How long does it take to absorb? Only a week to charge it fully, though if you're a really experienced Diana, you can charge it faster than that, by finding the most powerful spots in the forest to go to. But I never got good at sensing those areas. And I needed to be able to access my source in the forest easily, so I buried it not far from the southeasternmost tip. It was walking distance from the Thursday estate.

Anyway, when it's not buried, a source needs to be somewhere easy to get to with lots of running water. And I was actually in the hot room during Coach Rosa's class when I suddenly realized there must be pumps that feed into the underground maze. All that steam would need running water, right? And once I figured out where the plumbing was—by following Rosa one day after class—it wasn't hard to actually steal Rosa's key and slip inside.

I spent almost a full two hours exploring this space that day. Because I mean, look at this! It's huge in here. Not only does it feed the hot room, but also the training lake and the pool. And then the entire school too, and the Sunday library. There's one spot, though, that no one knows about. Like, it's so forgotten there are three water heaters blocking it, and the only way someone would know about it is if they study old blueprints.

So how did I find it?

Because Jenna found it first.

35

Dampener: A metal tin filled with moss used to hide a Diana's source from Luminary detection and to slow the drain of collected spirit power over time. Often a fish hook is added to the moss to act as a "vent," since power sometimes drains in explosive spurts instead of steady drips.

There are some places that are so profoundly private, other people are never meant to find them. Secret corners where children play unwatched by adult eyes. Forgotten tombs meant only for spirits of the dead. The bathypelagic depths of the ocean.

And hidden rooms built for witchcraft.

Which is what greets Winnie after she wedges herself into a liminal space the original plumbers had no use for, so they blocked it off with three massive water heaters that radiate warmth like a dracon puffing fire.

"I never would have looked here," Erica explains, "if not for one line in Jenna's diary about *my secret place behind the three.* I didn't know what that meant at all until I was down here, saw three tanks, and that line came back to me. I poked around, and . . ."

"And," Winnie agrees because *and* is all there is to describe this spot, away from prying eyes. A place to do magic no one can sense. A place for an artist soul who needs to get away from it all.

It's not that Winnie feels safe here—she doesn't. The only things separating this random ten-foot-by-ten-foot area are three brutally hot water

heaters, so while Erica is right that it's almost impossible to get here without prior knowledge . . .

It's still not an *actual* room with an *actual* door that they can lock
against approaching scorpions. Plus, it wouldn't surprise Winnie if Jeremiah does dig up blueprints once Winnie and Erica aren't found on the
Sunday grounds.

Still, despite that inherent weakness, there is a sense that this place is
separate from the outside world. Like time has stopped and history is moving on without her. Only subterranean silence will ever exist here.

It even smells like Jenna, like the summer rain perfume she used to
wear.

Much like the old cabin on the Thursday estate, there is a shelf and folding chair in one corner. A fan too, which is probably necessary if the heat
off the water tanks gets too intense. A simple pink-and-white quilt has
been laid over the floor like a rug, and there's a second blanket that hangs
behind the heaters in a crude semblance of a curtain.

Erica lowers that blanket now, making sure there are no gaps around the
edges to let out light or sound. Then she moves to the shelf where a lamp
awaits. She flips it on. A warm glow unfolds, rendering the phone's sharp
light unnecessary.

"Grayson came here," Winnie says. "He must have come here."

Erica blinks from her spot crouched beside the shelf and lamp. "Why do
you say that?"

"Because Jay knew about the pump room," Winnie explains. "And he
learned about it from Grayson, who showed it to him a few years ago. That
can't just be coincidence."

"Oh." Erica frowns. Her cheeks are scarlet from the race to get here,
and the slightly crazed glint that had filled her russet eyes now snuffs out
beneath a grieving gust.

And Winnie understands that grief. She has been staring it in the face
ever since the old museum. Ever since she watched Jay turn to face the
Whisperer. *I love you. I'm sorry.*

"Jay," she begins . . . but then nothing else comes.

"I know," Erica replies. She carefully, thoughtfully eases her black duffel
to the concrete floor. "I saw him transform. Other people did too. He . . .
turned into a nightmare. And then the Whisperer was there."

"Did you see what . . ." Winnie can't finish that question. *What happened next?*

But Erica understands. "No. None of us did. We talked about it after—me, L.A., Trevor, Katie, and the twins. Everyone saw Jay turn into a wolf, but no one saw what came next."

Winnie swallows. Shoves at her glasses, which have all sorts of red body paint smeared across them. "I don't think he's dead."

"Okay."

Winnie pretends she doesn't hear the pity. "He's *not* dead, Erica."

"Okay," Erica repeats, and this time, she turns away to crouch beside her bookcase. After pulling off binders with handwritten labels like *Guitar Chords* or *Original Songs,* she gets to a false back identical to the one on the bookcase in the old cabin. She pries it off . . .

To reveal a square, metal tin.

Winnie knows right away what it is. She knows because she has seen a dampener before. After all, it was the first item that Dad's map led her to: Jenna's dampener hidden in a stream in the forest. But that dampener had been underwater for many years. The cookie tin holding the moss was dented and dinged, and the moss itself immediately began to rot upon exposure to air.

The dampener that Erica holds is spotless and gleaming. It's a simple silver tin—square, where Jenna's had been round—and there's no denting, no rusting, no damage.

Without thinking, Winnie reaches up and grips her locket. "That's your source, isn't it."

"Yeah," Erica replies, and there's a familiar hardness glazing onto her posture. A lowering of the castle portcullis because—as Winnie is now starting to recognize—Erica is afraid of what Winnie might do next.

But Erica shouldn't be afraid. If she thinks a source is going to scare Winnie off, then she really hasn't been paying attention these past few days.

Winnie shuffles forward. Then sinks cross-legged onto the middle of the blanket. "So how does it work? Does it have magic inside?"

Erica thaws slightly. "Yeah, there's magic. My source was charging up until the night . . . well, the night the Dianas went after Jay."

Right. *That* night, almost two weeks ago. The same night Winnie finally realized what Jay really was—and what Erica really was. *Anyone could be a Diana. A Diana could be anyone.*

"So how long can you keep it here?" Winnie asks because she'd rather think about magic than about Jay and all the ways she has failed him. "How long before all the stored power drains away?"

"A few months. Even a few years, if it's preserved in the right way." She strides toward Winnie and drops down before her. It's the same pose they shared in the cabin, when they had a sheet hung over them and Winnie thought the Crow was the greatest threat before them.

T minus "I don't know if I care anymore."

Erica opens her dampener. Static undulates outward, plucking at the hairs on Winnie's arms, neck, face. They feel tugged by a thousand tweezers. Then the sensation passes, and Winnie is left staring at a Diana source.

It's the first source she has ever seen, yet not the first time she has seen this particular sphere of obsidian that once lived beside the Thursday family piano.

Part of Winnie wants to laugh. *You took Marcia's crystal after all. Amazing.* Another part wants to recoil. *A source. This is dangerous, run away.*

But try as she might, she can't quite reach the appropriate feelings. There is simply too much happening. Inside of her, outside of her, in concentric shock waves around Hemlock Falls. So Winnie stares at Erica instead and lets her fumble to find her own emotions.

"I was so . . . angry when Jenna died." Erica slides her hands beneath the obsidian. It rests atop a nest of moss, but unlike Jenna's dampener, there is no fish hook nearby to vent power.

Which, Winnie supposes makes sense, given that Erica is not a strong Diana.

"Why was Jenna on her second trial?" Erica continues. "*Why* did she go out there, into the forest, if all she wanted was to leave the Luminaries and leave Hemlock Falls?"

The source glisters, veins of gray sliding through it. Winnie thinks again of bioluminescence. She thinks again of secret places where adults can't watch. And she thinks of those words from long ago that she and Erica uttered as girls in the cabin: *Sumus ūnus in somnō et somniīs.*

"The Saturdays were managing the trial that night." Erica's voice is a detached confessional, as if she is narrating one of her own letters. *Yours sincerely, Erica Antonia Thursday.* "So I never understood why it was the Tuesday clan who brought my family the news about Jenna's death. Yes, Tuesdays eventually contain a kill site, but shouldn't that come later? It was the Saturdays who must have found her first.

"It was only later, when I found Jenna's spell . . . Well, someone else must have realized what she was. And Dianas are always the domain of the Lambda scorpions." Here Erica pauses long enough to withdraw a torn piece of notebook paper from the dampener. Its blue and red lines have faded to teal and pink, as has the ink scrawled across it.

"Is this it?" Winnie asks. "The spell?"

Erica nods. She doesn't offer it to Winnie. Instead, she holds the spell in one hand, her source in the other. Lady Justice with her scales in perfect balance.

"You told us you got rid of it."

Erica winces. "I know. And I'm sorry I lied. I did *mean* to destroy it, four years ago. But I . . . I just couldn't in the end. Jenna took the risk of leaving it in her diary—where anyone could find it. And I just . . . well, it felt like maybe that was the point. Like maybe she *wanted* me to uncover it."

"And do what with it? What's the spell for?"

"I don't know."

"You haven't asked the other Dianas?"

Erica's head shakes. Then she blinks, as if tears are stinging. "I haven't asked them. I'm afraid to. Because I still don't know how Jenna died, you know? My family never saw a body before Jenna was cremated. Was it really a vampira horde that killed her? Or did Tuesdays find out what she was and finish her off? Or . . ."

"Or did the Dianas kill her?" Winnie fills in, and she thinks back to what Signora Martedì told her—that a spell killed Jenna. And that the spell is still bound to her source. *Maybe this is the spell. Maybe this is what created the Whisperer.*

But Winnie can't say this to Erica any more than she can suddenly say, *The Crow is a powerful Tuesday!*

Erica's fingers tighten on the paper. "All I really know is that this spell, whatever it is, is an important one. We're told never to write spells down. We learn them like songs instead, so that no one can ever take them from us." She laughs here, an almost hateful sound. "Remember those blisters you saw on my fingers?" She makes jazz hands. "They *were* from a guitar because I was trying to memorize spells by giving them tunes."

"And that one?" Winnie points at the spell. "Does it have a tune?"

Erica frowns. "If it does, I don't know it."

Winnie would bet *she* knows it. Because there's only one song it can be, right? *The* song that haunted her beneath the waves of the waterfall—the one she thought saved her while hypothermia crushed in. She must have had it wrong; it wasn't Jenna's ghost protecting her underwater. It was the Whisperer, still hunting even as water and cold dragged Winnie down.

And it's the same song that has now dragged Jay down too.

"I don't know what the spell does," Erica continues. "What few books there are in the library on Dianas sure don't mention the *Incantamentum Purum Cor.* And until I have an answer—I'm afraid to even make up a melody of my own."

Winnie swallows. Then folds forward, her ribs bowing down into her stomach. She wants to tell Erica everything. Never has she wanted it more. *I know the song. I know how Jenna died. I don't understand why, but Erica, I have at least a few answers for you.*

But of course Winnie can't grit any of those thoughts past her circling-words spell. As soon as she opens her mouth and tries, she feels the Compendium awakening instead.

Erica watches Winnie, her eyelids lowered to half-mast. Her nostrils flaring with something that is almost tipping toward rage. "I'm sorry I haven't found a way to break that spell on you. You have no idea how sorry, Winnie."

It's fine, Winnie wants to respond. *I'm sorry too.* But the words won't come—and now that she considers it, there's a weird feeling tickling at the back of her neck. A shuddery sensation that makes her think of a CD of her dad's that had overtone chanting. The recorded monks were able to manipulate their vocal tracts to create more than one pitch at a time.

Here is Erica's apology, says one pitch. *And now here is something else too.*

Erica lowers her arms. After easing her source back onto its nest of moss, she tenderly rests the spell above it. The paper is clearly precious to her—and understandably so. That spell and a locket with a stain on it are all she has left of her sister.

Winnie blinks. Sits taller. All thoughts of overtone chanting have fled now. *A locket with a stain on it.* "Show me your locket," she blurts, and with as little caution as Erica just used on her source, Winnie leans over the dampener.

Erica's head chickens backward, her face scrunching with surprise. But she does let Winnie tug out the locket and tip it toward the light.

"Four stars," Winnie murmurs. "For the yew tree, which symbolizes hunters or danger. Or . . ." Her eyes flick to Erica's. "Maybe it symbolizes nothing at all."

"Um, I have no idea what you're talking about right now, Winnie. Is this the circling-words spell again?"

"No." Winnie rocks back, laughing. A wheezy, pained thing fueled by too much terror, too little sleep, and days of *nothing* making sense in Hemlock Falls.

Witch, Whisperer, werewolf, Wednesday.

Mom, Dad, Grayson, Jenna.

Four stars. Yew trees. *And a rolling ball fountain that my dad built.*

"The maze," Winnie breathes. "Erica, Jenna's source is in the hedge maze on the Saturday estate."

C H A P T E R

36

Winnie wants to leave now. Immediately. Fire the starter gun and *go*. Because she knows—finally, finally—what Dad's last message was: *The source is in the yew trees.*

"He must have assumed we'd stay friends." Winnie is pacing. With her glasses off, the whole space feels like an orange-lit fever dream. "He must have assumed I would see Jenna's locket on you."

"Except Grayson had Jenna's locket four years ago."

"I know, but . . . he must have known Grayson would give it to you." Winnie imagines the Hummer at the bottom of the Little Lake, surrounded by candy. *Save the Fish. Save Grayson.*

Too late.

"And Dad must have assumed we'd then figure out the four stars on your locket."

Erica has taken off the locket, and she studies it on her palm, lips puckered to one side. With her hair askew and Winnie's vision blurred, she looks like the cat version of herself again. A thoughtful, considering cat with a splash of gold upon her paw.

Winnie shakes her head. *You're delirious. You haven't slept in a long time. Stay focused, Winnie.* "We need to go get that source."

"And then what?" Erica levels her gaze back to Winnie.

Who grinds to a halt. "What do you mean, 'then what?' The source is what you've wanted all along, isn't it? And their feathers can be ground into gray powder that is a stimulant when consumed . . . *grrrrrr.*"

Erica doesn't respond, and nothing in her posture suggests the same breathy urgency that now rattles through Winnie like live wires strapped to her fingertips.

So Winnie tries a different tack: "You said finding Jenna's source would help you figure out what happened the night she died. Isn't that right?"

"Yes. Of course it is." Erica swipes at her face, a movement Winnie has seen Antonio make a thousand times. Every instance when Marcia's nagging became too much for him. And then, just like her father, Erica also mutters, *"Ay, Dios mío."*

Her heart's not in the words, though. And her posture is like the piglet's straw house after the wolf blew it over.

"I don't understand." Winnie drops to her knees before Erica. The dampener remains open, although the folded spell covers the source below. "What's wrong?"

"Nothing." Erica shakes herself. Swipes at her face again, smearing ancient, flaked mascara in the process. "I've just been searching for so long, and . . . I don't know, Winnie. You ever want something so bad, and then you finally get it, but it's just . . ." She doesn't finish.

One second passes. Two.

Then: "What if it isn't what you think it will be?"

Winnie almost laughs at this, a guttural bark of air because that has been her literal life for the past month. Four years wanting to be a Luminary again, and yet nothing lived up to her daydreams.

But Winnie doesn't laugh. Because again, she has the sense that there are two pitches coming out of Erica's mouth. A harmonic chant she can't tease apart. A double meaning she isn't picking up on.

"Do you want to leave the source, then? Because we can pretend we never figured out where it is." What Winnie can't add is: *But if the Whisperer really is bound to that source, then finding it will protect all of Hemlock Falls.*

"No." Erica's posture chinks higher. "I want to find it. I can't just walk away. Not after so long."

At those words, Winnie thinks of Jay's song. Of the chorus: *I miss you more now. Now that it's been so long.* She pushes at her glasses. She can't think of Jay. She can't get trapped again in her loop of the old museum. She knows where Jenna's source is; there is only moving forward, following the photons down a trail her dad left four years ago. And Winnie says as much: "We have to finish what we started, E. We have to get Jenna's source."

"Yeah." Another nod. Another lift in Erica's spine. The straw house is becoming a brick one. "You're right, Winona. I know you are." She fastens the locket around her neck. An elegant movement by a Thursday who is poise through and through. "I can get us out of here," she continues, her voice picking up speed. "But I'll need a little time to get it ready."

"Get what ready?"

"A *mundanus*. For hiding." Locket in place, Erica grabs the dampener and tugs it to her crossed legs. "It's, like, one of the only spells I can do, and it won't keep us covered for long, but I think it will get us out of here."

"Okay." Winnie isn't opposed to this, but again: she wants to leave *now*. "How long will it take?"

"I have to pull together the pieces of the spell, assemble it, then place it in the source. Once that's done, I can cast it and we'll get out of here. It'll take at least an hour to assemble, so you can nap or something."

"Nap? Are you serious right now?"

"No one will find us."

Winnie chokes out a laugh. The last thing she wants to do is sleep. Seriously, if she wanted to do that, she could have done it during her many hours locked underground in the Tuesday estate.

Erica seems to realize her advice isn't being taken. She also seems annoyed by it. *I gave you a command, Winona. Now you're supposed to follow it.* "Fine," she snips. "Don't nap. Wash up instead." She motions to her duffel. "I've got baby wipes in there. And your training clothes are on top. Plus, there's a brush somewhere, which . . . you really need a brush, Winnie."

"What about paper? Do you have any paper?"

Erica's eyebrows rise. The impatience is practically rolling off her now. She is no longer a little pig trapped in a house but the wolf blowing it down.

Winnie can relate. She would *really* like to get out of here. "Paper," she repeats.

"Sure, yeah. That unlabeled binder on the shelf has paper. And there's a pen in there too. Now can you stop asking for things? I need to concentrate." Erica reaches out to grab her source as she did before, two-handed . . . Except she hesitates. Then flashes a warning glance at Winnie. "Don't watch me, okay? I'm not very good at magic, and . . . I just really don't want an audience."

Winnie flips up her hands, already rising so she can find that blank paper. "No worries, E. Pretend I'm not here. Although . . . what do I do if I hear someone coming?"

"I'm not going into a trance, Winona." Erica slips her hands under the source. "If the Tuesdays come, I'll hear it just like you. But seriously: don't worry. This place kept Jenna safe, and it'll keep us safe too."

Winnie takes Erica's advice and cleans up. She won't win any awards for freshness, but she does get the paint off her face. It also feels truly excellent to put on clean underwear, plus clean black sweatpants, a clean T-shirt, and the black zip-up hoodie she always wears during training.

Erica, having grabbed her source, has done absolutely nothing but close her eyes and concentrate. It's identical to the pose she and Winnie mimicked as kids; all that's missing is the dramatic bedsheet costume.

Okay, and the recitation of words like "eye of newt and blood of stone" or "tongue of harpy whispering home." What Winnie hears coming from Erica are the soft mutterings of a language she can't understand. She assumes Latin, but it might be Klingon for all she knows. It is with that gentle murmur behind her, rustling like spring in the forest, that Winnie finds a spot away from the heaters and leans against the wall. She folds up her knees, and with a binder on her lap, she starts to draw.

The pen is a ballpoint (the worst) and requires a few frustrated scratches to work. The paper, meanwhile, is lined, but with the blue still blue and the red still red. Not that any of that matters. What matters is the connection of pen to paper and the pressure of Winnie's hand on the binder.

First, she sketches Erica, seated like she was before, with a source in one hand and Jenna's spell in the other. She adds a blindfold because Justice is blind and neither Erica nor Winnie knows what will come next after they find Jenna's source.

Then Winnie draws her family. A crude mimicry of the old photograph that hung in their living room, and that Dad sketched in Darian's birthday cards. While Dad's drawings were faceless, Winnie adds detail. Darian, laughing over pickle breath. Mom, setting her jaw against a spell that won't defeat her.

Winnie keeps her own face featureless. No mouth, no nose, no eyes.

Justice is blind, after all.

She keeps Dad's face blank too because she has no idea what he looks like now. Is he alive? Is he nearby? Or is he long gone, replaced by a tiny person in a hound mask? *Anyone could be a Diana. A Diana could be anyone.*

Lastly, Winnie draws Jay.

She doesn't want to, and if she's honest with herself, she's afraid to even try. To *commit* his essence to paper like she did three nights ago. Because she has no idea what actually remains of the boy she loves. But once the distillation process begins, there's no stopping it. Heat sends vapor rising through the copper still, until the alcohol is separated. Then gravity pulls it down, down, spiraling it through tubing, until *drip!*

There is the finished product.

This is what Winnie saw in the old museum. Not boy, not man, not wolf, but a silhouette with shadows to writhe around him like prey engulfed by an amoeba.

I love you. I'm sorry.

Why? she wants to scream at him. *Why are you sorry when I'm the one who left you behind? Sumus ūnus in somnō et somniīs.*

Winnie blinks. She didn't think those last words; she heard them because Erica just uttered them. Static laps across the room, gentle as a hot blanket pulled fresh from a dryer, and with the faintest dusting of mist to curl out from Erica's source, still clasped in her hands.

For half a breath, that mist curls past Erica, obscuring her face like the blindfold. Then it is gone. Her eyes open. "You're watching." She blushes. "I told you not to."

"I wasn't." Winnie sets down the pen, the binder. Paper crunches as she folds it. "Just at the end, when you said those words—*Sumus ūnus in somnō et somniīs.* Katie was right? That's really how you end a spell?"

Erica nods, and with more care than she showed earlier, she slides the source back into the dampener. Jenna's spell, Winnie notices, is no longer tucked inside.

"How does it work?" she asks as Erica stands, legs wobbly. "The magic—what did you just do?"

Erica sniffs. Classic Ice Queen. "Now is not the time for Spells 101."

"Okay, give me the SparkNotes version, then."

"Give me the duffel first." Erica holds out her arms, and Winnie complies, crossing the small space in two steps. She watches as Erica tugs out a pair of black leggings, and there's no missing a shiny red pucker on the tips of Erica's fingers. Next, Erica rolls up her shirt to reveal her abdomen. "Since my mask is in a toilet tank half a mile away, I've got to make a sling."

"Why?"

"Because your source has to be on your body to use it. The closer to you, the better."

"But can't you just hold it in your hands, then?"

"Sure." *Tug.* "But judging by our wild escape to get here . . ." *Knot. Tighten. Release.* She glances at Winnie. "I figure I'm going to want both hands free."

Bilateral symmetry, Winnie thinks. "So you'll just put the source in that . . . swaddle?"

"Yep." Erica demonstrates by swooping down, fetching her source—which no longer oozes mist—and tucking it right into the leggings now wrapped around her midriff. Then she grins. "Perfect."

"Okay, but now how will you summon the hiding spell?"

"I just say the right words, and the spell will be there." She wets her lips. "Probably."

Later, Winnie will consider that word—*probably*—and wish she'd paid closer attention to it. She will wish she'd paid closer attention to lots of things Erica said, and that she'd examined the harmonic overtone too.

In the moment, though, Winnie is thinking only of Signora Martedì. Of where the woman could have hidden her source on her body. People conceal weapons all the time, so Winnie supposes it wouldn't have been hard for the signora to stash a chunk of stone or metal in her clothes.

"Anyone can put power into a source," Erica explains, tucking her shirt over the new swaddle. "You just bury your source in the forest. The *hard* part is getting the magic back out. I'm . . . not good at that part."

Again, Winnie really should be paying attention.

Again, she isn't. *If I could find the Crow's source, could I take it off her? Would that nullify her magic?*

"Imagine the mist," Erica continues, "now imagine if you could shape it into whatever you want, instead of what the spirit wants. Right now, we want be hidden. So that's what I've told the magic to do."

Winnie finally homes in on Erica again. "So that's why I saw mist when you finished? There is *actual* spirit mist inside the source?"

"Yeah. That's what *all* magic is. At its most fundamental base, it's the mist. The spirits use mist to create their dreams, and Dianas use mist to create their spells." Erica rummages in the duffel. "Is there anything in here you want to bring? Otherwise, I'm leaving it behind."

Just my sketch, Winnie thinks, *which I already have.* She shakes her head. "We're good."

"Then"—Erica smiles, a grim, almost frightening thing—"let's get moving."

37

There's a story of a Korean hunter who lived an entire night inside a swamp serpent's esophagus. When the mist appeared at dawn and scattered the serpent away, the hunter reemerged. Except he was transformed into a half man, half swamp serpent.

Winnie has never believed that story because—gastric acids that should kill you aside—why on earth would being inside a nightmare's stomach mutate someone into a half nightmare? And shouldn't the consumed hunter have been transported away with the dawn mist too?

Of course, whether or not the Korean hunter actually mutated is moot. Winnie can appreciate the moral of the story: if you can't kill a nightmare, then run the heck away. She thinks of that moral as she and Erica creep through the pump room. As the plumbing and heaters gurgle like a digestive tract ready to suck them down.

Kill or flee.

Winnie has already killed once. Would she do it again?

She has no idea what time it is outside. Midnight, dawn—it doesn't really matter. Jenna's secret corner was a time capsule; now Winnie and Erica are the contents ejected into a new age.

They reach the hot room without incident. Another small hatch leads them into a corner of the maze Winnie doesn't recognize. Then again, without the steam or any light, everything looks different. Feels different. *Breathes* different. There is only Erica's phone beaming around to guide them, and Winnie feels like she's trapped in a horror film. The kind where a monster will jump out from any one of these bleak, concrete corners filled with shadows.

Except right now, Winnie would rather face actual monsters because at least she understands nightmares. But Tuesdays? Jeremiah? They're incomprehensible.

She would also rather face nightmares than the thoughts this maze stirs inside her. She imagines she can smell bergamot and lime. She imagines Jay holding her while water sluices off them.

What happens if I change while other people are around, Win? Then what? What do I do?

You die.

He's not dead though, because Winnie won't let him be.

The gurgles of the hot room are gone now. The swamp serpent has vanished, and soon Winnie and Erica are just two hunters trying to navigate back into life. The mist can't have them. The scorpions can't either. And they will not emerge from here mutated into nightmares.

The air gets colder, sharper as they continue onward with Winnie in the lead. She thinks she hears footsteps. She definitely hears voices, which means the exit must be near. Erica snaps off her flashlight; Winnie tows her close, close, close enough to hug. "Guards, probably," she whispers. "Cast the spell, and we can sneak by."

Winnie feels Erica nod, but doesn't see it. They are once more in darkness, and although the rods in Winnie's eyes grapple and claw to find photons, so far they are coming up empty. Then she feels more than *hears* as Erica offers the words of her spell.

Static skates over Winnie, plucking at her arm hairs all over again.

And her locket, she notes, heats up. Not a scalding, violent heat, but a noticeable warmth against the spring bite nipping around them.

Winnie's glad she's still holding Erica, because now that they are enmeshed by this spell, she can't even *look* in Erica's direction. It's like her brain won't let her. Every time she tries to find her friend, her eyes get shoved aside by magnets.

Winnie sinks back into her creeping stance. She tugs Erica onward. And photons do gradually sift into her pupils. In minutes or maybe only seconds, she has hauled Erica to the stairs out of the hot room. Two days ago, she met an ambush at the bottom of these steps; now she hopes to avoid one at the top.

There are no voices, but there is a gravity ahead, a sense of movement and weight that signifies people. How many, Winnie can't guess. She just hopes she and Erica are quiet enough not to alert them.

She shouldn't have worried. It's only two scorpions framing the door in the dead of night. They are fully armored with their faces masked and guns in hand. Large, terrifying guns that Winnie knows nothing about because hunters only use firearms as a last resort—they're too loud. Too violent, even for the nightmares of the forest.

Kill or flee, she thinks again.

The two soldiers are relaxed but ready, both staring out over the surrounding forest filled with shadows. They aren't expecting their targets to creep past them with magic—which is silly, now that Winnie ponders it. Jeremiah believes Winnie is a Diana, so wouldn't he *expect* spells and sources and power?

Maybe that's why the scorpions have guns. She doesn't know why she is disturbed by this thought. She doesn't know why she has a sudden urge to cry. *Kill or flee. Kill or flee.*

Winnie releases Erica, trusting her friend to know that *straight ahead* is the best option for them until they are far enough from these scorpions to pick up the pace and run pell-mell for the Saturday estate.

Winnie creeps forward, feeling as clumsy as a pounding droll. Loud as a slathering hellion. The scorpions definitely hear her. They both shift their weight and look *exactly* where Winnie is. She dares not slow, though. Dares not see if their eyes skate off her like hers did with Erica. She moves faster, each footstep an overloud drumbeat.

And that is when it happens. That is when the spell fails them. *That* is when Winnie sees her own body suddenly burst into the night, and the two scorpions see her too. One barks out, more sound than word—but the meaning is clear: *There she is!* And the other scorpion instantly snaps up their gun. Menacing, massive, *wrong.*

Kill or flee. Kill or flee.

Kill, Erica decides, and now Winnie sees her friend is not behind her at all but standing in the doorway where the scorpions haven't noticed her yet. Horror blanches her skin as mist coils from her abdomen like tentacles on a squid. Then two arrows form and rocket outward. A smell like burning plastic cuts into Winnie's nose.

Her locket scalds instantly.

One arrow hits the guard on the right. They scream, dropping to their knees. The second hits the other guard, the one with their gun aimed and ready. The scorpion pulls the trigger, but not before the *sagitta aurea* stabs through.

Their aim goes wide. They fall, shriek, collapse.

And Erica is now sprinting toward Winnie while accidental gunshots reverberate into the night.

"I thought you only prepared one spell!" Winnie doesn't mean to shout this, but it's like the volume dial on her throat got spun up to max. "Did you *kill* them?"

"It wasn't me." Erica rushes to Winnie's side and grips her arm with iron, panicked strength. "I didn't *do* that."

"But it was your source—"

"It wasn't me!" Her dial is turned up to high too, and it's clear from the terrorized bulge in her eyes that she's telling the truth: that spell was *not* hers. Yet either way—no matter who cast it—the consequences are now dominoing around them.

A radio crackles on a fallen Tuesday. *"COME IN, LINDSAY. WHAT WAS THAT?"*

Shouts ricochet off tree trunks. *"THEY'RE THIS WAY!"*

In the timeless, hunter corner of Winnie's brain—right at the nape of the neck, where instinct spouts louder than logic—Winnie suddenly realizes they will never reach the Saturday estate on foot. Straight ahead is the obstacle course and the main building, where shapes are now charging with precise, organized force. To the left, the north, is the Sunday library, but that too is out of reach. Scorpions, scorpions, their masks glinting in the moon.

Then there it is: an answer. A way out provided by Winnie's brainstem, where reflexes exist unfiltered. "The garage," she says, and an early morning from two weeks ago jets across her prefrontal cortex, providing context for her instincts. "There are corpse-duty four-wheelers in the garage."

"Can we get to them?"

"Only one way to find out." Now Winnie is the one to grab Erica, hauling her to the right, toward a garage she *really* hopes isn't guarded. Or
locked. Or burned to the ground by golden arrows that apparently *Erica*
didn't cast.

Their feet thunder on hard earth and pine needles. There is no underbrush here; there are only trees and soldiers closing in from behind.

"It wasn't me," Erica says over gasping breaths. "It wasn't me. I didn't
cast that."

"I believe you," Winnie says. "But is there any way you *can* cast your
hiding spell again? Because . . ." She points ahead, to where lines of light
are visible, outlining four wide doors on the brick garage. A single window reveals a backlit soldier, and something about the stance—casual, but
square—clues Winnie in to who it is.

So we meet again, Jeremiah.

"Yeah. I can try to hide us again." Erica digs her heels to a stop. They are
only ten more steps from the tree line, and only thirty more steps to that
silhouette skulking in the garage. She cups her hands to her abdomen, to
where the source swells out like some messed-up baby. "Focus," she hisses
at herself. "Focus, Erica Antonia."

She sounds like Marcia. She sounds cruel and controlling.

"*Latate.*"

Nothing happens. Nothing except shouts pinging this way. Then a garage door groans, and the shadow in the window moves.

Erica tries again. "*Latate.*"

Still nothing.

"*Fuck,* Erica," she half screams at herself. "You're useless, useless—"

Winnie grabs her friend by the shoulders. "Shut up. Now." She squeezes
and stares with all her bear might into Erica's eyes. "Erica Antonia Thursday, I have missed you *so* much these last four years. More than I missed
Jay. Because you *aren't* useless. You are necessary—especially to me—and
right now, you're going to cast that spell and get us into that garage door
that's rolling open on the left. So look at me. *Look* at me."

Erica looks at Winnie. Her posture softens, away from angry wolf, away
from frightened pig or straw house, until she is simply Erica. The bell to
Winnie's bear. The T to Winnie's W. And the *witch* to Winnie's *Wednesday.*

"Say it," Winnie commands. "Say the spell."

Erica nods. *"Latate."*

Then together, just as they did all those years ago in the old cabin, they whisper, *"Sumus ūnus in somnō et somniīs."*

And there it is: the spark to fire between them. Then comes the static, the mist, the heat on Winnie's sternum. Until she is no longer visible, and Erica isn't either. They both turn, just in time to see Jeremiah Tuesday march out of the glaringly bright open door along with four faceless scorpions.

Winnie slides her hand down until she finds Erica's. She squeezes. Erica squeezes back. They set off toward the garage.

38

They can't speak because there are soldiers everywhere—and Jeremiah too, who shouts orders on every other breath. *They're here. Look for signs of magic!* Or, *Check the trees—they were just here.* Or lastly, *Get that garage door shut!*

But he's too late on the garage. Winnie and Erica might not be able to talk, but they don't need to. Their clasped hands are a tether to hint at where each girl might go before they move. Winnie leads them into the garage. Erica leads them to the four-wheeler. Then Winnie briefly pulls away to release the flatbed attached at the back.

It's loud—so loud—but there's also enough commotion outside to mask them because more scorpions are coming, enclosed in Hummers and snarling down the narrow road that leads to this garage.

People will wonder where I am. That was the last thing Winnie said to Jeremiah before he ended the interrogation. How hilarious that now *he* is the one wondering.

Winnie sneaks to the front of the vehicle, feeling her way around Erica—then feeling as Erica slides her arms around her waist and the source presses into her back, blocked by layers of clothes.

"Ready?" It's the only thing Winnie has said in minutes.

"Ready."

Two things happen simultaneously: first, Winnie revs the four-wheeler to life in rumbling shockwaves that alert every nearby scorpion that chaos is about to cut through them like a battering ram.

The second thing that happens is Erica laughs. It's bright and brilliant, and suddenly it's not just she and Winnie who are hidden, it's the entire four-wheeler too. Winnie feels the magic shiver over her. Hot mist curls around her. Her locket heats up anew. Then they are an unseeable unit barreling out of the Sunday estate toward a line of Hummers and soldiers and Jeremiah Tuesday spinning around confused.

He roars something, but Winnie is already fixing her attention on the driveway ahead. She speeds off it, avoiding the careering approach of a Hummer. And she stays off-road—that's what these vehicles are for, after all, and the smooth lawn of the Sunday swans is nothing compared to the forest.

"We're leaving tread marks!" Erica's voice stabs into Winnie's ear. "And I'm . . . I'm losing the spell!"

"Okay." Winnie doubts Erica hears her—and it doesn't really matter. The facts are what they are, and Winnie is going to adapt accordingly. They are almost to the road now; all they need to do is cross it. On the other side, directly opposite, is the Saturday estate. If Winnie can just get them to the maze, she is almost *certain* she can lose the Tuesdays.

They don't know the secret ways inside like she does. They don't know the twists and turns mapped out for Dryden. If Winnie can just *get her and Erica* that far, then everything will be okay. They'll lose the Tuesdays. They'll find Jenna's source. And then . . .

And then . . .

Witch, Wednesday, werewolf.

Trust the Pure Heart.

Hope is the thing with feathers.

Winnie's inner monologue fritzes and fries, no longer spewing out Compendium facts or Diana insights. Just random snippets from past musings and plans and fixations. Bits of scrap paper that mean nothing on their own, and that cannot be assembled into a coherent whole upon a conspiracy board.

Darkness, darkness, light.

The cause above all else.

MEETING AT THE OLD MUSEUM.

The four-wheeler hits the street. There is no traffic at this hour. The only light is from the streetlamps—and from two Hummers that have managed to turn around and give chase.

Winnie and Erica are halfway across the road when Erica's spell fails. When Winnie abruptly *sees* the four-wheeler, her arms, her hands. She thinks she hears Erica wail, *Sorry!*, but she can't be sure because more Hummers are turning. More engines are revving. Which is fine. The scorpions won't reach Winnie and Erica before Winnie and Erica reach the Saturday estate.

The topography changes. Gone is smooth asphalt, replaced by juddering cobbles—with a six-inch curb. Cursed Saturdays and their need for *over-the-top fancy.* Winnie can't escape the driveway; these wheels just aren't going to cut it.

The headlights burn brighter, illuminating every stone in the driveway. Igniting each bush and hedge and perfectly shaped tree, and revealing *absolutely* no way off this roller-coaster ride.

Black wings streak past, so fast Winnie thinks she imagines them. Except now Erica is shrieking in her ear, "THERE! WINNIE, THERE!" Winnie sees it too: a dip in the curb and a walking path that veers into manicured woods. She doesn't know that trail, but those trees sure won't let a Hummer through—and how hard can it be to navigate from there to the maze?

Winnie swerves the four-wheeler right. Cold air slices against her face. Engines boom and howl. For several fractions of a second, headlights sear into the side of her face. She thinks she hears a horn.

Then they are off the driveway and on the path. Headlights fade behind them. Trees launch up around them like bars to keep intruders out. *Or bars to keep us caged.*

"Can you see the maze?" she shouts over the engine. The four-wheeler's own small headlights, which were subsumed by the Hummers', now spray over the narrow path. *Very* narrow and very clearly meant only for walkers. A bench framed by potted roses streaks past. Then an absurd array of statues shaped like toga-wearing cupids holding golden keys. "Through the trees," Winnie adds. "Do you see the maze?"

"It's too dark, but there's a—" Erica breaks off as Winnie slams on the brakes. The path has ended and a marble gazebo now glows white before them.

Winnie doesn't bother to cut the engine. She knows where they are now, even if she's never been here. Erica seems to know too, and as they both scrabble off the four-wheeler, Erica says: "The maze is that way." She points to a lantern-lined path.

"Yeah," Winnie agrees, and though her legs are Jell-O from clenching onto the four-wheeler and her ears still quake from the engine, she staggers toward the lanterns.

One by one, the lanterns ignite. Unseen motion sensors trigger them to life, sending orange light outward. It should be beautiful. It should be an elegant display of darkness, darkness, light and everything the Luminaries stand for. Instead, it's like tens of giant arrows pointing, *RIGHT HERE! YOUR TARGETS ARE RIGHT HERE, JEREMIAH!*

Winnie and Erica start sprinting again. The lanterns stop blinking into existence. The final steps of the path grind out. Then there is the outer wall of the maze, the green of the yew hedge turned to black at this hour.

Winnie and Erica thunder inside.

Immediately, the world quiets. They are soundproofed by yew trees. The lanterns that flared behind them disappear. There is only darkness again. The air is colder in this place, as if sunlight never quite muscles in to warm the leaves, the gravel, the shadows.

"This way," Winnie says, whispering even though she doesn't need to. "Stay close."

"Duh, Winona."

Winnie smiles.

In her mind, she can see the maze as a sketch upon the family desk. It's like it's right there, like she is a child again and Dad never left. Winnie remembers wondering *why* the Saturdays needed a maze. Like, sure it seems fun, but who actually *uses* one?

Dad, it turns out.

Winnie jogs steadily onward, the map in her mind swiveling with each turn. For once, she's glad she has never had a fancy phone; she's *glad* for all the practice she's had reading maps for corpse duty; and she's *glad* that Dryden wouldn't rest until the maze was exactly as he wanted.

Complete with an ugly fountain made of purple granite.

"There," Winnie says, and she finally, finally slows.

"Oh." This is all Erica says, and there's a resonance to the word. When Winnie looks over, she finds her friend is crying. Not a bitten-back sort of cry, nor an effusive sob. Nor even the silent, stiff cry of someone who is ashamed to be seen.

These are happy tears. The kind you let loose when you finally, *finally* know you're free. When finally, *finally* the weight of an impossible task is lifted off of you.

Winnie swallows. Then fixes her glasses, which are practically falling from her nose at this point. And as her lenses slot into place, Erica crystallizes into the girl she used to be. The one who spent every Friday night with Winnie in an old cabin that smelled like cut grass.

The fountain burbles, oblivious to Tuesdays on the hunt or the source it has been holding for four years: a simple, metallic sphere that spins and rolls atop running water.

"It's genius." Erica's voice is thick with reverence. With joy. She inches closer. "I still have no idea why your dad hid Jenna's source, but . . . this was a *genius* place to do it."

Winnie doesn't disagree. Her fingers fumble her locket from her black sweatshirt. "Now what?" Her voice is so quiet, the fountain's water seems to steal it. The source seems to absorb it.

To think, only four days ago, she and Signora Martedì were standing *right here* beside the one thing they both wanted to find.

"Now we pull it out . . . I guess."

"You *guess*?" Winnie's fingers tighten on the locket.

Erica winces. "I don't know. Sorry. I just . . . this is a lot, okay?"

Winnie can definitely agree with that. She can also agree that she and Erica are sitting ducks right now. "Do you know how to pick up the source? Safely, I mean? I saw a diagram once, but . . ." She trails off.

And Erica gives a hard nod. "I can pull it out. We're blood relatives, so I can touch Jenna's source. Besides, it's been sitting here so long, exposed to the water—I don't think it has any magic left." A twisted, sideways smile. "Still, I wouldn't be a Thursday if I weren't prepared, just in case." She withdraws a pair of latex gloves from her pocket. They're garishly blue in the shadows and make Winnie think of four-petaled poppies. They make her think of what Erica said back in the pump room: *You ever want something so bad, and then you finally get it, and it's just . . . not the same anymore?*

Winnie knew then, and now she knows it all over again—because Erica was right to worry in the pump room. This is the last clue. This is Winnie's *last* piece of Dad. So what on earth will she do next?

Erica eases her gloved hands around the ball—which is no larger than a baseball—and lifts up her sweater as if to tuck this source into the swaddle alongside her own. For half a breath, she is Lady Justice again, with her left hand balanced to one side holding Jenna's source and her right hand towing her sweater aside.

That is when Winnie feels it: her locket, clutched in her hand, turns to fire. *The Crow*, she thinks. Then there she is, an actual crow swooping down. A harbinger on flapping wings that erupts into a thick mist . . . before resolving into a human.

Caterina Martedì now stands before Winnie, dressed as she was in the forest before she tried to kill Winnie: scaled armor reminiscent of a hunter, a black mask with an unnatural golden beak.

In a scientific, but currently useless corner of Winnie's brain, she thinks, *Wow, so there are spells that can turn you into animals. I wonder what they're called.* In the more practical, plugged-into-this-moment part, she thinks, *Oh shit, this just got so much worse.*

For one, a familiar whispering scratch is snarling out from the Crow's mask.

For two, Erica hasn't yet tucked Jenna's source into her swaddle and she is only just lifting her gaze to see what has arrived.

For three, Winnie's locket is smoking. Like *actually* smoking, and the heat is so intense she can do nothing but drop the golden circle—and then feel it scorching through terry cloth on her chest.

"Well done, Erica." Martedì's voice is wreathed by whispers—and her arms are wreathed in mist. "Hand it to me now, please, and we can go."

Erica stares, still as a statue. Her sweater remains tugged to one side and her left hand hasn't released the glittering silver ball. And Winnie realizes in a dawning, surging sort of horror that there is no surprise on Erica's face.

She knew, Winnie thinks. *She knew this was coming.*

"Now," the Crow adds, "before the scorpions arrive, Erica."

"No." Erica's voice shakes. She releases her sweater. Stands taller. And it's like watching her tug on a mask of her own; she becomes the Ice Queen. She becomes her mother. "I've changed my mind."

"No one changes their mind, Erica. Your sister couldn't, and you can't either." The Crow laughs her cartoon laugh—except this isn't an animated Saturday-morning kids' show and Winnie isn't tied to train tracks.

In other words, Winnie can move. She can stagger around to gape at Erica. "You knew this was coming?" It's a stupid question because the answer is obvious. But she needs to hear Erica say it.

Erica shakes her head. "Winnie, stay back."

"Yes, Winnie," Martedì agrees. "Stay back. Because Erica here knows what she has to do, and I will absolutely kill you if I must." The mist continues to swirl around the Crow's arms—yet it now pools downward to her feet, as well. Shapes form, knee-high mounds of fog.

"No," Erica repeats. "I've changed my mind, Signora. I won't do it."

Winnie's head is wagging now. She stumbles back a single, stupefied step. Erica knows who the Crow is; she *has* known and she was playing Winnie all this time. The Winnie-em theorem. Input *x* for *loyalty*, and you will always get *y* for *stupidity*.

Jay was right, Winnie thinks. *Jay was right, and you didn't listen to him.*

"How," Winnie tries, but the words won't come. *How could you do this? To me? To Jay?*

"I'm sorry, Winnie." Erica's gloved hands tighten on her sister's source. Her muscles are tensing as if she might make a run for it. "It's not what I wanted to do—"

"Oh, don't lie to the girl, Erica. It was your idea, pitched to me in the forest with a full moon beaming down. Now hand me the source, and let's finish what we started. What Jenna started."

No. Winnie's head is still shaking, but it's getting slower. Sluggish. As if her whole body is being weighed down by bricks. No wolf will ever blow her over, because she will be crushed beneath the house before it can.

She should have listened to Jay. She should have *listened* to the boy she loves.

"Enough of this," Martedì declares, "we are out of time, Erica, and I don't want to lose the night." She smiles at Winnie now, and there's no ignoring that the mist puddling before her is taking on shapes—canine shapes. And Winnie has a skittery, painful sense that she recognizes one of them. That one of these creatures was a professor with a telescope fixed on shooting stars.

Canēs, Winnie's mind provides. *These are the lowest level in the Diana hierarchy, specialized in hunting nightmares for spells and spreading the Diana cause.*

"A for effort, Winnie," the Crow continues. "You did what I asked quite beautifully. But now . . . well, I can't let you get in my way. I've had enough of your family interfering. *Go.*" Her arms sling toward Winnie, and suddenly the mist-born hounds are slathering and snarling right for her.

Yes, Winnie thinks. *Go.* Without a thought, she twists around. And maybe it's the Winnie-em theorem just plugging in x for y, or maybe it's foolish denial—or maybe it's a foolish hope that her friend didn't actually want this . . .

Either way, Winnie grabs Erica by the arm, and for the ten thousandth time that night, she yanks her friend into a run.

But Winnie isn't fast enough. At least not to outrun the magicked dogs. Paws land on her. She flies face-first toward gravel. Erica screams, a sound to saturate Winnie's mind. To infuse the entire night like the Lyrids across the April sky. There is no overtone chanting here: there is only one meaning, and it is pain.

Rocks smash into Winnie's face. Teeth latch onto her neck. Drool slathers, and though she rolls and writhes, these hounds are supernaturally strong. She can't stop them.

Not until a command cuts into Winnie's eardrums like a serrated knife. *"RUN!"* Then suddenly the mist is melting off Winnie. No weight, no snarls.

She lifts her head. Erica has been captured by mist vines; she is being dragged away like a calf by a cowboy. But her mouth is still free, and she screams again: *"RUN, WINNIE!"*

Then she is gone. The Crow has hauled her around a corner and out of sight.

Winnie gropes to her feet. She is bleeding on her palms. Her ankle barks out pain. But those are problems for future Winnie. Current Winnie has to get Erica, because in the end, her friend changed her mind. Because in the end, her friend got those hounds off of Winnie. And because in the end, her friend is *still her friend,* and Winnie won't leave her behind.

She staggers away from the fountain—now just a burble of water, so calm. So *cruelly* tender as Winnie lugs herself toward where the Crow dragged Erica. Her vision spins, as if her eyes are playing tricks on her. As if mist and shadows swirl like gasoline on water. In the distance, she hears Tuesdays shouting and maybe a voice like Dryden, furious and demanding.

Winnie steers left, but there's no one there. She shambles onward anyway, pushing herself faster. Searching, searching. She turns right. She turns left. This is the way out, so surely this is the way the Crow came with Erica.

But she sees nothing. She *finds* nothing.

Until worse—so much worse—a smell like cooked rubber and forest fills Winnie's nasal cavity. Then a sense of music sweeps over her, except it is no longer Jenna's haunting melody; in its place is a different song, this one from a night when *yes* after *yes* fell from Jay's tongue.

> *The more I forget you, the deeper you sink in*
> *Fangs at the neck and red paint on a lost cabin*

Winnie stops her forward movement. Stops her frantic search for Erica. Gooseflesh ripples across her skin, almost painful, and her eyes are watering. Her breaths start to shake. While ahead, between yew hedges, movement glitters like a portal is being torn apart.

Then she smells something new and unexpected and so, so awful: bergamot and lime.

> *Ten dollars to kiss, a bet I can never win*
> *Snow on your lips*
> *It's feast or it's full famine*

The song quavers here. Stopping as if the Whisperer has forgotten the lyrics, forgotten the tune. Until suddenly it remembers. Until suddenly, it no longer sings but speaks. *PURE HEART,* it says. *I AM READY.*

The reaction is instant. An explosion rips free, hard enough to topple stars. Bright enough to mimic dawn. Loud enough to silence the approach of Tuesdays. It flings Winnie backward. She hits the yew hedge, missing a nearby bench by sheer luck.

PURE HEART, it repeats. *I AM READY.*

Winnie has no choice now: she hauls herself once more to her feet and runs. But now, she runs in the other direction. Back toward the fountain, away from the girl who was taken by a Crow.

And away from the boy trapped and singing inside the Whisperer.

39

Winnie's glasses are broken. Her face is bruised and throbbing. And her earlier stages of grief are back, stronger than ever. Because this cannot be happening right now. The Whisperer cannot *be* Jay and now hunting Winnie as if nothing will ever fill him up.

With heat on your skin I spin until I can't see us
I find no relief, inside I'm still a hopeless curse

None of this can be possible. None of this can be real. The crack on Winnie's left lens, the pain on her torn-up palms, the shots of heat near her ankle—none of that can be *real*. Jay lost, Erica taken. Here one moment, gone the next. And somehow, this whole clusterfuck *still* isn't over.

Because the source was only the first thing that Diana Crow wanted from Winnie, wasn't it? Clearly Caterina Martedì also wanted Jay, also wanted Erica. Her threats to take them both from Winnie were promises all along.

But why? Why does she need Jay inside the Whisperer? Why does she need Erica shackled in mist vines? What are you still not seeing, Winnie Wednesday?

The Whisperer chomps through yew leaves and branches like they are blades of grass. It will reach Winnie faster than she can escape these infernal bends and turns that Dad etched onto a page all those years ago. Unless she can find something to distract this monster chasing from behind.

Such as Tuesdays. She sees their shapes ahead. A regimented line to guard an intersection in the maze.

"Don't shoot!" Winnie screams, which is a pointless endeavor because the Whisperer is a vortex too loud for any sound to bypass.

And now guns are pointed at Winnie. *Guns.* It's so ridiculous she actually marvels at it—in a weird, slow-motion sort of way. The Tuesdays still think *she,* Winnie Wednesday, is the problem? They still think shooting *her* is going to stop the god-awful acid trip that this night has become?

Muzzles flash, sparking like violent versions of the lanterns from the Saturday trail. Yet no pain bursts inside of Winnie. None of her limbs stop their forward drive. Instead, it really *is* like the Saturday trail, with lights to guide her on. *Because the guns aren't pointed at me,* she realizes. In fact, the Tuesdays *don't* still think she is the problem at all; they have instead finally realized the true threat is the devastation chasing behind.

The stench of gunpowder sears over burning plastic. Scorpion masks glitter in the strobing light of their weapons. Winnie doesn't know who these Luminaries are, but she is suddenly struck by the weight of their lives. They were the enemy half an hour ago; now, they are on the same side against an enemy no guns can ever defeat.

"Run," she screams into the mask of one soldier. She grabs their shoulders, forcing them to stop their gunfire. *"RUN."*

There is nothing else she can do. Nothing else she can say. Denial is ham-fisting its way to the top of her brain: *They aren't so stupid as to let this consume them. No way they will let the Whisperer just come. They will run any second now.*

They don't, though. None of them run, and Winnie will never know if that one scorpion heard her shouts or not. She will only ever know that *she* kept running, and no . . . no. The Tuesdays did not.

The Tuesdays held the line.

And it is their strength that lets Winnie roll left into Dad's secret exit through the same hidden slice of hedges she used a few days ago. A crooked slingshot tucked between the hard lines of Dryden's maze. It will spit her out beside the front entrance to the mansion. Fifty steps from the awning where she was deposited last Saturday for a breakfast she didn't want to attend.

The breakfast where she also let herself fall into the clutches of a Diana Crow. *Unlike you, I'm an excellent liar.*

Here comes the fury now. It's a golden locket stamped with a moon and stars. So heavy it scratches at the lottery ticket of grief, straight through denial and into rage. Rage at the Crow in her *stupid* mask. Rage at Erica for lying. And above all, rage at herself. Winnie should have listened to Jay; she should have prodded more at those harmonic overtones in Erica's voice. Erica might have changed her mind at the eleventh hour, but the eleventh hour could have been avoided altogether if Winnie had only *looked past* her relentless loyalty.

Winnie runs on. This route is narrow. Her shoulders scrape on branches that have been tended, if crudely, to prevent the path from growing in—and whatever devoted gardener maintained Dad's secret trail, Winnie owes them a thousand thank-yous that she isn't sure she will survive long enough to ever relay.

Gunfire still erupts from behind.

Winnie bursts out of the darkness onto a driveway crawling with scorpions, backlit by headlights. A line of Hummers is parked against the curb, although there is one Hummer—only one—that doesn't face the same direction. Its lights are aimed away, and its back door hangs open as if someone just climbed out of it.

That is when Winnie sees a small scorpion rushing toward her. The person's arms sling out with expert precision to intercept Winnie.

Winnie tries to duck, but the arms leash around her. Yet, rather than try to stop her, arrest her, control her, detain her, the arms *propel* her right into that open Hummer door and a familiar voice bellows: *"GET IN!"* Then Winnie is pushed inside with all the force of a bulldozer.

And her captor?—savior?—climbs into the driver's seat. Tires squeal, a sound that barely cuts through the Whisperer. The *famēs* spell has eaten its way out of the maze now, and though Winnie can't see it, she *smells* it. She *feels* it.

> *The more I forget you, the deeper you sink in*
> *Fangs at the neck and red paint on a lost cabin*

The scorpion speeds the Hummer down the driveway. Wind jet-streams into the open back door, until the force is too strong. The door crashes shut, prompting Winnie to finally claw her way into sitting. To try to *see* who the hell is driving her away from the Whisperer.

"Buckle up!" the person shouts. "Winnie, BUCKLE UP."

Winnie buckles up. And just in time. They skid so hard onto the main street, aiming north, that only the seat belt keeps Winnie from slamming full power against the window.

And now her savior—and they *are* a savior—finally removes their helmet, revealing a face so out of context, Winnie almost doesn't recognize her. "Ms. Morgan?" Her voice is a mere squeak over the Hummer's V-8 engine. "What are you doing here?"

"Saving you, obviously. And it's about to *really* suck, Winnie."

"What do you mean?"

"I mean you had it right when you jumped off the waterfall on your third trial. This spell ain't stopping unless you drown it."

Winnie gawps at the sweating, shadowed face of her homeroom teacher as the Hummer vibrates like an earthquake around them, as Ms. Morgan goes hell for leather through one intersection after another—the same intersections Winnie and Erica burned through hours ago, going the other direction . . .

Erica, who is now in the clutches of the Crow. *Enough of this,* Martedì said, *we are out of time, Erica, and I don't want to lose the night.*

There's no chance for Winnie to mull over those words. Or to mull over the Whisperer—did she really hear Jay singing in that pixelated, magicked maelstrom? Or was that just her desperation, her denial, her delusion? The reality is that the Whisperer hunts right now. It *wants* to kill Winnie. It wants to *obliterate* this Hummer.

The dam bridge appears ahead like a dark blade to guillotine the night. And that's when Winnie's mind rockets to a different time, a different memory. Because oh god, it's all so *obvious* now—what happened four years ago, on the night Jenna died.

"Grayson was on his second trial," she says to herself, exactly as she said while she gripped her green sweater and stared at the same waters ahead. "When he stole a Tuesday Hummer and drove it off the dam."

Ms. Morgan doesn't answer. Presumably because she can't hear, and anyway, what is she going to say?

Jenna Thursday created the Whisperer, and it killed her. Grayson was either with her on the trial or else nearby, and the Whisperer tried to kill him too. So he ran. He *ran* and took whatever vehicle he found first: a Tuesday Hummer just like this one.

No, Winnie doesn't have all the gaps filled in yet, such as why Jenna cast such a monstrous spell, why she did so on the night of her second trial, or what the Crow has to do with any of it, but Winnie knows, deep in the beating ventricles of her heart, that this is why Grayson drove a Hummer off the bridge.

And that she is about to follow the exact same path.

A speed bump launches the Hummer skyward. They are almost to the dam. "You're a Diana, aren't you?" Winnie has to shriek to be heard.

And Ms. Morgan's eyes find Winnie's in the rearview. "Defected!" she answers. "Winnie, do you trust me?"

Yes, Winnie thinks, and she nods to prove it. Because even if her brain can't arrange all these puzzle pieces, she can't deny that Ms. Morgan really has always been on her side.

"Good." Ms. Morgan's eyes latch onto the road again—onto the dam bridge straight ahead. "Because I meant what I said before: this is about to *suck*." She cudgels her heel to the gas. They reach the dam. They career fifteen feet onto the bridge.

And Ms. Morgan wrenches the steering wheel left.

Time slows like an action sequence in a movie, except every sensory organ is engaged—organs Winnie never knew she had because they're not on human anatomical diagrams. Like the ability to sense inertia, tugging her backward while gravity and gasoline rip her forward. Or the sense that space and time really *are* connected, meaning Winnie is not a three-dimensional being so much as a four-dimensional one wound tightly inside the confines of gravity.

Her eyes, despite the crack in her glasses, are suddenly aware of all sorts of details she has never registered before on the dam: how the railing on either side is rusted iron with rivets as large as her fist. How the concrete curb is painted yellow, or how signs every ten feet proclaim: *Warning, Dam Outflow. Water level change when alarm sounds.*

Winnie has never actually heard that alarm, has she?

The Hummer hits the railing. It is a sound louder than any alarm. And although the iron *tries* to hold back this charging bull, it is no match for five thousand pounds of SUV. It crunches through the iron as easily as the Whisperer did through the maze.

The Little Lake shines, beautiful with the round-the-clock lights from the Floating Carnival to dance and scatter on the waves.

RIP, fishes, Winnie thinks as the four dimensions of the universe tip her downward. As the lights and waves vanish and all Winnie sees is the darkness of water ready to feast.

40

Distantly, Winnie knows that bracing is bad. That if she can stay re-laxed she's more likely to reduce injury upon impact. But *sure*. Relax muscles when a hungry lake closes in.

Then the Hummer completes its high dive, and the front bumper slams so hard against the water that Winnie's head snaps backward with a vi-cious, audible popping. The seat belt sucks in tight.

And the slowness of time somehow stretches *more*. Winnie has enough space to think, *I was just here a few days ago, floating on this lake like a swan. Now I am sinking, like a whale carcass into that lightless bathypelagic.*

I wonder if I'll see any candy bars.

Chassis groans. Glass creaks. The water is rising so fast, and holy *shit*, why is Ms. Morgan rolling down the passenger window? She's scream-ing too, over and over: *"Get your seat belt off, Winnie! Get your seat belt off!"*

Winnie's fingers are smarter than her mind. They obey, releasing the buckle in a sharp click that will vibrate in her body for the rest of her life. A cosmic microwave background caused by a new Big Bang that will change the trajectory of her future forever.

Water gushes like a waterfall into the passenger window. Ms. Morgan is crawling toward it, her hands and lower legs already submerged. She screams new words that sound like, *"Follow me! We have to swim!"* But might also be, *"This way to your death, Winnie!"*

And it *is* death that way. The water is toppling onto Winnie, and it's so *fucking cold*. There's no melusine to save her. No Jay to haul her to shore and keep her warm. There is only hypothermia and darkness and silence.

Ms. Morgan's hand lands on Winnie's leg. She has crawled backward and is grabbing Winnie just as Jay grabbed Winnie in the conservatory. Just as Winnie grabbed Erica in the maze.

"*EAT THE PIZZA!*" she hears, although that voice must be in her head. A command summoned by a soul not ready to die. Because Winnie *isn't* ready to die, and the ghosts of dead fishes and dead Hummers, of past trials and past pain cannot have her.

Winnie moves.

The water is to her waist now, icy and heavy and unwilling to let her go. But if the ghosts can't have her, then the water *sure* as hell can't either.

Ms. Morgan is withdrawing. Grappling toward the window and pulling herself through. She kicks into the Little Lake, vanishing like a kelpie into the waves.

Winnie is only a few seconds behind. *Eat the pizza, eat the pizza. Move and swim and get away.* She tugs off her glasses, stuffs them in her zipped-up hoodie, and finally launches into the lake.

The water is so cold, so heavy, she instantly loses dexterity. Worse, it is so dark, she cannot tell which way is up. What little light is in the sky cannot reach here, especially with the water so churned. It's like cloud cover, like thunderstorms. And there are no lanterns from the Saturday woods to guide Winnie, no gunfire flashes from Tuesdays holding the line.

Until Mom's voice tickles against her submerged brain.

To determine which way to swim, exhale into your hand and feel which way the bubbles move. Air will always rise up.

Winnie covers her mouth, her fingers numb and clumsy. She exhales, and yes. It's hard to tell, but yes. The bubbles are at the top of her hand; she is facing the right way.

She swings out her arms, scissors her legs, and swims.

Swims and swims and swims until she no longer needs Mom's voice to guide her—for new lights now glimmer. Blinking from the Floating Carnival.

Winnie breaks the surface. Freezing air steers over her. Then she hears Ms. Morgan nearby, "This way, Winnie. Come on, we're near the dock."

This is not the first time Winnie has been to the Floating Carnival at night. She came as a girl, of course, and then more recently when her Midnight Crown forced her to watch fireworks surrounded by Sundays.

This *is*, however, the first time Winnie has been here with absolutely no one else around. It's eerie. Super eerie, like a continuation of the horror film she imagined in the hot room.

INT. HOT ROOM, the script read two hours ago. *Winnie and Erica sneak through an empty hot room while unseen monsters shiver and hide in dark, concrete corners—and while Tuesday soldiers hunt.*

Now it reads: *EXT. FLOATING CARNIVAL. Winnie and her English teacher creep through the empty carnival. The full-moon Ferris wheel winks a golden glow across the booths and stands. Fairy lights glimmer, strung down aisles. In the distance, engines rev from Tuesday search boats launching on the other side of the Little Lake. Voices echo, the words inaudible but urgent.*

Urgent is what Winnie feels too. She and Ms. Morgan haven't died of hypothermia, but they will soon if they don't get moving. If they don't find dry clothes and heat.

Except that isn't what Winnie is actually fixated on right now. Survival? Whatever. She's a lot more worried about all the things she *couldn't* process as she sprinted for her life. Like how the Crow has Erica—but *why*? What is Erica to Martedì? And where is she taking Erica?

And then there is the Whisperer. There is Jay.

Winnie swivels her body on the dock. Cold air pierces all the frozen parts of her. She squints at the bridge. It's lit by tens of headlights now, as well as an ambulance from the Monday hospital. Putting on her busted glasses doesn't improve the view. "Is the Whisperer gone?" she croaks.

"For now," Ms. Morgan replies, her voice just as waterlogged. "It'll come back, though. They always come back."

"Good," Winnie murmurs.

Ms. Morgan blinks. "Good?"

Winnie nods. Then says it again: "Good."

"Winnie, that *famēs* spell just ate half the freaking bridge. And now you're saying you want it to come back? Are you okay?"

But what if it's not a famēs *spell?* Winnie wants to ask. *What if it's Jay and I can bring him home?* She doesn't offer this out loud. There's a heat sparking to life inside her. Steel striking against flint at the word *famēs*.

"So you knew it was a Diana spell all along, Ms. Morgan? For this past month, you've known exactly what the Whisperer was, and you've done nothing to stop it? Nothing to help me? And when you called it the Rustler at school, you were just saying that to mess with me—"

"It's not like that." Ms. Morgan's hands whip up.

"Then what *is* it like? Because I spent weeks with no one believing me—" Winnie breaks off as a massive searchlight carves down from the bridge. A circle of light that pendulums across the water, exactly where the Hummer went down. Then it skirts toward the western shore, suggesting it's only a matter of time before it swings east too.

Winnie doesn't care.

When she thought the Crow was the lesser of two evils compared to Jeremiah Tuesday and his scorpions, she was wrong. She was more wrong than she could *ever* have guessed.

You ever want something so bad, Erica asked her, *and then you finally get it, but it's just . . . What if it isn't what you think it will be?*

Winnie should have listened more closely to that question. She should have noticed that Erica *was* singing a second pitch.

"Erica," she tries to tell Ms. Morgan. "She's been taken by a Diana Crow, and we need to *find* her." But of course, that isn't what crawls off Winnie's tongue. "The sadhuzag is a rare but massive stag with seventy-four antler prongs and razor-sharp hooves."

Ms. Morgan stiffens. "Winnie—are you okay?" She slips a hand behind Winnie's back. "Oh gosh, you're so cold. Come on. We need to warm up." She pushes unsteadily to her feet, hauling Winnie with her. Water pours off them.

They are both shaking.

Which is the only reason Winnie lets herself get carted into the Floating Carnival. Her sopping clothes leave a trail through the fairy-lit avenues. Her teeth chatter. Her lungs quake. And her left ankle hurts with each step. It's the same one she twisted on her first trial a month ago.

As for her hands, they're so cold, she can't feel the small gashes scraped across them.

Next to her, Ms. Morgan's scorpion armor squeaks and drips. "That's Mason's gear, isn't it," Winnie says. A statement, not a question.

And Ms. Morgan nods. "There are some perks to dating the Lead

Tuesday Hunter." She offers a weak laugh, but when Winnie doesn't return it, she sighs. "Mason told me you were arrested, Winnie, and since then, I've been doing everything I could to find you." She gives a full-body shudder now. Then tugs Winnie along faster. "I'm sorry I couldn't help sooner."

Winnie compresses her lips. None of this makes sense. No matter how hard Winnie glares at it, she can't find a cipher to decrypt it all. "What about Erica? Were you trying to help her too, Ms. Morgan?"

"Leona." Another nervous laugh. "Call me Leona. And no—I didn't know about Erica. Was she arrested too?"

Winnie shakes her head. Both as an answer to Ms. Morgan's question and as a refusal to call her *Leona*. Because right now, Winnie needs to cling to something familiar. *This lady is named Ms. Morgan. She teaches me English at the high school. She moved here from outside Hemlock Falls because she met Mason Tuesday and fell in love. My own aunt vetted her . . .*

Oh god.

"Wait a minute." Now Winnie skids to a halt. Water drip-drips around her. "My aunt vetted you. I know she did because *you* told me that years ago. So how did Rachel not catch that you were a Diana?"

"Oh, she knew." Ms. Morgan swats a seaweed-like tendril of hair from her face. "Your aunt *definitely* knew. But sometimes Luminaries are willing to look past a person's origins. After all, it's not only Dianas who recruit Luminaries. The conscription can go both ways. But look. We can find clothes over there." She points at the Kelpie Carousel fifty paces away. Its wooden nightmares are wrapped in shadows; only a string of green lights runs in loops around the top.

Winnie can't decide if the absence of calliope music makes it more creepy or less.

Beyond the carousel is what Ms. Morgan actually points to: a souvenir shop lit by blue bulbs, where—in addition to stuffed toy kelpies—you can also buy T-shirts.

Ms. Morgan grabs two shirts as soon as they scurry in. They're both long-sleeve and navy blue, with the words *Gone Fishing* written over a swirly, vortex lake with a massive eye opening at the center.

Which *wow*, that's some peak Luminaries humor, right there. *Let's joke about the sleeping spirit waking up! You know, the one thing we never want to happen in Hemlock Falls or anywhere else and the one thing Dianas do want!*

A Diana like the one standing next to Winnie and stripping off her upper layers of stolen armor. Winnie's fingers close into a fist around the shirt. "When you say 'defected,' what does that mean? That you don't want this anymore?" She shakes the shirt at Ms. Morgan.

"Yes," Ms. Morgan replies, her head stuck halfway inside the shirt as she tries to find the neck hole. "It means that I don't want to wake up the sleeping spirit and free all its magic into the world. Though to be honest"—her head finally pokes through—"that's not *really* what Dianas want either. Or at least they don't want it because they're wicked and power-hungry."

Winnie blinks, an old quote coming to mind from *Understanding Sources* by Theodosia Monday: *Both carnivores and herbivores are essential for a healthy ecosystem, and this author posits that so too are our disparate societies of Dianas and Luminaries. The question however is: Which society is the predator? And which society is the prey?*

Winnie peels off her soaked hoodie, then her soaked T-shirt too. She forgets to remove her glasses; they clatter to the floor—overloud in this horror film.

And Winnie swears she can hear Erica as if she's right there. *Oh Jesus, you look so much worse now, Winona. You need a shower.*

Winnie swallows. Then sticks her tongue between her teeth so they won't start clicking. She's still freezing, even after she tows on the Gone Fishing T-shirt. Ms. Morgan, meanwhile, crooks down and retrieves Winnie's glasses. She offers them to Winnie, pasting on a smile that can only be described as *Concerned Adult*.

Winnie takes her glasses, but doesn't smile back.

Ms. Morgan sighs again. Then shivers. "I . . . think Archie sells sweatshirts, so let's go there next."

And then what? Winnie wants to ask. *Then where the hell are we going to go? Where am I going to go?* Dad's trail has ended in nothing. No pot at the end of the rainbow; no missing father to jump out of a shadow and say, *You did it, Winnie! You won the prize and you found me!*

She doesn't know where the Crow went. She doesn't know where Erica is. She doesn't know where the Whisperer will reappear next, or if Jay will again be inside that supermassive black hole that feasts on galaxies.

So Winnie follows Ms. Morgan out of the gift shop. One wet foot in front of the other. Her cracked glasses distort the carnival. They turn the full-moon Ferris wheel into a Wheel of Fortune. *Pick your nightmare, spin the wheel! Or you'll end up as your boyfriend's meal!*

The wheel doesn't turn at this hour, but it does glow. Carts drift and wobble on the breeze. It is beautiful—which only makes Winnie want to laugh. To clap her hands and say, *Oh boy, you sure had me fooled, you liars!*

How could she ever believe the lights of downtown were honest? That it was bioluminescence creating photons in the depths?

"Why are you helping me?" Winnie asks. "If you're a defected Diana, then why do you care what happens to me?"

"Of course I care about you, Winnie." Ms. Morgan shivers, her arms hugged to her chest. "I mean it every time I say I'm on your side."

"That's not an answer."

"It's a long story."

"Well, do you have something better to do?" Winnie flings out her arms. The spirit on her shirt looks like it's winking.

"We need to keep moving—and get more clothes."

"No." Winnie stops now. The Ferris wheel rocks and sways. "Explain to me why you're here. Too many people have kept secrets from me lately, and I'm not moving until you tell me exactly what's going on."

Ms. Morgan grimaces. Then rubs at her eyes. Then finally mumbles, "Okay. It's . . . well." She waves toward Winnie's neck. "When you put a message in your locket a few days ago, your grandmother Harriet received it. She contacted Professor Funday, who then found me. I gathered up the rest of the birthday cards and met you at the old museum—where I was shocked to discover another Diana in Hemlock Falls who cast that hotspot spell. Now, here we are."

Winnie stares at Ms. Morgan. Her jaw sags. "Here . . . we are? You just went from A to Z without any of the alphabet in between. What does Professor Funday have to do with anything? How does my grandma Harriet have a locket? And why the hell do you have birthday cards from my dad?"

Ms. Morgan's grimace deepens. Because Winnie is almost yelling now. Which is foolish, since sound carries over water—and the Tuesdays will hear if she isn't quieter. But she can't make herself care. The flint sparks have turned into a bonfire.

"There were three of us originally," Ms. Morgan answers, her voice appeasing and gentle. "Defected Dianas, I mean, living in Hemlock Falls. One was Theodosia Monday."

"The lady who wrote all those books on Dianas?"

"Yes. She goes by Funday now because that's just the sort of person she is. Then, I was the second Diana. And the third . . ." Here Ms. Morgan dithers, as if she really doesn't want to finish this sentence. As if she hates to be the bringer of bad tidings.

But Winnie already knows what's coming next. The alphabet is filling in, and she can see where at least half the letters are headed. *B = Grandma Harriet had a locket. C = Dad had a locket too. That means D is . . .*

Her spine gives way, so fast she barely staggers to a bench beside the Ferris wheel. She slumps over. Her glasses slip down her nose. And her brain starts blasting out: *I NEED AN ADULT!*

Ms. Morgan eases beside Winnie. But where Winnie is a spineless lump, Ms. Morgan is all stiff bones and stiffer muscles to hold them.

And at last, the letter *D* arrives. Two circles on Winnie's Venn diagram. On her three-petaled trilliums, drawn and redrawn a thousand times.

"Your dad," Ms. Morgan says, her voice scarcely louder than the boat engines in the distance. "The third Diana was your dad, Winnie."

D for Dad.

D for Diana.

41

"Four years ago," Ms. Morgan continues, "your mom caught your dad doing magic. It was bad, and your family was hauled in for questioning. But you weren't the only ones who got interrogated that night. Funday and I were brought in too—it's how I learned Teddy was a defected Diana like me. It's also how I learned that your dad cast a spying spell to steal Luminary secrets." She glances at Winnie, as if expecting a reaction.

But Winnie can't move. All these years she thought her dad was a Diana . . . and he was. *Anyone could be a Diana. A Diana could be anyone.* Winnie's eyes close. Her glasses have almost fallen off her nose.

"After hours of interrogation," Ms. Morgan continues, "the Tuesdays decided that Teddy and I knew nothing. We were sent home. But with the expectation that we never, *ever* step out of line."

Winnie coughs now. A sound of incredulity because *really*? Ms. Morgan and Professor Funday were told to *behave* while Mom, Darian, and Winnie became outcasts? "Why did they believe *you* knew nothing, but they wouldn't believe my family?"

Ms. Morgan rubs her lips together, like they're dry. Like they're hurting her. "I . . . honestly don't know, Winnie. I cannot tell you how many times I've wondered the same thing. But I've never dared ask. I'm sorry."

Winnie sits up. "That doesn't make sense though. I'm still missing letters of the alphabet. You just said you had my dad's birthday cards. Which means *you* are the one who's been delivering them for four years, right? But why? And how?"

Ms. Morgan gulps. "Look, Winnie," she begins. But then a long pause follows, as if she's already lost her words. As if they somehow got separated into a twisty crossword puzzle, and all she has now are the clues. *Eleven across: Another word for clusterfuck.*

"A . . . few days after your dad disappeared," she begins haltingly, "I found a stack of cards in my mailbox—along with instructions on what to do with them . . . And, well, I got scared. When a Diana defects, we become the enemy to all other Dianas. A kill-on-sight situation. Plus, since your dad was a *lēgātum*—"

"A what?"

Ms. Morgan looks ill now. Like saving Winnie from certain death was one thing, but having to explain the birds and the bees of Dianas? No way.

"Right," she says. "You don't know what that word means. But like, imagine Diana royalty. That's what the *lēgāta* are: legacy families who have been in the society for generations. Everyone knows who they are—so once I learned your dad was a Diana, I realized he was *that* Bryant from the Silvestri family. As did Teddy. And we both just assumed that what Jeremiah told us was true: your dad had cast a spying spell, and . . ."

"Oh no." Winnie doubles over again. Because she can fill in the next letters on her own. *E, F, G! Next time won't you sing with me!* "You thought Dad killed Jenna, didn't you?" she croaks out. "You thought he was a Diana spy and a murderer."

"Yeah." Now Ms. Morgan sounds as ill as she looked. "And so you can see why I was terrified not to do as Bryant asked. When I found those cards in my mailbox—"

"*Did* he kill Jenna?" Winnie interrupts. She clutches at her knees. *Breathe, breathe.* "*Did* he cast a spying spell to the Dianas?"

"I thought he had. For four years, I really thought he had, Winnie. And that's what I believed right up until a few days ago, when you contacted Harriet and she contacted Teddy."

"But what changed your mind?" Winnie's voice sounds so far away. "What did Grandma Harriet tell you that convinced you my dad wasn't the bad guy?"

"First, Harriet explained that Bryant wasn't casting a spying spell, but rather contacting her on the night he disappeared. He was trying to warn her of an active witch in Hemlock Falls, but he never said who it was or what they were doing before your mother interrupted the spell."

Winnie pushes at the bench. Her torn hands screech at her, but she savors the pain. It sharpens her. Grounds her. And with a grunt, she cranks herself upright again. "But why believe Harriet? For all you know, my grandmother was lying."

"To tell you the truth," Ms. Morgan admits, "I didn't believe her. Not until we were at the old museum. Not until I saw that golden arrow coming for me, and I *saw* a hotspot open up. I mean, raising a hotspot—that's some serious magic. And *bad* magic."

"So that's when you decided to help me?"

"I'm certainly *trying* to help you." Ms. Morgan tries again for a Concerned Adult smile. "I'm not sure I'm succeeding, though. You're way too cold, Winnie—and honestly, so am I. We need to find those sweatshirts and get out of here."

"Right." Winnie can't argue with this, so when Ms. Morgan stands and offers her hand, Winnie takes it. And when she pulls Winnie into a trudging walk, she doesn't resist. Her ankle stabs with each step.

But again, she finds the pain clarifying. A filter that she can pour this jumbled-up alphabet through. When Winnie stood on the bridge, her green sweater in hand, sleeves fluttering on the breeze—the same breeze currently sucking all warmth from Winnie—*this* was the missing link, wasn't it? The missing connective tissue: *D* for Dad, *D* for Diana.

And, apparently, *L* for *lēgātum*, too.

The petal labeled *Grayson* was connected to Jenna because they were in love.

Jenna's petal connected to Dad because, like Ms. Morgan, she must have figured out that Dad was basically Diana royalty. And knowing that Dad had defected, maybe Jenna believed he could help her. Because she didn't *only* want to leave the Luminaries four years ago; Jenna must have wanted to leave the witches.

And of course, Dad's petal then connected to Mom because they were in love too. *I didn't move to Hemlock Falls for my degrees, Win-Ben.*

Soon, the lantern-shaped carts of the Tilt-A-Whirl glow into Winnie's vision. Beyond is Archie's Funnel Cake booth, where sure enough, a stack of black sweatshirts rests on one side of the counter.

Ms. Morgan hurries ahead, grabs a sweatshirt, and flings it at Winnie. It is, of course, *another* hoodie. Bretta would laugh. Fatima would too.

And Erica. So would Erica. *Why did we do all that shopping, Winona, if you're just going to wear hoodies in the end?*

Revenant's Daughter, this one reads in the same script as the sign outside the restaurant. It smells vaguely like fried food and powdered sugar. It makes Winnie think of Mom. It makes her think of how she has failed her—and everyone else too. Erica, Jay, the entirety of Hemlock Falls. After following all the steps in Dad's long, convoluted plan, it has led Winnie here: nearly drowned and stuck inside a horror-film carnival.

Signora Martedì won.

She *won,* and now it's more than Winnie's back that's pressed against the wall. It's her face and stomach and legs. She is locked up in a straitjacket. She is buried in a tomb, and that *fucking* Diana Crow with her *fucking* golden-beaked mask won. Dad couldn't beat her, even though he was apparently a powerful *lēgātum,* so really, what chance did Winnie have four years later?

"Winnie." Ms. Morgan's voice sounds thick and inhuman. Like Winnie is again under the Little Lake, again under crushing waves. "No, no— Winnie! Look at me!"

Winnie's vision swims, but she doesn't look at Ms. Morgan. Instead she grabs—frantically—at her back pocket. Does she still have her last drawing? For some reason, it seems important right now. Like she *needs* to see her final picture of Erica, of Jay, of her family. Otherwise all the ghosts Winnie sealed up are going to seal up Winnie instead. Mummify her organs and shove her into a sarcophagus.

The paper is waterlogged, just like her pants, and she is too rough as she fumbles it open. It tears.

Yet where Winnie expects to find a sketch of Lady Justice or Jay or her family, instead, there are words written in round, curlicued script. *Jenna's spell.*

Winnie has *no idea* when Erica put this in her pocket. Maybe when they were on the four-wheeler fleeing the Sunday garage. Maybe when they were running helter-skelter into the maze. Maybe in that last moment, when Winnie tried to drag her away from the Crow.

The *when* doesn't matter, though. It's the *what* that makes all the difference.

"Winnie," Ms. Morgan says, but Winnie is outside her body now.

Somewhere several feet to the right. She doesn't feel Ms. Morgan's hand on her shoulder. She doesn't feel the glacial caress of a spring night. "Are you okay? What's wrong?"

"What do these words mean?" Winnie's voice is even farther away than her body. An echo in a canyon. *What do these words mean, mean, mean?* She points to a title written at the top of the page. "What does this mean, Ms. Morgan?"

The teacher frowns, squinting at the paper. "We need to *move*, Winnie. We can look at that paper once we're away from here—"

"This is Latin, right? So what does this mean in English? *Incantamentum Purum Cor?*"

Ms. Morgan blinks. "What did you just say?"

"*Incantamentum Purum Cor,*" Winnie repeats, and she once more holds out the paper for Ms. Morgan to see.

Ms. Morgan snatches the paper from Winnie's grasp, her eyes growing rounder by the second. She holds the page up, trying to get enough light from Archie's funnel cake stand. "Oh god," she breathes, and the words are more prayer than curse. "Oh god, Winnie. Where did you get this?"

"It means Pure Heart, doesn't it? *Incantamentum Purum Cor* translates into 'Pure Heart spell.'"

Ms. Morgan eyes shutter. "Yeah. That's exactly what it means."

"And what does it do?" Winnie has a pretty good guess where this going. The letter *E* in her alphabet, for *explosion*. For *eruption*. For *end of everything*. "This isn't a self-feeding *famēs* spell, is it, Ms. Morgan?"

"No, Winnie. It's not. It's far more powerful." Ms. Morgan rolls up her hoodie until her Gone Fishing shirt is revealed underneath. "In fact, it's *the* most powerful spell Dianas have ever discovered, meant to awaken the sleeping spirit.

"And if the *Purum Cor* is what your dad was trying to stop four years ago—if *that's* what just chased us off the bridge, then dear god, Winnie. This is so much worse than I was fearing."

The Pure Heart Spell

(Translation by Leona Morgan)

In the forest, dead of night
With Lyrid stars falling bright
Granite safety, walls for height
The mist will gather in.

Nightmare father, gone and slain
Lantern mother, spirit's bane
Son of forest, son of pain,
Pure Heart
Trust the Pure Heart.

Feed it, tend it, hunger strong
Let it grow, spread its song
Pure Heart,
Trust the Pure Heart.

Dawn will rise, casting light
No more Lyrids falling bright
Where waters fed will wake the night
And mist inside the Pure Heart

Pure Heart
Trust the Pure Heart

For we are one in sleep and dreams
For we are one in waking.

THE SISTER

On the final night of the Lyrids, the girl goes into the forest. She has pretended she wants to be a hunter, and she passed the first trial without difficulty. It's easy to kill a nightmare when you have magic. When all you have to do is whisper the right words and watch as a golden arrow hits its target without error. It's even easier if you've had your source buried in the forest for months, weakening the nearby nightmares.

She killed a siren. Her stepfather was so proud.

The girl feels only shame over that death. It wasn't right to kill that creature—as a hunter or as a witch. But it was what she had to do if she wanted to get out of the Dianas. To finish the agreement she was bound to years ago that *has* to be fulfilled or everyone she loves will die.

She understands—loosely—why it must be her to cast the spell. It's a long spell, longer than any other she has been taught, and the words are slippery. Her tongue doesn't want to hold on to them, her brain doesn't want to memorize them. It has taken her almost two years of practice and it's only when she writes a song to go with the Latin that it all finally sticks.

She liked the melody so much, she ended up writing innocent words to go along with it. She sang it last month at an open mic night; her little sister told her it was the best song she's ever composed.

The hills at the northern edge of the forest are sharp crests of granite. They break from the earth like fins. The girl climbs and dips, climbs and dips. Her heart pounds. Her fingers imagine strumming a guitar that isn't there.

Light quivers through trees. A nest of will-o'-wisps. They watch her pass. They do not flee. The girl's heart tightens. This is the last time she'll ever see them.

Soon she reaches the granite hole in the ground, a dark gash in these shadows. It is a special place. *One of a kind,* said the Diana *cornīx* who first recruited her, and who first tasked her with this spell. *Centuries ago, we Dianas interpreted the* Purum Cor *from the spirits' magic, and we have waited ever since to find the necessary pieces. Now we have them: the granite walls, the Lyrids, the half human, half nightmare—and you, Jenna, with your pretty voice and pretty music, able to control it all.*

The *lēgātum* has told the girl, of course, what the spell will actually do. *Incantamentum Purum Cor.* The Pure Heart spell. He knows its power. And the girl knows that if she *really* casts it, she will be sucked into the spell and die. Because it's not her pretty voice that most appeals to the *cornīx*; it's her expendability.

But that is why the *lēgātum* is helping her.

Now here he is, stepping out from between a rowan and an elm. He is dressed in all black, with a cap pulled over his head. He's usually so well-dressed and polished—even when knee-deep in compost—but tonight he looks disheveled. Disastrous. And she fears for half a second that he *isn't* going to help her. That he has come to tell her he has changed his mind.

He hugs his hand to him, and even in the shadows, it's clear the skin is burned raw. It has sloughed off to leave glistening flesh exposed to the frozen night.

That's what magic does. A *lot* of magic.

"Your hand—what happened?"

He shakes his head. "I . . . had to cast a *verba circumvolēns.*"

"On who?" Circling-word spells are complicated—and magically intensive, requiring strict boundaries on what and who a person can speak to. Still, they should not leave scars like that behind.

The *lēgātum* ignores her question. "Is Grayson ready?"

"Yes, he's ready. When the spell is finished, he has a ride for us. That way." The girl points north, to the forest border where her boyfriend waits.

"Good. You'll need to be fast when this finishes—run like you've never run before, Jenna. And I will handle the *cornīx.*"

Yes, right. The reason the girl is here. She nods obediently, even as her throat is closing up while she settles on the edge of the granite pit. She has always been struck by the strangeness of this place. In a forest made of *weird,* somehow this rectangle in the ground is even weirder. And she has never been quite clear if it was made by natural geology or spirit dreams or something else entirely. It's so perfectly carved into the earth.

She has also never been quite clear how a half human, half nightmare came to live in Hemlock Falls. Whoever they are, were they naturally born? Or were they somehow created?

Jenna slips inside the pit. Her feet crunch on decaying leaves, compressed and rotted by winter. They are a soft, damp carpet of a tree's shed memories. *That's a good line for a song,* she thinks. *Maybe I'll write it once Grayson and I reach California.* That's where her birth dad lives. He's a composer like Jenna wants to be.

On the higher ground nearby, the *lēgātum* paces. Whatever just happened to him, it was bad. But they both know that the *Incantamentum Purum Cor* is so much worse.

"I'm going to get started," she calls from inside the pit.

"Yes," the man agrees. He flips up his burned, ruined hand. Then he vanishes, and half a breath later, static scuttles over Jenna.

She feels instant grief, instant shame. The *lēgātum* doesn't do magic anymore—that was the requirement if he moved to Hemlock Falls. And throughout this entire year that he has been helping Jenna, he has *never* broken that promise.

Until tonight.

Focus, she tells herself. Then she opens her locket, the one she usually lets Grayson wear, and she inserts the expected message. *Ready.*

The locket frizzes.

She shoves it into her pocket.

It takes a while—much longer than she expects—for the *cornīx* to finally arrive. So Jenna watches the sky while she waits. She watches the Lyrids fall, a meteor shower that has been observed and recorded longer than any other in human time.

A flash of shadow. A gust of wings. Then a smell like hot rubber, and the Crow materializes in a burst of mist. She wears her mask, as always.

Once upon a time, Jenna saw that mask as aspirational. She could become powerful as a Diana. She could work with the nightmares instead of against them. All she had to do was keep learning. Keep absorbing power and building spells.

A lie. Just like the Luminaries. All of it eventually ends in violence.

"You are here early." The Crow's voice is modulated by her mask, and for once, she is not dressed in black armor, but a billowy, silvery gown that slithers around her like the forest mist.

"I'm sorry." Jenna points to the sky. To Vega beaming bright. "I saw the stars, and I got worried about mixing up the time."

The Crow's mask tilts. The golden beak glisters. "Indeed." Though her voice is made of only hisses and snarls, Jenna senses skepticism.

It makes her stomach flip. "Can . . ." *Swallow.* "Can I begin?"

"Not quite yet." The Crow advances on the granite pit. Jenna cowers, although she hates herself for it. "I would remind you, Jenna, to consider who will suffer tonight if you do not do as you agreed."

"I'm going to do as I agreed—"

The Crow cuts Jenna off with a wave. "Your sister is with that Wednesday girl right now, did you know that? And I have no qualms about eliminating both of them if I must. Do you understand?"

Oh yes, Jenna understands. She also understands Bryant won't like this, since the Wednesday girl is *his* daughter. And she understands that this version of the Crow is the real one. Not the patient one who trained Jenna, but this threatening woman in rippling silver.

Jenna steps gingerly through detritus to the lip of the pit. Her feet are so cold. Her toes so numb. "I'm going to do as I agreed," she repeats, pumping all the certainty she can into her words.

And the Crow nods. Her head is at least ten feet higher than Jenna's, an obvious representation of her power. Of who between them will walk free and who between them is caged. In the dark sky behind her head, Lyrid meteorites shoot by.

"Good, Jenna Thursday. I am relieved to hear it." The Crow raises an arm. "You all may come out now." At these words, shapes melt into the clearing, undulating and solidifying as if hiding spells are shedding off of them.

Jenna's breath catches. She counts six hounds, two more crows, and three sorts of witches she has heard of but never seen: three owls, two boars, and a lynx. Fifteen Dianas in total, all right here.

Suddenly her plan feels impossible. Suddenly, Jenna feels so, so tiny. So, so trapped. What was she thinking? Why did she *ever* believe she could outsmart a *cornīx* and break free from this mistake?

"Now, Jenna," the Crow murmurs, her voice less whispery, less modulated. As if she has given up trying to hide who she is since this child before her will die imminently. "Now you can begin."

Jenna swallows. She has always known she would have an audience, even if she thought it would be an audience of one. The notes of her song are writ on her muscles at this point, and as she steps to the center of the pit, her pulse decelerates. Her breaths steady. This is just one more open mic night. One more concert for a Thursday clan dinner. Her audience of witches are like standing stones. The only movement is the breeze, twining through gowns and suits and pajamas and armor. Whoever these witches are, they come from all corners of Hemlock Falls—and possibly far beyond.

Overhead, the Lyrids fall in sharp lines. Arrows shot from a bow-shaped moon.

Jenna takes up a wide-legged stance on the frosted leaves. Gripping her source in her left hand, she pretends it is her guitar. Here are the frets, here are the strings. With her right hand she strums air. It would feel ridiculous if not for the intensity with which everyone watches her. Even the sleeping spirit seems to hold its breath.

Jenna inhales, letting her diaphragm pull in air and her soft palate rise. Then she sings the slippery words that are so hard for her brain to latch onto—or for anyone else's brain. Because the words are anathema to logic. Anathema to self-preservation. *This will kill you,* her instincts tell her. *This is how you and many others will die.*

Mist swells around her, looking like bark peeling from a birch tree. Her source grows warmer against her sliding, squeezing, guitar-playing fingers.

Distantly, she hears a whisper, which is her signal. This is what Bryant warned her of.

"When you hear the whispers—that's when you change the first word, Jenna. All it takes is one syllable. Change it, and the spell will begin to unravel."

"But they expect me to die. The cornīx *will see when I'm still alive at the end."*

"No, she won't, Jenna. Because I will be there, and I will make sure she sees nothing at all."

Jenna is to the main summons portion of the spell. The first requirement beyond her voice and her source, beyond the Lyrids and the granite. She knows what the words *literally* mean, but she doesn't know what will happen when she says them. *Nightmare father, gone and slain. Lantern mother, spirit's bane. Son of forest, son of pain.*

It is on the first line that she is going to change a syllable. *Incubo* is what she should say; what she will say instead is *encuba*. It should be so subtle none of these looming Dianas notice . . .

Except when the words arrive, when the spell's magic rattles into her with its fiery force—as more mist spews and snakes around her—she doesn't change the word at all. She *can't*. Because suddenly she is not the only one singing. All the Dianas in the clearing have joined in the song, and the power of *their* words crushes out Jenna's resistance. Her song is now *their* song, and it has taken on a mind of its own. Their whispers are speaking through her. Horrifying layers that entangle her voice.

Jenna says *incubo* because that is what the whispers say.

And so, Jenna summons the Pure Heart.

She watches as it happens—she *sees* with eyes that are impossible to blink as the message of her summons goes shooting into the forest. It looks like a small sparrow made of mist—and in its beak it is holding something. *A wolf's jawbone,* she thinks, although she has no idea why she would know this. The misted sparrow flies so fast, and it's not as if she has ever seen a wolf's jawbone before.

The words continue pouring out, Latin and unchanged. No, no—this isn't supposed to happen. But she can't change her tongue and mouth. She can't stop her song. The mist swirls around her. It is pure fire, scalding brighter than the forest's own mist.

She *will* die here.

Of all the figures, the Crow stands closest. Her gown flips and flies around her as if she too is engulfed in this boiling mist. She is also the loudest, her beak rising, defiant and domineering.

Pure Heart. Trust the Pure Heart.

The spell was not supposed to get this far. Jenna was *never* supposed to reach these words. She was supposed to be running away by now. Bryant was supposed to have jumped in to help her. Where is he? Why isn't he here?

I am going to die.

Grayson will wait for no one.

Erica will never, ever see me again.

It is in that moment that something finally shifts. A flashing light that Jenna recognizes even as most of her brain and body are consumed by this spell still spewing from her throat in Latin.

Pure Heart.

Trust the Pure Heart.

The lights flash brighter. A host of blue fire carried on tiny, flittering wings. It is the nest of will-o'-wisps, and in their center is a mass vaguely human that Jenna's gaze simply will not fix onto. *Bryant and his hiding spell.*

The will-o'-wisps attack the witches.

And the Dianas finally stop singing. They stir, they scream, they scatter. Golden arrows flash, clashing against the will-o'-wisps' fury.

The Crow, however, keeps singing—and so Jenna does too. She smells her hair burning and sees flickers of shadow fire leap off her skin. She hears—far, far away—a voice that sounds like Bryant's. *Jenna,* he shouts. *Release it. Stop the spell now. Do not say the final words—*

Bryant's voice strangles off as if he has been discovered, defeated, destroyed. His help, his support . . . It vanishes like nightmares in the mist.

Jenna's mouth continues to shape each vowel, each consonant of the final Latin phrases. The promise that every spell makes. The nail to close out the coffin. "Sumus"—*no, no, no*—"ūnus"—*no, NO, NO*—"in somnō . . ."

A will-o'-wisp bursts from the spell's mist before Jenna. Inches from her face, it is a beacon of blue fire and perfect light. A tiny skeleton wreathed in power and dreamed up by the sleeping spirit. So beautiful, so fragile. Its eyes—empty holes inside a bleached skull—stare at Jenna with a sentience she feels more than sees.

She has never been this close to a will-o'-wisp before.

She has never had one take her measure and assess what course it will choose next. *Are you a danger to me? Do you deserve to die?*

Most nights, the will-o'-wisps *know* Jenna Thursday is no danger to them. They ignore her, just as she ignores them. But tonight . . . Tonight she *is* a danger. An explosive, apocalyptic danger to herself and everything else inside this forest. Inside this world.

I don't want to die, she thinks. *I want to live.*

Yes, the nightmare seems to say. *But you know it's too late for that.*

It's true. Even if Jenna doesn't really understand where everything went wrong, even if all she wants to do is warn Grayson half a mile to the north—even if all she wants to do is *hug* her little sister one more time and say, *I will always love you even if I can't be there . . .*

Well, this will have to be the way Jenna says it. This will have to be the way she shows how much she loves them all.

Not all nightmares deserve to die. Not all Luminaries or Dianas either. But sometimes, it's the only way to fix a mistake made many years ago, when a much younger Jenna didn't know what she was agreeing to.

No! she thinks she hears Bryant say. Though if he yells that at her or at the Crow or at the will-o'-wisp, Jenna will never know. Because she says the opposite.

"Yes," she tells the will-o'-wisp, and it's the first word in what feels like eons that is *not* Latin, that is *not* part of the *Incantamentum Purum Cor.* She has stopped the spell. It will not finish.

The will-o'-wisps attack Jenna. They feast. They kill. Blood, blood, so much blood to stain the granite and that soft, damp carpet of a tree's shed memories.

Piece by piece, drop by drop, note by note, the will-o'-wisps consume a vibrant, singing spirit that once belonged to Jenna Thursday. She becomes one more ghost sucked into the forest. One more dream fed to the spirit's night.

And one more body for Luminaries to clean up tomorrow.

C H A P T E R

42

W e have to get help." Ms. Morgan is wheezing. This might be caused by panic or might be from the fact that she and Winnie are now running. "We'll go to Teddy—she can help us. And . . . and your grandmother. We'll send her a message."

"My grandmother," Winnie replies, her own breaths shallowing out, "isn't here. Plus, Harriet didn't exactly help my family when Dad vanished, even though she knew he was the good guy. So why would she help us now?"

"Because the world is ending?"

Winnie's jog slows. Her ankle isn't happy about this pace as she aims herself and Ms. Morgan for the striped tent. There's a phone in there Ms. Morgan wants to use. "But we just dumped the Whisperer in the lake. Surely that bought us time?"

"When I thought the Whisperer was a run-of-the-mill *famēs* spell, sure. I would have said we bought time. But"—*pant, pant*—"I have no idea anymore, Winnie. All bets are off. We have to assume the worst."

"And the worst is the world is ending?"

"No one knows." Ms. Morgan flips up her hands. "That's kind of the whole point." *Pant, pant.* "Dianas think waking the spirit will be good for the world; Luminaries . . . think . . . it will be bad."

"And you?"

"I think we have a . . . good balance here, so why mess with it?"

Winnie thinks again of the words from *Understanding Sources*—written by none other than Professor Funday. *Both carnivores and herbivores are essential for healthy ecosystems,* it reads, *and this author posits that so too are our disparate organizations.*

"What if the Dianas are right, though? What if waking the spirit *is* a good thing?"

"I mean, it's possible." *Wheeze.* "Dianas believe . . . Luminaries hoard and control the sleeping spirit's power. And they're not totally wrong. You have life-saving technology here, like . . . melusine blood—and you don't share it with . . . the wider world."

"Okay, but sharing all the magic will also share all the nightmares." Winnie's glasses are bouncing on her nose. It makes the stripes on the tent ahead look like an EKG.

"Again, we don't know . . . Jesus, Winnie. Can we slow down?" Ms. Morgan's footsteps drop to a trot. Then a shamble. She's really breathing heavily. "I'm not . . . a hunter. I do *not* run sprints. Like, ever."

"You're the one who said the world was ending!"

"Well, it won't help if I go into cardiac arrest. Do *you* know how to stop the Pure Heart?"

"I thought you didn't know either."

"No, but Teddy might, and I'm the one who has her phone number."

Winnie groans. Her adrenaline is kicked up to eleven, and her blinders have been so firmly slotted on, she can't see anything but the path ahead—which goes right into the carnival tent. The flaps are lowered. Winnie thrusts them aside.

Where she almost gasps because all the lights are on. It's like stepping into a snow globe. A crystal ball. A fairy land of gold. Winnie thinks of bioluminescence and photons. She thinks of the guiding lights of downtown. *They're all here, sparkling inside this tent.*

"Look. There's the phone I was talking about." Ms. Morgan points to a nearby booth. It's a first aid station, only a few steps away. And sure enough, there's a corded phone on the outside wall, glittering like it's made of gold.

"I'll call Teddy now." Ms. Morgan is still half gasping. "And you can . . . send a message to your grandmother with the locket."

"I don't want to send a message to my grandmother."

Ms. Morgan frowns. Her cheeks are shining. "Winnie, now is not the time to be upset she missed Christmas dinners—"

"That is *not* my reasoning."

"Are you sure about that?" Ms. Morgan's lips purse, but she says no more before retrieving the phone and hammering in a number.

Winnie doesn't join her teacher. Instead, she stares into the glittering lights of the tent—a booth selling handcrafted jewelry, a stand for tarot card readings, a food truck offering frozen treats. Her eyes sink out of focus, like she's turning the knob on Professor Samuel's telescope to blur out the night sky. She pretends there are no Tuesday boats zooming across the water or Hummers revving down the streets. No Crow with a stolen source or Erica held prisoner.

And above all, no Jay trapped inside a Whisperer that isn't a *famēs* spell.

Guess I have all the evidence Mario needs now, Winnie thinks, fighting off a bitter laugh. She might not understand how a werewolf seventeen years ago became Jay's father—or how a wolf's jawbone appeared under Jay's pillow—but she can't deny what's right in front of her. It doesn't take a genius to draw the connecting line.

The *Incantamentum Purum Cor* requires someone with a "nightmare father, gone and slain" and a "lantern mother, spirit's bane." Jay's father was a werewolf; his mother was a Luminary. That makes Jay the "son of forest, the son of pain."

Pure Heart. There you are.

"Teddy?" Ms. Morgan pants into the phone. "It's me. Sorry to wake you, but we're in big trouble. Like, *big* trouble."

Winnie slips off her glasses. Another telescope knob turns. The lights become bulbous, as if they are bubbles under the water. All Winnie has to do is press a hand over her mouth and she can follow them.

Follow them where, though?

"No, not with the Tuesdays," Ms. Morgan is saying from twenty thousand leagues away. "With the Dianas. It's the *Incantamentum Purum Cor.*"

A plastic trash bin hovers to the left beside a stall selling homemade soap. It's blue like poppies. Blue like Erica's gloves.

"Yeah," Ms. Morgan continues nearby, "Winnie doesn't want to contact Harriet, but I agree: we have no other choice. You can send the message, if she won't."

Winnie won't. She absolutely won't. For four years, Grandma Harriet didn't help her family. Neither did Ms. Morgan or Professor Funday. Or Aunt Rachel. The *only* person who helped was Dad, albeit in the most convoluted way possible.

Although Winnie understands why he had to use codes and maps and drawings. He must have been trying to hide the source from Martedì so the Crow couldn't finish the *Incantamentum Purum Cor.* And he did a really good job of it. No one ever found anything until Winnie started poking around a month ago. And the only reason she ever poked around was because Darian gave her a locket by *accident* on her sixteenth birthday.

But there's one big question Winnie still hasn't answered: Why leave the clues at all? Why not let Jenna's source stay hidden forever?

There's something important there. Something Winnie is still missing. The *why* at the heart of her Venn diagram.

"Yeah, Teddy, I'm almost positive Winnie is under a *verba circumvolēns* spell. Still, I've managed to piece together the important parts—and that we're probably dealing with a *lēgātum.*"

Winnie stares again at the blue trash can. Her ghosts are far away; she is an emotionless robot; her fingers don't itch to draw. She just needs to keep thinking, keep following the bubbles.

Right now, Ms. Morgan has drawn the conclusion: *This whole town is in danger. The sleeping spirit is about to wake up.*

The Tuesdays, meanwhile, have decided: *This whole town is in danger because Winnie Wednesday is a Diana who is casting spells and killing people.*

The Luminaries Council has decided: *There is no danger worth disrupting the Nightmare Masquerade for.*

And Winnie, meanwhile—well, what has she decided? Where is her data leading her? Or for that matter, what conclusions is Signora Martedì making right now? The Crow has a witch and a source, she has the son of forest, the son of pain . . .

> *The more I forget you, the deeper you sink in*
> *Fangs at the neck and red paint on a lost cabin*

Winnie startles. She just heard those words as if they were right beside her, sung directly into her ears by Jay's rasping throat. She looks around. But of course, the tent is empty save for her and Ms. Morgan.

> *Ten dollars to kiss, a bet I can never win*
> *Snow on your lips*
> *It's feast or it's full famine*

Winnie doesn't actually notice when her feet begin moving. She just knows she is suddenly pivoting toward the tent flaps, marching once more toward the pier.

"Winnie?" Ms. Morgan calls after her. "Where are you going?"

"Do you hear that?"

"Hear what?"

"That song. Jay. He's this way."

"Winnie, there is no song."

No, there is definitely a song. It is Jay, singing *the* song he wrote about Winnie. Just like she heard him in the maze. Just like she heard him at Joe Squared two weeks ago. And it's coming from outside the tent.

She pushes back into the early morning. Wind, cruel and venomous, bites at her face. It's so at odds with the grayscale twilight rippling over white-tipped waves. Tuesday boats still chug; lights still beam off the dam; her ankle still throbs.

I miss you more now
Now that it's been so long

Ms. Morgan barges out of the tent to join Winnie. "What are you doing, Winnie? What do you hear?"

"I already told you. Jay's song. 'Backlit.'" Winnie reels about, feeling like a compass drawn by the earth's magnetic field. And just like a compass, her finger abruptly points north. "It's coming from that direction."

"Winnie, I don't hear anything."

"I told you: the Whisperer ate Jay. I *told* you I heard him in the maze. And I . . . I hear him again now. He's not dead, Ms. Morgan. He's not gone."

"I never said he was, but—wait." Ms. Morgan grabs at Winnie's shoulder because Winnie is yet again moving. "You can't just walk all the way up to the forest. Assuming Jay *is* there, what will you do once you find him? We need a better plan."

Yes, Winnie thinks. *We do. A plan like Dad would make.*

Her feet stop again. Her eyes stare at nothing. Her mind clicks and whirs as new punch cards get fed through her processor. *Agent Wednesday. What would Agent Wednesday do?* She can see her drawing of Jay before the Whisperer ate him. She can see her drawing of Erica channeling Lady Justice.

And she can see all the pieces of the last week—of the carnival, of the Masquerade, and of Hemlock Falls connecting like constellations through her telescope. *Here is Lyra. Here is Hercules. And here are the Lyrids, shooting across the sky.*

"I . . . have an idea," Winnie says, and now her compass swivels south. Toward the dam, toward all those Tuesdays hunting for her. "We'll have to split up—"

"*No.*"

"—because I'm going to need you to make a distraction."

"Winnie, *no.* We can't split up. It's too dangerous."

> *To kiss across shadows into a bright fever*
> *The dawn mist rises inside me like a wildfire*

Winnie's compass fastens onto Ms. Morgan. She takes in how tired, how drenched, how cold and broken the teacher is right now. This is not the woman who called her homeroom students *childish assholes* and begged them to boycott the Nightmare Court. This is not the woman who invited Winnie to apply to an art program at Heritage or snuck her an early pamphlet on a Compendium contest.

This is a defected Diana who just translated the Pure Heart spell and now thinks the world is going to end. Ms. Morgan really *is* just trying to keep Winnie safe.

But Winnie has her own people to look after.

> *With heat on your skin I spin*
> *Until I can't see us*
> *I find no relief, inside I'm still a hopeless curse*

"Please, Ms. Morgan. If you're always on my side like you keep saying, then please help me do this. I need to get into the forest." *I need to get to Jay and Erica.* "And I need *you* to make a distraction that will let me get there."

Ms. Morgan's nose twitches. Her parted lips tremble. Several more tired gasps escape her chest. Then she nods. "Fine, Winnie. God, I hope I don't regret this, but . . . tell me what you want me to do."

NOPE

WINNIE'S SCHEDULE FOR THE NIGHTMARE MASQUERADE

WEDNESDAY

8 A.M.: *Masquerade Fun Run*
- *Winnie is expected downtown at the Carnival—participation is optional. Dress is sportswear, if you decide to join.*
- *Winnie will fire the starter gun along with the entire Council.*

9 A.M.–12 P.M.: *Sunday Estate Training*

1 P.M.: *Hunters' Feast Kickoff*
- *Winnie is expected at the Wednesday estate ten minutes before—dress is casual. Darian suggests an elastic waistband for eating!*

1:30 P.M.: *Interview with Johnny Saturday and Wednesday hunters in Armory*
- *Rachel suggests you get there a few minutes early so she can prep you.*

2–5 P.M.: *Hunters' Feast*
- *Winnie can mingle and eat and hang out with her clan.*
- *Again, expect photographs and interviews!*

6 P.M.–9 P.M.: *Global Music on Garden Stage*
- *Winnie is expected for photographs beforehand with the visiting performers.*

9 P.M.: *Floating Carnival*
- *Wednesday firework display on the Little Lake*

CHAPTER

43

No estate in Hemlock Falls is ever in total darkness.

Timed lights trigger on driveways or trails. Motion sensors flicker lamps at the slightest twirl of a leaf on the breeze. And always, always there are night owls working through the spirit's hours, sitting at their desk and wondering how their colleagues are doing in the forest only a few miles away. While the hunters face mist and monsters, they will nurse a hot tea and finish up their reports on Luminary Supply Chain Logistics in South Brazil.

Two such lights burn in the Wednesday estate: one on the highest floor, where the councilor lives and is currently being debriefed on the phone by Jeremiah Tuesday about An Incident that happened in the night.

The second is from an open door to the basement where hunters train. They're only just getting started with their drill sergeant of a Lead Hunter, who barks out different combinations of rolls and swings and punches. The two newest recruits are struggling to keep up, and the taller of the two can't help but moan *Thank god* when the Lead Hunter hollers, "Forest loop!"

She doesn't actually know what *forest loop* means, but it's got to be better than the hundred and fifty pushups she just did.

The hunters head out, falling into a familiar rhythm and order they've tracked out countless times. Hundreds of hunters before them have jogged this route; hundreds after them will too—although usually, they run in the evening, when the gray light that falls over the garden comes from the west instead of the east. And when there aren't tens of booths and stages for a Hunters' Feast to snake around.

And usually the hunters run *before* the mist rises, not *after* it has fallen at dawn. But these differences are so subtle that no one pays too much attention. Their muscles know which paths to take through the gardens; their feet know which forks to follow on the paths; and if there's an unusual bite in the air as they tromp over pine needles and red soil, they just chalk it up to a freeze that came in the night before.

That is until they reach the stakes and electric sensors that mark the edge of the forest boundary.

Because here, mist scuttles outward like crabs across the ocean floor. Mist that should never stretch this far; mist that should have vanished an hour ago.

Worse—so, *so* much worse—is what crawls out *with* the mist: vampira. An entire horde of at least thirty monsters with their praying mantis arms and vicious mandibles. And although the sensors nearby are blink-blink-*blinking* with a franticness that means a thousand alarms are currently tripping at the Tuesday estate . . .

Well, there aren't enough Tuesdays at the estate to do anything about it. They've all been sent out to deal with a delinquent Diana who stole a Hummer.

Besides, it's not just here, near the Wednesday estate, that the sensors are losing their collective shit. It is *every sensor that encircles the forest.* They are all submerged by a mist that should not be there. A mist that is assembling nightmares *after* dawn.

The Lead Hunter is the first to understand what's happening. No, she doesn't understand the why or the how of it, but the what—oh yeah, she's got that figured out. And as the Luminaries rules say: *Any nightmare found outside the forest boundary must be killed on sight.* That is *the* reason the Luminaries exist, and the Wednesdays are nothing if not the cause above all else.

So Rachel Wednesday cups her hands and roars, *"Bellwether! Take down the bellwether!"*

Three miles away, near the western shore of the Big Lake, the Tuesday night hunters, tired and busted after a night on the hunt, are limping into the forest parking lot.

Despite a full night facing nightmares, poor Isaac Tuesday's ears are still ringing from the *royal* bless-downs he got less than twelve hours ago. First from Mason, then from Jeremiah. As punishment, Isaac doesn't get to go home after the hunt this morning. He's expected back on duty at the Tuesday estate to deal with a backlog of filing he's pretty sure didn't exist until last night.

Does it matter he tussled with a full-grown manticore at three A.M.? Nope. He better get his ass back to the estate by eight.

Isaac rubs at his right shoulder and leans against a Hummer's cold hood. His rotator cuff has been giving him grief again. His eyes too, from lack of sleep, which will only continue to worsen as the dawn stretches into day.

God, he's so tired, his mind is playing tricks on him. He's seeing things that aren't there, like a white fog unspooling from the forest.

He scrubs his eyes.

It's not going away. That is definitely a fog billowing out from the forest. And that is *definitely* a massive, hulking shape stomping and slashing this way.

Fuck me, he thinks. *Not her again.*

"MANTICORE!" he shouts, lurching away from the hood. Thank god he still has his gear strapped on. Thank god he hasn't taken off his helmet. "MANTICORE!" he repeats, and this time he tugs a flash grenade off his belt.

He's not fast enough. The manticore remembers him. *You chopped off one of my antennae,* she seems to say as she charges right for Isaac at the Hummer. He fumbles the grenade and dives for the other side of the vehicle. He ducks down right as the manticore slams into the metal chassis and hood with so much strength it shoves the Hummer back a whopping three feet. Isaac barely has time to roll under the Jeep parked next to it before the two vehicles collide.

Gunshots fire. Shouts ripple and ping. Someone else launches a flash grenade.

And Isaac can't help but wonder as he crocodile-slithers out from under the Jeep, *Why me? Why does this shit always happen to me?*

A few miles south of the forest parking lot, four high-powered motorboats steam back and forth across the Little Lake. They beam spotlights into the water near the bridge, where all flow through the dam has been halted. The Tuesday Lambdas have already determined, thanks to divers, that there are no survivors trapped inside the Hummer. But they've yet to find where Winnie Wednesday and her accomplice have gotten to. They might be dead . . . but more likely, they're alive. After all, Grayson Friday pulled this same prank four years ago and made it out just fine.

Dryden Saturday is going to be furious. Marcia Thursday, too—especially since her daughter was also an accomplice in Winnie's escape. But Jeremiah hasn't told them yet; he has only talked to Leila Wednesday at this point, because he needs her to be on the lookout for Winnie. When fugitives hide, they often flee to places they're familiar with.

"Call me if she shows up," Jeremiah commands from atop the bridge. Dawn rises in the east, but it's a clouded dawn. And there's a tenacity to the wind that portends storms.

His phone rings. It's Lizzy Friday. But he sends her straight to voicemail. Her cameras and inventions drive him to distraction; right now, he needs to stay focused on Winnie Wednesday. On the damage control in his near future.

It is as Lizzy is calling him a *second* time, that a sound cuts into his ears. It's so startlingly unexpected that it takes Jeremiah a solid five seconds to process what his ears are hearing.

A high-pitched wail echoes from downtown. It keens up, keens down. Again, again, again.

The Diana siren.

Well, now Jeremiah knows where Ms. Wednesday has fled to. And, grudgingly, he is impressed. She not only survived the crash off the dam, but she made it all the way to city hall. She is so, *so* much more formidable than her father ever was.

But Jeremiah will crush her. Because he must. She's *far* too dangerous to leave free.

Jeremiah yanks a radio off his belt. "Downtown," he barks, alerting the lead Lambda below. "Everyone. Now." Then he stalks to his Hummer, his entourage of Lambdas standing sentry along the bridge scatter for their own vehicles like the good scorpions they are.

Below, four boat engines rev loudly, abandoning their search.

The siren still continues howling. It will wake up everyone in the town, and Jeremiah is about to have a real shitstorm on his hands. One led by certain Saturday and Thursday councilors.

But oh, how short-sighted this will prove to be for Jeremiah Tuesday. Because as the four scorpion speedboats zoom toward the northeastern shore where a concrete landing feeds into downtown, on the *south*eastern shore a pontoon boat putters to life. It has been made to look like a swan, complete with white wings and a graceful neck—although its current pilot ruins the effect by bonking into the dock three times. Then breaking off the tip of the left wing on a steel piling.

No one notices, though, because no one is looking at the Little Lake anymore. And *definitely* no one is looking at the Floating Carnival.

The swan sets off to the north, where clouds coagulate over the forest like scabs atop a wound.

CHAPTER

44

Winnie has been many things in her life: Wednesday, Luminary, outcast, bear, girlfriend, best friend, science nerd, Midnight Crown . . . What she has never been is a thief. Until today.

First, she stole the T-shirt. Then the sweatshirt, and now she's jumping right up the corporate ladder to *vehicular thief*.

Number of boats stolen a month ago? Zero.

Number of boats stolen now? One.

Oh, and the fireworks—she can add those to her list as well, since there are three crates of them in the pontoon boat. Does Winnie have any idea how to detonate the fireworks? Nope. But surely the box of matches in her pocket that advertise the Très Jolie will do the trick.

Wind slaps over Winnie, cold and stinking of ancient soil. The swan's neck, head, and wings act like a funnel, targeting all the frozen air into her face. It snatches away the whine of the Diana siren downtown, so all she hears is the wind.

She thinks she smells dead things.

And she definitely feels Jay's song, summoning her like a different sort of siren.

Siren: These nightmares are known for luring their prey in with a song so seductive, no one can resist.

Ms. Morgan never did hear Jay's voice, and she was *adamantly opposed* (her words) to Winnie's plan. But Winnie didn't care about her teacher's approval back at the Floating Carnival, and she sure doesn't care now, halfway across the Little Lake. Jay's song is so seductive, Winnie can't resist it.

Besides, it's not Ms. Morgan's boyfriend who is trapped inside the Pure Heart. It's not *her* boyfriend who is the son of forest, son of pain. And it's not *her* boyfriend who said, *I love you. I'm sorry.*

Winnie's plan is a pretty simple one, in the end: while Ms. Morgan gets Jeremiah Tuesday aiming for downtown, Winnie will sail upstream toward the Big Lake. She actually wants the Tuesdays to follow her eventually— just not yet. Winnie needs a head start. Because no way in hell is this majestic Sunday swan going to outrun the scorpion speedboats.

Storm clouds have fully assembled in the north; the morning that should be peeking out in the east is being stamped down again. *Never mind, sunshine. Go back to sleep. You're not welcome here today.*

Winnie's hands—gloved in scorpion armor that belong to Mason—are frozen atop the pontoon steering wheel. The gear, although top-of-the-line, was definitely still wet when Winnie slugged it onto herself at the pier. It fits her taller frame no better than it fit Ms. Morgan's, hanging loose on Winnie's shoulders and thighs. The exo-scales *should* be form-fitting.

Still, some armor is better than no armor.

Her ankle thrums with a rhythm like Morse code. *SOS. Bandage immediately and elevate.* Winnie's response to that would be, *LOL. Not happening.* As long as her fibula, tibia, and talus bones can still support her weight, then she's going to keep using them.

Her left sleeve is rolled up to her mid forearm, allowing constant access to her watch's digital screen. What it says right now is *T minus one hour and seventeen minutes until the Crow makes good on her threats.*

So yeah, no stopping for injuries. No stopping for potty breaks or hitchhikers either, since here's the way Winnie sees it: there was a reason Martedì gave her an 8 A.M. deadline. That can't just be an arbitrary time on an arbitrary day. So by Winnie's logic, maybe the Pure Heart spell has until 8 A.M. to be cast.

Which also means it has until 8 A.M. to be canceled.

Winnie pushes at her glasses. The crack over her left eye seems to pinwheel. *Pick your nightmare! Spin the wheel! Ignore how Jay's song makes you feel!* She is almost out of the Little Lake, and although she can't see it from here, the Tuesday estate is beyond those dark fir trees and burgeoning maples.

And okay, there's undeniably a white fog trickling downriver now—one that is not merely water vapor condensing as the morning temperature ascends. *Awesome.* If Winnie had any doubt the forest spirit was waking up, that mist just dispelled it.

She grabs a life vest from under the captain's seat, and with the straps and foam, she locks the steering wheel in place. Then she scoots to the back of the boat.

To think, she stood here on this same platform only a few days ago and refused to toss out candy. Now she is about to aggressively launch pollutants into the lake.

Number of fish saved six years ago? Zero.

Number of fish saved today? Probably in the negative hundreds.

After all, Winnie caused a *second* Hummer to sink down to the lake's substrate, where it can leak out toxic chemicals and gasoline for all of time. Well done, Little Environmentalist!

She finds her matches. The armor makes her clumsy; the cold even more so. She has to remove her gloves to get the flimsy box open. Then it takes her six tries and three ruined matches to get a flame going long enough for her to shove it into a crate of fireworks. *Don't try this at home,* she thinks once she drops in the burning match, hefts up the open-top crate, and finally tosses it all overboard. It won't float forever, but hopefully no fuses will catch inside the box before Winnie gets twenty . . . thirty . . . forty feet away . . .

The fuses catch fire.

And the display that follows is filled with so much Wednesday green—since it's intended for after the Hunters' Feast—it sears the color onto Winnie's eyeballs permanently. Like, she's pretty sure her irises are no longer brown but hazel. And while half the fireworks go rocketing into the sky, the other half definitely don't make it out of the crate.

That should get some Tuesday attention.

Winnie scoots back to the steering wheel, where she detaches a walkie-talkie from her belt. It has dried out enough now from its dunk in the lake to switch on. Chatter and static topple out of the tiny speaker.

Fireworks. North of the Little Lake. All Lambda units move.

There are other messages spewing out too, now that Winnie is nearer to the forest. These voices are muffled and broken by a spirit that doesn't want to let them leave. *Help—forest—manticore—spread—salamander—lightning—mist—*

Well, shit. Winnie sure hopes this next part of her plan goes accordingly. She's no Thursday, so *haphazard* is a fair descriptor for the next few bullet points on her to-do list.

She hits the walkie-talkie's transmit button. "Hey, Jeremiah!" she shouts. The wind tries to steal her voice. "Hey, J.T. J-Dog. Pickle-breath—you around for a chat?"

Winnie presses the speaker to her ear. Behind her, one final firework sparkles into the gray, clotted sky. A bursting circle of Wednesday green.

"Ms. Wednesday," a voice answers momentarily. "I assume you just set off the fireworks?"

"Guilty as charged. Did you find Leona Morgan yet? Has she explained by now that we've got a spirit waking up in the forest?"

"She has, and it's an interesting tale. About as interesting as all those Compendium facts you shared with me underground yesterday."

Jesus, Winnie thinks. *That was only yesterday?*

"So I guess this means you don't believe her?"

"Not particularly."

Winnie groans directly into the mic. Jeremiah is excruciatingly predictable. Worthy of a Jeremian theorem: input *x*, and he will always think *y* is a lie!

"Well, if you want to catch me, J-Dog, you're going to have to come this way. I'm headed north. Swan float. Hard to miss."

Winnie gives an emphatic wave toward the lights of downtown.

"Also, I'm going to guess you're not getting the messages out of the forest right now. Otherwise, you'd probably believe what I'm telling you. So I'll just give you the basics: it's bad. Really bad. It sounds like the hunters are facing a manticore and a salamander right now. So you're going to want to get back to the Tuesday estate and load up on all that shiny gear from your Masquerade displays."

"Ms. Wednesday, turn around the pontoon boat."

"No, J.T. Can't do that." Winnie frowns at a shadow forming in the nearby mist. Then water splashes. *Kelpie,* she thinks. *Great.*

"Also, you've got mist and nightmares incoming. So . . . you know: get ready."

Winnie turns off the radio. The mist is so thick, she's not sure her final message went through. Plus, she's officially out of the Little Lake now. The banks are closing in on either side; the current is picking up speed. And to complicate things, the mist is quickly erasing all shoreline. Only the vague shapes of trees keep Winnie aimed in the right direction.

There are other vague shapes lurking in there too. They hulk and prowl, moving like zoo animals finally freed from their habitats. They parade south, toward Hemlock Falls.

The wind, at least, is gentler. The *only* improvement, since the mist cloys at Winnie with carrion smells. It strokes against her legs with hungry heat. And Jay's song—she still hears it, still feels it.

Elliott Monday hypothesized in 1974 that a siren's song switches on key dopamine receptors in the brain, and it is in fact this hunger for dopamine that drives people to follow the song.

Winnie dips away from the steering wheel to light another match. This one catches on the first try, and she tosses another crate of fireworks overboard.

Once again, Wednesday green lights up the sky. Beacons for scorpions to follow. Lying lights to lead them into danger.

> *The more I forget you, the deeper you sink in*
> *Fangs at the neck and red paint on a lost cabin*
> *Ten dollars to kiss, a bet I can never win*
> *Snow on your lips*
> *It's feast or it's full famine*
> *I miss you more now*
> *Now that it's been so long*

CHAPTER

45

Winnie runs the pontoon boat aground. She doesn't have much choice. There are too many rocks as she goes upstream, and the river rapids are too turbulent for the swan to sail against. This vessel was built for show, not power. So she veers the boat onto the eastern shore and runs the poor Sunday beast aground.

The pontoon boat launches upward like it's hit a ramp. The right wing cracks against a hemlock. Winnie topples backward, falling alongside her final crate of fireworks toward the railing at the boat's end.

She hits the railing. The crate hits too, bonking right against her swollen ankle. She yelps. Then clasps her hands over her mouth to stay quiet. And other than a brief lurch when the current headbutts the swan farther onto its rock, Winnie and the fireworks don't move again.

Her heart gallops inside her skull. Her ankle is really shouting *SOS* now. But if it ain't bleeding—which would attract nightmares—then Winnie still ain't stopping. At least there's no mist here, and Winnie can only assume that's because it has finished its job. It has built the nightmares it needed, so now it glides southward, raising nightmares far beyond the spirit's usual realm like a gardener plucking weeds from a vegetable patch.

She peers around the crooked pontoon boat; its electric engine is still thrumming. The shoreline is almost all conifers. This has never been a place dense with monsters because running water deters land nightmares—which is why Winnie made *this* her route into the forest in the first place. Unfortunately, she's on the wrong shore. She wanted west because that is where the trail switchbacks up to the overlook and the Big Lake beyond. But oh well. East she is, so east she shall go.

Wind kicks upward in blustery, unpredictable bursts, as if the spirit inhales. As if it *laughs. Finally, I am awake. Finally, I am free.* But Jay's song continues to call to Winnie too. Louder than the spirit's tempestuous laugh. *I miss you more now. Now that it's been so long.*

As Winnie clambers from the pontoon boat, the scent of petrichor pings around her like a pinball, promising rain at any moment. Her boots slide on slimy rocks. Water splashes to her calf. Her ankle snarls its rage. But with only a little wobble and no surprise drop-offs, she reaches the shore in seconds.

Where she immediately sets off north. Toward the lake, toward the Crow and Erica and . . .

Jay.

To kiss across shadows into a bright fever
The dawn mist rises inside me like a wildfire

Winnie unstraps a hunting knife as she creeps forward. A fine, serrated thing that Mason probably spent a lot of time selecting for himself. It even has his initials on the hilt (MRT). Briefly, she considers unstrapping a second blade for bilateral symmetry, but a low-hanging branch that almost swats her into the river ends that thought. She'll need one hand empty for climbing and grabbing.

Lights flicker to her left. A nest of will-o'-wisps jets across the river like dragonflies before zapping out of sight. In the distance, she thinks she hears gunshots.

T minus forty-nine minutes until the Crow makes good on her threats.

Winnie stays as low to the ground as she can. As close to the shore too. Her eyes search the veiled, gusting dawn for any sign of game trails, worn into the ground by nightmares or hunters or both. But she spies nothing. And when she squints east, she sees flames in the distance. *Salamander,* she remembers from the radio, and if that is one, then she'll want to avoid it.

Actually, she needs to avoid it. Those things are massive and spit fire.

Salamander: These large amphibious nightmares are able to start fires thanks to special glands on their backs. They are cold-blooded, so salamanders hibernate underground in winter.

The waterfall gets louder the farther north Winnie aims. It's like static on an old TV—like the sleeping spirit has its finger on the volume and is just pushing it higher, higher, higher. The light changes too, brightening in a way that suggests sunshine is being allowed through.

But it's a green sunshine, toxic and terrifying, and it paints the forest in too much color. This is a world of grayscale or sepia, where running water not only deters nightmares, but also deters vibrance and saturation.

Sleeping spirits: Little is understood regarding these magical entities believed to be the source of all nightmares. Most theories are, in fact, philosophical instead of scientific. The lack of empirical—

A bolt of lightning sears past Winnie. Heat and light crack in, so close that she needs three full heartbeats to realize the lightning didn't actually hit her. Then she launches into a run.

Air sylphid: These humanoid creatures are childlike in size with bark for skin and stone for teeth and horns. Their mastery over wind allows them to fly. They can also summon lightning; hunters are advised to avoid.

Winnie's boots toss up rocks and mud. She is making way more noise than is wise, but whatever. She has already been spotted; might as well go full throttle. The sylphid plunges out of the trees. Sparks flare between its gnarled hands.

Lightning streaks toward Winnie's head. She ducks. The electricity hits the water, sizzling lines across the surface and illuminating waters below. *CURSES*, she screams internally. *Why couldn't you have grabbed a bow, Ms. Morgan?* That would be *so* much more helpful right now, instead of this knife with *MRT* stamped onto it.

Winnie teeters toward the water. The river is pure chop this close to the waterfall. Jagged rocks jut upward. Cold wind gnaws, thick with spray off the waves. And the waterfall's roar builds—as does the cold, heightened by this wind that still sucks upward.

It's as if a cosmic vacuum has been switched on over the Big Lake, ready to suck up dirt, pet hair, and protons in one fell swoop. And hell, for all Winnie knows, maybe the spirit really is just a giant Hoover and the Pure Heart spell is the plug that slots into a socket. She can even imagine the Compendium entry: *The spirit vacuum is especially powerful on carpets.*

Oh god, she thinks as she lopes along the jagged riverbank. The falls are getting unbearably loud. *You are losing it, Winnie. Focus. Stay sharp.* Her arms swing at her sides. Adrenaline is stamping out the pain from her ankle, but she needs more speed, more bilateral symmetry—and oh no. *There.* There's the waterfall.

Winnie has nowhere else left to run. *Aroo! Aroo! Was it fun jumping, Wolf Girl?*

Lightning discharges behind her. Inexplicably, it doesn't connect. She rips a glance back . . . only to find a weeping willow tumbling onto the riverbank.

Dryad: These nightmares are indistinguishable from trees or hedges until disturbed by humans. They will attack with branches that become claw-like and legs that extend from their roots.

Lucky for Winnie, this particular dryad is focused on the sylphid—and the sylphid is suddenly distracted by the dryad. Which means *now* is a good moment to break from the river and launch uphill.

Except then a second sylphid hurtles in. Because of *course* it freaking does. Fresh lightning scrapes over Winnie's head. She smells burning hair, although the stench is quickly vacuumed up by the spirit.

The sylphid sweeps closer. Bark skin, stone horns, sharp teeth laughing. It reaches for her while light and static build visibly between its hands. This near, there will be no avoiding the lightning. But this near, there is also no avoiding Winnie. She thrusts out Mason's blade.

And she stabs the sylphid in the skull.

Light and static electricity wink out. The sylphid screams. Its magicked flight fails, and the natural pull of gravity lugs it from the air, sliding it right off Winnie's stolen knife.

It lands on the wet, craggy shore before her, body quivering. Lightning from the other sylphid continues sizzling nearby; the dryad continues fighting with swinging branches. And even though Winnie should run, she can't look away from the dying sylphid.

It would have killed her. Gladly. And yet, she can't stop thinking of an afternoon almost a month ago when she found a gash on Jay's wrist. *What happened?* she asked him.

Harpy, he replied.

Oh. Did you kill it?

Her, he corrected, his eyes wintery and cold. Mournful and lost. *Yes, I killed her.*

How many nightmares has Jay had to slay as a hunter? How many times has he looked into a creature's eyes and thought, *I am like you, and it's only a matter of time before I die too.*

Son of forest, son of pain.

No. Winnie can't do this. She can't kill again and cry *Self-defense!* If there's one thing she has learned in the last week, it's that she has to live with her choices for the rest of time; she has to live with her ghosts.

Winnie grabs the sylphid by the arm and starts tugging. The creature is heavier than she expects—which is silly. She has lifted plenty of dead sylphids during corpse duty. Behind her, the dryad lashes out with willow branches. It is green—so green—and the first sylphid hisses and electrocutes.

Winnie drags its sibling toward the water. The white foam of the waterfall spits and sprays; the TV static sound is overpowering; and Jay's song whispers and kisses against Winnie's skin.

Green. Everything glows toxic green.

The water kicks at the shoreline. Here is where Jay saved Winnie on her third trial. Here is where she awoke with the scent of him to keep her safe.

She doesn't think it's all in her head when she catches a whiff of lime and bergamot now. Or when she hears, again, his song "Backlit" summoning her in a voice that isn't really there.

With heat on your skin I spin
Until I can't see us

Her boots reach the water. The sylphid isn't moving, and its oozing, silty blood has left a trail.

I find no relief, inside I'm still a hopeless curse

Winnie heaves the body all the way into the water, careful to keep herself from ever getting so deep that the natural whirlpool sucks her down . . .

It sucks down the sylphid in seconds. And Winnie stares hard, hard at the churning waters. "Help it," she begs the melusine who lives below.

"Heal it because I don't think—" Her voice cracks. She tries again. "I don't think it's a hopeless curse. I don't think it deserves to die."

Winnie has no idea if the melusine hears her. No idea if the mist even brought that particular to life this time. *I love you. I'm sorry.*

Winnie turns away from the shoreline and tromps uphill into the trees.

> *Melusine: These beautiful, mermaid-like creatures inhabit the rivers and lakes of the forest. They are not aggressive but will attack if humans get near. Their blood, a clear liquid, can heal external injuries when poured on a wound. When ingested, it is an effective antidote against venoms and poison. (Note from Winnie: It leaves a horrible hangover.)*

The melusine is following Winnie.

Winnie doesn't notice it for a full five minutes as she scrabbles up the unfriendly hill. As her left ankle gives out three times, and she nearly face-plants on roots or rocks. Only when she hears a loud *boom!* like a Tuesday grenade from the west does she look back . . .

And oh, there it is. Humanoid and hunching. Slippery and scaled. The melusine is only thirty feet away, and it's not even trying to hide itself. It blinks, eyes vertically pupilled (*Like a banshee,* Winnie notes). Its chest rises and falls. Its teal scales flicker with shades of purple, winks of blue, and above all, flashes of green.

But what surprises Winnie most—other than the fact that the melusine is *there*—is that it has legs. In all Winnie's readings, in all her obsessive study of illustrations, she has *never* seen or heard of a melusine with anything other than a fishlike tail.

But this is definitely a melusine; it definitely has legs; and it's definitely following Winnie.

They are not aggressive but will attack if humans get near. Welp, Winnie sure is near! And she can't help but recall a mutilated vampira she found two years ago on corpse duty. She was *so* sure a melusine had killed it, but Mario had simply shaken his head while the Council had simply laughed. *It's not your fault,* Marcia had told her, *that you're so out of practice.*

Well, Marcia, Winnie thinks, *I have a surprise for you! Not only do melusine kill, but they will track you before they do so!*

With a strangled groan, Winnie hefts up her knife and trudges onward uphill. Wind slants against her, stinking of rotting leaves and musty water. Of fresh-churned soil and gunpowder. Wood smoke too—she catches whiffs of burning trees.

She checks behind her. The melusine is no closer, but it's also not farther away.

She wants to scream at it. To shout, *Shoo, shoo! Leave me alone! I'm only here to help you!* But that would most certainly draw other nightmares— such as the salamander probably burning the forest south of here.

Another *boom!* like a grenade. Another glance behind her to check on the melusine.

It's closer this time. So Winnie claws uphill faster. Her ankle fights her. The ground fights her too, slick with rain that is just starting to topple out. Fat, hot drops that remind Winnie of the mist. That hurt each time they pelt against her skin.

She is almost to the top of the hill. Then she will be a mere forty feet from the Big Lake. If she can *just* get that far. If she can *just* see what's waiting up there. Is it Jay? Is it the Crow and Erica? Is it a single eye opening wide with the words *Gone Fishing* written in mist around it?

Winnie hauls herself over the final crest, pulling onto the root of a massive black walnut. The low branch of a much smaller white ash. She peers back.

She no longer sees the melusine.

Which feels like a very, *very* bad development. She whips forward once more, knife outstretched. Wind beats faster here, no longer blocked by the lower terrain. The hot rain falls harder. The roar of the falls is less TV static now, more microwave cosmic background. It all crushes together, compressing Winnie in green chaos. Branches waving. Trunks groaning.

The more I forget you, the deeper you sink in.

She limps forward. *SOS* throbs from her ankle. Ahead, a weeping willow thrashes more wildly than the elms or ash trees around it. Winnie skirts to avoid . . . only to watch as the willow follows her. Because—*duh, Winnie!*— it's the dryad from before. She was so focused on the melusine, she didn't pay attention to what else was stalking her up the hill.

Such as the *actual* forest.

Branches fling out. Claws form at the ends. Winnie arcs up her knife, tumbling left. But it's useless. The branches loop around her arm like vines, and in seconds, she is being dragged toward the dryad's trunk. She digs her boots into the soil. The earth is soft here, sand and pine needles that kick up greenish dust—before getting sucked into the currents slinging toward the lake.

"No!" Winnie screams. *"Let go!"* The fat scorching raindrops vanish as she is towed under branches. She thinks of Erica in mist vines from the Crow. She thinks of Jay eaten whole by the Whisperer. She was *so* close to the Big Lake. She was *so close* to the Pure Heart. "I'm on your side," she tries to shout, but the branches are creaking around her head, shoving wet leaves and rough bark into her mouth. Her glasses get crushed against her face. She can't even scream now, and there—oh god, there is a *mouth* forming in the middle of the dryad's trunk.

It has teeth, it has a tongue. Hot breath curls outward. The branches constrict Winnie tighter.

Then it stops.

It just *stops,* as if someone hit a pause button on the dryad. Rain still batters down. The wind still sucks over Winnie, frizzing with a song that sounds like Jay. And the waterfall still thunders and snarls downhill.

But as quickly as the dryad overpowered Winnie, it now releases her. She topples to the sandy earth, coughing. Smoke-flavored air courses over her. Rain, still hot and charged, lands on her face. Her glasses are bent and warped.

A shadow stretches over her. Then a pair of scaled legs. It is the melusine, and when Winnie tries to scoot away, it doesn't stop her. It simply watches as she crab-legs backward. And though it has no eyes, Winnie can 100 percent feel the dryad watching her too.

"Oh shit," she croaks, clutching at her throat. Her neck is bleeding. Her face as well, and the rain is washing blood down in burning stripes. But neither the melusine nor the dryad make a move to attack again. So Winnie doesn't grab for her second knife, nor does she get up and start sprinting. She simply wipes the blood and rain from her eyes. Adjusts her glasses as best she can. Then pushes all the way to her feet, ankle bones juddering and howling.

Smoke billows upward, a gray curtain to haze out the southern sky.

And there's a rhythmic thump in the sand like a heartbeat. Gently tangible through the strange, tugging storm that wants to consume Winnie—and everything else—around the Big Lake.

"I'm . . . going now," Winnie tells the melusine. She lifts her hands. *No weapons, see?* "I think that's what you want me to do. I *think* that's why you just helped me. And uh . . . well, if you can find any other helpers, that would be great. Because I'm not sure what's happening at the shore, and I'm only one person against a really powerful Diana."

The melusine coughs, a violent sound that draws up from its aquatic throat while its scales coruscate in a wave of colors. It lifts its arm; Winnie sees it's holding her knife.

"For me?"

The melusine blinks. Its irises, Winnie notes, are glowing silvery gray like Jay's.

"Okay. Thanks . . . I guess." Winnie inches forward. Her exo-scales— modeled on this creature right here—look laughably clumsy next to the nightmare's own scales.

Winnie grips the hilt. The melusine's fingers briefly brush against hers.

And a ripple of strength courses through her. Up her arm, into her skull. It's like coffee with a splash of starlight. Like kisses underneath a Lyrid sky.

Melusine scales provide all the euphoric feelings of melusine blood but with only limited active healing properties. That's what the Compendium says, but now Winnie adds a note of her own: *However, when the melusine chooses to share its healing powers, all it requires is a single touch to transfer the magic.*

Winnie feels amazing.

Like, *amazing.* All the pain in her ankle is gone, as if there was never a Morse code machine pulsating through her blood vessels. The shredded skin on her face and neck stitches back together—she feels it happening, as if there are zippers on her flesh sliding shut. Within seconds, it's as if Winnie never got hurt in the Saturday maze or by a sylphid at the falls. Like she was never in a Tuesday cell with too little food and even less sleep.

Yet unlike when she drank melusine blood, she feels no silly drunkenness. No giggly ecstasy. The touch of the melusine was healing, empowering, restoring—and nothing more.

"Thanks." Winnie chokes out a laugh. A slightly deranged laugh as she finishes accepting the knife. Steel glints in the green and orange light. Rain plops onto it and slides down.

The melusine doesn't move, and as Winnie carefully backs away, it lets her. As does the dryad, so immobile now it looks more tree than nightmare. Only its branches move, clashing on the unnatural, Pure Heart wind. On that heartbeat rumbling into its roots.

Winnie turns. Winnie runs. And this time, when the melusine follows—and the dryad too—she lets them.

46

In theory, Winnie knows what she will find at the Big Lake is not *actually* going to be a single spirit eye opening while the words *Gone Fishing* hover in mist nearby. But now that the thought is in Winnie's head, it's basically all she can imagine.

Pure Heart. Trust the Pure Heart.

I love you. I'm sorry.

What Winnie actually finds when she bursts through the tree line is the end of the world. Ms. Morgan wasn't overblowing her panic; the *Incantamentum Purum Cor* really is destroying everything. There's a hurricane spinning over the Big Lake made of green clouds and lightning. The forest behind Winnie burns, flames spread by this wind—and not at all tamped down by the rain. And all along the shore, in droves beyond imagining, are nightmares.

There are Luminaries in there too, although they are vastly, pitifully outnumbered. Through her near-ruined glasses, Winnie spots familiar faces battling against more nightmares than she ever knew the forest could contain. It's as if the Xeroxed Compendium at the bottom of her closet just started vomiting out every page. *There's Chad Wednesday against an arassas with a cat head and lizard body. There's a hidebehind, long and thin and laughing as it attacks Isaac. There's a hellion pack, a banshee, a kelpie.*

And oh god—there's Aunt Rachel against countless swarming manticore hatchlings.

With Bretta and Fatima beside her.

Winnie wants to plow right to them, knives slashing through carapace and antennae. She even bursts out of the trees, ready to rampage over . . . until wind freight-trains into her, cackling like a combine harvester eating an eclipse. It hurls the full force of the acid rain onto Winnie's face; her nose hairs singe on a stench like a chemistry lab that's gone up in flames.

It is the Whisperer unleashed.

And it is Jay, still singing: *I miss you more now. Now that it's been so long. T minus nineteen minutes.*

Nearby, the melusine emerges from the trees. It stays tucked in the same shadows as Winnie—a shadow that stretches longer once the dryad joins them.

Which, *wow,* is weird enough to jolt Winnie fully back to the task at hand: to the Crow, to Erica, to Jay. *The enemy of my enemy is my friend,* she thinks as she searches for *any* sign of where Martedì might be.

Except . . . as soon as those words flicker across Winnie's brain, they get punted back out again. Rejected like faulty code. Because there's something that doesn't feel quite right about them. Something she can't pinpoint at this *exact* moment while the apocalypse rages before her . . . But something.

"Focus," she hisses to herself. Hot rain sears her lips. "If you were a Diana casting a spell, where would you go?"

Okay, that answer is easy: She would go somewhere all these fighting nightmares and Luminaries couldn't reach . . . But also somewhere near enough to the lake that the Pure Heart spell in Jenna's source could finish casting. Because as the final lines of the spell read:

> *Dawn will rise, casting light*
> *No more Lyrids falling bright*
> *Where waters fed will wake the night*
> *And mist inside the Pure Heart*

Winnie wishes she had binoculars. She wishes she had harpy-sharp vision. She wishes her left lens wasn't shattered and her right lens all crooked, turning this epic collapse into an epically collapsing kaleidoscope.

And she *wishes* that she hadn't seen two corners of her Wednesday square—and her aunt too—fighting only a tenth of a mile away. Near enough for her to help, near enough for her to save.

She searches for them once more . . . but rather than spot Wednesday forms fighting off hatchlings, she instead spots the sadhuzag bucking down the beach. Its seventy-four prongs stab anything in its path. Its razor hooves slice up shoreline.

Though not flesh eaters, they will kill any who enter their territory, including other nightmares. Addendum: Some evidence suggests the sadhuzag is drawn to residual magic, such as areas where Diana spells have been cast.

"Oh," Winnie says on a sigh, watching as the stag-like beast thunders this way. When Jenna cast the first portion of the *Incantamentum* four years ago, that residual magic attracted the sadhuzag to a bloodied pit in the forest.

Now the spell is finishing, so maybe the sadhuzag will be drawn to all that magic again.

"I have to follow the sadhuzag," Winnie tells the melusine, who is five feet to her right and curled in on itself, as if it craves the end of this cataclysm and the return of a comforting night. "Will you come with me?"

Somehow, talking to the melusine is even weirder than simply standing with it. But the melusine does oblige—and the dryad too, lumbering onto the shore while sand digs beneath its root legs. Its branches corkscrew outward. Wood groans, loud enough to puncture the storm's subatomic thunder.

Then branches stretch around Winnie, around the melusine.

And the sadhuzag scuds right past them, massive and majestic. It doesn't see them. It just careers ahead, while the sand beneath its razor hooves gets punched up . . . then sucked into the vortex of the waking spirit.

"*Follow it!*" Winnie hollers, and the dryad's limbs creak apart to let Winnie and the melusine hurry onto a path Winnie has taken before. On her third trial, she came this way, trying to cross the lake where water flowed shallowest toward the waterfall. *Trying* to outrun the Whisperer as it chased her.

This time, she is the one doing the chasing.

The sadhuzag leaps into the lake, clattering onto the same submerged rock that Winnie used a month ago. Its hooves seethe up water, and Winnie is shocked to see sparks of green winking with each splash. It's like the Wednesday fireworks exploding in every wave. *Bioluminescence,* she thinks.

She lurches into the water after the sadhuzag. Her feet also froth up microscopic lights. And oh goodness, how the scientist part of her wishes she could take a sample. Wishes she could stop and observe this never-before-seen galactic light forming in every splash her boots disturb.

The melusine does not run beside Winnie. It dives into darker, choppier depths and vanishes. The dryad, meanwhile, follows much more slowly. Its root legs can't gain purchase on the slick, underwater rock. The winds want to tug its branches the wrong way.

So Winnie leaves it behind. The sadhuzag is already to the other shore, and if she loses sight of it, she'll lose her only chance at finding the Crow and Erica.

And Jay, and Jay, and Jay.

> *To kiss across shadows into a bright fever*
> *The dawn mist rises inside me like a wildfire*

Yes, it really is a wildfire now because the salamander's flames have reached the shoreline in some spots, choking out smoke and sparks.

The water is to Winnie's knees, warm and feral like a hot tub with all the jets on. The current pries at her, wanting her to go toward the waterfall.

You either trust the forest or you don't, Winnie. You have to make up your mind.

She trusts it. She trusts it to the very purest heart of her. But to follow the current—to let it tow her over . . . That is not the way she's meant to go today. The forest is going to have to trust *her* instead.

Green continues to burst around Winnie's legs. Even the waking spirit and its hot, hot rain and merciless winds cannot stop these lights from shining. Honest lights. True lights.

Ahead, the sadhuzag has been forced to slow because more nightmares infest the western shore. More Compendium entries spewing out willy-nilly.

There are Tuesday scorpions here too, and as Winnie drags onto the shore, shedding water like a sodden bear, she thinks she spies a graying redhead fighting against a manticore hatchling.

Well done, J.T. Winnie smiles grimly as she pushes into a walk. Then a canter. Then a run. *You finally picked the right team.*

Except . . . no. There it is again. That burst of faulty code that says, *You're missing a semicolon. Try again, Winnie.*

She rushes on. The TV static volume is turned so high now, it's a disharmonic overtone to an unshackled superstorm. Her hair is wet from the rain, wet from sweat. Hemlock Falls never gets this hot; the forest won't let it. *But the forest,* she thinks, *isn't in charge anymore.*

And it seems to have realized this. Because as Winnie and the melusine rush down the sandier western shore, the nightmares they encounter stop fighting. They leap back from their Tuesday targets or from each other. Whatever match they are locked in, they cease entirely. They fix gazes onto Winnie—some beady-eyed, some eight-eyed, and some with no eyes at all but simply cold sentience. Then one by one, they scuttle or paw or lope after her.

Some Tuesdays take advantage of this, shooting or stabbing at a back that flees. But most gape, just as the nightmares did, at Winnie while she cannons past. She tries to smile at Mason, whose knife she has . . . well, not stolen, but *borrowed.* She doesn't think he sees the grin.

It is right as the sadhuzag flings itself into the stretch of forest that dips all the way down to the shore—the place where Winnie came with Mario only two nights ago for the safari—that she has a sudden vivid memory of a rowan tree with leaves bursting fresh along its spindly branches.

Some Dianas will craft small coins from rowan wood that has been harvested in a spirit forest, believing such amulets can protect against nightmares.

Winnie could almost smack herself for not remembering this sooner. There was a rowan tree beside the granite pit, as if planted there to protect while a spell was cast. So of course, the rowan tree by the shore might also have been strategically grown. Which means *that* is where the Crow—and Erica and Jay—must be.

Winnie glances behind her. She has hundreds—*hundreds*—of nightmares following her. She hopes the rowan tree doesn't harm them. She hopes the Crow doesn't either.

T minus thirteen minutes.

The forest here looks like it did on Monday night. The light is that same awful gloaming that Winnie's eyes hate, and the shapes in the trees might as well be her fellow science nerds. She can almost pretend that wulver over there is Mario.

Wulver: These creatures are often mistaken for werewolves, but in fact are full nightmares with no daywalking abilities. With furred, humanoid bodies and lupine heads, they are not aggressive unless provoked.

Ripped-up earth and roots mark the sadhuzag's passage—and Winnie follows it. The green light feels weaker here, and now that Winnie is paying attention, the wind is softer too. She thought it was just a result of entering the trees. That these aspens and silver firs were protecting her. But no, there is actually less wind.

Static scrapes over her skin. A whispery keen that means magic happens nearby. And Jay's song grows louder. But it's like he's singing through a wind farm; like she can *hear* that he's right there, but everything is distorted by the waking spirit.

I'm coming, Jay. Wait for me.

Then Winnie sees it: the sadhuzag. It has stopped fifty feet ahead, more silhouette than vibrant beast, its proud body at attention, head and antlers upright.

Two hellions charge by on Winnie's left, spraying tendrils of flame and tearing up underbrush. Next, a banshee on her right in a streak of silver and green.

Grief wells in Winnie. Unbidden, burning. *Jay, Erica, Dad.* But it dissolves as soon as the banshee is past.

The hidebehind leaps from tree trunk to tree trunk—laughing and laughing. Then come three vampira on their stilt legs with mandibles wide. Even two ghost-raccoons smear by like glowing exhales.

What is happening? Winnie thinks. Her brain accepted that the melusine and the dryad were helping her. It accepted that all the nightmares of the forest were following her. But now it has decided to revolt and go, *THIS IS WEIRD. MAYBE YOU SHOULD WORRY.*

Winnie unstraps her second knife. Nightmares are still marching or crawling or zipping by her, and one by one, they're stopping behind or around the sadhuzag. Assembling like soldiers in a row . . .

No, like flies on sticky paper.

Now that Winnie really squints, she can make out a faint mist curling and coiling around each nightmare. *Vines,* Winnie thinks. *Like the ones that held Erica.* And the nightmares are leaping right into that trap, getting glued into place one by one.

Well, no one ever said nightmares were smart. *To judge a nightmare with human emotion,* the Compendium states, *or to anthropomorphize them in any way is to fundamentally misunderstand their inner motivations and decision-making. They do not operate according to Maslow's pyramid of needs, but rather to an arrangement of needs that is entirely their own.*

Winnie hastens forward. She at least knows there is a trap there, and that means she can avoid it. She cuts left, circling deeper into the trees, away from the lake. The wind and rain have all but stopped now.

And oh yes, now she feels her locket. It's buzzing like a wasp inside a bottle, and it's *definitely* getting hot.

T minus seven minutes.

Nightmares continue to get snared by the fly trap. Tens of them pinioned between trees or under hedges or on top of branches. Each immobile while mist swerves around them. But actually, the farther Winnie treks, the more grateful she is that the nightmares are there. Because thanks to their arrangement, she can see exactly where the trap's boundaries are— and avoid the boundaries in turn.

"I take it back," she murmurs to the caught hidebehind as she shimmies around a red cedar. "You nightmares are *really* stinking smart. Please forgive me and every other Luminary who ever thought otherwise."

Winnie gets all the way to the overly cheerful stream that will lead down to the shore, its waters burbling a bit higher now thanks to the rain. The nightmares don't cross, of course, but neither, Winnie notes, does the mist.

This is a crack in the witch's trap. *This* is how Winnie is going to get close to the Crow.

She fights the urge to check the Timex as she stalks forward. She doesn't need a second-by-second countdown anymore. The time is basically panic o'clock. The heat cast from her locket tells her that. As does the total stillness that has draped the forest. No rain, no wind, no movement or noise or distant chaos. Just . . .

Quiet.

It's like the silencing spell the Crow cast in the maze. Everything has suddenly become muffled. Even her boots splashing in the stream stop creating enough sound.

Mist continues to writhe over the shore, holding nightmares in its clutches like an entomologist with new bugs. Winnie's Compendium can't stop cataloguing them. *Basilisk, changeling larvae, urus, vampira, ghost-deer, velue, earth sylphid, manticore hatchling.* She even thinks she sees the fiery wings of a phoenix.

Then suddenly, Winnie is back at the shore. At that half-moon stretch of beach where the safari went. Where Grayson's funeral was and Jay was forced to hear congratulations and condolences at the same time. *Youngest Lead Hunter! You must be so proud!*

To think, that was the least of the problems rolling down the pipeline toward Jay.

The Big Lake is visible again—and there's no winking eye. Nor any hurricane. Nor any *waves.* The whole thing is placid as glass, except for a rhythmic ripple each time the ground quivers with the spirit's geologic heartbeat.

Ba-doom.

Ripple.

Ba-doom.

The Crow stands at the water's edge, her hands on her hips and her attention on the lake. She is dressed as she was in the maze with armor and mask—but she isn't the only Diana now. Winnie hastily counts twelve other figures: four hounds, two more crows (although their masks have black beaks instead of gold), and then figures like she has never seen before.

Strigēs, she thinks, remembering back to *Understanding Sources. These Dianas are ranked just below cornīcēs and wear owl masks. Since spells are not created so much as interpreted from the forest's own magic, these witches specialize in translating magic into spoken words.*

Aprēs: These Dianas wear boar masks and are colloquially referred to as "sniffers." They are tasked with finding new types of magic in the forest that owls can then translate into spells. Hierarchically, they are one level below strigēs.

Lyncēs: These Dianas wear lynx masks and frequently command hosts of hounds. Like a Diana version of a Tuesday scorpion, they are meant to guard witch society from Luminaries.

Well, so much for Winnie's attempts to uncover all the Dianas in Hemlock Falls. She has *no idea* who any of these people are. They could be friends, they could be relatives, they could be strangers from a thousand miles away. She has no idea, and dressed as they all are in this nondescript armor, there's nothing at all for Winnie to latch onto for recognition.

Other than the chattering stream and throbbing lake, the one lynx and four hounds are the only movement on the beach. Mist oozes from their left hands to serpentine into the trees. And now that Winnie squints, she can see second ropes of mist connect each witch with the rowan tree. Silva, Winnie recalls. *A spell that can only be cast within the forest, relying on immediately absorbed spirit power.*

If Winnie can stop those witches from drawing that power, then she can probably stop the fly-trap spell that's imprisoning all the nightmares. And *then* she could give all these Dianas something else to fixate on.

Winnie's front teeth tap together silently as she tries to make the math of two knives against five targets work. Presumably the lynx is in charge, so maybe she can take them down first—

A splash shatters the stillness. Erica bursts from the water, towed onto the shore by mist vines. She gasps and chokes, as if she was just anchored underwater to the point of drowning. Her body reaches the shore. The vines tow her to the Crow's feet, sand shoveling out from beneath her. A scar to mark the otherwise untouched beach.

"Let's try this again," Martedì declares, her voice unmodified by her mask. "Finish it, Erica. Finish what Jenna started *now,* or join her at the bottom of the lake. We had an agreement, remember? And you should know by now that there is no escaping a Diana bargain.

"So do as you promised, or next time, I'm not towing you out again."

Winnie's teeth don't move now. Her breath is held tight. *Erica hasn't finished the* Incantamentum. *There is still time to keep the spirit from awakening.*

"Finish the spell, Erica. You've done so well up until now. All that's left are the final words. We'll say them with you, won't we?" Martedì opens her arms to the other Dianas, like a maestro ordering her choir to perform. As one, they all sing—except the hounds and the lynx: *Sumus ūnus in somnō et somniīs.*

A wave of power rocks outward, knocking Winnie onto her heels. It makes her locket sear so hot, she grabs for it. So *hot* she rips it out from under her armor without conscious thought. *It hurts, it hurts, it hurts! Get it off me!*

She makes noise. Way too much of it. But no one hears her because at that same moment, Erica makes noise too. A giddy, croaking howl. "You won't hurt me. I'm the only one who can use Jenna's source, I'm the only one who can finish—"

The vines rip Erica back underwater. In less than a second, she is submerged with only bubbles to show where she went down.

Winnie's locket continues burning. It glows orange now—and she can smell the exo-scales under the gold melting. Heat claws upward, drawing more sweat from her face. The locket is going to roast through her armor. It's going to brand her skin.

She bites her fist to keep from crying out, but as each second passes, the locket glows brighter. So even if she can keep her voice contained, she can't hide this glow.

It's like a beacon. Like a lantern. *Or like fireworks.*

Winnie's lungs and spine soften at that thought, and suddenly, she sees a way to make her math add up: before she left the pontoon boat, she grabbed—on sheer instinct—a single capsule of fireworks plastered with *Danger!* labels.

Well, danger is exactly what Winnie wants right now.

She digs into a side pocket of her armor until she finds the paper filled with gunpowder and stars. It's slightly damp from her run through the lake, but not soaked. As long as she can get the fuse hot enough . . .

Except no. When she tugs out her matches, they are fully sodden. Fully useless. *Think, Winnie. You're a scientist. You're a problem solver. All you need is . . .*

Heat.

She fights off the desire to laugh—a giddy, croaking howl just like Erica's. Then she cants forward, her eyes never leaving the shoreline or the Dianas. Erica is still plunged underwater, and the words *Sumus ūnus in somnō et somniīs* still shiver through the air, lapping in time to the heartbeat waves against the beach.

The locket cooks Winnie's face, heat rising off it like a candle. She lifts the fuse to the locket. The gold dangles and sways. But after sixteen Mississippis, the laws of thermodynamics finally take hold.

Fire sparks. The fuse catches. The fuse burns.

Winnie chucks the firework at the rowan tree.

CHAPTER

47

While Winnie's new plan, crafted from a truly desperate assemblage of bullet points, won't impress the Thursdays anytime soon, it *does* give Winnie precisely the mathematical outcome she desires.

The fireworks detonate, spraying out green sparkles that *pop-crack-boom!* around the rowan tree or across the half-moon stretch of shore. One hound gets it in the abdomen, another in the leg. And the lynx, meanwhile—well, they get a faceful of Winnie because as soon as the fireworks start going, she starts running. Bilaterally symmetric, her knives swing like she is a vampira with blade arms.

She aims one knife at the lynx's face. *Swipe.* She slices off a pointed ear. Then her other knife she punches across the lynx's abdomen. These aren't killing blows so much as flourishes meant to stop the *silva* spell channeled from the rowan tree.

It works. Winnie knows it works because she sees the mist evaporate like a line of falling dominoes. Then a bellow fills the morning, so loud, it rattles into Winnie's bones—a familiar sound that was directed at Winnie only fifteen days ago . . .

And that is now beautifully, *viciously* directed at the Dianas.

The sadhuzag charges this way.

Now Winnie does laugh with a full-throated cackle. She is a hunter. She is on the move. And although the Dianas are trying to launch attacks at her, only one actually connects with Winnie before the sadhuzag—and all its fellow nightmares—come pouring out of the forest.

The spell that hits Winnie is a bad one, though. The worst: a golden arrow that shafts right into her chest. Pain, heat, *screams*. They suffuse her body, all the way from her anterior fontanelle down to her distal phalanges. She becomes the *sagitta aurea*, her vision turning gold as molten sunlight.

Her locket burns like fresh magma. Fully red. Fully smoking. But, inexplicably, Winnie doesn't die. The gold and the pain clear, and other than a melted depression on her armor, there is no wound.

So she runs onward. Her knives drip blood. Her focus, even with green fireworks to burst in her periphery, stays lasered on the Crow. Martedì has seen what is happening, so is tearing Erica out of the water again. This time, there is no struggle in the girl.

"Do it!" Martedì shouts in a voice made of thunderclaps. As if her mask magnifies her words, turning her into an all-powerful godling. "Do it now, Erica, or I will make sure everyone you love is destroyed."

Winnie throws her knife, but it's useless. The blade simply bounces off the Crow, deflected as if hitting a force field.

"*DO IT, ERICA. NOW.*" Martedì whips Erica higher, and a cry rips from Erica's throat. Partly pained, mostly defeated.

Then come the words Winnie doesn't want to hear. The words that mean, *We are one in sleep and dreams. We are one in waking.*

The explosion that ripples out is devastating. It flings Winnie back—along with everyone else on the shore. Nightmare, Luminary, Diana. Everyone topples like wheat beneath a scythe. All except Martedì, who leans into the wave as if she knew this was coming. As if she *loves* it, and by the power of the forest, give her *more*.

Worse—so much worse—a tunnel begins opening into the water. It pulls at Erica, sucking her into the lake as if she really is nothing more than protons and dirt dug into the carpet.

Winnie rises. She runs. The earth no longer pulses with a heartbeat. Now, there is only the chaos of the resuming supercell storm.

She drops her second knife because it's no use against the Crow or the waking spirit. All Winnie needs are her smarts, all she needs are her instincts. "*Stop!*" she screeches at Martedì, who stalks toward the watery tunnel carving into the waves. "*Stop!*"

Martedì doesn't stop. She probably can't hear Winnie over the universe collapsing. So Winnie pushes herself harder. She's close to the Crow now. Close to this uncanny hole spiraling into the Big Lake.

That is when two things happen. First, a bird drops out of the sky and starts squawking. It flaps and claws into Martedì's face, forcing the woman to stop right at the tunnel's edge. Which gives Winnie enough time to catch up. To rush onto the first stretch of exposed silt and rocks and weeds.

Then the second thing happens: the melusine returns. It propels itself from the water like a wave come to life. Its tail morphs into legs. *Webbed feet,* Winnie notices for the first time. *And very sharp claws.* It attacks the Crow—and this time, Martedì has no choice but to stop and fight back.

Winnie stampedes past them. The melusine doesn't notice her, nor does Martedì. But the crow—the *avian* one . . . It screams a throaty caw at Winnie before flapping away. And sure, why not? A sentient crow on top of everything else makes total sense here.

Winnie looks back only once, to check the battle that has laid claim to the beach and forest. Golden arrows fly against nightmares, against Luminaries—and a lone signora still fights against a melusine with scales that shine like a sunrise.

Winnie enters the Big Lake.

Possession: Though rare, there are reports of forest spirits briefly possessing humans and using them to accomplish tasks that nightmares cannot complete, such as destroying sensory equipment or killing hunters. The hosts rarely survive the encounter.

The ground is silty and sopping as it slopes downward. Already Erica is fifty feet ahead. She doesn't look conscious. She doesn't even look alive. But if Winnie won't give up on Jay, then she sure won't give up on Erica either.

She pushes the muscles of her quadriceps, hamstrings, glutes faster. She channels every ounce of speed into legs that haven't felt relief in hours. That haven't had calories in even longer. But that is what the melusine's caress was for. *Keep going. Keep going.*

T minus this is the end.

I miss you more now. Now that it's been so long.

Water fuses into a liquid wall behind Winnie, and though light still pours down from above, the deeper she runs, the less light reaches her. It reminds her of an aquarium she went to once, when she was eleven. There was a tunnel that went right through the shark tank. Now, instead of Chondrichthyes to swim around Winnie, there are sirens, kelpies, river sylphids. They whip and flash, keeping pace with Winnie in a way she really hopes isn't predatory.

Each time the shadows move, green bioluminescence ignites. It doesn't make her think of fireworks now. Instead, she thinks of fish food. She thinks of Grayson's funeral and his ashes tossed into the Big Lake. *May Grayson find peace in his long sleep at the heart of the forest.* That was how the eulogy ended because that is how they always end.

Winnie's boots slomp in the silt and trip through plants drooped across the substrate. *Erica, Erica.* She just has to reach Erica. She just has to stay ahead of the water stalking behind.

Her breathing turns pained. The air is humid like a spa. Like the hot room. And all the gurgling from the encroaching lake—they're just pumps and pipes and furnaces to keep Winnie hidden away from Tuesdays.

God, if only she could go back to that moment in Jenna's secret corner. If only Winnie could *listen* to the harmonic overtones in Erica's words and push her friend for more answers. For more truth.

There's something important in that thought. Something that is digging at Winnie's frontal lobe like it's another scratch-off lottery ticket. But she has no time to scrape in search of matching numbers. She is still running down into a lake that wants to crush her.

The descent flattens, and Erica slides like a sea slug, her body carving a groove through silt. Each rock she bumps into makes her eyelids open.

If she's alive, there is no sign of it.

A droplet plops onto Winnie's head. It's so hot, so startling that she looks up. *Oh shit.* The lake has sealed over her. And any light still letting her see, move, run—it isn't coming from overhead. It's coming from the center of the lake, from a silvery glow that . . .

Oh yes, is pulsing.

Pure Heart. Trust the Pure Heart.

This, Winnie decides, must be the sleeping spirit. Not an eye nor even a heart, but a silver glow like the full-moon Ferris wheel surrounded by lapping waves and dry ice.

A mist floats here too. An ethereal fog that lacks the talons of usual mist. It's not hot, nor even warm. It's simply vapor that Winnie scrambles through.

More hot water rains onto her head.

The light brightens. There's a greenish tint that swirls through like two paints being mixed upon a palette. *Forest green,* reads one tube. *Full moon silver,* reads the other. And all Winnie has to do is dab her brush in, then smear, swipe, create whatever nightmare her mind's eye can imagine.

Brighter, brighter. Winnie has to screw her eyes to almost shut. Erica is losing definition, becoming a silhouette. Backlit, like Jay's song—a title Winnie still doesn't understand, even though she asked him about it nine days ago. *I miss you more now. Now that it's been so long.*

She does miss him. And if Jay isn't here, if Winnie can't save him or Erica now that she's literally *at the bottom of the Big Lake,* then what was the point of everything? Of Dad's clues or a stolen swan boat or a ruined maze and a derailed Hummer?

Erica stops moving. It's sudden. One moment, she's prostrate. The next, she's rising, pivoting, as if invisible hands have scooped her up. *There, there, little witch. Let's get you back on your feet.*

The water still prods at Winnie from behind, shepherding her forward. She is a fish in a net, pushed along toward doom. Until she too reaches the greenish, throbbing light, where a second silhouette awaits. A figure she has drawn and redrawn more times than she can remember. He fills her sketchbooks, he saturates her thoughts. And his song—it continues to sing, controlling her just like a possession as described by the Compendium.

"Jay?" she asked him nine days ago as they lay on Winnie's bed, her body tucked against his. Her fingers reveling in the shape of this boy she'd lost for so many years.

"Yes, Winnie?"

"Why's your song called 'Backlit'? You never say that word in the lyrics."

"Not all song titles have to be in the lyrics, Win. I'm an artiste like that."

"You mean, you're a dork."

"A cute one?"

"A very cute one."

"Do cute dorks get kisses?"

"Not until they answer my question. Why 'Backlit'—what does it mean?"

"It means . . ."

"Stop squirming. Answer the question."

"Fine. It means 'I don't know.' I just . . . heard the tune, and for whatever reason, that title was there. 'Backlit.' It felt important. Like I needed to write it down. I didn't have lyrics yet—just the tune and the title."

"But then why make the song about me?"

"Because . . ."

"You don't need to blush like that, Jay. I promise I won't laugh."

"I'm not worried you'll laugh. It just doesn't make sense, is all. When I heard that tune, I saw you. There was all this light radiating off you, like you'd stepped out of a star. And . . . yeah, yeah. I know how weird that sounds. But once I saw you like that . . . well, there wasn't anyone else I could possibly write the song for.

"There, are you happy now, Win? Does that satisfy your ladyship?"

"Stepped out of a star?"

"I knew you'd laugh."

"I'm not laughing, Jay. I promise. It's just . . . hard to imagine myself like that."

"Not for me it isn't. Now can this dork have his kisses?"

Well, Winnie can imagine the light of a star now. Holy hellions and banshees, can she imagine it. Jay wasn't just having some weird dream about her; he was *seeing* what would come. He was seeing this moment, right here.

Just like how you keep dreaming of the Pure Heart.

There goes the scratching at the lottery ticket again. Winnie can see the first numbers. Important numbers that add up to something bigger, like a jackpot for her friends, her family, for all of Hemlock Falls . . .

Water sloshes behind her. Impatient. Filled with galaxies and fish food and nightmares. *Go on, little hunter. Make your move or we will make it for you.*

Wednesday, witch, werewolf.

Bear, bell, sparrow.

Three circles on a Venn diagram; three petals on Dad's favorite nodding wakerobin.

Luminaries. Dianas. Nightmares.

Oh. *Oh.* There goes the last of the scratch-off silver. Because *oh,* this must be why Dad left Winnie all those clues. Why he didn't simply hide Jenna's source away forever, but left a complex scavenger hunt for his daughter to follow. A secret exit from a twisty maze.

The enemy of my enemy is not my friend. Yet neither are they my enemy. Because in a system, there are no enemies. There are no friends. There are predators, there are prey, and there is survival—all kept in a careful, cautious balance. To remove one piece of the system means the whole thing will collapse.

The spirit was awoken because the balance was broken by a Diana who fed it a half nightmare made from pure, Friday heart. Now if Winnie wants to reassemble the balance again . . .

She sucks in a sweltering breath. The green lights dart around her, blasting photons that no one will ever see. They aren't swamp fires, but rather fairies who will guide Winnie where she needs to be.

You either trust the forest or you don't, little hunter. You have to make up your mind.

Winnie steps into the light.

C H A P T E R

48

Ghost-deer, ghost-squirrel, ghost-raccoon, etc.: Much dispute remains around their origins: Are they creations of the dreaming spirit? Or are they phantoms left over from the creatures that inhabited the wood prior to the spirit's arrival? In the forests surrounding the Earth's oldest spirits, there are apparitions of primitive creatures long since lost to time.

What happens next will be the topic of discussion for decades to come. Papers, dissertations, conferences, and debates amongst scientists and philosophers—both Diana and Luminary alike—as they try to break down the exact mechanisms at play. There will be terms like *ecological niche* and *system collapse* and *magical biotic potential*.

But no one will agree.

Because no one will ever really know what happened at the Big Lake or inside the spirit.

Not even Winnie, despite being the one who chose to step inside. All she will ever be able to articulate is this: she enters the spirit. It feels like she has always imagined stepping into a car wash might feel—specifically that part at the end where all the dryers blast you. Except instead of air, there is light. There is static. There is a silence so complete, it is matched only by the vacuum of outer space.

Above all, there is the greenish full-moon light. It engulfs her, it consumes her, it breaks her apart into the most basic of subatomic particles.

Yet somehow, Winnie has enough awareness and physicality to still search for her best friends' hands.

First she finds Erica, the girl she spent every Friday night with, giggling under bedsheets. As soon as their fingers connect, Erica's eyes pop wide. Her russet brown irises glow like phoenix flames as she takes in the situation. Takes in Winnie, Jay, the endless and total light.

Jay? she asks without a real voice.

Yes, Winnie answers, and together, they each grab one of his hands.

Then Jay, the boy who was cursed before he was even born, but who never stopped loving his friends, finally opens his eyes too. They are the exact same shade as the green moonlight that surrounds him. *Winnie,* he says—also without a voice. *Erica. What's going on?*

It's kind of hard to explain, Winnie replies. *But I'm pretty sure we're inside the sleeping spirit.*

This is all she can say before suddenly the three of them begin moving. Spinning as if they are in a centrifuge. Faster, faster while their base components get separated even further apart. *Here are the solids. Here are the liquids. Here is the forest. Here are the last four years of pain.*

Distantly, Winnie thinks she should feel sick. But no nausea touches her. Her senses are simply too deluged by the sleeping spirit. Her extrasensory organs toggle on: the one for inertia. The one for the four dimensions of space-time. They tell her that she's rising and that the rules of gravity no longer apply.

Tears rip from Winnie's eyes. Her ears still absorb no sound. And she wonders if her collection of atoms might end up trapped forever like this, orbiting in this centrifuge.

Until gradually, the light does fade, and Winnie can see that she and her triangle are back underwater—although they aren't actually *in* the water. Instead, the depths of the Big Lake churn around them. Dark, cold, ravenous. *Pick your nightmare, spin the wheel! You'll need all three pieces to finally heal.*

A rumbling roar soon takes over the spirit's silence. A mauling cold supplants its static. And stormy shadows seep in to replace the green moonlight.

Winnie, Erica, and Jay begin rising through the water column. They still spin, although slower now, and soon they break through the surface of the

Big Lake. Water stops crashing around them, replaced by storm, winds, lightning. The hurricane has resumed over the forest, yet now three friends are its eye.

Gone fishing, Winnie thinks, and she wants to laugh at that. Because she's still wearing her stolen T-shirt under this armor, like she's some kind of sleeping spirit fangirl.

Erica is the first to speak. Later, she will be unable to explain *why* she is compelled to say anything. The words are simply there, ready to be spoken. Waiting to trip off her tongue.

Which, later, Winnie will decide is a sure sign that Erica was possessed. And she, Winnie, was possessed too, along with Jay, since each of them begin acting in accordance to what the spirit needs them to do.

We are one in sleep and dreams, Erica says in English. Then again, *We are one in sleep and dreams.*

She chants it three times before Winnie is compelled to join her—and as soon as Winnie also starts chanting, she feels her atoms move, melt, quake with a newly electrified life.

Jay is the last to join. *We are one in sleep and dreams.* The magic amps upward. The volume dial twists to max. Like Erica, like Winnie, Jay also says the invocation three times. *We are one in sleep and dreams.* And on his third recitation, the whirling cyclone of their triangle hits its crescendo. A great climax that no one—especially not Winnie or Erica or Jay—will ever be able to describe. So much storm. So much sound. So much space-time compressed and simultaneously ripped apart at the quantum seams.

Then, like all songs, all eruptions, all dreams, the storm ends. The spirit winds pluck out the final notes in a melody that Jenna Thursday composed four years ago. And a new mist rises, ready to reclaim the nightmares of the forest.

For several eternal seconds, Winnie, Erica, and Jay finding themselves unbound by physics. They no longer spin but simply float above the Big Lake. And in those dilated moments of spacetime, they each see something—as does every Tuesday, every Wednesday, every hunter that charged into the forest when the siren went off downtown.

They see figures coalescing in the rising mist.

They see ghosts.

Erica sees Jenna, her form hovering where the melusine just stood.

Jay sees Grayson, bowing his head like a sadhuzag. Aunt Rachel sees her mother, Grandma Winona, grinning where a dryad was. And Winnie, to her shock, sees Professor Samuel, hunched where the wulver just stood.

On that morning, each Luminary and each Diana who ever lost a person to the forest and its nightmares . . . They see that person they knew. For two heartbeats. Then the ghosts fade away, eaten up by the mist. Returned to the spirit, who once more sleeps at the heart of the lake.

Winnie will have a theory, of course. An "inspired one" she'll bet Mario a week's worth of coffee over, even though they both know she'll never be able to prove it. Her theory includes the law of conservation of mass along with ashes that sink down like fish food.

As soon as the ghosts wink away, Winnie, Jay, and Erica fall. At a speed of 9.8 meters per square second, they plummet back toward the Big Lake that just spat them out. It's not far to fall—thirty feet at most—but certainly far enough to hurt. To send them plunging deep, deep, deep beneath choppy waves.

Winnie loses her glasses as water courses over her, and she can't help but think, as she grapples and swims back to the surface: *Wow. It's amazing I didn't lose my glasses sooner.* Then she bursts from the Big Lake, sputtering, gasping, coughing up all the water that just shoved down into her nose. Erica is already treading water nearby, gulping at the morning air.

"WTF," Winnie gasps out.

Erica coughs a laugh. "Seriously." She is shivering. Her hair is matted, her makeup gone. "WTF just happened to us."

Jay explodes from the water. Like them, he gasps, he chokes, he spits up lungfuls of lake. But it's clear he's struggling. Sapped by his time in the Whisperer . . . and perhaps transformed into something even less human than before.

His eyes glow like green full moons.

Winnie paddles to him. Water flips and flings around her. "Let's get you out of this water." She grabs Jay's arm. He's weak. His skin is deathly pale.

"People," he rasps, pointing. "So many . . . people."

Winnie squints at the shore. Without her glasses, it's hard to see specifics. But yes—there are people. Tens of them. Maybe even hundreds. She turns back to Jay. *Son of forest, son of pain.* "I won't let them hurt you," she says. "I swear, Jay, I won't let anyone hurt you."

"How will you stop them?"

"With my help," Erica replies, and she pushes through the water until she too can hold fast to Jay.

He sighs at her touch, as if something inside releases. Color daubs across his cheeks. The glow in his eyes drains, drips, washes away, until soon, only forest gray remains.

A fresh surge of strength ripples through him. "Okay," he tells them. "Let's get out of this water."

Together, the triangle of friends swim toward shore.

Meanwhile, down, down, beneath heavy waves where only nightmares and starlight are meant to tread, the spirit of Hemlock Falls smiles. Its lone eye finally closes.

Now, it thinks, *spring can finally come to the forest. Just after winter like it's supposed to.*

C H A P T E R

49

Interview with Wednesday (Winnie) Winona Wednesday

[0:00]

Jeremiah: [seated at coffee table in back corner of Joe Squared with Winnie Wednesday. Notepad in front of him.] Interview begins now, at 9:45 A.M. on Thursday, April twenty-fifth. Thank you for meeting with me, Ms. Wednesday. I . . . *appreciate* that you didn't have to, and I hope we can one day work through our history.

[Winnie snorts. Then sips her tea.]

Jeremiah: I have been debriefed by Erica Thursday on your current curse. It still holds, I presume?

[Winnie's mouth opens twice before she actually speaks.]

[0:20]

Winnie: Human by day and monster by night, these rare daywalkers blend in easily and are unrecognizable from other humans in their daytime form.

Jeremiah: Right. [Jeremiah makes a note.] For the record, I have approved Ms. Thursday's request for a Contained Spell Casting. Once she finds a way to remove the curse, then she will be allowed to—under supervision—craft a new source and cast the spell.

As for Mr. Friday, I have come to an agreement with the Council, and we will keep the information about him secret. Assuming of course that his mutation does not grow . . . *violent.*

Winnie: It won't. [She glares.] I, however, might, if
any Tuesdays ever go near him.

Jeremiah: Ms. Wednesday, I realize you believe you
have leverage now—

Winnie: Because I do.

Jeremiah: —but I am still a councilor, still a Tuesday
scorpion. If Jay Friday becomes a threat, then he will
be eliminated. The same holds true for Erica, for you,
and for anyone else in Hemlock Falls. I hope we're
clear on that.

[Jeremiah's eyebrows rise. He sips from a latte,
clearly waiting for Winnie to respond. She does not.
Jeremiah sighs.]

[1:22]

Jeremiah: As I was saying, Ms. Wednesday—

Winnie: Winnie. Just call me Winnie.

Jeremiah: —you don't need to worry. All hunters and
scorpions have a no-kill order on werewolves. They are
required to leave werewolves encountered inside or
outside the forest alone.

Winnie: And what about Erica? You just said you
approved her for a Contained Spell Casting. So does
that mean she isn't in trouble either?

Jeremiah: Not at the moment, no. And so long as she
continues to cooperate fully with our Lambdas, then
she too will be added to our list of known defectors.

Winnie: And the three Dianas you captured? What's
happening to them?

Jeremiah: That is confidential, Ms. Wednesday. But I
can share that we're building a complete picture of
what happened with the, um . . .

[Jeremiah hesitates.]

Winnie: With the Whisperer? With the Pure Heart spell?
With all that stuff you didn't believe was real when
you thought my dad and I were Dianas?

Jeremiah: Your father was a Diana.

Winnie: Defected.

[Jeremiah doesn't respond. His head tips back and he watches Winnie for several seconds, his fingers tapping on the notepad.]

[2:14]

Winnie: What? What does that expression mean? My dad *was* defected. He's on your fancy list.

Jeremiah: Yes, when he moved to Hemlock Falls he was on that list. But . . . here. There was a reason we suspected him four years ago. Now that I know you're no longer a threat—

Winnie: I was *never* a threat.

Jeremiah: —then perhaps this might be of interest to you.

[Jeremiah withdraws a manila envelope from his back pocket. It has been curved in half to fit, and now he smooths it out.]

[2:47]

Jeremiah: These are files from the night your father disappeared. Your mother caught him in your house, but she wasn't able to give us a full picture—yes, *yes*. I now know there was this circling-words spell on her that jumbled what she said. Still, my Lambdas and I did have another witness that night.

[Winnie yanks the envelope to her and tears out pages. It is a printed interrogation as well as a photograph of Grayson Friday, wet and bruised. Winnie quickly skims the pages.]

[3:27]

Jeremiah: You will see that Grayson Friday and Jenna Thursday had a plan to leave town, but it failed. Grayson didn't understand the full extent of the plan, only that your father, Bryant, was helping Jenna exe-cute it. He said he saw Bryant that night, during the second trial, and your father was doing magic. A hid-ing spell that fell away when he reached Grayson.

The Whisperer was also chasing your father at that time, and he and Grayson were able to use a stolen Tuesday Hummer to reach the dam bridge—much as you did on early Wednesday morning. However, Grayson said that while he was able to escape from the Hummer, he didn't fully understand what was happening with your father.

He believed your father was likely dead. We . . .
suspected otherwise.

This is, of course, classified information, Ms. Wednesday.
So please do not share.

[Winnie rolls her eyes. Then sets down the pages and
photograph so she can study them on the table.]

[4:32]

Winnie: You thought my dad did magic and killed Jenna,
right? That's what Ms. Morgan told me. [She looks at
Jeremiah.]

Jeremiah: It was our working theory at the time.

Winnie: Well, your working theory was stupid.

[Jeremiah's chest expands. He takes another sip of his
coffee, visibly trying to control his temper. Then he
carefully nods.]

[4:51]

Jeremiah: Yes, Winnie. It was not a good theory. In our
defense, we were working with incomplete information—
and the network of Dianas were incredibly good at cov-
ering their tracks.

They still are. But thanks to your, erm . . . *continued*
efforts, I suspect we will make great progress in
uncovering that network moving forward. The international Luminaries have offered substantial aid, and
while our networks have always worked closely together,
now that you have thwarted what would have been the
worst disaster in all of Luminaries history—

Winnie: Is that a "thank you"?

Jeremiah: —there is an increased effort to fund and
coordinate Diana hunting around the globe.

Winnie: [shaking her head] Well, don't go overboard. We
do need the Dianas, remember? That's sort of the whole
point of what I just went through.

Jeremiah: Yes, you've said that before. [He flips to an
earlier page in his notebook and reads.] I believe you
told Mario Monday, quote: It's all about ecological
balance, Mario. We need each other to keep the system
in check. End quote. Does that sound accurate?

[Winnie nods.]

Jeremiah: And that will be taken into consideration, Ms. Wednesday. I can assure you Monday scientists like Mario will be heavily focused on researching this new revelation.

[Winnie grunts, a sound that isn't impressed. Jeremiah's face tightens in return.]

[5:57]

Jeremiah: As mentioned, I do appreciate you taking the time to speak with me for a quick debrief. Please keep that file private, and if you need me . . . Well, you know where to find me.

Winnie: Yep.

[She turns her attention back to the interview records while Jeremiah rises and gathers his things.]

[6:20]

Winnie: Wait. [Her attention snaps up.] Right here, it says Grayson saw my dad turn into a crow?

Jeremiah: He did mention that, yes. It's an ability we know the strongest Dianas possess.

Winnie: Yeah, but it says that my dad transformed right *before* the Hummer went underwater and Grayson never saw my dad again after that. Does that mean my dad could, like . . . still be a crow?

Jeremiah: I wouldn't know.

Winnie: My *god*, Jeremiah. You should know! [She shoves away from the table, sloshing her tea and Jeremiah's coffee.] You're supposed to be a Diana-hunting scorpion, yet somehow you know even less about witches than I do!

I mean, you arrested me, my mom, and Darian four years ago even though we were so *obviously* innocent. And then you arrested us *a second time* three days ago! Like, come on, man. If you were even halfway decent at your job you would realize how many answers Grayson gave you right here.

Jeremiah: Ms. Wednesday, that's enough—

Winnie: No. It really isn't. If you'd just believed my family when we said we were innocent, you could have used these last four years to pursue real clues and catch the real Dianas.

Jeremiah: Ms. Wednesday, if you are quite finished, I would like to—

Winnie: No. I'm not *quite* finished. I mean, come on, Jeremiah! A crow—my dad turned into a crow, and you never wondered about that? Or looked into it further?

Jeremiah: No, Ms. Wednesday. We did not. How exactly should we have gone about that?

Winnie: [shrugs] You're the Lambda, not me.

Jeremiah: Now are you finished?

[Winnie nods curtly.]

Jeremiah: Good. Because I have one more thing to give you before I go. [He crooks down to remove a plastic bag from under the table. It is puffy and large.]

[7:51]

Jeremiah: I believe these clothes belong to you. A hoodie and a leather jacket. We found them in the All-Terrain Race tent, under a table. Would you like them back?

[Winnie frowns at the bag for several seconds before snatching it to her.]

[8:01]

Winnie: Obviously I want them back. [She turns away. But then pauses and glances over her shoulder at Jeremiah.] Actually, there's one more thing I want to say before I go: Isaac deserves a promotion. Or . . . maybe just a raise, since you know. He's Isaac. But still, make it a big one. That guy went through hell for me. [She lifts her chin.] Okay, *now* I'm done. [She swivels once more and stalks away without saying goodbye.]

Jeremiah: [sighs] Interview concluded at 9:54 A.M.

[End 8:39]

As angry as Dryden Saturday is to have his maze destroyed, it quickly becomes a tourist destination for both visiting Luminaries and the residents of Hemlock Falls too. And although Dryden tries to get Winnie to film a quick interview within the shredded remains of the yew hedges, she tells him she'd rather jump off the waterfall.

Because she would.

The fact is, she hasn't yet seen the damage the Whisperer left behind in the maze. She hasn't yet *seen* where the Tuesdays held the line. A scorpion died in there, and Winnie would prefer to face that particular ghost during her first therapy session next week, and not during a live TV interview, thanks.

"In fact, Dryden," Winnie tells the councilor, "I'd rather step inside the sleeping spirit again than ever chat with you about anything. So leave me alone. I'm not your Midnight Crown anymore."

It's true: L.A. Saturday has fully claimed the Midnight Crown (although no, she did not actually get as many votes as Winnie). And at Winnie's firm (read: unrelenting) insistence, the rest of the Court has been reinstated as well. Emma Wednesday has won the Golden Crown; Kiki Monday has earned the Silver; and Bronze goes to Eugene Saturday.

They all look quite stunning on Friday morning, when they are brought onto the Saturday clan's newly erected Nightmare Stage by the river. Emma smiles widest for the group photo. L.A. opts for a broody smirk.

Winnie, meanwhile, is nowhere near the Saturday estate. Or the Friday estate, where the day's Masquerade festivities are kicking off in earnest. (Lizzy goes *all out* for the Haunted House each year.) Jay isn't at his own party either. Because he's with Winnie.

So is Erica.

So is Mom.

So is Darian.

And so is the crow from the family rooftop.

They are all assembled in the old cabin at the edge of the Thursday estate, and for once, the place does not smell like cut grass or fertilizer. The scent of hamburger overpowers everything. The scent of fries too, since Erica is currently shoveling three into her mouth.

She sits in her chair near the shelf, while Winnie kneels on one side and Jay crouches on the other. They are, each of them, focused very intently on the crow that currently hides in a birdcage borrowed from Animal Control (aka Lauren Wednesday). Winnie holds a burger toward it. Erica holds a fry. And Jay just watches on silently, his pewter eyes filled with a combination of sympathy and pity.

Nearby, Mom paces. In one hand she holds the photograph that was hanging in her office until last night. In the other hand, she holds the now-empty bag of Revenant's Daughter takeout. Darian, meanwhile, sits on a lawnmower. He is bent over, his hands in his hair. "We need a permit for this," he says to his loafers for the thirty-seventh time. "We need a permit—"

"*Enough.*" Winnie glowers at her brother. "I know we need a permit, Darian, but by the time Jeremiah approves another request for a Contained Spell Casting, months will have passed. I don't want to wait that long for Dad, do you?"

Darian hoists upward, his hair disheveled and face green. "Sure, but what are you gonna do when we get caught, Win? Because we *will* get caught! People are going to notice when Dad just shows up, walking around town again."

"It's called double jeopardy." Winnie plants a hand on her hip. "Ever heard of it, Darian? We can't get punished twice for the same crime."

"That is a non law, Winnie, not a Luminary one."

"I'm pretty sure, though," Jay inserts, "that your sister is above the law at this point. At least for right now while the entire town is obsessed with her."

Winnie makes a gagging sound. "Don't remind me."

"But Winnie is not the one doing the magic." Mom's voice is very pitchy as she points this out. She waggles the empty paper bag. "It's Erica, and I would hate for Erica to get in trouble trying to help our family—"

"It's okay," Erica cuts in. She bares a weak smile, her mouth half-full of french fry. "Bryant got in a lot of trouble helping Jenna, so trying to turn him human is, like . . . Well, it's the bare minimum of what I can do—Oh! Here he comes."

All attention snaps to the crow, now hopping out of his cage toward the hamburger.

Winnie's eyes bulge. They are very bloodshot thanks to a combination of recent sleep deprivation *and* the fact that she is wearing contacts since her glasses got lost in the sleeping spirit's vortex. It'll take another day for new lenses to arrive.

Jay keeps saying she looks so different.

Then kissing her to make sure she knows how very much he doesn't mind if she looks different.

Winnie, in turn, keeps trying to adjust invisible glasses that aren't there. Or rubbing at her eyes and knocking the stupid contacts out.

The crow hops two more steps toward the hamburger, his beak parting and the little gray feathers across his face fluttering. Winnie drops the burger. He starts chowing down.

And Mom stops pacing for the first time since entering the cabin ten minutes ago. "What if that's not him? What if that is just *some bird*?"

"Or what if it is him," Winnie counters.

"Stop arguing, everyone." Erica wiggles to the edge of her folding chair. "He's out now, so I'm going to try doing this. Which means, um . . ." Her cheeks redden. "Please go outside?"

Darian hurries out, still muttering. Mom traces behind, and Jay ambles out third.

The last to leave is Winnie. She stares down at Erica, who holds a new source, crafted in a pinch last night from another crystal that Marcia spent too much money on. This one is amethyst and very sparkly in the old cabin's dim light. It only has a single night's charge, but Erica thinks that'll be enough.

"Thanks for doing this, E."

"Like I said, Winona"—Erica grins in a way that's almost a grimace—"I owe you. And I *really* owe your dad. Now let's just hope this spell actually works." She slides a white postcard from her jacket. It's exactly like the birthday cards—except *not* a birthday card.

Rather, this is Dad's final clue.

It was hiding in plain sight all these years. He even said as much in the very first card Winnie found:

Happy 1-3-Th birthday, Winnie! I wish I was there to see you. It was only last year that things were normal and right, framed like that picture of us in the living room. Stay safe.

Love, Dad

There was more there than just a coded message that read, *I Was Framed*. It was an arrow pointing to the old family photo, moved into Mom's new office on the Wednesday estate. When Winnie opened the back, she found the postcard. And on the card is a spell for transmutation into an animal.

It would seem Dad knew he might have to change into his crow form; he also seemed to know he might be in no position to ever change back out of it. Because without a source, without access to magic . . .

Well, he has been like this for four years.

Winnie gives Erica's shoulder a squeeze. "Thanks," she murmurs. "And good luck." Then she turns away to join Mom, Darian, and Jay outside. The nodding wakerobins watch her stalk by. *Tsk, tsk, tsk. You sure you should be doing this?*

"Shut up," Winnie tells them.

"Huh?" Jay blinks at her. He leans against the shed, his pose not so different from one he made against her locker a month ago. He looks just as haggard, just as pale. Because no matter what happened two days ago in the sleeping spirit, he remains a nightmare. He remains only half human.

Son of forest, son of pain.

Winnie hasn't told him about Mario's theory yet. She will eventually, but now isn't the right time. Jay has more than enough to process. They both do, in fact, which is why she moves to him and glides her hands over his flannel-covered waist. He is warm. He is solid. He is safe.

Winnie kisses his neck, on a secret spot beneath his ear, then she withdraws.

Jay sighs, but he releases her so she can go to her mom—who puts her arm over Winnie's shoulder while Darian slots into place on Mom's other side. Together, the three Wednesdays stare at the lone window above the shed door. Winnie thinks she sees light flickering within. She *definitely* feels magic plucking at her arm—and the smell like burning plastic now overpowers the smell of delicious cholesterol.

Jay soon joins the trio, taking Winnie's hand in his. And they all stand there like that, three bears and a sparrow, waiting for a bell to finish bringing a Diana home.

A yelp cracks out from the cabin. Then a thud like an anvil falling in a cartoon. Then a screechy, "OH MY GOD IT WORKED, BUT WINNIE HE HAS NO CLOTHES ON. OH MY GOD. YOUR DAD HAS NO

CLOTHES. I DIDN'T SEE ANYTHING. I'VE COVERED MY EYES.
BUT PLEASE HELP ME!"

Mom leaps forward, Darian beside her. And Winnie, her heart bursting
into her skull and punching light beams out of her ears, can't do anything
but laugh and laugh and laugh. Clap and clap and clap. And wait for Darian to bellow a choked-up, "He's dressed now! And holy shit, Win, it's
really Dad!"

Then Winnie, with Jay just behind, darts for the shed door. Finally, *finally* Agent Wednesday solved the case. Finally, *finally,* she has finished
what Dad started four years ago.

Well done, the nodding wakerobins say as she charges past. *Now please
tell your father we need more fertilizer. The Thursdays haven't been taking
good care of us at all.*

50

What Winnie soon learns is that on the night her dad disappeared, events unfolded as follows:

When Mom found Dad in the middle of the living room with a glowing light in one hand and a piece of paper in the other, Dad *did not* in fact try to run. And Mom *did not* in fact give chase—because her ankle was busted.

Instead Dad said, "I am so sorry, Fran. I'm only trying to save the town."

"What do you mean?"

"Dianas," he answered. "A *lēgātum*. But if it all goes to plan, I'll be back soon to explain. If it doesn't . . ." He shook his head. Then magic slashed out. A *verba circumvolēns* spell mixed with a mild attack spell—to keep Mom from explaining what she saw.

To protect her, in the end, in case a Crow like Martedì ever came calling.

When Mom awoke, she *did* drag herself to the Tuesday estate—hoping she could get help for her husband. Hoping she could alert Jeremiah to a *lēgātum* in Hemlock Falls. But she couldn't explain herself, and by then it was all too late. Dad's plan failed; Jenna died; Dad got Grayson away . . .

But then he had to ensure Martedì's attention never turned onto the poor boy who knew nothing of what Jenna really was, but simply loved her with all his heart. First, Dad gave Jenna's locket to Grayson with the order to give it to Erica.

Then Dad became a crow and flew away.

The rest . . . ah, well, the rest is shitty history. Dad was four years out of practice with magic, and he couldn't change back into a person. He'd known this might happen—he'd also known there was a very good chance he might die—so he had crafted a contingency plan. But Ms. Morgan didn't follow her instructions. She was supposed to give the cards directly to Winnie and Darian. Instead, she delivered them to a mailbox, and then Mom tucked them away into the attic.

Human error. One step gone wrong. One semicolon forgotten on the line of code. Until a lucky, fateful day when Darian gave Winnie a locket for her sixteenth birthday . . . and Winnie went into the attic to dig for clues.

Dad *was* framed, just not in the way Winnie thought.

And now he is back. Now he is home.

And sweetest in the gale is heard;
And sore must be the storm
That could abash the little bird
That kept so many warm.

I've heard it in the chillest land,
And on the strangest sea;
Yet, never, in extremity,
It asked a crumb of me.

On the top floor of the Wednesday estate, a fabric shop has exploded inside of Fatima's bedroom. And a crafts shop too. And also, forty-six jars of sequins. Her sleigh bed is hidden beneath so many silks, satins, feathers, lace, and sparkly plastic pieces that Winnie isn't sure Fatima will ever find her lavender-colored bedsheets again.

Winnie keeps trying to neaten things. Fatima keeps swatting at her to stop. "Oh my *goodness*, Winnie. Just stay still. Is that really too much to ask?"

"Winnie." Bretta shoots a glance from across the room. She stands in front of Fatima's mirror, while Emma carefully—like, *really* carefully—attaches oak branches to her head. "You have the easiest costume out of all of us, so you should be able to follow instructions."

"Exactly," Fatima agrees, concentrating on the seam she is trying to get some final stitches onto. "And I wouldn't be here finishing this . . ." She glares at Winnie. The thick midnight liner around her eyes make her blue irises pop with almost terrifying intensity. "If you had just told us everything that was going on in your life."

Winnie cringes.

"Because if we'd known," Fatima continues, repeating a rant she has expressed several times since Wednesday morning, "we could have helped you *and* we could have worked on this costume way sooner than the *day of the freaking Nightmare Ball!*" She stabs her needle into emerald silk.

Emma clucks her tongue, pausing her application of branches onto her sister's head. "Everyone leave Winnie alone, okay? She was just doing the best she could. We love you, Winnie."

Now Winnie really cringes, and shame is basically oozing out of her ears, her tear ducts, her nostrils. "No, no. Fatima's right—"

"Yeah, she is," Bretta mutters. Emma pokes her with a branch.

"—and I will just keep apologizing for the rest of time. Because it's what you all deserve, okay?"

"And *we* will keep on accepting those apologies," Emma answers. She pokes Bretta again.

"Ouch!" Bretta scowls. Then sighs. Then groans and drags her dryad-self away from the mirror. Her gown of gray and brown velvet streams behind her, the train cut into spirals to look like roots. So far, only three of the planned seven branches poke off her head. Emma has to chase behind to keep the fourth branch from falling before she has finished pinning it.

"Oh, you better not be walking over here, Bretta Wednesday!" Fatima doesn't look up from her stitching. "I spent weeks making that costume, and if you tear it, I'll feed you to a real dryad."

"You are way too stressed right now, Fatima." Bretta comes to a stop next to her—which puts her diagonal to Winnie. And Emma too, as keeper of the branches.

Bretta grins, her dimples digging deep. "Winnie: I *do* still love you, okay? I'm mostly just mad I didn't get to kick more Diana butt. So next time—because I just . . . I just have the feeling there *will* be a next time with you—you'd better include us in your plans."

Winnie bites her lip. Her shame is turning soupy.

"Oh no! You've made Winnie cry!" Emma tries to slide around her sister, but she can't release the branches. "Oh, Winnie, hon. Don't cry."

Fatima finally looks up, her cheeks fully aflame. "Winnie, if you get tears on this silk, then *you'll* be the one I feed to a dryad."

"N-no," Winnie blubbers. "I'm not . . . crying." She sniffles. Then because she has been forbidden to move, she just lets the tears and a little snot slide down her face.

Bretta howls out a laugh, swiveling around to return to the mirror. "I made Wolf Girl cry!" she chants, clapping in time to the words. "Don't tell Jay, he'll eat me alive!"

A knock sounds at the door. Tentative. Almost drowned out by Bretta's repeated chanting *I made Wolf Girl cry! Don't tell Jay, he'll eat me alive!*

"Come in!" Fatima calls.

The doorknob turns. The hinges creak. And there is Erica, poking in her head. "Hey, uh . . . we're here."

"Wheee!" Emma declares, bouncing on her toes—and in turn, making Bretta's branches bounce too. "Join us, join us!"

Erica obeys, pushing through the door. Behind her are Katie Tuesday and Angélica Martes. All of them carry their costumes in long garment bags, and in mere moments, the bedroom is doused with noise. With laughter and voices and squeals. With questions and teasing and the *shk-kkkk* of hairspray.

And although Fatima continues to snarl at Winnie, *Stay still!*, and Winnie's stomach can't quite stop gurgling with guilt, she also can't *not* join in with the laughter and the squeals and the teasing. Her costume might be the simplest one in the room by far, but it's still so much more than she could have *ever* asked for.

She is the Hunter, just like she and Fatima drew (minus the popcorn hands), complete with a jeweled belt and the sleek lines of an Ancient Roman gown—in emerald silk, of course, since Winnie *is* the Girl in Green.

Over the next two hours, all the girls dress. Bretta finishes transforming into an oak dryad, her head fully crowned with branches. And Winnie—under Fatima's somewhat snippy guidance—paints gray lines down Bretta's bare arms and across her face.

Emma becomes a phoenix, with fully feathered crimson wings to float off her back, and a gown made of slippery orange satin. Her lips are orange, and Winnie gives her feathery swirls across her face. Lastly, the Golden Crown shines like a lantern atop Emma's head.

Fatima, meanwhile, is a siren in a fully sequined gown that fits her whole body like a shiny glove—and then slithers behind her in a long, magical tail. Her hijab is the same midnight blue as her eyeliner, and the rubber bands on her braces are teal. (Apparently Trevor, who is her date, has a matching costume that is, in Bretta's words: *smokin' hot sexy*.)

Erica metamorphoses into an arassas with (now-familiar) black cat ears, a form-fitting scaly dress, and her usual steel-toed boots. She glows with a radiance Winnie hasn't seen in years, and rather than straighten her hair as she usually does, to look like Jenna's, Erica has let the natural waves curl down her back.

Katie and Angélica—who have recently started dating—wear matching white vinyl bodysuits with long whips that come off their hands. "We're manticores!" Angélica explains when Winnie raises a puzzled eyebrow. "Here's the stinger." She swings around to give a booty shake.

And yep. Okay. Winnie sees it now, and she applauds—and laughs—accordingly.

Once everyone is fully costumed, decorated, and accessorized, Winnie and her friends strut out of the bedroom, ready to take on the night. No longer a square of friends, but something bigger. And so, *so* much better.

Winnie spent four years as a hypotenuse cast adrift, and for those four, lonely years, she mistrusted anything more complicated than a line. All shapes—whether they were squares or triangles or trapezoids—looked to her like big red *STOP* signs.

But now she not only has a triangle, she not *only* has a square, she has a complete overhaul of geometry. She has a mixing of angles and lines, of blocks and diamonds, of parallelograms and polyhedrons.

So while Signora Martedì might still be out there somewhere, along with those nine other Dianas from the shore that were never captured, that Crow won't find such an easy target in Winnie Wednesday if she ever comes back again. No more lines, no more singular photons beaming into space at the speed of light.

Number of shapes Winnie could rely on a month ago? Zero.

Number of shapes Winnie can rely on now? Too many to count.

So with her silk dress gliding over her legs and her jewel knife sheath resting comfortably at her hips, Winnie hooks her arm into Erica's on one side. Into Fatima's on the other. And together with this complex fractal of friends to glitter around her, she sets off for the final event of the Masquerade.

51

It will go down in history as the greatest Nightmare Ball that ever was. Everyone who attends—be they local or foreign—will agree that never in all of Luminary history has the society shined so brightly.

It's not the false glow of people trying to outrun the night, trying to pretend the ghosts don't haunt them when they close their eyes or that all they have to do is eat enough pizza. This is the glow of people who *saw* the ghosts. Who opened up their compartments and pizza boxes and let the nightmares run free.

Winnie Wednesday shines the brightest of them all. She and her fractal arrive at the ball as an entourage, tumbling out of the twins' dad's van like they are real nightmares tumbling from the mist. Somehow Bretta's branches do not get crushed, nor do Emma's skirts get flattened. And when they pull up to the awning, Dryden's old assistant Cindy leaps over to valet park for them.

Because oh yes—didn't you hear? Darian quit his job. He was offered a new position in Italy with the Mercoledìs, so he and Andrew are moving there in a month. It's going to be *very* exciting. Especially since Dad was able to warn Darian of a certain Martedì to watch out for.

Not that anyone really expects to see her again.

The Saturday estate is bedazzled to a whole new level for the ball, the dramatic decorations from the breakfast now applied to the *entire* estate. Even the damaged maze has been decorated with lights and baubles that give it a distinctively *Wicked Fairy Tale* vibe.

The main lawn is also transformed, the Nightmare Stage complete and a massive temporary dance floor assembled on the grass. Crystalline torches (which also act as heaters) flicker with real flames, while nightmarish ice sculptures lurk in secret shadows made from towering cypress trees. Dry ice seeps outward in lazy spirals.

Because the Hunters' Feast was canceled this year, the various globally imported ensembles who were scheduled to play that day were unable to perform. So now all those bands get to play on the Nightmare Stage instead, while the usual four-string quartet has been punted over to the maze. *Explore the Wicked Fairy Tale and enjoy some Mozart!*

When Winnie and her friends reach the lawn's edge, a band from the Pakistani branch of the Luminaries sings in Urdu while hundreds of costumed "nightmares" dance and laugh and gleam.

At Winnie's request, the group huddles in one of the dark corners protected by cypresses. Dry ice pumps around them and a wyrm ice sculpture snarls menacingly. Winnie isn't ready to be recognized; she isn't ready to abandon the shadows. Johnny Saturday called her *the Hero of Hemlock Falls*, and thanks to her cousin Marcus, everyone has turned the previous *Aroo!* into a *Herooo!*

"Ooh, there's Xavier." Fatima points toward a collection of juniors at the closest refreshments table. "*Wow,* his costume is awesome."

"Seriously," Bretta agrees. "How did he get his hood to look so much like a banshee?"

"Let's go ask him." Fatima grabs Bretta's arm, then Winnie's wrist. "Come on. We can't hide here forever."

Winnie doesn't come on. "You all go without me, please. I'll join you in minute. I need to, um, find someone else first."

"Ooooh, Winnie wants to find her *booooooyyyyfriend.*" Bretta hip-bumps Winnie. Then curses when one of her branches gets stuck in Winnie's hair.

"No," Winnie insists while she and Bretta disentangle. "I actually want to find my mom . . . and my dad." It's strange to say that word. But also amazing.

"Aw," Emma coos, her posture melting and her phoenix flames sparkling. "Are they dressing up tonight?"

"I don't know. All my mom said was that I'd have no trouble finding her." Which, in Francesca Wednesday speak, could mean just about anything.

"Well, good luck." Fatima's eyebrows bounce. "We'll talk to Xavier and then head over to the stage." She grabs Bretta again, this time latching onto Emma instead of Winnie. Then the three girls—and Katie and Angélica with their swinging tails—hurry off.

Which leaves Winnie alone in her secret corner with Erica. Her Thursday friend takes two steps toward the lights. Then pauses. Then looks back and gives a high-pitched, self-conscious laugh. "So this is . . . uh, kind of weird, right? I mean, all of us just being friends like it's totally normal?"

"If by weird, you mean it's *awesome*." Winnie dips closer. "Then yes. Yes, it is."

Erica blushes. But it's a happy sort of blush, even as she rolls her eyes. "Okay, Winona. Don't get *too* Wednesday on me."

"Oh, you love that I'm a Wednesday." Winnie bats her eyelashes and leans in even closer. "Bears, after all, give the best hugs."

And now Erica gives a very round, very real laugh—one that bubbles out more brightly when Winnie wraps her arms around her friend and squeezes.

"Oh my god," Erica says between giggles, "you really haven't changed in the last four years. Same old Winona ignoring all my boundaries."

They both know that's not true, of course. Not even a little bit. Winnie herself erected such vicious boundaries that no one got past the tarps or barbed wire for four years. And for all that Erica has, quite literally, let her hair down tonight . . .

She's still got the Ice Queen inside her. She still has too much grief to simply shed in a few days.

Still, Winnie knows what Erica is *actually* trying to say. She hears the harmonic overtones, and she agrees. Because although neither girl is who they used to be, there are still pieces of them that haven't changed. That never will. After all, culture runs thicker than blood in Hemlock Falls.

And so does family. So do friends.

"Go find Jay," Erica commands, still laughing as she finally shimmies out of Winnie's hug.

"I'm *really* not looking for him, though!" Winnie tosses her hands. "Why does no one believe that I want to find my mom and dad?"

"So what if I say I see Jay right there?"

Winnie spins around, fast as a torpedo and with her heart ballooning. But of course, there's no Jay. There's absolutely nothing at all except an ice wyrm.

"*Man*, Winona!" Erica gives a full-blown guffaw, clapping like the trickster she is. "You should have seen your face just now."

"Oh, go away." Winnie glares. "That was mean, E!"

"No, *that* was hilarious." Erica winks. "See you soon, Winona." In seconds, she and her cat ears disappear into the crowds.

Leaving Winnie all alone. The night air breathes cold against her bare arms. It smells like dry ice and gas heaters. Like the rose garlands that cover the cypress trees. And like the distant forest, forever feasting on detritus and carrion in the north.

"Hey," a voice says, and Winnie torpedoes around *once more*—but this time, when her heart balloons, it gets to stay that way. Because Jay really *is* there, slipping into her corner from the main lawn. Crystalline light casts shapes across him; his eyes glow moonlight silver.

"Ugh, Jay!" Winnie declares as she takes in his lanky form. "You're not in costume!"

"I know. I'm sorry." He lifts his hands, wincing. "A tux was the best I could do. Plus, if I'm being honest, it feels weird to dress up like a nightmare, when . . . you know."

"Right." Winnie reaches him. "Well, good thing you look so sexy in a tux, then."

He flushes right up to his hairline. "I, uh, like your costume. Very sleek." He flicks a finger at her jeweled knife sheath. "Very dangerous."

"That's in case you turn into a wolf, Mr. Friday. I have to be ready to defend myself."

He chuckles now, skimming a hand over Winnie's waist before furling his fingers into her back. "New glasses, too, huh?" He tugs her close to him. He is warm. "They look good. Those frames suit you. But . . ." He reaches up. "May I?"

"Always," she answers. Then her glasses are off, and she and Jay are kissing. It is not the wild, desperate kissing they shared on Wednesday, after the dust settled and they could finally, *finally* consider all they'd been through. These are tender kisses. Little promises trailed along Winnie's jaw or traced along Jay's neck that say, *The forest can't have you. I am here to keep you safe.*

The Lead Hunter who is also a nightmare.

The Luminary who is also a *lēgātum.*

A buzzing in Jay's phone finally pries them apart. "That'll be L.A.," he groans, and sure enough, his phone reads *MOST IMPORTANT MEMBER OF THE FORGOTTEN* (she labeled herself in Jay's contacts, of course).

He sends the call to voicemail. Then he gives Winnie one more lingering kiss filled with promises. "I'll find you on the dance floor, okay?"

"Does that mean you're going to dance?"

"No." He grins. "But I'll definitely find you." One more kiss, this time on the cheek, before Jay Friday slips into the crowds. Into the lights.

After twelve selfies, two requests for an autograph, and a quick interview from the same Sunday blogger who drove the pontoon boat (Winnie can now appreciate how hard that swan is to steer), Winnie finally reaches her mom and dad. And Mom was right: Winnie had no trouble finding her.

Because Mom is dressed as a very—like *very*—furry black bear with a green sash across her chest. So is Aunt Rachel, who stands beside her at a fountain spewing punch. Dad, meanwhile, is dressed like a gardener, in coveralls and a goofy bucket hat, his old water canteen strapped at his waist, and with an old, *old* pair of glasses perched atop his nose. (Because of course, four years ago, he lost his glasses before turning into a crow.)

He looks like the dad Winnie remembers.

But he is also someone totally new. Because this Bryant is tired. He has aged. And he is just a little bit furtive after too many years in avian form.

"*This* is your costume?" Winnie demands. "*Dad.* This is even worse than Jay phoning it in with a tuxedo."

Dad laughs—and okay, it might be the best sound in the world. "I know, Winnie Benny. *Mea culpa.*" He slings an arm over her shoulder. "But I spent so many years as an actual bird with actual feathers, I just want to feel human for as long as I can."

Winnie can't argue with that. Especially since it's basically the same argument Jay just gave.

"Well, can I have your hat then?"

"Uh . . ."

Winnie doesn't give him a choice. She swipes the bucket hat off Dad's head, revealing gray-streaked auburn hair (*Address me as "my lord."*), then plops it over her own auburn waves. *Much better.* She has already tugged on her leather jacket for warmth, so now—she hopes—she won't stand out once she pushes again into the crowds.

Fatima is going to kill her. Winnie definitely looks less Badass Hunter from Ancient Rome, and more Angler Who Left Her Bait Kit at Home.

Gone Fishing, she thinks.

Dad studies her new ensemble, his expression as pained as it used to be when she made, in his opinion, poor clothing combinations. But wisely, he offers no criticism. Instead, he says: "I guess now *neither* of us will detract from your mom's display of loyalty. She's really proud of that costume, you know."

Yeah, Winnie can tell. Mom is preening and declaring to the third person in the last ten minutes: "I'm going back on the hunt. Have you heard? Rachel, tell Archie here."

"Yep," Rachel indulges. Also for the third time. "Our Frannie's a hunter again, Archie. Though she'll have to work her ass off if she's hoping to take back her old title."

"Oh, I'm coming for ya, baby sister."

"Bring it on, old lady. Especially since you've got your daughter over there to contend with." Rachel grins Winnie's way. Her bear ears seem to wiggle. "Everyone's saying you're headed for Lead Hunter one day, kid."

Winnie smiles back. First at Archie, who looks about as interested in this conversation as he would be in *Chrysomya megacephala* on a corpse. Then Winnie smiles at Mom, and lastly at Aunt Rachel. And to her surprise, it's not the false, pained grin she's used to wearing whenever Rachel talked about the hunt.

No, Winnie hasn't exorcised her ghosts. She hasn't learned to differentiate between compartmentalizing and accepting that ghosts are a part of her . . . But she's confident she'll get there one day. Just like Mom, just like Rachel, just like Grandma Winona. Because the hunt is in her blood.

And the forest is, too.

Plus, working through the ghosts is exactly what her future therapy sessions are for, right?

Dad gives Winnie another sideways hug. A quick squeeze that says, *Yeah, I get it, Win-Ben.* Then they're all moving, abandoning the fountain (Mom has had *way* too much punch) and aiming for the Nightmare Stage.

Winnie's latest disguise works beautifully, except for one awkward moment halfway across the lawn when she runs into Jeremiah. Like literally runs into him because he's the most *phoned-in* of all the costumes at the ball. He wears his usual black fatigues and even has a black cap too, so he fully blends into the shadows. Winnie doesn't see him until she steps on him.

He coughs. Jumps back. Then a scowl tugs at his red eyebrows. "Ms. Wednesday."

Mom shoves in before Winnie can answer. She stares daggers. "Piss off, Jeremiah. No one wants you here."

"Fran," Dad says tiredly. Then in a voice that's *way* nicer than Jeremiah deserves, he adds, "Hello, Councilor."

"Hello, Mr. Silvestri. Thank you again for all the information you gave us last night. We're grateful for your insights."

"I mean it, Jeremiah." Mom bares her teeth now. "Piss. Off."

"You heard the lady," Rachel inserts, her own eyes shooting death rays. "No one wants you here."

This time, Jeremiah does depart. But not without a frown. Not without a disdainful sniff.

"Pickle breath," Winnie mutters after him.

And beside her, Dad sighs. "My ladies and their tempers."

"It's not a temper," Mom counters, "if the target deserves your outrage—"

"Oh come on," Dad cuts in, now slinging his arms around her instead of Winnie. "Let's not let a silly Tuesday ruin our night. Onward! To the stage!"

"To the stage!" Rachel cheers. (She has also had too much punch.)

"To the stage!" Winnie agrees, although she does tug her hat a bit lower, just to be safe. Minutes later, when they reach the thickest clots of crowds, Winnie separates from her family, searching, searching until she finds her fractal of friends.

"Winnie, no!" Fatima screeches as soon as she spots her. She yanks the bucket hat from Winnie's head. "How *could* you?"

"I'm sorry."

"This has to go too," Emma insists, grabbing at the zipper on Winnie's jacket. "And not just because you should be showing off Fatima's creation, but because it's also really freaking hot down here."

It *is* really freaking hot, so after stuffing the hat in the jacket's pocket, Winnie ties the leather awkwardly around her waist—and just in time, too. Cheers go up a second later. A spotlight winks on. And there's L.A. Saturday on stage dressed in a purple velvet dress made to look like a dracon. Her tulle skirt is navy and violet, and as she strides toward a mic, it flickers like blue flames.

On her head, the Midnight Crown's ouroboros seems to slither.

"Hello, Hemlock Falls!" L.A. shouts into the mic. "You may know me as your Midnight Crown—the second and more *deserving* of the Midnight Crowns this year." She grins cheekily; the audience laughs on cue, including Winnie. "But in case you've yet to experience my beauty and talent, I'm L.A. Saturday, lead singer of the Forgotten. And oh my, have we got a show for you tonight."

Two more spotlights snap on. First onto Trevor, dressed in a leaves-nothing-to-the-imagination unitard of sequins that matches Fatima's gown. Then the final light snaps onto Jay, in his aggressively dull tuxedo. Not that *anyone* in the audience seems to care. They holler and wail for him like the adoring fans they are.

"Okay, okay," L.A. shouts into the mic. "We get it: you love us. But before we begin, we do have to give a special shout-out to a girl who—I can't believe I'm saying this—actually deserves all the hype."

Oh, awesome, Winnie thinks as a spotlight now locks onto her. She grimaces. The entirety of the ball starts screaming. Her friends are loudest of all, and as they boogie up right next to Winnie, the only one who looks even a little apologetic—and only a *little*—is Erica.

Winnie's family also claps and hoots nearby. There's Darian, dressed as a spidrin with eight spindly legs—and with Andrew as his silk-spun prey (honestly, he looks more like a mummy). There's Ms. Morgan and Mason, dressed as matching ghost-deer with antlers and white face paint.

Oh, and there's Funday too, festooned as the most colorful harpy that ever was. More like a parrot, really, than a nightmare. She beams at Winnie—and winks.

And you know what? Fine. Winnie is going to let her friends and family have this. Her fellow students, too. Even Casey. Even Peter. Even Dante and Marcus and everyone else she so bitterly resented for the last month.

She's done being a line. She's ready to embrace the fractal.

Winnie grits out a smile. Muscles out a wave. Then *finally* the light snaps off her and hundreds of rapt Luminaries rocket their attention back to the stage.

"Winnie Wednesday, this song is for you," L.A. declares. "It's a new composition I think you're going to like called 'Wolf Girl'—"

"No." Jay lurches toward L.A. His head is wagging. "No, you said we wouldn't do this one, L.A."

"Shut up." L.A. tries to elbow him aside.

"Oh my god, Win." Jay finds her in the crowd. His eyes are nearly as white as the spotlight. "I'm sorry. I told her we shouldn't do this one—"

"Enough." L.A. full-on shoves him. "You're just the boyfriend, and no one cares what you think. We don't, right?"

"*NOOOOO!*" the audience roars.

"That's what I thought. Trevor? Give me that beat."

Rocking with laughter, Trevor complies. He shoves a boot heel onto his drum machine. A raucous rhythm blasts out, sending the pitch of the crowd toward feverish. Until even Winnie finds she's laughing just as much as everyone around her.

Oh, there's a Wolf Girl,
(Heroooo! Herooooo!)
She jumps off of waterfalls
(Don't you know? The heroooo!)
She saves our town!
(Heroooo! Herooooo!)

The lyrics continue on in similarly absurd fashion, but Winnie can't deny the tune is catchy. Before she knows it, she's howling *Heroooo! Heroooo!* along with all the rest of the ball. And when the song ends, she claps so hard her hands hurt.

Then it's on to the next song—about a siren—and Winnie loses herself to the darkness, darkness, light. To the heat and the joy. To the complex geometry unfolding around her. Ghosts might float forever below the surface, but that *is* what makes these moments so lucent. So alive.

Winnie do-si-dos with Bretta, she hops around with Emma, and at one point, she and Erica twirl like ballroom dancers. Mom, meanwhile, bounces with Dad the whole time—even when she is dripping sweat and has to peel off the top half of her bear costume.

Winnie's favorite part comes halfway into the show when the Forgotten perform "Backlit." Jay doesn't sing this time, instead letting L.A. keep the limelight. But he does find Winnie in the crowd, he does watch her while his fingers move over the bass and his body sways.

His gunmetal-gray eyes grow hard, intense in that way only he can manage, and by the second verse, Winnie stops dancing. By the third verse, Jay does too. His body tightens, tightens, like he is a bow being aimed. Only his fingers keep moving.

He does not blink. And Winnie wonders when the bowstring will finally snap.

Never surprise a nightmare, she thinks. Then she smiles because she can't help it. It's Jay. The Friday sparrow she trusts completely. "I love you," she mouths at him—because she hasn't actually said that to him yet. She hasn't shared this final truth.

And it would seem that was the trigger he needed. Suddenly he has slung off his bass and is shoving it into L.A.'s hands. He leaps off the stage and strides right up to Winnie. He lifts her off her feet, which jostles the leather jacket off her waist. Then while hundreds upon hundreds of Luminaries shriek their heads off, he kisses her.

I miss you more now, L.A. keeps singing. *Now that it's been so long.*

Winnie kisses Jay back. With all the torment, all the strength, all the need that he offers and then some. She doesn't care what people think or how they'll *absolutely* talk about this tomorrow at Sunday training. How Bretta will probably start singing, *K-I-S-S-I-N-G!* in the van later. Or how Erica will use this moment to maximize her teasing.

Jay is her nightmare; Winnie is his hunter; and the forest north of Hemlock Falls is that magic, secret place they will always share.

"I love you too," Jay says, when he eventually pulls away. He is having to yell to be heard over the whistles and the laughter and the howls. "Like I *really* love you, Winnie."

"Good," Winnie yells back. "But there *is* one more thing I need from you to make this moment perfect."

Jay laughs, one of his raspy laughs. "Homeostasis?"

"Ah, Jay." She kisses him again. "I love you."

The crowd's pitch passes feverish. It reaches boiling. It reaches the Planck temperature. Until L.A. finally gets impatient and declares into the mic, "Okay, you guys are getting annoying now. We need our bassist back, please, Wolf Girl."

More laughter, more howls, more applause, and finally Jay withdraws. Seconds later, he's on stage again, his fingers once more flying across his bass. But now with his cheeks a violent pink, and his lips too.

The song croons on, L.A.'s sultry voice at the fore. Beneath it—the microwave cosmic background to so much light—are the Luminaries celebrating the start of spring. Celebrating that the forest and its sleeping spirit haven't gotten them yet.

That's why we're called the Luminaries, Winnie. We are lanterns the forest can never snuff out.

The sounds of music and revelry carry onto the river. Upstream they flow, gliding over the Little Lake like fireworks. Then farther upstream, until they hit the thunderous falls. But even that roar cannot kill the reverberations from the party. The sound rises to the top of the hill. Drifts onto the Big Lake, where the pure heart of the forest still resides.

Nightmares smile from within the blue spruce and silver maples, from within the balsam firs and hemlock trees. Hunters too, even if they're bummed to miss the party.

The last person the soundwaves reach is a single Diana, stalking northward through the forest—and even she can't keep a tiny smile from twitching across her face.

For they are one in sleep and dreams.

Although for now, there will be no waking.

Dear Harriet,

You really are a nuisance, aren't you? That was clever of you to put a protection spell on the locket—I was wondering why the girl kept getting up after everything I threw at her.

But you should know after all these years that I am not deterred so easily. There are thirteen other sleeping spirits, after all. Thirteen other forests, thirteen other Pure Hearts just waiting for me to nudge at them.

You only have one son, though, Harriet. You only have one granddaughter.

Yours in sleep and dreams,
Caterina Martedi

THE HEMLOCK FALLS GAZETTE
Reporting on Local News Since 1922

Winner Chosen in the Nightmare Compendium Illustrations Contest

By Helena Thursday

After several rounds of voting by a panel of Sunday and Monday Luminaries from around the globe, a winner was selected from the forty-nine different illustrated entries.

First place, whose art will be printed in the next edition of the Nightmare Compendium, goes to our very own local hero, Winnie Wednesday, for her illustration titled, *An Anatomically Correct Basilisk.*

Second place, which will be printed in the Sunday Encyclopedia, has gone to an anonymous entry with the title, *A Sadhuzag with All Seventy-Four Prongs Because I'm Not Lazy.*

The third-place winner, whose art will also be printed in the Sunday Encyclopedia, is another anonymous entry, this one titled, *A Werewolf that Actually Looks Properly Menacing.*

The runners up—who will win small cash prizes—are as follows:
- *A Melusine With Legs Instead of a Tail* by Anonymous
- *Will-O'-Wisp Nest in Mourning* by Anonymous
- *Male Spidrin with Chest Hair* by Anonymous

All anonymous winners are requested to contact the Monday or Sunday clans for receipt of their prizes and proper attribution in the Sunday Encyclopedia.

The panel of judges also wishes to extend a warm, gracious thank-you to all contest participants, even if forty-three of the forty-nine were anonymously submitted.

And congratulations again to Winnie Wednesday for claiming the coveted first prize!

ACKNOWLEDGMENTS

Despite publishing twelve books, this is only my second series closer—and oh! The pressure! It's a good pressure, though. The kind that really pushed me to do justice to the characters, to the plot seeds planted long ago, and above all, to the readers. I know many of you started with the Luminaries voting adventure from back when Twitter still existed, so I hope you appreciated all the inside jokes and Easter eggs. And thank you *so much* for sticking with me and this world for so long!

☐ (That is meant to be a heart, but my computer is like Winnie's phone.)

Because of the ~~terrifying~~ intense pressure to do right by both the WTF gang and all you LumiNerds—as well as all the ~~terrifying~~ intense deadlines I was facing, I had to tap a lot of friends and family to help me with *The Whispering Night*.

Rachel Hansen, my longtime brainstorming wifey, dear friend, and fellow Wednesday: thank you for reading my early drafts and spending those many hours brainstorming with me. You are a tough critic in the *best possible way* and your feedback always takes my storytelling to the next level. Plus, you're just the most excellent sounding board for my ideas. Thank you, thank you, thank you!

Alex Bracken, I owe you many thanks for those longs walks in the autumnal forest where you endured not only my stressed-out venting (Must. Get. This. Right!) but also helped me see the story didn't have to be nearly as daunting as I was making it.

To Joanna Volpe, you continue to do more for me than I deserve! You're so much more than my agent—you're an editor, a brainstorm-buddy, an emotional support, and above all, an incredible, *incredible* friend through what has been a very tough time of my life. Thank you. I can't say it enough.

An enormous thank-you to all my other readers and sounding boards: Lindsay Howard, Keifer Ludwig, Callum Car, Kaite Krell, Sam Tan, Sanya Macadam, and Erin Bowman. You guys helped me not only polish the story, but also cheered me along.

And now, because I am *horrible* and left Sam Walma out in the last book, I'm going to mention you twice now. Thank you to Sam Walma, for always supporting me. You're truly awesome. (And now one more time, to make up for *The Hunting Moon*: thank you, Sam.)

For my friends who listened to me vent and moan along the way: Shanna Alderliesten, Victoria Aveyard, Leigh Bardugo, Tanaz Bhathena, Kat Brauer, Alexa Donne, Amie Kaufman, Brigid Kimmerer, Lizzy Mason, Jodi Meadows, Nicki Pau Preto, Beth Revis, Meghan Vanderlee, and Abigail Welbourn.

I also need to thank the people who helped me make sure this book was accurate in language and representation: Dajin Choi, Emily Goldstein, Fatima Macadam, Shahid Macadam, Srishti Kesarwani, Carly Pappas, and Dmitriy Antselevich. And to Asteria: thank you, thank you for all the many Latin translations and your patience as I pestered you for more and more!

For Bayley, Kim, Adriyanna, Emily, and Sanya: thank you, *thank you* for looking over our DenNerds and keeping our community safe. You're the best, and I am so grateful to you and for you.

I also want to throw out a thank-you to Caitlin Davies for her incredible narration of the series audiobooks! Caitlin: you channel Winnie so perfectly that I now hear your voice when I write her! Thank you so much for bringing the world to life.

For my mom and dad: you went above and beyond to help me get through this book (and my two others due in the same year). You flew across the country to help out, multiple times, and listened to many a venting—and occasionally crying—session. Life was tough in our little household over 2023 and 2024, and I'm so grateful I always have your support. (And to David and Jen: you're fine, I guess.)

And finally, to the incredible team at Tor Teen who take my books and turn them into beautiful products on the shelf, thank you! We have my in-house knight Lindsey Hall and her page Aislyn Fredsall; my marketing geniuses: Anthony Parisi, Isa Caban, and Eileen Lawrence; my awesome publicity people: Giselle Gonzalez, Alexis Saarela, and Sarah Reidy; the incredible ad and promo designer: Megan Barnard; the incomparable cover artists and designers: Sasha Vinogradova, Lesley Worrell, and Greg Collins; the ever-patient copyeditor: Christina MacDonald; the wise managing editors and editorial directors: Rafal Gibek, Will Hinton, and Claire Eddy; the top-notch production team: Ryan T. Jenkins, Jim Kapp, Michelle Foytek, Rebecca Naimon, and Erin Robinson; the clever publishing strategists: Alex Cameron and Lizzy Hosty; and lastly, the fancy (and awesome) people at the top: Lucille Rettino and Devi Pillai. Again: thank you all so much! I've been at Tor Teen for eleven years, and what a ride it has been!

Oh, and I guess I can't close these acknowledgments without thanking my husband and partner. Frenchie, you're great. We went through the wringer over the last two years, but I never felt afraid or alone. You were always there, whether it be in the human hospital while we dealt with one unexpected health scare after another or at the animal hospital when we had to say goodbye to both our beloved dogs. We found a lot of joy through all those moments, and I'm thankful to have you.

Lastly but not certainly leastly: Cricket, this series was always for you at the end of the day. I started the Twitter adventure when I was doing IVF. You were born exactly one year after that began. And then during that first year of your life, I wrote *The Luminaries*. Now here we are: you're four years old and this series is ending. I hope one day we have the relationship Winnie and her mom have (minus the crow-for-dad and nightmares, of course), and remember: *I LOVE YOU UNTIL THE END OF TIME!—MOM*

ABOUT THE AUTHOR

Susan Dennard is the award-winning, *New York Times* bestselling author of the Witchlands series (now in development for TV from the Jim Henson Company), the Luminaries series, the Something Strange and Deadly series, in addition to short fiction published online. She also runs a popular newsletter for writers, *Misfits & Daydreamers*. When not writing or teaching writing, she can be found mashing buttons on one of her way too many consoles.

susandennard.com
Instagram: stdennard